CALIGULA

CALIGULA

Can a slave decide the fate of an emperor?

Gaius Julius Caesar Augustus Germanicus, third Roman Emperor, is better known by another name: Caligula. Rufus, a young slave, grows up far from the corruption of the imperial court. His master is a trainer of animals for the gladiatorial area, and Rufus discovers he has a natural talent for controlling and schooling the animals. He attracts the cruel gaze of the Emperor, who wants a keeper for the imperial elephant. He is bought and taken to the imperial palace, where he and his friend, the gladiator Cupido, find themselves unwittingly at the centre of a conspiracy to assassinate Caligula.

CALIGULA

by

Douglas Jackson

Magna Large Print Books
Long Preston, North Yorkshire,
BD23 4ND, England.

British Library Cataloguing in Publication Data.

Jackson, Douglas
    Caligula.

    A catalogue record of this book is
    available from the British Library

    ISBN   978-0-7505-3117-7

First published in Great Britain in 2008 by Bantam Press
an imprint of Transworld Publishers

Copyright © Douglas Jackson 2008

Cover illustration © Larry Rostant

Douglas Jackson has asserted his right under the Copyright, Designs
and Patents Act, 1988 to be identified as the author of this work

Published in Large Print 2009 by arrangement with
Transworld Publishers

Magna Large Print is an imprint of Library Magna Books Ltd.

Printed and bound in Great Britain by
T.J. (International) Ltd., Cornwall, PL28 8RW

0454661

For Alison, Kara, Nikki and Gregor –
who always believed

Prologue

The Rhine frontier AD 18

The boy crept stealthily through the low bushes, eyes darting right and left for any sign of the enemy. Today he imagined himself the last survivor of the battle of the Teutoburg Forest, the only man from the three massacred legions who could still complete his mission and kill the Cherusci king, Arminius. He came to the edge of a small clearing and stopped. There was his quarry. He drew the small dagger that doubled as his legionary's *gladius* and charged the Cheruscan hordes, smiting their champions one by one. There! And there! Die, Arminius! Die for your treachery!

When the victory was complete, he stood among the fallen bodies of his enemies, breast heaving beneath the light armour that protected his chest. Except for the helmet, he wore the complete uniform of a light infantryman of the Twentieth legion: red tunic, mail vest, a thick belt that held loops for his equipment, leather greaves covering his shins, and sandals. The uniform had been specially made by the quartermaster to fit a six-year-old and when he wore it his heart filled to bursting with pride.

He brushed the unruly dark hair from his eyes and began to pick up the enemy dead. The thin green saplings would have to dry first, but they would do for the fire. Collecting firewood gave him the excuse he needed to come to the woods. He loved the woods; loved their sharp, resin smell and the way the wind moved through the tree-tops, loved the way the sun pierced the leaf canopy to create strange, shifting patterns on the forest floor. The birds and the beasts fascinated him, and he was always on the lookout for some-thing new to discover. His mother didn't like him coming here. She worried too much, and would have preferred him to stay close to the camp and try to make some friends of his own age.

What did he need with friends when he had the soldiers? The soldiers loved him as they did his father, Germanicus. Germanicus was a great leader and a favourite of the Emperor. The boy could list every one of his victories and had even touched the two eagles his father had won back from the Cheruscans as he wreaked vengeance in the years following the Teutoburg disaster. He loved his father, especially when he gave him presents like the uniform.

When he'd collected all the saplings and a few fallen twigs he began to make his way back to the camp. He had only a vague idea of the direction, but he wasn't afraid. He followed a faint deer path through the undergrowth which should bring him to a small stream. Once he was there, he would know his way.

A blackbird exploded from a low thorn bush be-side the track, making him jump, and he grinned at his own foolishness. He laid the bundle of sticks on the ground and inspected the bush closely, taking care not to catch himself on any of the dangerous, inch-long spikes. There it was, close to the ground, a tight-knit structure of grass and moss. He crouched low and crept forward. There might be a clutch of the pale blue, brown-freckled eggs.

Once he was in position to see into the nest he realized with a thrill that the eggs had recently hatched. Huddled together in the centre of the grass bowl were four tiny baby blackbirds. Very carefully he reached in and picked up one of the wriggling little creatures and placed it gently in the palm of his hand. He studied it carefully. It was small and naked and vulnerable. A long-necked bundle of pink flesh that was so light he could barely feel it on his hand. Its head was the same size as its body and the little wings were barely formed flaps of skin with bumps that were the first signs of feathers. It had an almost imperceptible pale yellow beak and the eyes were just dark circles beneath the translucent pink skin. The sensation of it, warm and helpless and so alive he could sense the beating of its tiny heart, sent a liquid feeling of pleasure through him.

But there was another feeling too, an underlying tension he didn't recognize, but that made him feel quite breathless. Could he? With his free hand he reached out and plucked one of the inch-long spikes from the thorn bush. The breathless sensation slowly left him, and it was as if he grew larger and the baby bird in his hand diminished. He hesitated, still not certain, waiting for a sign. The little bird opened its beak.

He smiled and very deliberately forced the

needle-sharp thorn through the fleshy covering and into the centre of the helpless chick's eyeball. It squirmed between his fingers, but he held it tight. The tiny mouth opened and closed in soundless agony. He selected another needle from the bush.

It was very informative. Each chick reacted in a slightly different way to the application of the thorns. One reared and attempted to wriggle away. Another curled up and simply accepted the torture. As he completed each experiment he dropped the dying birds on to the leaf mould at his feet with the wooden spikes still protruding from their blind eyes.

'Gaiuuus!' His mother's cry came from the direction of the camp and he realized he was late.

He dropped the last chick to join its siblings and lifted his foot to bring the nailed sandal they called a *caliga* down hard on the tiny pink bodies, twisting and turning the sole until what had once been perfectly formed baby blackbirds were just a red mess among the disturbed dirt.

'Coming, Mother,' he shouted. In his excitement he almost forgot the bundle of sticks, but he picked them up and began to run towards the sound of her voice. It would soon be time for dinner.

I

Rome AD 36

Rufus sat with his back to the warm bark of a pear tree and pondered his future. For the first time in his life he was tortured by the luxury of choice.

Should he stay with Cerialis, or should he accept the animal trader's offer? The question had vexed him all morning, and he was no nearer the answer now than he had been two hours ago.

The household of the fat baker had been his family since he was six years old and he considered himself fortunate. How else could he feel when Cerialis showed enough regard for him to allow a slave to decide his own future? He was learning a trade. He did not go hungry and he had never been beaten.

So, stay with Cerialis. It was obvious.

But on the opposite side of the scales was the prospect, the unbelievable prospect, of freedom. Freedom. The word made his senses spin. Did he really want to be free? Free to do what? To starve? To beg on the streets?

In any case, the animal trader was not offering freedom now. It might be years before he fulfilled his bargain.

It was the bear's fault. If it wasn't for the bear he would be at his ovens baking the finest bread in Rome, instead of sitting in the gardens of the Porticus Liviae with his head pounding like the inside of a drum.

Two butterflies, one a delicate pale blue, and the other a beautiful mix of red and brown, flitted across the edge of his vision towards the flowerbed. He grinned and touched the charm at his throat.

So be it. Let the gods decide.

Cornelius Aurius Fronto was endowed with a laugh that bent forests and shattered roof tiles and he was laughing now.

'So, the baker's boy has finally made up his mind? He has chosen the certainty of greatness with Fronto over the drudgery of picking weevils out of stale bread for that lard-arsed shopkeeper. How could it be otherwise?'

This last, with a theatrical whirl, was addressed to the half-dozen slaves and freedmen who emerged at his shout to welcome Rufus. They appeared, showing various attitudes of boredom or interest, at the gateway of a walled enclosure which hid the animals that were Fronto's stock-in-trade. Rufus wondered what the animal keeper would think if he knew that he had placed his destiny in the flight of a blue butterfly.

As the slaves gathered, he reflected on the contrast between Fronto's welcome and the previous occasion on which he had changed masters. The ordeal at the enormous slave market outside Ostia when he arrived on the ship from Carthage was one he would never forget. He had been a small, terrified boy, alone among more people than he ever dreamed existed. He remembered looking for somewhere to hide among that great ebb and flow of humanity, but it had been hopeless. Eventually, he had sat down close to the wall and cried until he could cry no more. It was a relief when he was bought by Cerialis the next day.

He returned the stares of the little group, noting whose smile was open and who among them saw him as a potential enemy. They were evenly split.

'Did I tell you how he saved my life?' Fronto demanded, and a few wide grins told Rufus that the answer was 'yes' – several times over – but they knew they must endure the story one more time.

'It was a large bear, but not one of my finest. No, the finest must be kept for the arena. In truth this one was old and mangy and worm-ridden. But it still had its claws. Great hooked claws that would tear the top from a man's head. Is that not so, young Rufus?'

Rufus remembered that the bear's claws were clipped short, but thought it would be impolite to cast doubt upon his new master. So he nodded. The beast's yellowing fangs were terrifying enough.

He had been escorting Lucretia, the cook, to the fruit market along one of the narrow streets off the Sacer Clivus when it happened. One moment the street was filled with laughing, jeering peasants, the next it was emptied by a single scream. The bear stood on its hind legs, a broken length of chain hanging from a metal collar round its neck, its dark brown fur matted with patches of dried blood.

'And that poor child,' Fronto was almost weeping now, 'abandoned by her wet nurse, alone and defenceless with that ferocious monster drooling over her. Poor little...' He faltered for a moment.

'Tullia,' chorused his audience helpfully.

Tullia. She was blonde and tiny; the bear enormous and angry.

'Certain death,' the animal trader roared. 'Certain death awaited her, but for this brave boy.' An arm as thick as a tree branch swept towards Rufus.

He meant to run away from the bear with Lucretia. Instead, he found himself scrambling towards it.

'And do you know what he did? He danced.' Fronto roared with laughter, his great belly shaking. 'He danced with a bear.'

At the time, it seemed the only thing to do. He couldn't fight the bear – it was twice his size and many times his strength. But to remain still was to die.

'How did you think of that, boy?' Fronto demanded. 'What made you dance with my bear?'

Rufus remembered the terrifying moment when he had stood at the great beast's mercy, but he shrugged as if dancing with bears was an everyday occurrence.

'When I was small a travelling circus visited our village,' he explained. 'It was nothing like the circuses in Rome, just some bad actors and their flea-bitten animals. They owned a bear, a little thing the same height as I was. They had taught it to dance. Just a few steps, but it would dance, and people would dance with it. It seemed to enjoy it. I suppose in my head I was dancing with the same little bear.'

He had danced around the bear, and the bear followed, its obsidian eyes never leaving him, as if it was concentrating every part of its brain on copying his movements. As it turned, a group of men appeared behind it. One motioned to him to keep dancing, while the others untangled a large net. They crept closer to the bear while he opened up the distance between himself and the animal a few precious inches at a time. Then the net whirled and the bear became a spitting, growling ball of fury, paws clawing at the all-enveloping mesh.

'You saved your own life, and, though you did not know it, you saved Fronto's, and Fronto pays his debts.' The trader wrapped an enormous arm round Rufus's shoulders and he felt he might collapse under the weight of it. 'I pledged my word to Vitellius Genias Cerialis, and I pledge it to you now. You have a way with animals, and I can use that. I buy them and I train them for the arena and the circus. I'll teach you every trick I know, and, if you come up to scratch, in a few years I will make you my heir and sit back and watch in comfort as you make me rich. We will draw up the papers tomorrow.'

A murmur ran through the group of workers. Rufus noted the frowns and understood that Fronto's generosity wasn't received with universal approval. He saw their point. He doubted if they were impressed by the tousle-haired seventeen-year-old in the ragged tunic. The ambitious

19

among them would resent him and attempt to obstruct him, but he was not concerned. Years of lifting sacks of grain at the bakery had made him strong. He would be ready for them. It was his good fortune that Tullia was the daughter of a very senior senator. Her father was as well known for his devotion to his youngest child as for the cold-blooded manner in which he disposed of his political rivals. If the bear had harmed her, Fronto would have ended up in a sewer with an assassin's knife in his liver.

'What if I don't come up to scratch?' he asked.

'I'll feed you to the lions.'

There was a long silence.

'Only joking, boy ... feed you to the lions.' The laughter shook Fronto's great frame once more. 'You should see your face.'

Fronto's business was to the south of Rome, across the four arches of the Pons Sublicius. It was far enough from the city to deter crowds from coming out to gawk, but close enough to the cattle market at the Forum Boarium to ensure the trader a constant supply of food for his carnivores.

Inside the animal compound Rufus's heart quickened as Fronto proudly listed the exotic treasures he bought and sold to perform at the great spectacles in the arena. The grass-eaters browsed peacefully in a series of wide paddocks. The trader pointed out the different types.

'Antelope.' He indicated a herd of graceful animals standing placidly in one enclosure. They were several shades of dusty brown, and varied in size from tiny fragile creatures the height of a small dog to broad-chested giants with long spiralling horns and dark patches on their haunches.

'What are those?' Rufus asked, pointing to another small group. 'I've never seen a horse with stripes.'

'They're a type of wild ass. I tried to train them to pull chariots, but they are much more stupid than horses.'

'And those?' Rufus pointed to a dark brown, hunch-backed, front-heavy creature built on the scale of a small donkey, but with short incurved horns, heavy brows, wide-set narrow eyes and a nose that trailed streamers of snot.

'Those?' Fronto grinned. 'We just call those ugly.'

Beyond the paddocks and in a separate compound were squat huts built of heavy timbers. Fronto led the way towards them. As they approached the buildings, Rufus was aware of a vaguely familiar scent, a powerful, pungent aroma which dominated everything around it. It was a few seconds before his memory swept him back more than a decade.

Lion.

The galley from Carthage to Ostia had carried them as cargo. Two big females and two cubs. Now he was staring into those same murderous eyes, pale golden yellow flecked with shadows of grey and shooting back pure hatred.

He still did not truly understand why he had been sold to the slaver. His father was a Spanish auxiliary who had settled in Mauretania at the completion of his service. He had been a better soldier than farmer. Their little homestead in the foothills of the Atlas Mountains was a parched, dusty place in the summer where the rocks cracked with the frost in winter. His mother was a vague memory now, but he knew with certainty that she had loved him, if only because of the contentment he felt whenever he thought of her. If he closed his eyes he could almost recall her face and the damp, morning smell of her long black hair. They were always hungry, but could she have stood by while he was dragged away crying? He supposed she must have. That, he calculated, was in the eleventh year of the reign of the Emperor Tiberius.

Fronto had a dozen lions, including three magnificent black-maned males. But there were also slim, athletic cheetah, and three lithe, spotted cats of a species unfamiliar to Rufus.

'They are leopard,' Fronto explained. 'The crowd loves them. Big as a lion. Twice as fast. Once they get on top of a man, it doesn't matter how well protected he is, he's dead. Their teeth go for his throat and their claws go for his belly. You've seen a kitten worrying a dead pigeon, little paws scraping away like mad? Same thing with a leopard. If they can't get his belly, they'll get his balls. If not his balls, they'll strip his legs to the bone. Doesn't matter really. Just means it's over more quickly if they get his belly.'

Finally, they came to what Fronto called his monster.

'Amazing, isn't it? You'd never think something like that only eats grass.'

Rufus gazed at the grey goliath standing alone in its paddock. The animal was about twice the size of a bull, with thick, leathery skin. Its head was large even compared to its body, but its legs were almost comically short. It had tiny eyes and from low on its wide, shovel nose projected two horns, one behind the other. The larger, at the front, was nine inches across at the base and tapered over about the length of two feet to a deadly point. The second was half the size, but looked even sharper.

'I don't know what to do with it. It looks dangerous, but it never seems to do anything except stand around. You can pat it like a dog. Why don't you give it a try?'

The eyes which studied Rufus brimmed with sincerity. Fronto wore the look of a man who had never done wrong in his life; a man who would go to his grave without a stain on his reputation. A man Rufus did not trust an inch.

Fronto was testing him, and he believed he knew why. The shrewd trader was giving him his opportunity to prove himself in front of the men who might one day call him master. He looked again at the monster, which seemed to have grown even larger. The question was, would he survive the test?

With more confidence than he felt, he grinned cheekily and said: 'Of course.'

Titus, one of the slaves who formed Fronto's welcoming party, held the gate open for him, then, as he shut it again, whispered:

'Watch his ears.'

Rufus walked slowly into the enclosure. The tension made his heart race, but the world seemed a clearer place and his stomach tightened

23

with anticipation. He saw that the walls of this paddock, although built like the others of wooden planks about the height of a tall man, were strengthened by horizontal beams. In places, raw white patches stood out clearly as if the wood had recently been splintered.

The heat of the sun beat on his back like a hammer as he marched further into the enclosure. Where the monster waited.

After about twenty paces he noticed what might have been a flick of movement at the side of the animal's head. Yes, there it was again, an almost imperceptible twitch of the left ear.

Never taking his eyes off the beast, he subtly changed direction. Now, each step took him diagonally across its front, rather than directly towards it.

He couldn't believe something so big could move so fast. One moment the monster was motionless, its small eyes staring unseeing into the middle distance. The next its short legs were a blur of speed and it had covered half the distance between them with its head lowered and that lethal scimitar of a horn pointed directly at his groin.

To turn and run directly towards the fence was pointless. He would never outpace this animal. But his change of direction had taken him slightly out of its path and that gave him a fraction of a second to sidestep the charge.

He waited until he could have touched the lower horn with his outstretched hand before he dived low and to the right. With one movement he was on his feet again and his long legs flew as he sprinted towards the fence.

As he ran, he could hear the beast's thundering hooves close behind and knew it had turned its huge bulk in an instant and was pursuing him. He could see the gnarled knots in the wood of the fence and the rusty heads of the nails which held it together. Behind him, the explosions of breath from the animal's nostrils told him it was closer still.

One moment of hesitation and he was dead. He picked his spot on the fence, kicking up one leg and pushing with the other, so that for the final two paces before he hit it he was in the air. His front foot met one of the horizontal bars and he used every muscle he possessed to turn forward momentum into an upward leap that would carry him safely over. Another inch and he would have made it. Instead, the knee of his trailing leg smashed into the top plank, generating a fiery stab of pain and turning a controlled jump into an untidy, somersaulting flight. While he was airborne, he distinctly heard the thundering crash of something enormous and fast-moving hitting something even more solid and unyielding. Half a second later he landed with an impact that knocked the breath from his body, loosened several teeth and left him wondering how many bones he had broken.

He lay, stunned, with the metallic taste of blood filling his mouth and dust clogging his nose.

'You show a fair turn of pace for a baker, but your vault could have been more elegant.'

Rufus opened one eye. Fronto was standing over him, his bulk blocking the sunlight.

'Come on, get up and let's see what you've done to the poor old monster.' He gave Rufus his arm and pulled him to his feet.

Wincing with pain, the boy limped to the fence, which now sported a splintered hole the size of a man's fist. Rufus looked through the gap and flinched as he stared into the angry eye of the monster. It gave a shake of its head before trotting back towards the centre of the paddock.

'She'll have a bit of a headache, but she should be fine,' Fronto said proudly.

'What about me?' Rufus demanded. 'She could have killed me. You said I could pat her like a dog.'

'I may have exaggerated a little,' Fronto admitted. 'But that is lesson number one for you, boy. You've proved you're not frightened of animals, but you must learn to respect them. Next time you go into a paddock or a cage, study what is in it first. These animals are all dangerous in one way or another. Even the small antelopes will knock you into the middle of next week if they're protecting their young.'

He picked up a piece of dung that lay at his feet and held it up to Rufus's face.

'See? It's all about profit. It doesn't matter whether it stinks like shit or smells of perfume – if it makes a profit it smells sweet. Now, we'll start you at the bottom. Titus, show him how to muck out the wild pigs.'

II

The bottom made Rufus's previous existence seem a positive paradise. Then, he had smelled fresh bread every day. Here, he was assaulted by a dozen different kinds of animal dung. But every moment he spent with the animals he learned.

He learned how to feed and water them. Each species had a carefully planned diet to ensure it was kept in the peak of condition. Too much meat and the cats would become fat and lazy. Too little and they would lose their great strength.

He learned to look for the symptoms that would tell him when an antelope was sick with one of the wasting diseases which plagued their kind. One sign of sores around the mouth or hooves and the entire herd might have to be slaughtered.

He learned to spot the slight swelling which showed that a doe was pregnant and needed to be moved from the paddock.

And he learned what happens to a man who gets careless in the company of lions. He would never forget the rags of torn flesh and splinters of bone that were all that was left of poor, slow-witted Titus after he failed to recognize a lion's growls of pain from a broken tooth. The other slaves did not hear his screams until it was too late and the overseer decided it was more economic to allow the animal to devour him – he was already dead – than to bury him. There was no question of killing the lion. Its value was ten times that of Titus and, as Fronto pointed out, its destiny was to kill men.

Day by day and week by week, his respect for Fronto grew. The animal trader had an unquenchable thirst for life that made even his competitors like him, and Rufus was sucked along on a tidal wave of enthusiasm which often left his head spinning. But when Fronto returned from his next trip to Africa to purchase stock to replenish the pens and paddocks, the grin that normally split his face was replaced by a weary frown.

'It's getting worse,' he complained, as they leaned together on a fence watching two gazelle bucks butting heads in a mock test of strength. 'Always our buyers look for something bigger, something better, something more spectacular, something more exotic, and each time I see my suppliers they claim that the animals are scarcer or the herds and the packs that feed on them have moved further south, and they put their prices higher. I'd say they were holding out on me but I know from other traders that it's the same wherever you go. The only consolation is, I can pass on the costs, but for how long, only Jupiter knows.'

'Can't you breed them?' Rufus asked.

'Breed them? I'm a trader, not a nursemaid. Buy cheap and sell at a profit. Anyway, most of them won't breed. It's been tried. You can do it with the antelope if you're careful and give them a bit of space and peace and quiet. But the rare ones, the ones where the real profit is? Never.

Those big cats? In their own territory they breed like rats. No predators apart from their own kind. But put them in a cage and it's as if they forget how it's done. Come with me.'

Rufus followed Fronto as he marched purposefully towards one of the far pens. 'They tell me you learn fast, boy. That's good.' He unchained the gate. 'This one arrived today, from Africa. From now on she is your responsibility. Feed her. Understand her. Win her trust. Gain her respect.'

Rufus had his own leopard.

The cat was about six months old, the spots already showing on her flanks through the fading down of her cub fur.

'Her mother died on the passage from Africa. If I put her in a pen with a family of older leopards she'll be torn apart.'

As yet, she had none of the pent-up violence and hatred of humans that characterized an adult leopard. Instead, she exuded a kitten-like playfulness as she wrestled and toyed with anything moveable. To watch her in her innocent pleasure gave Rufus a feeling of joy such as he had never experienced.

He called her Circe.

Circe was the first thing of value Rufus had ever owned and he vowed to form a bond with the cat which would never be broken. As Fronto conceded, he had learned quickly and learned well from the other animal handlers. He knew when to approach and when to leave well alone, when to pet and when to punish. He would tame the cub, turn her to his will.

He didn't notice the sly smiles of his workmates

as they watched him with the cat.

A month later, when Fronto next returned, he looked at the leopard lying at Rufus's feet and slowly shook his head.

'Come. It's time you visited the arena.'

The animal trader dressed in his finest for the occasion, and master and slave travelled to the capital in a one-horse cart.

'What are you gaping at, boy?'

Rufus knew this journey well, but the approach to Rome never failed to awe him. At first, the world's greatest city was a gigantic mirage of orange and white shimmering in the heat, but, as they moved closer, the images took on structure and shape, and finally – unbelievably – solidity.

The city rose before him, ridge after ridge like the craggy foothills of a mountain. Yet there was nothing natural about this magnificence. Every part of it had been created by human hands. There were buildings of such vast scale and splendour that they could only be the palaces of gods. Rows of huge pillars held up massive triangular roofs; great curved walls of stone rose like cliffs. And such colours: oranges and reds, silver and gold. The whole city glowed in the afternoon sunshine as if it was on fire.

Rufus's errands between the bakery and the baker's villa had allowed him to explore the crowded alleys and wide avenues. He was fascinated by the great triumphal arches and pillared, monumental buildings. He looked enviously at the inscriptions. Of course he could not read them, but he knew they were dedicated to the great heroes of the past: Julius Caesar, Augustus,

Crassus and Pompey. The vast palace complex on the Palatine Hill, which he studied from the Sacer Clivus, drew him like a moth to a flame. He never dared to approach the narrow stairway which would have taken him to its centre, but he knew in his heart that here was a paradise fit for Jupiter himself.

And, as he explored, he made an important discovery. Rome was a slave city.

It was true. Slaves outnumbered Roman citizens by a margin of ten to one and if the Romans ruled Rome, slaves ran it. Slaves or former slaves were doctors, lawyers and moneylenders. They managed businesses for their masters. They made things, bought things and sold things. Many slaves were enormously rich and many more were trying to be. It was rumoured that slaves even had the ear of the Emperor.

Rome would be nothing without its slaves.

At the city gates, Rufus and Fronto were forced to dismount from the cart, for only wagons carrying imperial couriers or transporting goods to the markets were allowed within the walls during daylight. The animal trader hired a curtained sedan chair carried by four muscular Syrians and directed them to the great Amphitheatre Taurus. They set off at a steady trot with Rufus running alongside, battling his way through the crowds.

The babble of noise that accompanied the frenzied comings and goings in the city was an assault on the ears. Every Roman seemed to be talking at once and not all of them in the same language. Vendors shouted their wares from myriad stalls lining the street. The variety was mind-boggling. Within a few yards you could buy shoes, the leather they were made from and the knife you would use to cut it.

In front of a spice shop, the air would be filled with the scent of cinnamon, pepper and frankincense. Mutilated beggars called for offerings of food from the entrances to narrow side streets while next door fat shopkeepers offered honeyed almonds at exorbitant prices.

The Taurus was close to the Campus Martius, on the northern side of the city. Only its lower storeys were made of stone, while the upper part was wooden, unlike the monumental Circus Maximus and the crumbling but still impressive Magnum, the 30,000-seat theatre of Pompey.

Taurus had been gifted to the city fifty years before. Now, it was showing its age like an old whore whose best days are behind her. Tiberius was rumoured to have plans for a new and even greater arena, but a building on such a scale would take many years to construct, if the notoriously frugal Emperor ever sanctioned the cost at all.

The amphitheatre had forty entrances for the paying public, but Fronto led Rufus to a small, unmarked door which opened on to a narrow, torchlit wooden stairway descending into the bowels of the complex. As he followed his master, Rufus felt the same excitement he experienced when he entered the monster's paddock. Fronto led the way through a labyrinth of passages, large and small rooms, and animal cages, all cloaked in a fetid atmosphere that was rank with the odours of stale sweat, urine and excrement, animal and human. There was also another smell, which overwhelmed the others and made his nostrils twitch. It puzzled him, until he was struck by a vision of the white bone and scraps of red meat which were all that was left of Titus after the lion had killed him. The smell was blood.

The realization of where he was sent a flutter through his chest. During his years in the bakery Rufus had dreamed of the moment when he would sit in the stands above and cheer on the favourites whose names and careers he knew by heart.

'When will we see the gladiators?' he asked, his voice betraying his excitement. Fronto turned to him, and Rufus was surprised at the intensity of his gaze.

'You will see them in the arena and not before. Men – and women – pay good money to share their quarters with them before they enter the theatre of combat. There is an atmosphere, a tension, in that room, Rufus, unknown in any other place on this earth. I have seen couples with some of the finest bloodlines in Rome so over-powered by the stink of raw fear and excitement that they rutted on the earth floor before them.'

He breathed heavily from his nose, as if he had just finished some hard physical labour.

'Do you know what those men on the verge of their deaths did? They turned their eyes away and looked at the walls. There is more dignity and honour in the meanest condemned slave than in such so-called nobles.'

They took a stairway leading upwards and came to a door that opened directly on to the killing ground. Rufus gazed across a flat earth-covered surface ringed with smooth planks to twice the height of a man. Whoever entered this trap would not escape by climbing its walls.

'What you see here is nothing,' Fronto whispered, his voice suddenly cold, and Rufus felt a faint shiver run down his spine. 'This is an appetizer for the poor and the bored who have no money or nothing better to do. Remember. It is nothing.'

From behind them came the distinctive clank of metal upon metal. Rufus turned to see three terrifying figures.

III

At first glance, they did not appear human. The leader wore a bronze helmet which covered his entire head, with slits for eyes and mouth, and strands of hair delicately woven in metal across the scalp. Otherwise he was clad only in a loin-cloth and a wide belt which cut diagonally across his left shoulder before running round his waist. In his right hand he carried a short-handled, wide-bladed axe, with a second in a loop attached to the belt.

Behind him stood a giant, bigger than any man Rufus had seen. His features were hidden behind a full-face visor dotted with a pattern of small holes. His wide-brimmed iron helmet was crowned with a knife-edged comb, as if he were some kind of enormous fighting cock. Mesh armour protected his left side from shoulder to waist and he was armed with a trident in one hand and a net the size of a small blanket in the other.

The third gladiator was the smallest of the three, but his presence outshone his companions. His face was also hidden, but this time by a golden helmet moulded in the handsome features of a young god, and the magnificence of the mask was mirrored in the immaculately sculpted torso of the man who wore it. The oiled muscles of his biceps bulged and the veins stood out upon them like a pattern of tree roots. He fought without armour, the better to allow the crowd to feast on his beauty, and he carried a long straight sword comfortably in his left hand. His right held a small, rounded shield with an intricate gilt boss decorated with the image of the war god Mars.

Fronto and Rufus stepped aside to allow the gladiators access to the doorway. They stood silently, waiting, but each seemed to have a pattern of small movements designed to keep their bodies from tightening. They swayed from one foot to the other, stretching first one set of muscles then the next, or rolled their heads in an arc, working neck and shoulder joints. Their bodies gleamed and Rufus could smell the not unpleasant scent of some sort of oil or balm that coated their flesh.

From within the arena he heard a murmur as the crowd noticed movement which was hidden from the group in the doorway. Rufus sidled forward, keeping as far from the intimidating figures of the gladiators as he could in the narrow passageway. Through a crack in the doors he saw a mixed herd of antelope and deer erupt from the centre of the arena floor, driven from the pens below.

As they emerged from the darkness, the terrified beasts were met with a solid wall of light and sound which drove them to panic and made them instinctively seek any avenue of escape. They charged round the walls in a group, eyes white with fear, nostrils flaring, and the sound of their flashing hooves, magnified by the wooden boards beneath the few inches of packed earth, echoed like thunder around the arena. The larger animals used their bulk to force their way past the smaller and weaker, but their efforts gained them nothing. There was no way out.

Eventually, the panic-stricken gallop slowed to a trot, then a walk. Finally the herd halted, confused and exhausted. A panting, nervous mass, their flanks gleamed with sweat and steam rose from their bodies in clouds.

Rufus too was panting, caught up in the excitement and terror of the animals. The noise in the arena had softened, but the very air seemed to crackle with the pent-up energy of a gathering storm.

Suddenly a roar erupted, and the animals exploded into movement. Rufus saw a light brown blur flash across the arena. A lion leapt on to the back of one of the smaller antelopes and hooked its claws into the squealing beast's flanks. From the far corner of the ring came the roar of another lion, and then Rufus felt a thrill of excitement shiver down his spine as he heard the unmistakable harsh, sawing cough of the leopard. His leopard.

The slaughter had begun.

In the wild, antelope use their speed, agility and numbers to outwit their hunters. In the arena their instincts counted for nothing. The big cats killed at leisure, each attack drawing louder cheers from the crowd as claws sank into flesh and then teeth closed on windpipes, bringing death by slow suffocation.

The smell of blood drove the antelope and deer into an ever greater frenzy. Some now ran awkwardly, having smashed their legs as they tried to climb and even leap the amphitheatre walls in their desperation to survive. The audience bayed for more.

But Fronto knew it would not last. He had seen it before. The lions and the leopard would become bored with killing and would settle down to feast on the carcasses of their victims. The antelope would reach a point where they could run no further, lungs bursting and hearts close to exploding in their chests. So the promoters of the arena had found an answer.

The hunters would become the hunted.

Rufus had watched with pride as Circe had killed first one and then a second antelope. He had become so engrossed in the entertainment that he was surprised when the double doors opened in front of him and the three gladiators marched past him into the centre of the arena, raising the noise of the crowd to an even greater pitch.

The two lions raised their heads from their prey and roared defiance at the threat. The leopard flattened herself down behind her last victim and waited. Only now, as each gladiator lined himself up with one of the big cats, did Rufus fully understand what was about to happen.

'Lesson number two, Rufus,' Fronto whispered into his ear. 'Never get too close to your work. The leopard could have made me a lot of money, but you ruined it. You turned it into a pet. Pets don't fight well in the ring. Look at it. It's confused and fearful. It doesn't know what's happening. But the lions have learned that man is a danger to them. Watch them. They will fight. The leopard will only die.'

But Fronto was wrong. The two lions did fight, but so did Circe.

The first move was made by the huge gladiator in the cockscomb helmet.

'He is known as Sabatis,' explained Fronto. 'And he is a veteran of the arena. He will be the first of the *venatores*, the hunters.'

Sabatis raised his trident to acknowledge the crowd's acclaim before he approached his lion, the big spear held steadily in front of him. At first, his chosen victim only snarled her defiance and tried to protect her feast. She had learned to fear humans, but hoped this one would go away and leave her in peace. As the armoured figure came closer the lion was forced into a decision. She charged.

'Watch how quick he is,' Fronto said.

Sabatis waited until the lion was within three paces before he stooped low, one knee on the ground. The cat's leap should have taken him full in the body, but its hooked claws went inches over his head as he speared upward with the trident, the three barbed points sinking deep into the female's unprotected belly. The lion squealed in agony as her momentum took her above and past the gladiator, threatening to tear the trident from his grasp. But Sabatis tightened his grip on the triple-headed spear and twisted, ripping it clear of the animal's flesh in a spray of blood and leaving her trailing feet of intestine from the terrible gash in her stomach.

The lioness landed in a cloud of dust and rolled over half a dozen times before slowly regaining her feet. Her whole body shook as the pain coursed through her and she licked pathetically at the huge wound in her belly. Her strength was ebbing from her along with the great gouts of arterial blood that stained the earth. She was mortally wounded, but she was also angry and at her most dangerous.

This time there was no precipitous attack. She painstakingly manoeuvred into position for the leap that would take her great fangs to the gladiator's throat. But her movements were difficult and every breath drove the pain deeper into her body. What she thought was a deadly leap was nothing more than a lurch which bared her chest to Sabatis, who thrust forward with the trident, forcing two of the prongs deep into her heart. Blood poured from her mouth as she died with a shudder and toppled to the ground the spear still in her.

The crowd screamed in adulation and roared

the second gladiator to his task.

'This fellow hasn't quite got Sabatis's style,' Fronto murmured.

The axe man had been impressed by the speed of the lioness's initial attack on Sabatis. He had intended to show his skill with the razor-edged hatchet, but now the crowd could sense his uncertainty.

He walked back to the edge of the ring and returned with a long spear in each hand. The tips of the spears were wide-bladed, narrowing to a needle point, with a crosspiece set a foot from the blade so that the charging lion could not fight its way down the shaft and tear at its attacker even in its death throes.

The mood in the tiered wooden stands changed as the crowd saw the spears. They had anticipated a more equal, more dangerous contest and they registered their displeasure with boos and hisses.

Already nervous, the gladiator misjudged his initial thrust at the dark-maned male lion and only succeeded in ripping the muscles of its shoulder, hurting it but leaving its movements unaffected. His second attempt was equally clumsy. The spear bit deep into the lion's belly cavity, but failed to find any of its vital organs. Worse, the axe man lost his grip on the weapon and in his panic dropped the second spear as well.

If the gladiator had stood his ground, the lion might have been content to lick its wounds. But, armed only with a dagger, he decided to put as much distance between himself and his nemesis as possible. Its hunting instinct aroused, the lion charged.

Now the roars of the crowd were roars of laughter. In his fear, the gladiator lost all sense of direction and ran in circles, scattering antelope as he went, with the lion gaining on him at every stride. The laughter grew hysterical when he looked over his shoulder, tore off his bronze mask and soiled his loincloth all in the same instant. Then the lion was on him, pinning the screaming man face down, shaking its head and working its great jaws at his shoulder. The screams grew louder as the lion bit through leather and into skin, but the thick shoulder strap saved the gladiator from greater damage for a few vital seconds.

Rufus watched with horrified fascination, unable to tear his eyes away from the doomed fighter. He barely noticed the slim figure who danced lightly across the arena to stand over the lion and its victim.

'This should be good,' Fronto said to him.

The man in the golden mask could have killed the lion with a single thrust, but he gauged the crowd's humour with the same precision he employed to calculate the damage the lion was doing his fellow performer.

Instead of striking instantly, he mimicked indecision with the mischievous confidence of an accomplished actor. The lifeless eyes of the young god mask merely added to the comic appeal. Should he strike? No, perhaps not. Was this his friend lying here on the ground in the process of being devoured? Perhaps yes. But the poor lion had to eat, didn't it? Well then, I'll leave the decision up to you, the audience.

Most would have been happy to see the lion's

victim die. But when the young gladiator forced his blade home into the base of the animal's neck, killing it instantly, the blow was received with universal approval.

Now he had his own performance to complete, and it was a piece of theatre that broke Rufus's heart.

Circe fought because the young gladiator left her no other choice. She lay behind the carcass of her final kill, ears flat against her head, and watched suspiciously as he advanced. Even when he was close enough to touch her with his sword, she stayed motionless, unable to decide whether the strange apparition was harmless or something altogether different.

Rufus felt bile rising in his throat. He understood there was only one outcome to the contest, but he could not stop himself from calling out to the leopard.

'Attack, Circe. Kill him, or you're going to die. Please, do something...' His anguished cry tailed into silence as Fronto gripped him by the arm. He turned to bury his head in the folds of the animal trader's cloak, but Fronto's strong hands forced his face upward and turned him to watch the spectacle unfold.

Circe did not die a brave death, or even a dignified one. She was butchered, slowly, one piece at a time, for the entertainment of the crowd.

With a barely perceptible flick of his wrist, the golden-masked figure drew the tip of his sword across the tender flesh of the leopard's nose, drawing blood and making the animal scream with pain as she retreated backwards from the protection of the antelope corpse. Still she did not attack, and the gladiator marched relentlessly forward with a measured pace that gave the spotted cat no time to consider her next move.

The sword flicked again, slicing away part of Circe's ear and leaving her half blinded by a flood of red which covered her face mask. Now the pain was unbearable and the cat launched itself at her tormentor, a spring-heeled, snarling, yellow and black harbinger of hell, whose needle-pointed claws raked at the soft, vulnerable skin of his stomach.

But the gladiator had been waiting for just such an attempt.

To the mesmerized crowd in the tiered stands, it was as if his whole being flowed in the same instant from one spot on the arena floor to another a few feet away. To the cat it was as if she was attacking one of the insubstantial white strips of cloud which scarred the azure sky above them. One moment he was there, so close she could almost feel her claws sinking into his flesh, the next he was gone and the rear of her body went rigid with shock and turned into a searing ball of unbelievable agony.

The crowd shrieked with amazement and Fronto shouted with them.

'*Di omnes*. Will you look at that?'

As he melted away from the cat's attack, the gladiator had positioned himself to deliver a single sweep of the long sword which severed her tail an inch from the root.

Circe spun in circles, almost insane with pain, squealing pathetically and trying without success

43

to lick the stump of her tail. Eventually she came to a shambling halt and turned again to face her torturer.

Rufus watched Circe's suffering in an agony of torment. Even at the risk of his own life, he would have rushed into the centre of the arena to stand between her and her executioner, but Fronto's vice grip on his shoulder held him where he was. Gradually the horror of what he was witnessing became too much, and it was replaced by a great emptiness. He willed the gladiator with the god's face to bring the uneven contest to a merciful end, but knew he would not. Every cut of the fighter's sword drove the crowd to new heights of ecstasy and each blow turned the once-proud animal into a shambling, bleeding mass of raw meat.

He removed an eye with a spearing thrust. A casual slash chopped off the other ear. As the tormented animal tried to close with him, he flayed her, expertly replacing the dark rosettes which had made her one of nature's most beautiful animals with obscene patches of scarlet flesh and white bone. Soon, Circe was swaying on her feet, exhausted by her efforts and by the loss of the blood which dripped into the packed earth.

The gladiator turned to walk away. Somehow Circe found the strength to break into a tired loping trot and then a full-blown charge that carried her towards the fighter's exposed back.

The crowd screamed a warning, but Rufus knew the gladiator had no need of it. He had choreographed this moment, just as he had choreographed every second of the one-sided contest.

He turned in a single graceful movement with the sword already extended in front of him, and sank the long blade into the leaping animal's throat, driving a yard of iron down the length of Circe's body. The blow split her heart, killing her instantly.

Rufus, sobbing now, but still drawn irresistibly to the dreadful slaughterhouse of the arena, could visualize the grinning, triumphant features behind the mask as the gladiator marched from the arena, acknowledging the tributes of the crowd. But as he traded the harsh glare of the arena for the shade of the corridor, the fighter's confident stride faltered, as if he somehow gained his energy and strength from the sun itself. Hatred welled up inside Rufus like the magma of an erupting volcano and for an instant he was on the point of launching himself at Circe's killer.

Then the gladiator removed his golden helmet.

IV

The saddest eyes Rufus had ever seen gazed from a face as handsome as the mask which had hidden it, and more so, for this was the face of a living, breathing thing and not some soulless metal façade that killed without compassion or conscience. His hair was the colour of a cornfield in high summer, but his eyes were the dull grey of a winter's morning. The sadness in them had depths that Rufus knew he could never – or hoped never to – fathom.

The second surprise was that the gladiator, who had looked and acted like a veteran of a hundred combats, was only a few years older than Rufus himself, probably in his early twenties.

When he spoke, it was in a guttural German-accented Latin that Rufus at first found difficult to understand, and his words were addressed to Fronto.

'This is the boy?'

'Yes. This is him.'

The young gladiator stared at Rufus for a second. 'I am Cupido,' he said, an unspoken question in his voice.

Rufus hesitated, but Fronto replied for him.

'This one is Rufus. He is my slave, but one day, if he learns, he will be my partner.'

'So, Rufus, you hate me now? For what I did to your animal?'

Rufus blinked away a tear, but said nothing.

'I was told you must be taught the reality of the arena. The cruelty? It was part of your training, I think.' Cupido fixed Fronto with a long stare, making the big man shiver. 'It was not something I took pleasure in. It was what I was paid to do. So, I tell you now in good faith, so that we will not be enemies, there is another lesson you must learn – do not waste your hatred on someone who does not have the luxury of choice.'

With a nod, he walked away.

As time passed, Rufus's feelings swung from one extreme to another whenever he went over in his mind what had happened. At first he hated

Fronto for his callous treatment of an animal that had done nothing to deserve the terrible death it suffered. He even considered running away from the trader, but he had no idea where he would go. Finally he realized the lesson of Circe was one he would have had to learn for himself. There could be no room for emotion when animals were destined for the arena. Their hearts might beat and they breathed the same clean air as men, but they were doomed from the moment they were captured on the savannahs or in the jungles of their homelands. From now on he must harden his heart and treat them as tools to be worked with. With that realization came another: Fronto was more than his owner. In the few months they had been together he had become a friend, and when Rufus thought back over a lifetime of often being alone, and occasionally even an outcast, that fact counted enormously.

That knowledge opened another door, and introduced a wonderful, unfamiliar feeling. A desire to change his life for the better. His time with the animal trader had been a success. He knew that if he worked hard and made progress he had a real opportunity to become Fronto's freedman and share in his business, perhaps even set up a business himself. Fronto had promised to take him with him on one of his trips to Carthage. Was it possible he might see his mother again? Was she even alive?

The next step of his development came unexpectedly, in October, when the first thunder clouds swept in from the coast, making the animals nervously pace their cages and compounds.

Fronto ordered Rufus to pack his few belongings and move them to his villa on the edge of the city. When he had settled in Rufus was summoned before his master. Fronto was not alone. With him was a small, plump man with sparkling, intelligent eyes and unruly tufts of hair growing above each ear, giving him the appearance of a well-fed squirrel.

'This is Septimus. He's Greek. He will teach you your letters.'

So began a long and often difficult journey that opened Rufus's eyes to the wonders of a new world and took him to places beyond his imagination. It was a slow process, but beginning with the simplest children's stories, Septimus taught him the magic of the written word. Fronto had compiled a well-stocked library: tight-wrapped scrolls in protective leather cases stacked neatly round the walls of the room. Rufus enjoyed nothing better than to browse through them, even if many of the words and what they described were beyond his understanding.

After six months he began to accompany Fronto to meetings with the men who organized the great games in the arena. Men who answered to senators and consuls, even to the Emperor himself. At first, he sat silently in the background concentrating on what was being said, and, sometimes more important, not said, trying to understand the intricate detail of the negotiations. Near-invisible signals of hand or eye could mean a difference of thousands of sesterces. They were hard men, all members of the same guild, who survived by their wits and their ability to drive a tougher bargain than their rivals. He grasped very quickly that to underestimate them or to treat them lightly was to court disaster.

By and by, there was a subtle change in his status. Now Fronto would occasionally bring him into the conversation, asking his opinion on some small matter or his advice on the qualities of one of the animals he knew so intimately. It was never mentioned directly, but everyone on the couches round the negotiating table was aware of it. Slave or not, Fronto had adopted Rufus as his heir.

As he worked with his animals, Rufus often thought of the young gladiator. He had long since stopped blaming Cupido for Circe's death. The leopard was always destined for the arena. It was his, Rufus's, own stupidity which had hastened her end.

They met by chance in early spring, at one of the first shows of the new season. By now the name Cupido was spoken with reverence among enthusiasts of the amphitheatre. He was fêted by the rich and the powerful. Rufus was surprised and flattered when the gladiator approached him and asked politely how he was.

'I am well, but I hear you are better. They say you have killed twenty men.'

The grey-eyed fighter gave a dismissive laugh. 'What do they know, these pederasts and wife-beaters who bay for blood from the cheap seats? Not every fight is to the death, and not every fight that seems to end in death produces a corpse.'

Rufus had heard rumours that it was not always the crowd who decided who lived and who died in the arena. Cupido seemed to be confirming this, but the gladiator clearly felt he had revealed enough and Rufus decided not to delve further. Instead, as they walked among the animal cages under the arena floor, he asked Cupido about his unusual name.

The fighter shrugged. 'That is my ring name. My true name is of no significance now. The person who owned that name is gone for ever. I was a prince of my people, but when the men of my father's tribe rose against the Romans and were defeated, I became a slave like all the others. The Romans put me on a farm. Not a healthy place. Many of us died in the quarries. They would have worked me to death if I'd stayed there.'

'How did you come to escape?'

'Escape? I didn't escape. The overseer was a man who used his whip and his feet too freely. He used them on me only once,' Cupido said, his tone proud. 'I took the whip from him and beat him until he screamed for mercy and the skin was stripped from his backbone. Perhaps I should have killed him. When he recovered he would surely have killed me. I was fortunate. The local magistrate gave me the choice of the cross or the ring. I chose the ring.'

The sad smile touched his lips. 'Now great men treat me like a prince again. One senator pays me to be his bodyguard, to impress his friends and as a warning to his enemies. He knows I despise him and all his kind, but still I must teach his children to use the sword and to defend them-selves, and he showers me with gifts. Last week, another rich knight sent me a beautiful woman because I had won him money. She seemed disappointed when I sent her away unused.'

Rufus was astonished that Cupido could take so little satisfaction from his achievements. He himself had often wondered what it would be like to experience the acclaim of a huge crowd in the arena. Sometimes, he dreamed he was in Cupido's place, his blade singing as he scythed down opponents, but there always came an awful moment when the sword point wavered and he woke up sweating in the certain knowledge that the next victim would have been himself.

'You have a wonderful talent, a great name and the acclaim of half of Rome. On a good day I work as a clerk and on a bad one I might wipe a hippopotamus's backside. Which life would you choose?'

The fighter turned to him with a flash of irritation. 'Yes, I have acclaim, but for what? One day the blood spilled in the arena will be mine. Then what good will all the past cheers of the mob do? I will be just another punctured bag of guts and bones to be dragged from the arena and fed to your lions. And yes, you are right, I do have a talent. A talent to take life and make it look easy. But such a talent comes at a price. Some of the men I would call my friends take pleasure from the kill. They live for that split second of another man's death. They savour the feeling as the blade pierces skin and the flesh closes round it and embraces it like a welcoming host. Nothing in life gives them greater satisfaction.

'And me? I despise myself, because killing is so easy. It's as if they offer themselves to me. In the arena there are only two types of men: the quick and the dead. The men who face me on the dirt are already dead. It is as if they fight with their feet trapped in mud. They wait until I have positioned myself for the thrust. They place themselves where I will them to be. Their weapons flash, but they are made of air, they cannot touch me. Then I kill them. Does a butcher have talent? Does a slaughterman? Then yes, I have talent.'

He turned and walked off, leaving Rufus utterly bemused.

V

In Rome, a rumour could pass from the Palatine to the Aventine quicker than a dog's bark. But the latest one turned out to be true. Tiberius was not the same man who had led his legions across the Rhine to conquer Germany. The Emperor took his ease now on the island of Capri, where there were stories of debauchery that would make even the most broad-minded Roman blanch. The ageing ruler had bested every rival for over twenty years and was secure in his power. He did not need to court the popularity of the mob and he was shrewd enough to take advantage of the fact. He refused to sponsor any further games.

Rufus thought Fronto would be concerned about the fall-off in trade, but where others saw a crisis the trader perceived opportunity.

'Don't worry, boy, the games will be back. They

say the youngster Tiberius has chosen as his heir can't get enough of the spectacle. Meanwhile, we are given the opportunity to improve our stock.'

Cupido, interested to learn more about the beasts being readied for the arena, became a regular visitor to Fronto's enclosures. Dressed in his white tunic, he might have been any other handsome young slave of average height and build, but there was a fierceness of spirit in him, a tension and an awareness, that made other men shy away.

He assessed the farm's stock with a professional eye, commenting on the hardiness of one antelope and the stamina or nimbleness of the next. They stopped at the stockade containing what Rufus now knew as the rhinoceros. Cupido laughed aloud when the young slave explained how Fronto had introduced him to the massive animal, which eyed them curiously as they stood by the fence.

'She must be much faster than she appears,' said the gladiator appreciatively. 'And that skin looks as tough as thrice-tanned leather. I wouldn't like to take her with only a sword: it would just bounce off. I think her horns are as much to frighten as to kill, but she'd crush a light infantryman, even a *hoplomachus*, without any trouble. Perhaps it would take a double team of a netsman and a heavily armoured *murmillo* like Sabatis to best her?'

Cupido commented on the many empty cages and stockades at the farm. Rufus explained that Fronto was on another trip to Africa to buy fresh stock and assured him they would be full again in a few weeks' time. A shadow clouded the gladiator's eyes.

'Do you think there are enough creatures in the world to keep the Romans amused? Look at them. They are as beautiful as they are wild. Each one has a purpose and a place, from the fiercest of the cats to the most docile of the antelopes. Do they not deserve life?'

'That is a curious point of view for someone who does what you do.'

'When I enter the arena, I leave my feelings in the arming room,' Cupido replied. 'Afterwards, when the blood-letting is finished, it is different. Every life I take, be it animal or man, weighs heavy on my mind. Each individual adds to the burden I carry. I know one day that burden will crush me. But do not be sad for me, Rufus. My fate was decided from the first moment I entered the arena. The *rudis* is not for me. Give me a clean death and a quick one and I will be satisfied.'

Rufus was surprised at his friend's fatalism. The *rudis* was the carved wooden sword presented to a gladiator on the day he won his freedom.

'But you are the most celebrated fighter in all Rome. The crowd loves you. Great men seek you out and reward you with gifts and money. The day will surely come when that gift is a wooden sword?'

Cupido shook his head and changed the subject.

'I remember the first day we met, when you cried for the leopard. Soon there will be no more leopards, or antelopes, or rhinoceros. They will all be gone, fed into the insatiable maw of the games. What will you do then?'

'Fronto knows what he is doing. He will find more animals for us,' Rufus said with more confidence than he felt.

'This time perhaps, and the next time. But there will come a day when he cannot. Think on that, Rufus. Think on a means of providing entertainment without blood. I have studied the mob. They don't come only for blood. If you can give them something different, something they have never seen before, perhaps they will be satisfied with a little less of it.'

It was a weary and disheartened Fronto who returned from his mission. The animal dealers at the trading camps on the coast all told the same story. They had few animals to sell and those they did possess were low in quality and high in price. He had hired guides and made the arduous trek into the mountains, but the news was the same. The game either was hunted out or had fled south, and the predators that lived off it had followed. He was venting his frustrations on Rufus by the menagerie gate when they were interrupted by a shout.

'Cornelius Aurius Fronto, you old lecher. You were in Mauretania, but you did not tell me you were going. I might have put some business your way.'

Fronto excused himself and went to meet his visitor, a tall, bald man in a threadbare tunic which hung loose on his thin frame. He spent thirty minutes in deep conversation with his guest, and when he returned to resume his discussion with Rufus the big man looked uncharacteristically thoughtful.

'Who was that?' Rufus asked, his curiosity getting the better of him. Fronto shrugged as if it was of no consequence, but Rufus persisted. 'One day it might be important for me to know this man. You are always telling me knowledge is profit.'

'His name is Narcissus,' the trader said reluctantly. 'He buys and sells commodities.'

'What kind of commodities?'

Fronto didn't answer directly. 'He is the freedman of one of our senators, a minor member of the imperial family. He is very clever, perhaps the cleverest man I know. He speaks seven languages and a dozen native dialects. Sometimes I use him as an interpreter. Sometimes I do him a favour.'

'A favour?'

'Yes. When it suits me I will carry a message to a certain person in a certain port. In return, I receive another message, which I pass to Narcissus.'

'So the commodity he buys and sells is information? Then he is a spy?'

Fronto turned to face Rufus with a dangerous look. 'No. Not a spy. A businessman. He buys and sells, just as I do. If the information eventually reaches the ears of Tiberius that is of no interest to me.'

'He must be an important man, this Narcissus,' Rufus said thoughtfully.

Fronto answered with a superior wave of his meaty hand. 'Oh, Narcissus would like to be important. And rich. But he will be neither. His senator is a crippled nobody and Narcissus's choice of horse is as poor as his choice of sponsor.

It is well known at the Circus that if Narcissus backs Red, the gods will favour Green. Come – we have work to do.'

VI

It did not take the animal trader long to discover that all was not as he left it.

Rufus was standing beside the lion pens speaking to Cassius, the head keeper, when a snorting sound behind him made him wonder if one of the enclosures had been left unbarred. But it was Fronto, and he was furious.

'What in the name of the immortal gods have you done? I didn't give you permission to separate the young cats from the adults. You'll ruin them as you did the leopard.'

Rufus had known this moment would come, but he was not prepared for the cataclysmic power of Fronto's wrath. He had hoped to be able to explain his plan earlier, but somehow the moment had never seemed right. Now their faces were so close that the younger man could feel the rage radiating from Fronto like heat from an open fire.

'I left you in charge here, because I believed I could trust you,' Fronto roared. 'All you had to do was keep things running smoothly, but you couldn't help yourself, could you? Don't deny it – I know all about it. I've heard what you have been doing with the lions. Petting them, sitting in the cage with them, feeding them by hand. Jupiter! You've even been wrestling with the bloody things. When they go into the ring they won't fight the gladiators, they'll try to hug them to death.'

Rufus opened his mouth to speak, but the modest sign of defiance only served to make Fronto angrier.

'You're too soft. I wanted you to have all this, but I didn't work my way from a farm in Etrusca to become a Roman citizen so that you could throw it all away. You will never be anything but a slave. You can move out of the house and back into the slave quarters tonight. Get out of my sight.'

Rufus refused to move as the bigger man tried to force his way past, and Fronto was as much surprised by the weight of the shoulder which halted him in his tracks as by the edge in the boy's voice. Boy? Perhaps no longer. This was a different Rufus from the one who had waved him off three months ago.

'I know how many animals you brought back on the ship. Eight. Six kudu and two mangy cheetah. How long do you think we can stay in business without animals? You're not a fool, Fronto. You know the answer as well as I do.'

'The answer is to go as far as it takes to find new stock,' Fronto spat back.

'No. The answer is to keep the stock we have alive, to find a way of winning the crowd without sacrificing them. We can use the animals again and again. It could earn us a fortune.'

Fronto laughed incredulously. 'Now who is the

fool? The mob only wants blood. It has only wanted blood for a hundred years. Do you think you can wean them off it with a few clumsy tricks?'

Rufus looked steadily into his eyes and the trader broke off, his anger beginning to ebb away like a wave retreating down a pebble beach.

'At least let me try.'

Fronto recognized the determination in Rufus's eyes. There was a certainty in them that left the contemptuous refusal on the tip of his tongue stillborn. For a moment he saw himself in the young man before him: stubborn, impetuous, unscarred by the thorns of failure. His anger faded completely and he shook his head at his own weakness.

'The gods save me, but tell me what you want to do.'

In the weeks that followed Rufus spent every waking moment with the big cats. He found they were as individual in their moods and habits as any human, and it seemed natural to give each of them a name, although he was careful not to allow Fronto to discover this.

'You will be called Diana,' he told the smaller, but more agile, lioness. 'For you will some day be a swift hunter.

'And you are Africanus,' he whispered in the ear of the big male, whose, mane would soon turn from its present fluffy fringe into the great symbol of power and strength that would awe everything, man or beast, he confronted. 'For you are a brave and mighty conqueror.'

When obedience had become a habit, he was certain he could make them do anything. The only question was what?

He sought out Cupido at the gladiator school, where he found the athlete going through a series of intricate movements under the watchful gaze of his *lanista*, the school's owner and the manager who organized his fights. Sabatis was watching from the edge of the training ground, and Rufus joined him, looking on fascinated as the naked Cupido pirouetted and danced, his sword glinting in the sunlight as it carved lightning patterns in the air around him.

'Make yourself comfortable: he'll do this all day. Wears me out just watching him,' the big man grunted.

It seemed impossible that anyone could keep up such a pace. But the gladiator never faltered as the sun grew higher in the morning sky, though Rufus could see that his muscles were shaking with the effort and sweat ran in glistening torrents down his tanned body. Finally, at a signal from the trainer, he halted, his chest heaving as his tortured lungs sucked in the warm air. Rufus stayed in the shadows and watched Cupido nod as the trainer spoke quietly to him, outlining where improvements could be made.

At last, the *lanista* handed the gladiator his tunic and walked off. Cupido joined Rufus in the shade. He sat back against the wall with his eyes closed and sipped from a flask of tepid water.

'So, you have come to join us, Rufus? You would like to fight beside me in the next games?'

Rufus laughed. They both knew his tenure in

60

the arena would be shorter than an Egyptian snowstorm.

'No. I came because I enjoy seeing you suffer, but also because your baby face cannot hide the fact that you are wise beyond your years and I am in desperate need of some wisdom.'

Cupido looked at him curiously. 'Very well, but let us walk. I cannot allow my muscles to stiffen.'

Saying farewell to Sabatis, they walked out into the city. Rufus loved the thronging narrow streets and it was clear that Cupido shared his pleasure. Beneath one awning was fine, shiny cloth in all the colours of the rainbow, which Cupido assured him came from a country in the east where the sun was so bright that people lived with their eyes permanently shut. The fruit stalls sold soft, ripe peaches of scarlet and gold, velvet-skinned apricots and squat, ugly pomegranates.

They found themselves on the street close to Cerialis's largest bakery and Rufus saw a face he knew in the booth outside the shop.

'Corvo! Are you still giving blind old Atticus the runaround?'

'Not me, Rufus. Now I am Corvo the dedicated. Work, work, work and then, maybe, just a little play.' The curly-haired vendor's face beamed with pleasure as he recognized his former workmate.

'But, more important, do you still bake the best bread in Rome?'

'Certainly,' Corvo agreed. 'Atticus may have the eyesight of a mole, but he grinds the best flour and I bake the best loaves.' He looked around and whispered: 'And we still keep a little under the counter for old friends.'

61

He reached below the cloth covering the table that held his stock of bread and brought out five separate sections of broken loaf, the largest of which was a half-circle with a distinctive line across its crust.

'Try them. See what you think.'

Rufus insisted that Cupido take first honour. He watched as the gladiator bit into a coarse loaf, the centre of which was a deep brown colour. 'It's good,' he said, mouth full. 'But I think you should get rid of these.' He spat a grit-hard grain of barley into his hand.

Corvo laughed. *'Panis rusticus* – peasant bread. So are those, *sordidus, castrensis* and *plebeius,* but a bit more refined. Now try that one.' He pointed at the largest portion, which was a deep golden brown. *'Panis siligineus.* Finest bread we make.'

Cupido bit through the crust of the loaf to the soft dough within. Slightly chewy in texture, it was pale cream in colour and had a clean, fresh flavour that only improved the longer he had it in his mouth. At last, he swallowed, reluctant to let the moment go.

'Not bad,' he said, trying without success to sound unimpressed, and Rufus joined in Corvo's disbelieving laughter as they left the baker and continued onwards in the direction of the Palatine. Many of the houses they passed had sheer frontages six storeys high, studded with dozens of windows, and Rufus told Cupido about the first time he had seen them.

'I thought the people in them must be very rich to live so near the clouds. Then I discovered it was just the opposite. This is where the poorest live; at least, the poorest who can afford a roof over their heads at all. The people who build them are thieves and the people who own them are gangsters. If you don't die when they fall down on your head, you burn to death when they catch fire.'

As they walked, he told Cupido enthusiastically about the big cats and how their training was progressing, but he was eventually forced to admit that he didn't know what his next step should be.

'I have discussed it with Fronto, but every idea we consider is worse than the last. We have only a single throw of the dice – if it fails, the lions will die and so, probably, will we.'

Cupido thought for a moment, his pewter eyes staring into the middle distance. 'The moods of the crowd are anything but certain,' he said eventually. 'But perhaps you have already seen the way to win them. Do you remember our first meeting?'

'How could I forget it?'

'Yes, but poor foolish Serpentius?'

'The gladiator who ran from the lion? Yes, I remember. He looked so pathetic running around the arena. What happened to him?'

'His next fight – his first proper fight – was his last. He was not really equipped for the arena.'

'I'm sorry.'

'Why? You didn't know him. He was just another slave. Just another piece of meat thrown to the mob. But look back. Remember their reaction when he ran. What did they do?'

'It was sad. They ridiculed the poor man.'

'No, it wasn't sad and they did not ridicule him. They thought it was funny and they laughed at him. Now do you see?'

Rufus looked puzzled for a moment, then the light of understanding sparked in his eyes, and a thrill of trepidation sent a shiver down his spine.

It was his time to enter the ring.

VII

If the past few weeks had been intensive, those which followed were doubly so. From dawn to dusk he worked with the lions in a paddock which was similar in size and shape to the arena.

Each evening when he lay back on his cot his muscles ached and the scratches on his skin stung beneath the salve Fronto had provided against the poison from a lion's claws, which could make any wound swell up and turn first red, then black, and lead to an agonizing death. But each day he learned more and taught more, and each day he became more confident that he could actually succeed.

It took a visit from Cupido to bring his soaring ego back down to earth.

'Yes, yes, the lions are very good,' he said. 'But it is not enough. If you are to convince the mob you must be able to show them something special, something they have never seen before. Think. What else is there? What can you do that will entertain a senator who has become bored watching two men trying to chop each other to pieces?'

Rufus shook his head, close to despair. 'I don't know. We've tried everything. Maybe I should just give up.'

'If you give up, you are as good as dead,' Cupido told him. 'And so are your animals. Come with me.' He marched across the packed dirt past the antelope enclosures, with Rufus at his heels. 'There, Rufus, there is your answer.'

Rufus stared. His heart seemed to have stopped. 'No,' he said, his voice faltering. 'No. I cannot.'

'You must,' Cupido said quietly. 'There is no other way. But tell no one, not even Fronto.'

Fronto monitored Rufus's progress with the lions and was secretly impressed by what he saw, but Rufus took Cupido's advice and there were certain aspects of the training that the trader didn't see. He still found it difficult to believe that the young man would succeed, but as he watched him work he felt himself drawn into the plan.

'I thought you were supposed to be making people laugh,' he complained helpfully. 'I've been watching you for an hour and all I feel like doing is crying.'

'If you think it's so easy why don't you try it?' Rufus replied wearily.

Fronto grinned. 'Fortunately, I'm too old and too fat. You are the young pup with the lust for fame and fortune.'

'Yes, but if I succeed it will only be fame. You'll be the one with the fortune.'

'Perhaps, but that is only fair. I am the one who's supplying all the livestock. Even you. Now get back to work.'

'Can you get me some wooden barrels?'

'If you need something to drink, drink water. Wine will only slow you down.'

'Empty barrels, about so big.' Rufus held his hand at waist height.

Fronto scratched his beard. 'It won't be easy. You're talking about a beer barrel and only barbarians drink beer. But I know someone who might have some to spare.'

Two days later, Fronto was back at the side of the paddock, looking pleased with himself.

Rufus was practising the most difficult part of his routine when the animal trader arrived. Things had been going well and he couldn't resist the temptation to show off. But in his efforts to impress, he lost concentration and missed his timing. What should have been an elegant landing ended with him rolling in the dust with the two lions, who looked at him with undisguised disapproval.

He picked himself up, patted Africanus on the back and limped slowly across to where Fronto stood. 'I hope you haven't come to gloat again,' he grunted.

'On the contrary,' Fronto said grandly. 'I have come to allow my newest entertainer to show me his work in all its perfection, though it seems I may have arrived at the wrong moment.'

Rufus's mood lightened and he smiled. 'You missed the best part.'

'I do hope so. Because in two weeks I will be sharing the experience with several thousand of my fellow citizens, and they may not be quite so forgiving.'

Rufus felt his stomach lurch. 'Two weeks? I can't be ready in two weeks.'

'I'm afraid you must, Rufus. The audience is invited. The ring is ready. The whispers already spread about this new phenomenon. It is much too late to turn back now. Besides, I spent all morning painting the posters.'

'But–'

'No buts. The deed is done. Now get back among your hairy friends and make me laugh.'

Fronto persuaded Cupido's *lanista* to give his less experienced gladiators the opportunity to perform in a bloodless contest before an audience who wouldn't demand their deaths if they were not properly entertained.

Rufus and his animals would provide the climax to the event. At least that was the plan.

Two weeks later, he sat alone in the darkness beneath the Taurus. Above him, he could hear the thunder of feet on the floor of the amphitheatre and the clash of iron as Cupido directed his gladiators in a mock battle of such terrifying reality that the mob roared their approval, despite the lack of gore. He had never been so scared in his life.

Twice he had emptied his bowels in the *latrina* which served the performers, and once he vomited bile from a stomach which burned and twitched with nerves. His hands shook so hard he could barely hold the short legionary sword he had been clutching convulsively for the last hour.

Everything was going to go wrong.

He tried to run through the details of the act in

his mind, but all he could think of was the consequence of failure. The humiliation and the shame. How could he face Fronto and Cupido after the faith they had placed in him? How could he have had the audacity, the stupidity, to think he was capable of this?

Five thousand people were out there beyond the darkness, waiting. Waiting for him. Rufus. Rufus the slave. Rufus, the slave who had never achieved anything in his life. Rufus the slave who would soon be standing frozen in the sunlight as the great mob bayed with laughter and howled for him to be dragged out of their sight and replaced with a true entertainer.

He could not do it. He would not do it.

He stood up, legs shaking uncontrollably, and began to stagger to the door, away from the terror that gnawed and tore at him as if he was already a victim of the arena.

Then the lions roared.

They roared with excitement. They roared because for the last week they had listened to these same sounds of battle in their enclosures beneath the ring. They roared because they were ready.

Rufus stopped, frozen in the act of reaching for the door. The lions roared again. And the sound echoing through the dark chambers returned to him the courage he feared had deserted him for ever.

His head, which had been filled with nothing but panic, cleared, and it was as if he had been blind and could suddenly see again. His hand stole to his throat and the lion's tooth charm that never left him. He took a deep breath, and his body was shaken by one last convulsive spasm.

He turned to find himself looking directly into two eyes still filled with the light of battle. Cupido removed his helmet and his hair was plastered to his head like a crown of molten gold. How long had he been there?

But the gladiator, if he had seen anything, was careful to say nothing.

'Five minutes, Rufus. My fellows are just going through their final set pieces. Here. Use this instead of the *gladius*.'

Rufus looked curiously at the cloth-wrapped bundle he was being offered.

'Take it.'

He took the parcel from the gladiator's out-stretched hands and unwrapped it. He was left holding a sword so long it could almost have been a spear and an outsize gladiator's helmet of the type used by the *murmillones*. Both objects looked as if they should be incredibly heavy, but Rufus discovered they were surprisingly light.

'Try them,' urged Cupido.

Rufus handed Cupido the sword and with two hands placed the helmet over his head. It was so big it covered his whole head and sat on his shoulders, but the eye holes were cunningly placed so that, although it looked from the outside as if he should be unable to see anything, his vision was hardly more impaired than if he had been wearing a normal helmet.

'Do I have to wear this?' he demanded, his voice muffled by the all-enveloping headgear. 'I must look stupid.'

'You do. That's the point. Try the sword.'

Rufus did as he was told and held the weapon in front of him.

'Wonderful. You look like a nobleman who has just been handed a turd. Wave the blade about a bit.'

Again Rufus did as he was asked. He was surprised to discover that when he swung the sword the blade quivered back and forth as if it had a life of its own.

'My armourer made it from a bad batch of iron,' Cupido explained. 'The edge is so dull it wouldn't hurt a fly. And when you try to stab something it will just bend back on itself. Go on, try it. Lunge at me.'

Cupido was wearing a polished iron breastplate and he insisted until Rufus could refuse no more.

'See, you couldn't pierce a piece of cheese. You might as well be waving a branch at me. Now, are you ready?'

Rufus removed the helmet and looked directly into the piercing grey eyes. He nodded.

'Yes, I'm ready.'

Cupido clapped a hand on his shoulder and squeezed hard. 'Then go and give the mob what they came for.'

The walk that brought Rufus to the trapdoor beneath the arena was the longest and loneliest he had ever made. The maze of tunnels seemed to go on for ever and, although he encountered several people he knew, they treated him as if he was invisible, turning their eyes away, as if to look at him was to share his fate.

Finally he stood on the wooden platform that

would lift him directly into the centre of the arena. Above him, the roars of the crowd were magnified by the empty shaft. He stood, head bowed, waiting for the signal that would tell him the instant the mob's attention was on the climax of the gladiatorial battle.

It came, a huge shout from fifty throats in the same instant: *'Roma victor.'* He nodded to the workman who operated the levers, and the platform began to rise a few inches at a time.

The brightness as he emerged slowly into the sunlight blinded him; then his vision cleared and he found himself in the loneliest place on earth.

He had been here before, when the stadium was empty, rehearsing for this day, but nothing had prepared him for the wall of screaming faces and the explosion of sound. For a moment the panic that had threatened to unman him in the depths of the arena returned, but then he heard Cupido's voice inside his head: 'Make them laugh and they will love you.'

Rufus the slave became Rufus the clown.

The crowd in the tiered stands saw a bewildered, childlike figure, small and lost in his oversized helmet, awkwardly holding a sword twice as long as a legionary's *gladius*. The helmet turned, slowly, taking in its strange surroundings. Why was it here? The helmet appeared to have a life of its own, which had little to do with the body beneath it. The helmet cocked to one side, searching the stands. Surely someone in this crowd of lords and ladies could give it a clue. What about you, sir? The helmet's eye slits looked directly at one of the toga-clad patrons in the expensive seats close to the edge of the arena.

By now, a few of the crowd were smiling, puzzled at this silent display, but others were becoming restless. Where was the action? What was this stupid game?

Suddenly, there was a gasp from the lower tiers and an ironic cheer from the upper stands. Rufus didn't hear the gate opening, but he knew he was now being stalked by Africanus. This was the game they had played during the long weeks of training.

But the helmet did not know and now the helmet was even more puzzled. Were they cheering it? Really, it? Oh, it was so undeserved. There was no need. The helmet acknowledged the acclaim with a wave of its unwieldy sword.

Africanus kept low to the ground, each deliberate movement of his huge paws taking him nearer the solitary, unsuspecting figure in the centre of the arena.

Still the helmet's vacant eyes remained fixed on the crowd. Ah, this was the only place to be, among the finest and most courtly people on earth. The helmet nodded its gratitude.

The suspense grew with each inch the lion moved closer to his victim. By now most of the mob was captivated by the heart-stopping hunt unfolding before them. They held their collective breath. But the helmet's eccentric vulnerability had endeared it to a few of the younger spectators and one could not help herself screaming out.

The helmet looked even more puzzled. Who? Where? What?

Rufus counted the seconds in his head. Now the voice had been joined by a hundred other shouts of warning. Africanus was crouched feet from his back. Three, two, one... Africanus was in the air, his hooked claws outstretched to tear the unsuspecting body in front of him.

Oh, look! The helmet had seen something glinting in the sand. It bent to pick it up.

Rufus felt the disturbed air as Africanus sailed across his back, missing him by less than the width of one of the loaves he had baked for Cerialis. He heard the roar of the crowd as the big lion rolled head over heels towards the edge of the arena.

The helmet turned towards the opposite side of the arena, shaking in wonder at all this un-deserved attention. Oh! They liked him too?

The roars turned to laughter and applause.

Then the second lion snarled her presence.

Now the suspense of the hunt was replaced by the thrill of the chase.

The helmet ran this way and that, sometimes from the lions, sometimes towards one or the other, but always somehow missing the lethal claws and fangs by a matter of inches. The lions roared in frustration; the helmet waved his long sword in defiance.

But what was this? The helmet was tiring, his stride faltering. He stopped.

The lions stopped too.

The helmet bent at the middle, chest heaving as it pumped in great breaths of air.

The lions lay, tongues hanging from their mouths.

The helmet straightened. It looked at the lions. The lions looked back. Agreement was reached. The chase was on again.

Half the crowd was urging on the lions. The other half was cheering the fool in the giant helmet. Both were happy.

Somehow, the helmet found itself in an open-ended barrel. The lions pushed the barrel around the arena in a great circle. The mob cheered the lions.

Somehow, the helmet escaped the barrel and stood its ground, its unwieldy sword drooping impotently. The mob still cheered the lions.

Now was the time for blood. The fool in the helmet was dead.

The lions roared in triumph, but the sound was instantly drowned by a thunder of hooves more powerful than anything the crowd had heard before.

The monster had come.

This was the moment Rufus had spent hundreds of frustrating, muscle-aching hours practising. The rhinoceros was notoriously unpredictable, but he discovered he could judge her moods just enough to trust her for the few fleeting seconds he needed. As the slab-sided grey bulk charged past him in a cloud of dust, he threw down the sword and helmet and sprang on to her broad back, somehow managing to keep his balance as the monster bucked and swayed beneath him and chased the lions from the arena.

Her job done, the great beast ambled to a halt in the centre of the arena with Rufus still crouched over her hindquarters. As the dust cleared, he

74

slowly straightened, raised his arms to the skies and bowed low at the waist.

At first, there was a shocked silence. Then a buzz of puzzled conversation. The buzz grew louder as the seconds passed, and turned into an explosion ... of laughter.

Rufus had won.

Cupido was the first to congratulate his young friend as he walked from the arena, quickly followed by an over-excited Fronto.

'We were wonderful,' the animal trader exulted, his face wreathed in smiles as his mind calculated the possibilities for future profit. 'I will organize the next performance for two weeks today. We will make it an appetizer for the main event. After all, the mob is going to want to see real blood at some point. We will play every arena in Rome, and when everyone in the city has seen us, we'll go on tour. I can just see it–'

'I'm not going out there again.'

Fronto gaped. 'But the crowds, the money, the... But...' He stuttered to a halt.

Rufus turned to Cupido. 'I can't go out there again.'

Cupido nodded gently. He, of all men, understood what Rufus was saying. For some, the cheers of the crowd were a drug. The waves of acclaim that flowed down from the stands mesmerized them, and when they strutted from the arena they lived only for their next performance, even though they knew it might be their last. But for others, the wall of sound chilled the blood and shattered the nerves. If these men were gladiators they died, reactions slowed by the same power that gave others incredible speed. If, like Rufus, they were given a choice, they never returned. He had used every ounce of his courage to perform before the mob. He had nothing left to give them.

Rufus turned to Fronto, who still stood with his mouth open. 'I won't go back,' he repeated. 'But I can train men who will.'

'What?' The word came out as a strangled croak and Fronto grasped dramatically at his chest. 'Are you trying to kill me, boy?'

'I'll train our animals to work with athletes and clowns who know how to please a crowd better than I ever could. And you're right, we should go on tour. When the Romans think they have seen everything we have to offer we will come back with a bigger and better performance. We can use other animals, other combinations. We cannot fail.'

Tears ran down Fronto's cheeks into his beard. He hugged Rufus to his chest. 'You are like a son to me. I always knew I could put my faith in you. Come, we will discuss this further over some wine.'

They walked away, leaving Cupido in the darkness. What might have been a smile touched his lips.

Rufus was proved right. Their initial celebrity proved a powerful attraction and entertainers flocked to the menagerie asking for work. Rufus trained man and beast hard and anyone who did not make the grade was quickly weeded out. The lions were soon joined in the arena by the other big cats, even bears, but it was the rhinoceros that always drew most cheers. Only the bravest would take to her broad back to escape the teeth and claws of the hunters.

They were successful, but their fame never matched that of Cupido, whose reputation grew with every kill he made. And he made many, particularly in the great games held in memory of the Emperor Tiberius, who died that year, the twenty-third of his reign. The games were sponsored by his joint heirs, his great-nephew Gaius and his grandson and namesake Tiberius Gemellus.

VIII

Gaius Caesar Augustus Germanicus studied the view from the great pillared window overlooking the house of the Vestals. He wondered idly what they did in there apart from keeping the flame. It might be interesting to find out. His eyes moved over the arched frontage of the venerable Basilica Aemilia, the walls of the forum of Augustus and the octagonal dome of the temple of Mars, and onward over the villas and mansions to the terracotta plain of pitched roofs that disguised the slums and cesspits of Subura the way a blanket covered the sores on a leper's legs. How many years was it since Romulus founded this city? He should know, but the date escaped him. Now it was all his. Or almost.

He turned to face the other man in the room. 'Well put, Tiberius; you have the wisdom of your grandfather. We must concentrate on the domestic issues that plague our people before we embark on the great building projects I have planned. The arch to my mother's memory can wait until we have constructed the new aqueduct system we discussed.'

He smiled at his cousin. Tiberius Julius Caesar Nero Gemellus really was a fine-looking young man. Intelligent too, and one of the most eloquent orators to grace the floor of the Senate. They had been friends since his great-uncle, Gemellus's grandfather, the Emperor Tiberius, took them both to his palace at Capri; they played together, fought together and swam together, were taught the skills of oratory and debate together and had been beaten together when they failed to convince. It was the Emperor's genius that he divined the separate talents which, in his joint heirs, would complement each other to create a Rome greater than ever before. They had learned how to govern.

How well it had worked. In six months, they had achieved more than the old Emperor had in the last ten years of his reign. And the *power*. Gaius had always known power, but this was different. The power to do anything. The power to sweep aside the mundane and the ordinary. The power over life and death. So much power he could feel it surging through his veins like an elixir, freeing his mind and filling it full of plans and schemes and ideas.

The brilliance of it all made him smile again.

His cousin smiled back.

A pity he had to die.

In the late spring of the following year Rufus took the troupe on a tour of the south, performing in a series of rude stadiums, before even ruder crowds. But Fronto sent him word of Cupido's progress and successes.

Rufus was pleased to receive the letters, but their contents, though they spoke of victories won, blood spilled and survival against great odds, gave him little pleasure. He remembered the day he had berated his friend for not appreciating his talent, and the mental scars he had exposed.

As the tour progressed there was a worrying trend to the notes. The victories continued, but Fronto, in his guarded way, hinted at hurdles placed before the crowd's favourite. Of displeasure in high places and of danger not only within the arena.

Fronto travelled south at the beginning of July to join Rufus in the thriving city of Pompeii, a prosperous harbour on the Bay of Neapolis. Pompeii lay in the shadow of a large mountain carpeted with vines and olive trees, and had a fine amphitheatre. Rufus had been surprised to discover its citizens were almost as cultured as those of Rome. The wealthiest Pompeiians owned elaborate villas overlooking the city from the lower slopes of the mountain, but Rufus was lodged in a former *hospitium* the city authorities used to billet visiting entertainers. Naturally, Fronto was too grand to stay in such humble surroundings and took himself off to the home of his cousin, Marcus Lucretius Fronto, a compact but rather fine house which fronted a wide alley off one of the main streets.

A house slave led Rufus through wide double doors into the atrium. It was a small, bright area, which opened directly on to the *tablinum*, and he could not take his eyes off the exquisite paintings that covered the walls of the room.

In one, a bronzed god in a toga of the most brilliant azure blue, wearing a golden helmet crested with eagle feathers, stood over a beautiful dark-haired goddess in a dress of shimmering turquoise. Rufus thought it must be a wedding scene, for the pair were surrounded by attendants in equally elaborate costumes. He was still gawking from the atrium when Fronto swept in.

He noticed Rufus studying the painting. 'Not bad, eh? Old Lucretius does well for himself. Who would have thought a backwater like this would be such a gold mine. We could do worse than stay here for a while, don't you think?'

Rufus was surprised; the itinerary had been finalized months before. Fronto's latest letter even suggested they might cut the tour short to return to Rome and cash in on the resurgence in the games under Tiberius's heirs.

'The new sequences are almost ready. The performers are at their peak. It's time they were given the chance to show what they can do on a bigger stage. You said yourself there has never been a better time to be in the entertainment business.'

Fronto sniffed and ran his hand over his beard. 'Yes, I did say that. But things have changed in Rome.'

'What do you mean? I thought Gaius Germanicus and his cousin loved the games?'

'Oh yes, Gaius loves the games. No one loves them more. Rome is one big spectacle day and night and the mob loves him for it. It's the type of games that's the problem. The young Tiberius has disappeared, by the way.'

'Disappeared?'

'It seems his grandfather reckoned on his being able to curb Gaius's wilder enthusiasms. He must have believed he was doing the boy an honour by making him joint heir, but all he did was sign his death warrant.'

Rufus thought for a moment. 'I can't see why that should be a problem. We are just businessmen. What happens to princes and kings doesn't concern us.'

'Don't be so naïve, Rufus. Anything affecting the games affects us. Gaius has changed everything. For the first few months the people loved him. When he arrived in Rome from Misenum they threw flowers at his feet and made sacrifices to him. And he's clever. He called a pay parade of the Praetorian Guard and handed over the money they were owed by Tiberius. A thousand sesterces each, they say. So now no ambitious young legionary commander can come marching in the back door and throw him out without a major battle.'

Rufus frowned. 'So why should any of this change our plans? You say he loves the games? Then let us give him a games such as he's never seen before. You haven't seen Marcus's latest trick. He–'

'Haven't you been listening?' Fronto interrupted. 'The games you knew are gone. With Gaius there is no more play-acting. No more little men running away from a couple of pet lions, being eaten, and appearing again to thunderous applause. With Gaius there is only blood – real blood. He pits cripples and old men against the most famous gladiators in Rome and laughs at the slaughter. He sends Roman knights of the finest families who have never raised a sword in anger against teams of his best fighters and mocks them as they die. The arenas haven't seen carnage like it since the days of Caesar.'

Rufus remembered the letters. 'Cupido? You wrote that Cupido had won many victories. That he was even more famous now, than before. But the Cupido I know would never be part of what you describe. He has too much honour.'

'You're a fool, Rufus,' Fronto said, but his tone was kindly. 'Cupido is a slave. Whatever honour he had he left behind in the ashes of his home on the day he was taken. He fights who he is told to fight, but...'

'But?'

Fronto shrugged. 'But Cupido too is a fool. He could have been one of the Emperor's favourites. All he had to do was do what he does best: kill, and kill with style. But not Cupido. When they sent the old men against him, he should have played with them as a cat does a mouse, entertaining Gaius and his band of sycophants. Instead, he ignored them. The golden idiot stood around flexing his muscles and doing his exercises and left the killing to the trainees. The

82

mob found it hilarious, but Gaius thought they were laughing at him.

'To punish him, Gaius arranged for Cupido to face half a dozen of the nobles he's had ruined since he came to power. He must have calculated that even aristocratic louts like them would give him a contest worth watching. So what does the boy do? He puts on an exhibition. Went through them like a whirlwind. Cut, thrust, stab. They didn't even have time to parry. It must have lasted all of five minutes. When it was over, Gaius had to stand up and applaud with the rest, or he'd have looked silly. Gaius isn't going to forget Cupido in a hurry, and that's not good.'

Rufus thought of the pain he had seen behind the storm-grey of Cupido's eyes, and the inner demons he had sensed. 'There must be something you can do to help him.'

Fronto shook his head. 'The only person who can help Cupido is Cupido himself. Now, we must get back to business. One thing works in our favour. Gaius has decided the old Taurus is out of fashion. Apparently, he has been telling people he will never go back there. The Emperor isn't the only one who can put on a games. We still have friends in the city to back us. We'll survive.'

So they returned to Rome, where the citizens had begun calling their young Emperor by a new name.

Caligula.

IX

He studied himself carefully in the big, silver gilt mirror. Yes, there was certainly another line on his forehead. And was his hair just a little thinner at the front? He turned his head to examine it from another angle, but it was difficult to tell. He waved the slave away and turned his attention to the two men standing nervously in the centre of the room.

Sweat ran in little rivulets down either side of Nigrinus's face, seeping from his hairline just in front of his fleshy ears. How had the man become so fat? His jowls hung in several overlapping chins on to his chest and even the expensive toga couldn't hide the enormous girth of his belly. Consul of Rome? Hippopotamus of Rome more like.

At least Proculus looked like a Roman. The strong features and long aquiline nose spoke of a lineage going back centuries. What a pity his abilities didn't match his bloodline.

It had all seemed so simple at first. Get rid of his cousin and everything would fall into place. No more obstacles to his grand plan. But it had all gone wrong. It was the Senate, of course.

'I didn't ask you here to tell me what you could not do, Nigrinus, but to show me you are capable of fulfilling your bargain. I backed you both for the consulship because you promised you could deliver the Senate. Now I discover that same Senate is obstructing me yet again.' He tried to keep his voice steady. He knew he had a habit of sounding petulant when he became angry, but it was so difficult to maintain one's temper when dealing with fools.

'But Caesar, it is the cost. If it was only one palace, not a dozen ... and the arch to commemorate your mother is on a scale unheard of. Your generosity to those made destitute by fire is admirable, but cannot be sustained. The great games you sponsor are becoming ruinous. We cannot squeeze another penny out of the Senate.' Proculus was truculent today. He obviously didn't like being reminded that someone else bought his office for him.

His headache was coming back. Sometimes it felt as if his brain was being split in two. He would have to ask Agrippina for one of her potions – that would do the trick. Though the last one hadn't been quite as effective as usual; indeed it had made him feel a little strange. He rubbed his temples in an attempt to ease the increasing pain.

'So Rome is to believe I don't mourn my mother? That I don't have the will to complete the temple in tribute to Divine Augustus, presently a hole in the ground in which not one brick has been laid upon another? Am I to go down in history as a pauper? No! You will find a way, Proculus, or you will be a consul no longer, for you will no longer have a head. If I need a replacement I will find one in my stables. My stallion Incitatus could do the job as well as either of you. Get out.'

It was so unfair. All this, and the mob was getting restless. The games no longer seemed to satisfy them. The organizers would have to introduce something truly spectacular. Something different. He had so much to do. He needed that money. He had outlawed dozens of aristocrats and confiscated their estates. There were plenty more where they came from, but the jails were already full to overflowing. What if...? The idea came like a bolt from Jupiter. Of course – it was perfect. And it solved two problems; he would empty the prisons and entertain the mob at the same time.

Their first performance back at the Taurus was like a homecoming for Rufus. The old stadium was less than half full, but word quickly spread among those who were happy to be amused as well as shocked, and the crowds soon returned.

But Fronto's business could not survive on a single performance. He was an animal trader and, under Caligula, there were never enough animals.

'It is no longer a question of deciding who I sell my stock to,' Fronto complained. 'The Emperor's procurers are everywhere. They come out to the farm with half a dozen guards, say "I want that, that and that" and off they go again without another word. Not that I'm complaining: the Emperor pays top prices. I want you to take the big black-maned lion – not Africanus, the other one – and two leopards and that half-lame cheetah to the new arena out by the Praetorian barracks.

They're to be used in some big spectacle the Emperor has planned. You might see your friend Cupido – he's on the same bill.'

When he arrived at the arena, Rufus recognized Sabatis and a few others from Cupido's school preparing weapons and armour, but the gladiator himself was absent, so he decided to return the next day. He approached one of the animal handlers and volunteered his services. Since his single appearance before the crowd Rufus had achieved something close to celebrity status among the keepers and cleaners who fed and cared for the arena animals, and the man was pleased to have his help.

When he reported for duty the following morning he was surprised to find many of the cages filled with a ragged assortment of half-starved and terrified prisoners.

'They are the *noxii*, condemned criminals. The Emperor has decreed that they must be executed in the arena so that their deaths can be witnessed by the populace,' the animal handler explained. 'They are mostly low-bred scum, but I've heard that some of them are knights who plotted against the Emperor. He is coming here to see them die.'

The spectacle would not start for some time, and Rufus sought out Cupido before he began his preparations. The fair-haired young gladiator was sitting with other members of his school, but when he saw Rufus he rose and the pair walked together to the main entrance, where they watched the stands fill.

'Look at them,' Cupido said, his voice thick with scorn. 'They are like sheep. They won't move all day, even to get up for a piss, in case someone steals their precious seat or they miss one bit of blood-letting.'

Rufus studied his friend as they stood in the shade of the doorway. The light streaming from the arena created shadows and hollows in his handsome face that made him seem much older than his years. A dark tinge round his eyes hinted at nights spent staring into the darkness waiting for sleep that never came.

'Fronto tells me you are more famous than ever,' he said lightly, trying to break the mood. 'But he says you are so fat on good living they will soon have to wheel you in on a cart.'

Cupido looked at Rufus and raised one blond eyebrow. 'And he tells me that you are even more famous than I am – but only in those places where they bathe but twice a year and have never been privileged to see a proper performance.'

Rufus laughed. 'Yes, Fronto is as big a liar as he always was.'

Rufus told the gladiator of his travels and the places he had seen, the great triumphs in small arenas and the way the troupe had been honed into a spectacle worthy of Rome's finest amphitheatres.

'But now it appears we are not wanted. The Emperor, it seems, is interested in blood, but not in entertainment.'

'Did Fronto say that?'

'Yes. He wanted us to stay in Pompeii. He fears the trained beasts will be forced to fight to the death again.'

'I think he is wrong. It is true there will never

be enough blood spilled to satisfy the Emperor, but Caligula devours art and spectacle of every form. He surrounds himself with actors and singers, as well as the gladiators who please him, and he spends as much time at the theatre as he does at the arena. To give a performance in front of him would be a risk, but the Emperor's favour can be a very valuable commodity.'

'And you, Cupido, have you won the Emperor's favour?'

Cupido shrugged. 'He can find someone else to kill the greybeards and the boys barely ready for the toga. There are plenty of people willing to do it for him.'

'Fronto says you are a fool to play games with this Emperor.'

'What does a fat swindler who stinks like a buffalo know of the arena?' Cupido replied evenly. 'I, and every one of my kind, face death each time we go through these doors. Those of us who survive do so on our own merit. Does he think anyone but the gods can make the arena a more dangerous place than it is now?'

'Perhaps you are right and he is wrong, Cupido,' Rufus admitted. 'But have you not always told me the best way to survive is to keep risk to a minimum wherever you can control that risk? Pleasing the Emperor is within your power, so at least consider it.'

The gladiator shook his head. 'Sometimes a man's pride, even a slave's pride, must decide between what he should do and what he must do. In the past, I had to fight to survive, because the men I faced were all capable of killing me. Since the passing of Tiberius I have become less a fighter and more an executioner. When I enter the arena today I will have a choice, and I will only make that choice when I see my opponents. I will live with that decision and so must the Emperor.'

As he checked the ramps and gateways later, Rufus became aware of movement in the pens holding the captive criminals. Guards separated five or six prisoners at a time and sent them in batches towards the arena floor. The shackled men prayed or pleaded for mercy. Rufus watched an overseer lash out with a spiked club, drawing a howl of agony from his wounded charge. Many of the prisoners were already injured, with blood flowing from open wounds. As the first batch of men were marched away, the order came to release the lions.

The screams were unbearable, even deep in the bowels of the arena.

Rufus had seen and heard men die, but the sound that reached him now was like nothing that had ever emerged from a human throat. It was not just the volume, which spoke of unbearable pain and unimaginable horror, but the duration of that agony which clutched like an iron fist at his heart. It seemed impossible that anyone could maintain such a sound for so long.

An hour later, his senses stunned, the piercing shrieks of men dying in unspeakable agony still rang in his ears. The selection from the cages continued, but now there was no more weeping. No more pleading. These were men without hope. They knew what awaited them, but they made no move to escape. It was as if their numbed minds could not come to terms with what lay ahead and had shut them off from the world.

But there was no sanctuary for Rufus. His mind would not shut out the screams and he truly believed he would go mad if he did not get out of the darkness. He could take no more of it. He stumbled up the stairs and the passageways to the doorway where he had earlier stood with Cupido. The sight that met his eyes was one he would never forget.

The arena resembled an abattoir.

A dozen lions, leopards and cheetah feasted on the carcasses of their prey, but Rufus could see that they were close to being sated by their human banquet. Their movements were lethargic and they chewed at the flesh and bones mechanically, as if more by habit than desire.

He turned away while the last of the terrified prisoners were led towards their fate, but his eyes were drawn to the purple-clad figure lounging on a throne surrounded by his guards in the stands. Even from the opposite side of the arena Rufus recognized that Caligula was an imposing figure, taller by half a head than anyone in the throng surrounding him. He also sensed something that astonished him: this man, who had watched a hundred condemned captives being torn apart by wild animals at his whim, was bored. There was no mistaking it. The young Emperor yawned. He looked at his manicured fingers. He made small talk to the senator seated to his left. Even when the screams resumed he barely glanced up to see what was happening.

But the entertainment had the opposite effect on the crowds surrounding him. They gasped as bones cracked. Howled in delight as flesh tore. Laughed as screams reached a greater pitch than before. In Tiberius's time these enthusiasts had seen dozens die in the arena, in single combat, or even in great battles. But this Emperor had given them something even they had never witnessed: human sacrifice on a grand scale.

Finally, the screaming stopped. The beasts were herded from the arena and, white-faced, Rufus joined the other workers in the gruesome task of clearing the arena of its human carrion. He breathed through his mouth in an attempt to avoid the sewer stink of a hundred eviscerated bowels, but his throat filled with burning liquid as he imagined he could taste the foulness that filled the air around him. He averted his eyes from the scattered remains, but his unwilling mind identified every piece of inanimate flesh that defiled his fingers.

When the job was completed, fresh sand was thrown across the blood pooled in the dirt, not to disguise what had taken place, but to ensure that the next actors in the gory drama which had been devised for the Emperor had firm footing to show all their deadly skills.

The gladiators.

Rufus listed the men of Cupido's school as they trotted into the arena. Buffalo-shouldered Sabatis with his distinctive mesh body guard, face hidden behind a *murmillo*'s fishtail-crested helmet; Flamma, the Syrian spearman, veteran of a score of contests, who fought in an unvisored bronze helmet of a style which had gone out of fashion a decade before; little Niger, the *retiarius*, net in one hand and trident in the other; and finally the golden one himself.

Cupido was magnificent. If he felt the weight of expectation, it was hidden behind the golden mask and no trace of weariness showed as he loped, across the heavily sanded floor. He fought without armour, but the harsh sunlight reflecting from his oiled muscles gave him a more martial appearance than any of the others in their brightly polished metalwork. He halted in the centre of the arena, head held erect behind the golden mask, the long sword steady in his left hand. He looked what he was. A killing machine.

But, Rufus wondered, would he kill today?

X

From a doorway directly opposite Rufus, a phalanx of perfectly matched gladiators jogged into the arena and turned to face the Emperor. Rufus counted them with disbelief: eight, ten, finally fourteen... Cupido and his fighters were hugely outnumbered.

Dressed in the leather greaves and griffin-crested helmets of Thracian light infantry, the enemy were matched physically in height and build as if they had been chosen for some human chariot team. As one, they knelt on a knee and roared: '*Ave, Caesar, morituri te salutant.*'

Cupido's group stood silent, the only sound the chink of metal as Sabatis adjusted the chain armour which protected his shoulder.

Caligula should have been offended by this show of defiance, but he gave a thin smile and waved a limp hand towards the editor, who proclaimed loudly: 'Let the combat begin.'

Unknown to the crowd, their Emperor had decided this would be no normal display of arms. A message had been sent to Menander, the Thracian leader, in the arming room: 'Strike every blow to cause the greatest pain and disfigurement. Cupido will pay for his insults to the Emperor, or you will.'

There would be no quick deaths today.

The two lines of Thracians moved smoothly to form a single ring round their opponents, but as the minutes passed it became obvious that Menander's strategy would be more difficult to execute than he had anticipated. Cupido's gladiators fought back to back, each covering the other's weakest side. Any attempt to split them by feint attacks or outflanking manoeuvres only made them move closer.

At a word of command, two Thracians at opposite sides of the circle dashed straight towards Cupido's group. If they struck the positions covered by Cupido or Flamma, the spearman, their momentum would have achieved Menander's aim: to smash open the little group and leave them individually vulnerable. But with a shuffle of feet it was Niger and Salamis who faced them.

94

The *retiarius* swung his net with a flick of the wrist and the first Thracian fell sprawling at his feet. With one movement Niger stabbed the man in the throat with his trident, retrieved his net, and resumed his position facing the enemy. In the same instant, Sabatis smashed his shield into the face of his charging attacker and knocked him backwards. With a single thrust, he pierced the off-balance gladiator's exposed belly with his *gladius* and left him writhing in the dust, blood spurting like wine from a punctured goatskin.

The crowd roared their appreciation and the depleted ring of Thracians retreated to their original positions. Menander glanced into the stands where Caligula watched with cold eyes and felt a deathly shiver run down his spine.

Rufus could see the Thracian leader's hesitation, and he knew that Cupido, who lived or died by his instincts, would have sensed it. But the four were still faced by a dozen.

Menander now knew that piecemeal attacks would only result in a slow stream of casualties and in growing frustration for the Emperor. He must stake everything on one throw, using the strength of his numbers. 'Form lines,' he ordered.

The Thracian ring transformed into two ranks, rectangular shields locked solidly together. Menander took up position on the far left of the first line and shouted: 'Advance!'

Rufus recognized that the tight-knit formation adopted by Cupido and his gladiators would not protect them against the classic battle tactics of the legion. When the two ranks reached the smaller band they would wrap around their flanks and while the front rank was testing their defences and taking the casualties, the second would exploit any gaps. Cupido would be overwhelmed.

Cupido had known this moment would come. He had hoped to be able to inflict more casualties on the Thracians, perhaps Menander himself, before he was forced to change tactics, but it was not to be.

'Flamma,' he said quietly.

The Syrian gave an almost imperceptible nod of acknowledgement.

'Wait until I give the order to break. They will be confused for a moment. One, perhaps even two, will give you an opening. Aim low. I want to hear them screaming for their mothers.'

Cupido waited until the advancing lines were less than ten paces away before he gave the command. 'Break!'

Immediately the huddle split, with Sabatis and Niger moving left, the big *murmillo* taking position just beyond the flank of the Thracian line, and Cupido moving right to do the same. As Cupido predicted, for an instant Menander and his men did not know how to react. The ranks halted, uncertain how to deal with this threat to both flanks.

The split second of confusion was enough for Flamma, who stood, balanced and ready to throw. The first javelin took the centre man of the front rank low in the groin, the leaf-shaped blade nicking an artery as it buried itself, leaving him writhing in the dust, shrieking in torment.

The second spear was in Flamma's hand almost before the first had reached its victim. It should have taken its target just below the ribs, but the Thracian's shield edge deflected the point downwards, through the cloth of his linen kilt, to pierce the muscle of his upper thigh, crippling him.

While the Thracians were still stunned by the death cries of their comrade, Flamma, now armed only with a dagger, took up position behind and to the right of his leader.

Menander cursed under his breath. It was time to end this cat and mouse game. Splitting his remaining men into three groups, he threw them forward, himself joining the unit attacking Cupido and Flamma.

The first precipitous rush cost Menander one of his gladiators, who died with Cupido's long sword in his throat, and left a second nursing a ragged slash that was his reward for under-estimating Flamma's ability with the dagger.

Rufus had been so mesmerized by what was happening to Cupido that he was blind to any-thing else in the arena. But now he could see that the overwhelming numbers pitted against Sabatis and Niger had begun to tell. The little *retiarius* was bleeding from at least three cuts and struggled to hold his surviving opponents. As Rufus watched, Niger plunged his trident deep into the chest of the nearest. But the other Thracians attacked simultaneously and he went down under a hail of blows. Above the baying of the crowd, Rufus could hear the sickening thud of blades hacking through flesh and bone before one of the men bent and picked up Niger's severed head by his shock of dark hair and raised it towards Caligula.

Sabatis, great Sabatis, had given his all. Three of the enemy crawled or lay in the dust around his kneeling form as he choked out his life in dark strings that stained the dirt, his body pierced by a dozen wounds, but still unwilling to die.

Only Cupido was untouched. Flamma had taken a slash which had cut deep into his knife arm. Now he was truly defenceless.

Menander ordered his men, reinforced reluctantly by Niger's killers, to hold Cupido's attention as he manoeuvred to take the golden gladiator in the flank. Cupido could sense his intention, but facing four swords he could do little to counter it. Seeing an opening, Cupido cut first right, and then left, into the necks of the two most vulnerable Thracians, but the commitment left him open to attack, and Menander needed no invitation.

The Thracian commander scythed at Cupido's exposed ribs, intending to cut him to the spine. But he had reckoned without Flamma. The little spearman threw his body between the sword and his leader, taking the blow across the nape of his neck and dying instantly. Flamma's sacrifice gave Cupido the instant he needed to force his remaining opponents back. One he cut down before the last, terror in his eyes, dropped his weapon and fled.

For a long moment Cupido stood, shoulders bowed. Rufus could see his chest heaving with the exertions of the prolonged combat, and rivulets of sweat created intricate designs in the opponents' blood which stained his skin.

The golden gladiator looked up into the stands

where Caligula stood, his face a confused mixture of anger and frustration, then turned to Menander.

The final combat took less than a minute. Menander knew he was no match for Cupido. His parries were sullen and slow and his feet seemed unwilling to move. Finally, Cupido, seemingly casually, slipped his leg between the Thracian's and flipped him over on to his back as if he was a novice at his first training session. Almost nonchalantly, he held his sword beneath Menander's chin, the point forcing his opponent's head backwards and exposing his throat.

Once more the empty-eyed gold mask turned to the stands, where the Emperor waited, hands clenched tight on the rail in front of him. Caligula raised his thumb, before ostentatiously hiding it in his fist to show that Cupido should sheathe his sword.

Cupido's eyes behind the golden mask never left the Emperor's. Their stares remained locked as he leaned forward and put all his weight on to his sword, forcing it home through flesh and bone with a crunching sound that could be heard in the stands.

The silence in the arena had the intensity of a solid object. Ten thousand hearts did not dare beat. Ten thousand mouths did not dare take a breath. Rufus waited with the rest, paralysed by fear. This was an insult Caligula would never forgive or forget. Every eye in the stadium was on the Emperor, waiting for the command that would bring his Praetorians on to the blood-pooled sands to avenge him.

As the seconds lengthened into minutes, the tension became unbearable. Above him, Rufus heard the sound of someone sobbing.

The Emperor rose to his feet. He had regained his composure now and his face was as much a mask as the sculpted gold which covered Cupido's. Slowly, he raised his arms ... and brought his hands together in a resounding crack which cut the silence like a clap of thunder, then again, and again, until the crowds caught his mood and realized this was not a death sentence, but an Emperor's acclaim for a warrior slave.

Rufus sensed Cupido's confusion as the mob's applause washed over him, knew the young German had expected, perhaps even wanted, to die. He watched as the gladiator shook his head slightly, as if to clear it, before walking from the arena without a backward glance while the crowd roared his name in adulation.

'Cupido, Cupido, Cupido.'

Rufus felt his heart clutched by a terrible fear. He turned to rush to the far side of the arena where he could be at his friend's side, but found his way blocked by a tall figure in a threadbare toga.

'Why, it is Fronto's protégé. Did you enjoy the spectacle, young man?'

Narcissus's voice was soft and his eyes were a deep, cobalt blue with an almost indefinable hypnotic quality. He stood smiling, his high, domed skull as bald as an egg and his scalp dappled with gleaming beads of sweat.

'I think the pretty gladiator has upset the Emperor, don't you? A sensible man would have entertained the crowd and died heroically, as was intended. It would have had a wonderful symmetry and added further lustre to his name. But now...'

'Excuse me, sir, but I must hurry.' Rufus tried to keep the urgency from his voice.

'Of course, I had forgotten. Your master advised me the brave gladiator was your friend. You would wish to help him celebrate the slaughter? But is that wise? Surely you don't find my company so poor?'

'No, sir,' Rufus said, confused. He couldn't understand why Narcissus should want to delay him.

'Then stay awhile and tell me about yourself. You have not always been with Cornelius Aurius Fronto, I'm sure. You must have a past?'

Rufus stared at him.

'But of course, I am being rude. I have not introduced myself. My name is Tiberius Claudius Narcissus, and I am Greek, born in the town of Pydna. Once, I was a slave like yourself; now I am the freedman of the senator, Tiberius Claudius Drusus Nero Germanicus, nephew of the late Emperor. I act as his secretary, and carry out what other tasks he wills. He is a fine man. Do not believe all you hear of him.'

Narcissus leaned forward, so that his mouth was close to Rufus's ear. 'It is not only your friend who is in danger. The gladiator has made his choice, and you would do well to allow him to reap the consequences alone. It is a pity; he could have been useful to me, and I to him. He refused my favour. Do not make the same mistake.'

'I must go to him,' Rufus cried.

'Go, then; be a fool. But take care. I may have work for you, and you cannot do it if you are dead.' But Rufus was already past him, pushing his way along the crowded corridor. By the time he reached the arming room, a squad of a dozen Praetorians was already formed up and moving away, with Cupido, now minus his golden mask, at their centre.

Rufus almost called out, but Cupido must have sensed his presence, because the young gladiator turned and looked directly into his eyes and gently shook his head. The message was plain: I am doomed; don't waste your life trying to save me. Then he was gone.

XI

'I have to find him.'

Rufus paced the main room in Fronto's villa. He had tracked Cupido's captors through the warren of narrow streets around the Castra Praetorium and into the centre of the city until they turned past the guard post and disappeared up the slope to the centre of the Palatine, where he did not have the courage to follow.

'He's dead. Forget him. If you try anything you'll only get yourself killed. Do you really believe Cupido would have wanted that? The boy lived with death every day of his existence. When he killed Menander he knew exactly what he was doing.'

Rufus knew it was true, but he couldn't bear the thought of the terrible fate that awaited his friend in the Emperor's dungeons.

Fronto smiled sadly. 'Think, Rufus. You knew him better than anyone. He had had enough of all this. He wanted to be somewhere else, anywhere else, a place without blood and killing, and he took the only honourable way he knew to get there. He did not bow to Caligula. You should be glad for him.'

'At least help me find out what has happened to him.'

The animal trader shook his head. 'What do you want me to do, walk into the palace and ask the Emperor?'

Rufus thought for a second, his mind going back to the strange confrontation in the arena corridor. 'The Greek would know.'

Fronto shook his head. 'Narcissus gives nothing for nothing. What do you have to trade? I don't think he'll be interested in Africanus's latest trick.'

'If I have nothing to give now, I will pledge something in the future, some gift, or some favour. I have a feeling this Narcissus is a man who collects favours the way other men collect gold pieces.'

The animal trader's look told him he was right. 'Perhaps, but you must understand, Rufus, that it is dangerous to be in debt to someone like Narcissus. He dabbles those long fingers in murky pools. It may be he will call in your debt at a time and a place which suits him, but not you.'

'I'm willing to risk it.'

Fronto bit his lip. 'But am I willing to risk you?'

For the next week Fronto did everything he could to dissuade Rufus from going ahead with the meeting. He pointed out how unlikely it was that Cupido could have survived in a place where so many others succumbed. Even if the gladiator was alive, he argued, it was certain he would be sent to one of the lead mines in the north, where he would die by inches.

But Rufus refused to be discouraged, and eventually the trader was forced to make the arrangements.

'I wanted to be with you, because Narcissus can be a tricky customer,' Fronto told him, 'but he insists you go alone. He will be on the steps of the temple of Hercules – that's the round one near the main entrance to the Maximus – at the seventh hour. Say little and agree to nothing. Promise me that, Rufus. You will agree to nothing he asks without first discussing it with me?'

Rufus agreed, but that night he dreamed he sold Africanus to Narcissus for a single sesterce, and he woke knowing he would get the worst of any bargain with the slippery Greek.

His belly fluttered with nerves as he approached the dome-roofed temple across the flattened earth of the Forum Boarium, but Narcissus greeted him with the easy smile of an old acquaintance and asked him how his animals did.

Rufus gave him a rambling answer, then paused. 'Cupido–?'

'No business yet,' the freedman interrupted. 'I have had a trying morning and it would please me to talk to you awhile, before we approach what I am sure are serious matters. Let us stroll in this direction, away from the river. It smells so much at this time of the day, don't you think?'

Rufus noticed there were few people in sight, and he realized that Narcissus had chosen the time and the place of their meeting with care. Most citizens, if they could, spent the time between the sixth and the seventh hours dining with their families. Only a dozen or so slaves were still at work clearing up offal left by traders from the morning meat market.

Their way led them behind the temple and into the shadow of the huge carved pillars flanking the entrance to the Circus Maximus. Narcissus walked steadily towards the gaudily uniformed gate guards, but Rufus hesitated, wary of their blank faces and nailed cudgels.

'Do not fear, I am known here.' The Greek took Rufus by the shoulder and steered him between the two men.

The panorama that greeted Rufus made him gasp. He was a veteran of the arena now, and had been in many stadiums, but the Maximus lived up to its name. It was vast, almost three times larger than any other in the Empire. A racetrack as wide as a triumphal avenue disappeared into the middle distance, its surface shimmering in the heat of the noonday sun, then curved to return behind a long row of pillars to where he stood. Rows of seats rose like cliffs on either side of the track. It was said that 150,000 people often packed the stands for the chariot races and other great spectacles and for a moment he was back in the centre of the Taurus with the waves of sound crashing around him. His heart fluttered in his chest and he felt a thrill of fear before Narcissus's calm voice returned him to the present.

'Come, we will sit in the shade.' He led Rufus to a spot opposite the starting gates where a dozen rows of benches provided a relatively cool resting place under an awning made of heavy sailcloth.

'Now,' he said. 'You had something to ask of me?'

Rufus faltered. What right did he, a slave, have to be demanding favours of a man like Narcissus? He looked into the steady blue eyes and realized the Greek was reading his thoughts.

'Cupido,' he blurted eventually. 'Cupido was taken by the Emperor's guards.'

Narcissus shook his head sadly. 'Yes. It was foolish to try the Emperor's patience in such a blatant manner. It could have been fatal.'

Could? Rufus registered the word and allowed himself to hope. 'He was – is – my friend. I was certain you would know his fate. I would always be in your debt...' The final sentence dropped into the silence like a boulder into a deep pool and Rufus knew he had taken a step into a dangerous unknown. For an instant he wished he could take the words back. But a word spoken aloud can never be retrieved. The gleam in Narcissus's eyes was the look of a hunter who has just snared his prey or a fisherman who has set his hook. But the Greek was in no hurry.

'It is possible I have this information, or can discover it, but first I must decide whether it is in my interest to reveal it. A secret can be a thing of great value; it can also be a thing of great danger.

Is Rufus, the animal trainer, the type of young man who can be trusted with secrets?'

He didn't give Rufus a chance to reply. 'When last we met our conversation was interrupted. We have more time now. Tell me about yourself. That charm, for instance. The workmanship is quite fine if I am any judge. Before I won my freedom no slave was given leave to own personal goods. These are enlightened days indeed.'

Rufus reached a hand to the thing at his throat. Fine? He had never thought of it as fine. Just a yellowing lion's tooth set in a metal which might have been silver, but probably was not. He found himself telling Narcissus how it had been given to him by the captain of the ship that brought him across the Mare Internum from Carthage.

'They had four lions in cages on the deck. One of them, a cub, was dying. It would not eat and it lay in the cage while its brothers played around it. They were going to throw it overboard, but I begged for the chance to try to save it.'

The cub had reminded him of himself, home-sick and fearful, sailing headlong into an uncertain future over which he had no control.

'I chewed its meat for it,' he explained, his gorge rising at the memory of the rancid leftover he had forced between his teeth. 'It grew strong and the captain was grateful, because the cub was worth money. He gave me the charm, said it was good luck and hoped it would bring me good fortune.'

'And has it?'

'The next day, in the slave market, a young man from Syracuse standing with the house slaves pulled me from the line of farm workers where the overseer had placed me, and told me I was a kitchen boy. If I had stayed in the first line I would be dead by now. So, yes, you could say I have been fortunate.'

Narcissus nodded, as if this confirmed something. 'So, you have a talent *and* the gods favour you. That is a rare combination, and one I might be able to put to use.' He paused, considering his next words.

'Your friend Cupido was placed in the torture cells for two days. When he was taken before the Emperor all who saw him believed he was a dead man, but Gaius Caligula's moods are as changeable as the four winds. Of all the virtues, he values courage most. The gladiator's must have impressed the Emperor considerably. He is now an honoured member of Caligula's personal bodyguard.'

Rufus didn't know whether to cry out with joy for Cupido's survival or shout his disbelief. Cupido in the Praetorian Guard? Cupido protecting the man he despised more than any other? He remembered the proud figure in the golden mask standing over the body of Menander and staring his defiance at the tyrant in the stands. How could it be? He looked up to find the Greek studying him.

'Sometimes the truth is more difficult to accept than the lie. You would have preferred it if he was dead?'

'No.'

'Then accept this as the will of the gods. I have found their designs are not always straightforward. Perhaps he has been placed there for a higher purpose. It is also possible the Emperor is simply toying with him. It would not be the first time.'

'What must I do? Will I be able to see him?'

Narcissus smiled his enigmatic smile. 'Do? You must do what your friend has done. Trust in the gods.'

XII

They came for him three weeks later, two very ordinary young men, their blandness effective as any cloak of anonymity. Fronto met them by the main gate, and Rufus could see their presence disturbed the animal trader. This was no harmless visit by forgotten creditors or circus promoters demanding compensation for a toothless carnivore.

After many minutes Fronto shook his head, not in defiance, but in defeat, and accepted a scroll from the taller of the two. He walked slowly to where Rufus stood.

The trader took a deep breath. 'I have sold you to the Emperor.'

Rufus thought he had misheard. Then the true meaning of the words burned their way into his brain. He looked around for somewhere to flee, but Fronto's calloused hands settled firmly on his shoulders.

'Courage, Rufus. It is not what you think. They

want you to work with his animals. Apparently he has something new, something special, and these men, his purchasers, were told about you. I'm sorry,' he said, 'truly sorry. I told them I was about to free you. I told them you were indispensable. I fought them until I saw my death in their faces. They have the Emperor's authority. I should have freed you when I had the opportunity, but I am a foolish old man. I thought you would leave me and I didn't want that to happen. Now I've lost you anyway.'

Rufus swayed on his feet, struggling to comprehend what was happening to him. This was his life: this place, the animals he cared for, the people who had become his friends. Fronto. He had learned so much and was on the brink of learning so much more. Now he was about to lose it all. The freedom the animal trader had promised him. Gone. All gone.

He shuddered – suddenly it was difficult to breathe. For a moment he felt himself close to breakdown, the tears sharp behind his eyes. Then some inner strength he didn't know existed took over. He looked into Fronto's face and saw the sadness there, and something deeper than sadness. Pity for a lost friendship? Grief at losing the son he never had? Love?

None of it mattered. He walked towards his new owners, Fronto at his side.

'The money I have been saving for you will always be there,' the animal trader whispered urgently. 'If you impress the Emperor, you can win your freedom. It does not have to end here; there must be another way. You can come back...'

Rufus hesitated at the entrance. He could see the two men were impatient to go, but he couldn't leave his friend like this. 'If there is a way I will find it, but I'm a slave, Fronto – I have always been a slave. So I'll go with them, because I have no choice. But don't be sad for me. You may not have given me my freedom, but at least while I was here with you I learned what it is to be free. No one can take that away from me, not even this Emperor.'

He expected to be taken directly to the animal enclosures close to the Circus Maximus, so he was surprised when the two men led him into the centre of the city, to the towering imperial palace complex on the Palatine Hill.

He knew he should be frightened, and was surprised to discover his emotions were mixed and his mind was clear. The sorrow he felt at what was lost stayed with him, but it was balanced by the pragmatism which had carried him unharmed through a lifetime of bondage. A slave must obey. Slaves who thought too much, or forgot that fundamental rule, disappeared into the quarries or the mines. He would obey. He would survive. Each step he took towards his new home was also a step closer to Cupido, and he knew instinctively that if they were both in the palace they would find each other. Then there was a third feeling, buried deep, but powerful just the same. Excitement. He was entering a new world and his life was changing for ever.

As he walked, his eyes were drawn to the fine-detailed glory of the great temples and palaces. From afar, the Palatine looked as if it must sink under the weight of the huge buildings upon it. But when they had climbed the hill, Rufus discovered that for every palace, there was a park, and for every temple a beautiful garden. It was a paradise. A home for the kings and gods who ruled over everything below them.

The escort took him through one of the palaces, along a wide marble corridor lined with ornaments cast in gold and silver, marble busts of Hercules and Apollo, Artemis and Hermes, and painted likenesses of past emperors. Beneath his feet beautiful pictures of red, blue and ochre were woven in stone across every inch of floor. But his eventual destination was no palace.

The barn was set close to the outer wall of the Palatine next to a park which had been created when Tiberius demolished the homes of two allies who forgot the simple truth that the friendship of an Emperor had the longevity of a sacrificial chicken. It had two large double doors to the front, but his escort led Rufus to a single small doorway set in the far wall, opened it with a large key, and pushed him inside.

'This will be your new charge. Your duties begin immediately.'

The interior was pitch black and filled with an animal smell like no other he had experienced. At first, Rufus didn't dare move. He sensed rather than saw the beast whose living space he now shared; a vast still presence identified only by the sound of easy breathing. Without warning, a powerful, python-like appendage swung out of the darkness and, with incredible tenderness, touched him on the forehead. He looked up into two of the most intelligent brown eyes he had ever seen.

It was not until he opened the main doors that Rufus appreciated the true scale of the animal. As broad in the chest as a four-wheeled cart, the Emperor's elephant towered over him, her vast bulk blocking out the sun. Her? Yes. Something about the way she stood and in the way she greeted him convinced him this was a female. She was large enough to strike terror in the bravest of men, but Rufus did not feel threatened. Fate had led him here. He had nothing to fear.

The elephant was tethered in her pen by a heavy chain wrapped round her rear left leg. It was just long enough to give her access to a large basket of hay hanging from one of the roof beams of the barn. A stone cistern filled with water stood in one corner.

He studied her closely. She had thick, wrinkled skin of a uniform, dull grey-brown, covered in stiff bristles. From the sides of her massive head, two huge ears flapped like giant fans. Long, yellowing tusks jutted from either side of a small mouth. His experience with other animals told him she was in good condition. The reason soon became apparent.

From behind a partition at the rear of the building emerged a skeleton-thin slave with skin so black it was almost purple. He carried a basket of rotting fruit, the scent of which quickly attracted the elephant's attention.

The dark man grinned, showing a mouth containing a few broken teeth. He offered the basket to the elephant. She ran the end of her trunk delicately over the individual fruits within, and, having made her selection, curled it like a hand round a bruised red apple and with infinite skill swung it into her mouth. The black slave placed the basket carefully in front of his charge, and he and Rufus sat in comfortable silence until she had finished everything inside. The tip of the trunk made one last circle round the bottom of the empty basket with a snuffling sound, then picked it up and threw it accurately at Rufus's companion, who caught it and shook his head.

'No more today. It is enough,' he said in a Latin so heavily accented that Rufus could barely make out the words.

Rufus learned that the little man was Varro, from an African province whose name made him none the wiser concerning its whereabouts. He had helped the beast's handler look after her until the man had died. Since then, Varro had been left to cope with the animal on his own, and had taken to hiding away whenever one of the Emperor's servants came near.

'And the elephant, what is her name?' Rufus asked.

'She is called Bersheba,' said the little man. 'It is a great name in her country.'

'Yes,' agreed Rufus solemnly. 'It is a great name.'

Bersheba lifted her trunk and sniffed the air, at the same time emitting a grunt from deep in her chest. When he heard her Varro stared at Rufus, eyes wide, and scuttled behind the partition to the rear of the barn.

The rhythmic clink of armour told Rufus he had visitors. He took a deep breath and stepped out into the sunlight. To meet his Emperor.

XIII

The young man who looked at him curiously from between twin armed guards could have been any other pampered aristocrat from a provincial city. Caligula, still a month short of his twenty-seventh birthday, had ruled Rome for almost two years. Dressed in a simple white toga with a single broad purple stripe, he was at least six inches taller than Rufus. He had the heavy chest and broad shoulders of a trained athlete, but his head was perched on a neck that seemed unnaturally long and his complexion had a sickly sheen. There was a softness, too, to his features, that was somehow childlike. Had Rufus not witnessed the horrors and heard the many stories, he might have been lulled into believing this smiling young man was showing a paternal interest in his latest acquisition. But he had witnessed, and he had heard, and it made him aware, aware that the smile never touched the dull, translucent blue eyes. And that the interest was that of a collector studying his latest specimen. Or of an executioner measuring his victim for a shroud.

'Is this our animal trainer? He looks too young.' The voice that had ordered a thousand executions should have dripped venom and clouded the air with sulphur. Instead, the Emperor's tone was conversational.

'I gave Sohaemus half of Arabia and he gave me

an elephant. What do I want with an elephant? It's not even a war elephant – the brute's been kept as a pet. I can't put it into the arena. Look what happened when Pompey did it. It ruined his reputation. What do you do with an elephant?'

The unblinking eyes never left Rufus and he realized he was expected to answer. He opened his mouth, his mind blank, but, before he could speak, the Emperor answered his own question with a short laugh.

'You teach it to do tricks, of course. I have plenty of people who can do tricks, but somehow the tricks always lose their attraction, and you have to find new people to do new tricks. Then the same thing happens and suddenly you find you've run out of people who can make you laugh.

'The same happens with animals,' he continued, eyes fixed wistfully on some distant spot. 'Dogs, bears, lions and horses. I've seen every trick they can do, but they all become boring in the end and you have to get rid of them.' The pale eyes re-focused on Rufus. 'But an elephant? Now an elephant that could do tricks would be impressive, don't you think?' He ran his eyes appreciatively over Bersheba's huge bulk. 'Can you teach an elephant to do tricks, boy? They think you're a sorcerer, you know, those people you work with. That old fart of an owner didn't want to part with you. Might have lost his head for trying to keep you. Didn't kill him, though. You can't just kill everybody. Had to give him a contract to supply animals to the Maximus. So you'd better be able to teach an elephant tricks.

You have a month.' He gave a curt nod and walked away towards the palace, his guards in his wake.

The Emperor had been gone for more than a minute before Rufus realized he had not even looked to see if either of the two men in Praetorian uniforms was Cupido.

XIV

Fortunately for Varro, and for Rufus, the elephant's handler had been able to impart the basic elements of his knowledge before his illness had reached its inevitable end. Bersheba, it turned out, was a patient creature of regular habits, who was normally happy to oblige when asked to perform any task she considered reasonable.

'Ask,' Varro repeated. 'Always you must ask. Not order. This elephant, she does not like to be ordered. She can be a very stubborn creature if you don't treat her with respect.'

But it soon became clear that no amount of asking was going to fulfil the Emperor's command that she be taught the kinds of tricks that would amuse a man who had already seen everything amusing his world could offer.

The animals Rufus had trained for the arena had been his to mould from infancy. He slept with them, played with them and was able to exert an element of control by giving or withholding their food. Once this discipline had been established, he found it relatively easy to teach them by the simple, if exhausting, method of constant repetition, and building from straightforward exercises to more complicated tricks and circus acts. But Bersheba was already trained. After a fashion.

When commanded, or rather asked, she would walk, halt, and bend on one knee to allow her handler and perhaps one other to mount; and, if she decided they were worthy, she would carry them where they wished. Rufus found he could direct her to the left or right by sharp slaps of the hand on her massive shoulders.

Varro also revealed, and Rufus felt this might offer him some kind of hope, that in her own country Bersheba had been used to haul or push large loads. Tricks? No, she had never been taught any tricks. Who would want to teach an elephant tricks? Varro made it clear he thought Rufus mad even to suggest such a thing. Tricks!

Rufus already felt he had reached a certain level of understanding with Bersheba. The way she looked at him with her small, knowing eyes convinced him that, if he could only find some way of communicating with her, she would be happy to do anything he was able to ask.

But how to ask?

After careful consideration, he decided he had only two choices, and one of these was so unthinkable it was not a choice at all. The quickest way would be to use force: repeated commands, accompanied by repeated use of the goad until pain or frustration made the animal carry out what she had been directed to do. But he would not raise a hand, never mind a staff, to such a

118

magnificent, intelligent creature.

The other course was gentle persuasion, and gentle persuasion took time. But if gentle persuasion was his only option, so be it.

The only question was how to persuade an elephant to extend a repertoire with which she seemed perfectly content. She would walk, but she wouldn't do anything as undignified as trot. She might be persuaded to 'fetch' something edible, but she would inevitably devour whatever she was fetching before she returned to her handler. She would pick up objects with her versatile trunk, including a giggling Varro, but never when Rufus wanted her to. He knew there was nothing intentional about her reluctance and occasionally he felt guilty about the demands he was making. If she detected even the slightest hint of annoyance in his voice she would look at him reproachfully with her brown eyes, which made him guiltier still.

Varro watched all this with a bemused smile, evidently convinced that all Romans were sun-addled. Sometimes when he grew bored he would throw one of the sweet little apples he hoarded for Bersheba and she would catch it dexterously in her trunk and swing it into her small mouth. One day, when Rufus was making yet another futile attempt to train her to roll over, he missed his throw and the apple landed on the roof of the barn, rolling gently down to catch on the very edge of the shingle.

Bersheba gave a groan of frustration. Ignoring Rufus, she ambled off towards the barn. When she reached the building she stopped for a moment, eyeing the apple, which was just visible on the edge of the roof. Her trunk curled out, questing delicately, but the fruit was just beyond her reach. While Rufus was wondering what she would do, she raised herself to her full height on her back legs, took two cautious steps forward and scooped up her prize.

Rufus laughed in astonishment. That was it. He would teach her to walk on her hind legs for the Emperor. Maybe he could even teach her to dance. Dogs trained for the circus sometimes danced, didn't they?

Five minutes later he was perched precariously on the peak of the roof just above the barn door, with one leg on either side. He held on to the tarred shingles with one hand while in the other he grasped a four-foot-long pole. At the end of the pole was a basket filled with the bruised apples Bersheba found so succulent. The first attempt almost ended in disaster. He hung the basket out just beyond the roof and shouted 'Apple', which brought her lumbering forward. But this time there was no gentle halt or cautious step. Rufus felt the whole building shudder as she hit it and used her front legs to climb to her full height. The timbers below him creaked ominously and he heard a distinct crack. He realized she was going to demolish the barn if he didn't act quickly.

'Here,' he shouted desperately, and threw the basket behind her.

For a moment he thought she wasn't going to move and that the barn would collapse and take him with it, but, just in time, she dropped to her feet and began snuffling for the dropped fruit.

'Too close,' Varro said helpfully. 'Apples too close.'

Rufus glared at him and climbed down for another basket.

It was nightfall when he finally gave up. By trying a longer pole, he could get her to rise on her hind legs, but nothing would make her walk. He was hoarse from repeating the word apple over and over again. Sometimes there were apples in the basket, sometimes not. If an apple was available, she would rear for it, but if she felt she had been cheated she lumbered off in a sulk and wouldn't repeat the trick for half an hour.

The days to the Emperor's deadline melted away, and Rufus descended into gloom, and from gloom to something approaching despair.

Dawn on the fateful day found him with little optimism. His only hope was that Caligula had forgotten him. Great emperors surely had more to do with their time than concern themselves with minor slaves and their amusing – or not – elephants.

But, if the worst happened, he was determined Caligula should see Bersheba at her finest. It would also put the elephant on her best be-haviour, for she enjoyed nothing more than having her thick, dirt-caked hide scrubbed down with the roughest materials available.

The two men led the elephant out into the soft light of the morning. They then filled a large wooden tub with enough water to soak the huge animal all over her body, using leather buckets Varro had obtained for the purpose. When the dust covering her was the consistency of thick mud it was time to bring out the home-made brushes the late trainer had devised. Fashioned of thick twigs tied firmly to the end of long branches, they allowed them to reach any part of Bersheba's body and loosen the grime, so she could then have a second sluicing with what was left of the water.

Soon, Rufus was so absorbed in his work and the snorting Bersheba's enjoyment of the soaking and scrubbing that he had almost forgotten its purpose. But his idyll was rudely shattered when he heard an unnaturally loud voice behind him.

He rested his aching arms and turned, sweat dripping from his chin, to see Caligula approaching across the grass, accompanied by a smaller figure, who walked with a pronounced limp. They were back-lit by the sun as it rose behind the trees and Rufus was unable to recognize the second man.

'I told you this would be worth rising early for, Claudius, you lazy old drunk. Did you think I'd let you forget your promise and leave you lying with that little slut you sneaked away with when you thought I wasn't looking?'

The braying tones, the stained clothes and the way the Emperor's head lolled on his long neck told Rufus that even if this Claudius had been to bed, Caligula himself had not yet called a halt to the night's revels.

'Boy! You, boy. Let us see what the beast can do. It had better be goo–'

The roar of an elephant whose morning toilet had been rudely interrupted obliterated the words.

Caligula blinked and rocked back on his heels. Then, with a loud laugh, he slapped his companion on the back so hard that the man was almost knocked off his feet.

'Nearly scared the shit out of you, eh? You were never very brave, Uncle Claudius. 'S why old Tiberius sent you away. Lucky I brought you back. Tricks, boy,' he said in a voice now with a worrying edge to it. 'I brought Senator Claudius here to see some tricks. And because he's got ears as big as an elephant's, haven't you, Claudius?'

The Emperor stood behind his companion, took a remarkably prominent earlobe in each hand and pulled outwards.

'See, just like an elephant. Uncle Claudius hasn't had a lot of luck in his life, have you, Uncle? Runt of the litter. Talks l-l-l-l-like that and is bloody useless in every way. Still, he's family,' he said, rubbing his hand affectionately through the older man's thinning hair. 'Tricks, now. We want to see some elephant tricks.'

Rufus felt something curl over his shoulder and pull impatiently at his arm. He said nervously: 'If the Emperor could wait a few moments longer, I–'

He was interrupted by Caligula's snarl. 'I don't wait, boy.'

Heart sinking, Rufus bowed. His only hope was to put Bersheba through her paces and pray that Caligula – at least he was still drunk – was somehow impressed. He was about to turn back towards the elephant when a tremendous jet of water shot past his shoulder. It was a mighty effort, an entire trunkful propelled with all the power of Bersheba's prodigious lungs. It took the shocked Claudius full in the chest and face, soaking him to the skin and rocking him back on his heels, and was instantly followed by a squeal of outraged indignation.

Rufus froze. It couldn't have happened. Not that. He was a dead man.

The two men, Emperor and uncle, could have been part of one of the marble tableaux that adorned Caligula's palace. They stood, stock-still, pale-faced, eyes wide in shock.

Then Caligula laughed.

It started deep in his belly, a pulsating unstoppable rumbling that surged into his chest and finally erupted in a series of hysterical whoops. The Emperor held his stomach with one hand, helpless to stop the relentless guffaws, while with the other he pointed at the hapless Claudius.

The older man's wispy grey hair was plastered across his pink scalp and his sodden toga dripped a steady stream of water on to the ground at his feet. His lips moved, but the words he searched for eluded him and his pale eyes stared at Rufus with a look of pure bewilderment.

By the time the Emperor's laughter subsided to a series of breathless sobs, Rufus's instinct for self-preservation had reasserted itself. He strode across to Bersheba and whispered the order to mount. She took a single step forward, bent one giant knee until it touched the ground, and bowed her head forward. But Rufus didn't use her leg to vault on to her back as he normally would. Instead, he stood motionless beside Bersheba until the Emperor recovered and looked in their direction. Then he gave a deep bow.

To Caligula it appeared as if both animal and slave were making their obeisance to him. He clapped his hands, crying: 'Wonderful. What a trick. I haven't seen anything that made me truly laugh for years. Now I shall bring all my friends to see the elephant and it can greet them as it greeted Uncle Claudius. Come, Claudius, let's get back and get you dried out,' he said, taking the still-dripping senator by the arm. 'But you're not even smiling? You must see the funny side, surely. A senator of Rome looking like a drowned rabbit. Ha, ha, ha...'

Claudius shook himself free of his nephew's arm and turned to stare at Rufus and the elephant. 'Wh-wh-wh-what is your name, slave?'

Rufus hesitated: 'It is Rufus, sir. I'm very sorry. Bersheba did not mean to harm you.'

Claudius stared at him for a second. 'R-r-r-rufus. I will r-r-r-remember that.'

Then the bedraggled figure limped slowly after the Emperor, whose broad shoulders still shook with laughter.

XV

For weeks, Rufus waited in dread for the Emperor's return, but Caligula never did bring anyone else to see the elephant. There was always the nagging fear that he would turn up and demand to see a new and even more hilarious trick, but Rufus was able to put the matter to the back of his mind and get to know better the ways of his new charge.

Bersheba's only obvious weakness was her sight. The small eyes, set to the front of the big, sail-eared head, gave her little peripheral vision. But if her eyesight was defective, her other senses amply compensated for it. The two hairy nostrils set into the fleshy pink end of her five-foot trunk were so finely tuned it scarcely seemed believable. Her hearing, too, verged on the supernatural. When visitors approached, Bersheba was aware of their presence minutes before either Varro or Rufus. The elephant's early-warning system kept them out of quite serious trouble on several occasions, when the Emperor's overseers came to call.

Of course, some visitors were more welcome than others.

He was exercising Bersheba on the parkland in front of the barn when he saw them. At first, he didn't know what to make of the noisy little group, but as they came closer he recognized the excited, high-pitched voices of young women.

There were six of them, accompanied by two Praetorians. Rufus scanned the faces of the two soldiers, but neither was Cupido. Caligula had hundreds of guards stationed on the Palatine and in the surrounding area. The gladiator could be anywhere, if he was still alive.

Careful not to make it obvious, he let his gaze stray across the women. When he realized who they were a shiver of apprehension ran down his spine. Bersheba must have sensed his unease, because her big shoulders shifted beneath him and her trunk came up to test the air. For once, Rufus did not need her talents. He knew danger when he saw it, and to underestimate this innocent gathering would be as fatal as stepping on a nest of mating cobras.

'Why haven't you brought us here before, Drusilla?' the oldest of the group demanded of the tall girl at her side.

'You know full well, Milonia, that your husband, my brother, forbade it. But while Gaius Caligula is off to outdo Xerxes at Baiae, Callistus would not dare oppose my wishes, nor yours, sweet sister.' Caligula's sister Drusilla gave a waspish smile. 'Of course, if he discovered you were risking the life of his baby daughter in the presence of the great beast, you would be making a living on your back again from passing soldiers, although I'm sure you wouldn't find it too unpleasant.'

Milonia, a strong-featured woman with a hawkish nose, huffed: 'Hark at the innocent one, to talk that way of me. Didn't you share my husband's bed long before I and does the whole world not know it?'

Drusilla laughed, and tossed her auburn hair. 'It was a mere sisterly duty, and a not unpleasant one at that. Can it be, Milonia, you fear my brother will tire of your ever so professional efforts and seek out a sweeter, more succulent fruit?'

'Must we always return to this subject?' the third of the group, a plump young woman in a pink dress, interrupted. 'My ears ache at your constant prattle and you know how the servants talk.'

'I think you are just jealous, Livilla, that you and

127

Agrippina are too plain to attract the Emperor's attentions,' Drusilla said. 'It is an honour as well as a pleasure to share his bed. Think of it, a pure bloodline direct from Augustus as our brother's heir. Better that than the fat little monkey who is the fruit of Agrippina's unattractive husband's loins.'

Agrippina gave Drusilla a cool smile. She had heard all this a dozen times before and was immune to her sister's mocking.

'The auguries have predicted that Nero will grow up to be a fine young man. He may never rule Rome, sister, but, under the direction of his mother, he will become a great Roman.'

'Oh, we all know your ambitions, Agrippina. It is fortunate, is it not, that Gaius is still unaware of their extent, but perhaps my tongue will slip when next we ... meet.' Drusilla rolled the final word across her lips with a sensuality that gave it only one meaning, attracting a sour look from Milonia.

'I thought we were here to see this beast which so fascinates my husband. I hope it does more than plod up and down with that dirty young man on its back.'

Drusilla followed her gaze. 'Are we to look up to a slave?'

Rufus belatedly realized he should have dismounted to greet them. He slid from Bersheba's back and stood by her shoulder. Drusilla was only feet from him. He dared not look directly into her eyes, so he stared over her shoulder and his breath caught in his throat.

The girl looking back at him was the most

beautiful woman he had ever seen. Dark, liquid eyes seemed to feed off his spirit and the amused glint in them informed him she was quite enjoying his discomfort. She was the tallest of the six women, but, he guessed, also the youngest. Lustrous golden hair fell in folds over her shoulders, and her cherry-red shift bulged with the promise of full, rounded breasts. She must have been sixteen or seventeen and she carried a squirming, dark-haired child of about nine months old.

He tore his gaze away with difficulty, and found himself staring into Drusilla's eyes, which held a message so obvious it drove all other thoughts from his mind. She stepped closer to him, so that his gaze was drawn to the low-cut dress and the dark cleft between her breasts. She was so close he could feel her breath on his cheek and the scent of her perfume overwhelmed his senses. There was something else, too: not a scent exactly, more a hint in the air, but so powerful it had an instant effect on him. He gasped as he felt a disturbance below his tunic, and bit his lip hard in an attempt to control the uncontrollable.

Milonia gave a coarse laugh. 'Don't you have enough puppy dogs, Drusilla? This one isn't even house-trained.' She turned to the blonde-haired girl whose beauty had so captivated Rufus. 'Aemilia, bring little Drusilla here. It is time for her feed.'

Rufus turned away, but Drusilla was still staring at him. 'What is your name?' she demanded.

'Rufus, lady.' His voice sounded as brittle as cracking ice.

129

'Well, Rufus,' she said, putting unnecessary emphasis on his name, 'tell us all about your pet.'

They stayed for an hour, watching as he showed off Bersheba's great strength and the delicate way she could use her trunk to pick up small objects. The only time Milonia and Livilla looked interested was when Bersheba let out an enormous fart. By this time they were competing to show how bored they were with both the elephant and its handler.

'Come, it is time we left,' Milonia said, attempting to reassert her position as the Emperor's consort.

'Wait, I have an idea.' All eyes turned to Agrippina and Milonia pursed her lips in annoyance. 'Our brother said the most amusing thing happened when the beast was bathed. Bathe the elephant for us, slave.

Drusilla clapped her hands and bounced on her feet like a child. 'Yes, bathe the elephant.'

Rufus hesitated. He normally only washed Bersheba in the morning and she was a creature of habit. He was not sure how she would react. On the other hand, he had no choice but to obey the Emperor's sisters. They stared blankly at him, waiting for him to move, but the girl Aemilia gave him an encouraging smile and his spirits rose.

'Come, Bersheba.' He led her back to the barn and chained her to her block.

He filled the first bucket and steadied himself to throw it over her back, but then hesitated. He still had his tunic on. He was reluctant to remove it in front of the women, who now sat together on a slight rise, but it was his only one and if it became soaked he would have nothing else to wear.

He went into the barn and stripped to his loincloth, folding his tunic carefully, before returning into the sunlight. He tried to ignore his audience, but he felt every eye on him, and at least one of the women let out a short gasp of appreciation. He was a little self-conscious about being almost naked in front of them, but he knew he had nothing to be ashamed of. There was not a spare ounce of flesh on his body, and the exercises Cupido had taught him had given him the firm muscles of an athlete.

He tried to concentrate on the job of first soaking Bersheba and then brushing her down, but there was something disconcerting about being studied like an animal in one of the Emperor's cages. He caught Drusilla's eye and his attention wavered. It meant he didn't see Bersheba dip her trunk into the bucket. The explosive jet that hit him knocked the breath from his body and froze him to the marrow.

The women squealed with laughter and Bersheba joined in with a trumpeting hoot. When his senses recovered Rufus could only reflect that now he knew how Claudius had felt. Then the tone of the laughter changed subtly and he sensed something different in the way they were watching him. Drusilla uncurled from her position the way a particularly healthy cat will, and approached him with a frank smile.

'Well, Rufus, the elephant man, we must thank you for a fine performance. My brother was right: elephants can be most entertaining, and,' her voice dropped to a whisper, 'we all found it very revealing, very revealing indeed.' She let her eyes drop to the level of his groin.

With a laugh, she turned away and led the giggling females up the slope towards Caligula's palace. As they went, Aemilia turned to give him a shy smile.

XVI

How could anyone be so beautiful? He breathed in the musky scent of her dark hair and couldn't stifle a tiny sob. Her hand reached up to gently stroke his brow. 'Hush, brother. You are home now.'

Home? Yes, this was home, this comfortable blood-warm, silken cocoon within Drusilla's arms where no one could ever hurt him. He had always felt safe here, even in the darkest times on Capri. Those were the times when Tiberius, rot his corrupt soul, had roamed the corridors of the palace like some scab-ridden hunting dog seeking new depths of depravity to plumb. The nights he knew that only by being invisible would he be safe. He remembered how he would wait until Gemellus was asleep in the room they shared then creep past the guards to his sister. Did they really not see him? Or did they retain some spark of decency despite all they witnessed on that debauched cesspit of an isle? At first, all he sought was comfort and the security of her presence. He would hold her hand through the dark hours and she would whisper her tales of their father; tales of honour and courage, of a goodness that seemed to belong to a different world from the one they inhabited. In their childish eyes, Germanicus, most noble of Romans, shone like a beacon in the stygian gloom of their existence. Later it was different.

Something stirred deep within him as his mind took him back to the night everything changed. Was he the instigator, or she? No, it was *they*, together, and at once innocent and knowing, a fusion of mind and body that neither could nor wished to deny.

She felt it too and purred like a cat at his side. 'So soon?'

Deep in the night he woke to find her silhouetted in the wide window that looked out over the Velabrum towards the Capitoline, her naked body cloaked in the warm glow of a harvest moon. She stood motionless, allowing its light to paint her flawless skin so it appeared she had just emerged from a bath of molten gold. Yes, she was a golden statue. Perfect. He didn't breathe. He didn't want her to move. When she finally did, turning back towards the satin-covered bed, his head filled with a sudden unbidden rage. How could she cheat him?

'You shouldn't have moved.' He tried to keep his voice level, but she recognized the edge to it.

'Tell me again about Baiae,' she said, slipping into bed and wrapping her body around him, so his flesh burned to the feel of hers. 'On the day you rode with the gods and defied Neptune.'

His mood changed as she knew it would. 'Was Alexander ever so fortunate, or Xerxes? I outdid them both. Two hundred ships bought or built, strung bow to stern in twin lines across the bay from the port at Baiae to the mole at Puteoli.' His heart soared with the memory of it. He had ordered a thousand carpenters to build a wooden pathway two chariots wide over the ships, and when it was complete five thousand slaves carried the earth that turned it into a road. A road across the sea. Two miles, at least; some men said three. Three, then. 'On the first day I donned the breastplate Alexander wore at Granicus, and my bejewelled cloak of purple, and I bade my Praetorians follow me as I galloped the length of the sea-bridge. On the second, I held a great spectacle and the two legions who escorted my chariot loved me for it. The people too. It was as if the whole world watched from the shore. Has any man been so fortunate?'

Drusilla stared at him, bright-eyed. 'You are no man, brother, but a god, an earth-bound god.'

He nodded. He knew she was right. She was always right.

'Yet the Senate would have thwarted me. The fools did not understand my purpose or that my glory is Rome's glory. Spend your own gold, they said, not Rome's. So I did. My inheritance is gone, but this I swear by Jupiter's lightning bolt. They will pay. They will pay a thousand-fold.'

As he spoke, he felt his face grow grim, and saw the fear in Drusilla's eyes as his hands caressed her neck. The fear pleased him.

'They hate me. Do you hate me, Drusilla?' He

allowed his fingers to tighten on her throat. Saw her mouth open and her eyes bulge. 'Do you hate me?'

She tried to shake her head, but his hands were compressing her windpipe and cutting off the air to her lungs. Her vision faded and turned first pink, then red with a halo of black. She knew that when the black halo filled, she would be dead. But there was no more fear, only exhilaration. To die at this man's hands was to be immortal!

Slowly, the grip on her throat slackened. The black faded to red, then to pink, and when she opened her eyes he was there above her, his eyes shining with desire.

'Yes,' she cried. 'Yes, Gaius. Please. Now.'

Aemilia's smile haunted Rufus. She followed him into his dreams, where her beauty tantalized him and he was tempted to places he had never imagined. But always she would be just beyond his reach, so he would feel the warmth radiating from her, but never the touch of her velvet flesh. See the glinting golden highlights of her hair, but never stroke its silken strands.

Even in daylight her presence seemed to be all around him. Every female voice he heard was hers. Every glimpse of a red dress through the trees or in the far distances made his heart race and his stomach churn. He imagined what they would do together, and what he would say to her. Even the simplest things would be a pleasure with Aemilia. Just to be with her would be enough.

Yet on those infrequent occasions when the red dress was hers he was left with a sense of failure.

Yes, she would smile at him, but she seemed to smile at everyone. Her greeting was warm, but was it *special?* She was never alone, so he couldn't ask her the things he longed to ask, or tell her the things she needed to be told. He thought he was making his feelings for her plain, but since she never responded or made *her* feelings known, how could he be sure? The merest hint would have been enough, yet the closest thing to a signal had been the faint suspicion of puzzlement in her eyes on a day when he had held his smile a few seconds longer than normal and she had asked him if he was unwell.

As the weeks passed, he realized he was being a fool and prayed for the feelings to go, but they never did. The only thing that drove her from his mind was the uncertain reality of life in Caligula's court.

The young Emperor exerted a baleful influence far beyond his immediate physical presence. Those closest to him lived, if not in fear, then certainly in a state of constant confusion as they attempted to preempt his ever-changing moods. This uncertainty filtered down from consul to senator, from freedman to clerk, and finally from palace servant to slave. Mistakes, even small ones, could be lethal. There was always room for one more sacrifice at Caligula's never-ending spectacles. People disappeared.

One day it was Varro.

Rufus discovered later that the little man had come to an agreement with a palace official to supply the farms that still studded Rome's suburbs with Bersheba's rich manure. Unfortunately, the little black man made the mistake of becoming too close to the wife of one of the farmers who was the recipient of the elephant's bounty. When she foolishly confessed to the liaison, her husband approached the overseer and threatened to end their productive relationship. A word to the palace guards had been enough.

Varro's fate shocked Rufus, but he had little time to mourn his friend. Now he had twice the work to do. And something much more dangerous to worry about.

He was mucking out the elephant's quarters as the autumn shadows lengthened early one evening when two Praetorian guardsmen approached the barn.

'You are to come with us,' the senior ordered.

Rufus froze. Was he to follow Varro to the arena? But he couldn't refuse. He turned towards the cistern, intending to wash the hard-caked elephant dung from his body.

'You've no time for that.'

The guards escorted him up the slope to the palace and through a series of lavish corridors to a room where a group of exquisitely dressed aristocrats stared at the new arrival as if he had just arrived from the wrong side of the River Styx.

'At last, the elephant boy. Our final guest has arrived; now we can begin.' The Emperor was seated on a couch at the far end of the room. The pale eyes studied Rufus for a few seconds that sent a shiver of fear through him, before a languid hand motioned towards an empty couch that was one of more than a dozen surrounding a long table which appeared to be crafted of solid silver. The Praetorian at his back gave Rufus a gentle push and left to take his place among twenty of his fellows positioned at intervals around the walls. Rufus noticed that each of them had his right hand on his sword hilt.

Was he dreaming? Anything seemed more likely than the reality. He walked slowly towards the table and sat bolt upright on the padded couch Caligula had designated.

'No, no,' Caligula said almost soothingly. 'Relax. Slave, bring my friend some wine.'

Rufus realized that everyone else in the room was lounging on one elbow on the couches, which were placed within easy reach of the main table so that their occupants could help themselves to the banquet. Awkwardly, he attempted to copy the nonchalant posture of the others, while a slave approached the table and placed a large drinking cup in front of him.

The Emperor raised his own goblet in a silent toast directed at Rufus, the cold eyes daring him to drink. Rufus reached out a shaking hand to lift the cup, which was filled with blood-red wine that had a strong fruity odour. The others supped deeply, but he ensured that not a drop passed his lips.

Caligula was now chatting animatedly with a sickly looking man of similar age who had the couch to his right, and Rufus was able to snatch a covert glance around the room, although he was careful not to meet the eye of any of his dining companions.

There appeared to be two distinct groups round

the table. One was made up of men who hung on the Emperor's every word, laughed uproariously at his jokes and matched him drink for drink. The other group was quieter, drank less, and picked at their food. These were all couples of the equestrian class, seated in pairs. They were not all young, but the women had a well-cultivated beauty regardless of age. Rufus noted that their faces wore the same hopeless expression he had last observed on the condemned prisoners he had seen beneath the arena.

Then his eyes locked on those of Claudius.

The Emperor's uncle lay on a couch at the far end of the table. He looked back at Rufus from beneath hooded lids as a dribble of wine escaped the corner of his mouth and ran lazily down the contours of his chin to stain an already un-redeemable toga. He appeared quite drunk, but a gleam in an eye that should have been dull indicated he was probably less so than he seemed. Rufus was surprised when the old man raised his goblet in a mock salute.

The food that was served would have fed a family of the poorer sort for a month. First came the small fare: exotic concoctions of the inner parts of birds and beasts, including their livers, tongues and brains; sea urchins, mussels of three distinct varieties, two kinds of sea snails, oysters and other sorts of shellfish; and a plate of roasted thrushes on asparagus. Then the greater: birds of all sizes, including chickens and pigeons, cooked golden brown (he also recognized a swan and a peacock because they had been decorated with their natural livery); meats of various shades and textures, which certainly included a sow's udder and the entire head of a wild boar; and an array of small bowls which held delicately sliced and chopped vegetables.

With every course, the wine flowed faster and the noise grew louder at the end of the table where Caligula held court. Rufus caught snatches of conversation from the Emperor, who was still engaged in an intense discussion with the man on the couch at his right side.

'Scribonius Proculus and his brother are becoming more than irritants, Protogenes, they are dangerous. I want them dealt with. Put them on the little list in your book.'

Protogenes, thin to the point of emaciation, with a sallow, pockmarked complexion, nodded agreement. He had hooded eyes that reminded Rufus of a snake and he felt a thrill of fear as they turned to focus on him. He knew instantly that Protogenes was aware the Emperor's words had been overheard and was equally certain that the man was deciding whether he was worth killing. The unblinking stare held his for a second before moving on. It seemed not.

By now, Rufus had recognized that he was as much part of the entertainment as the Illyrian dancing girls and the fire-eating jugglers who performed after the main courses. A pungently scented diversion to keep Caligula's guests the way he wanted them – off balance and nervous.

As much a part of the entertainment as Uncle Claudius.

During the early part of the banquet the Emperor had ignored the old senator, happy to trade conversation and banter with the sycophants who lounged close by him. But as the evening continued, Caligula began to taunt his uncle about his stutter and his appearance. When he tired of this verbal barrage, the Emperor began to throw pieces of food at the reclining figure, who could only blink as he was hit by slices of meat and half-eaten legs of chicken and, at one point, only just missed by a plate of fricasseed flamingo tongues. Still not satisfied, the Emperor encouraged his guests to follow his example, and, even though the attack was somewhat half-hearted, Claudius could eventually take no more. With a vacant smile he slowly closed his eyes and slipped back on the couch feigning stupor.

Caligula and his friends were by now finding that the fluency and ingenuity of their earlier conversation had deserted them. The Emperor, his face wreathed in a lazy grin, let his gaze range over his guests until it fell on a striking, raven-haired young woman who reclined, never raising her glance above table height, next to a crop-haired knight who was a little older than she, who Rufus assumed must be her husband. From that moment, Caligula's eyes never left her.

As the last of the food was cleared away, the Emperor rose from his couch. Rufus felt the guests around him tense and the guards along the wall seemed to stand a little straighter. Caligula swayed slightly, then walked carefully round the table until he was directly behind the dark girl, who, feeling his presence, began to whimper quietly behind the curtain of her long hair. At her side, her husband was deathly still.

'You will please me tonight, Cornelia,' Caligula said softly, his hand reaching out to caress the white skin of the woman's shoulder.

The young aristocrat beside her jerked violently and made as if to rise.

'You may join us if you wish, Calpurnius,' the Emperor offered. 'No? Perhaps I should insist. Never mind, I shall decide later. Come, Cornelia.'

The last words were an unmistakable command. Still weeping, the dark-haired woman stood up on shaking legs and, with Caligula's hand on her shoulder, walked with him from the room.

The mood of the remaining guests changed in an instant from unbearable tension to ecstatic release. A grey-faced young senator vomited on the marble floor, while nearby another aristocrat appeared to be having a seizure. The women at the table reacted in different ways. One or two seemed to be frozen where they lay, eyes fixed on something only they could see. The blonde matron who occupied the couch next to Rufus ran wailing from the room, pursued by her husband. From the corner of his eye, Rufus noticed Claudius, forgotten by all, raise his head warily.

A tap on the shoulder made Rufus jump and he looked up into a familiar grave face beneath a Praetorian helmet. Cupido.

XVII

He opened his mouth to speak, but the gladiator cut him off with a shake of the head.

'Fun's over, boy. Time to go home.'

A second Praetorian moved to join him as they turned from the room into a wide corridor, but Cupido waved him away.

'I think I can handle this one alone, Decimus, if I can stand the stink.'

The other man, a broad-faced giant, laughed and said something unintelligible.

'Cupido!' Rufus burst out when they reached the park. 'I–'

'Not here,' the young German hissed. 'Don't say anything until we reach the barn, and then only when I have checked.'

Rufus began to lead the way to the room at the rear of the elephant stall, but Cupido stopped him.

'More secure beside the beast, I think. Speak quietly; the Emperor has listeners everywhere and they are not always who you think they are. In future, visit me at my quarters. When I am off duty I have a room in the palace of Tiberius. I will leave word that you are welcome there.'

Rufus was a little confused by Cupido's excessive caution, but he grinned with the pleasure of seeing the young gladiator again.

'Same old Cupido, always taking the best from

life. Forgive me, my friend, but just to be in your presence again fills my heart, even in this dismal place. When they arrested you, I thought you were dead.'

The gladiator raised a sardonic eyebrow and for a moment he truly was the same old Cupido. Yet Rufus could see the months in the palace had changed his friend. The grey eyes contained an embittered weariness that had not been there previously. It was as if the sombre black tunic, which was the symbol of the Emperor's authority, had somehow worked its darkness into his spirit. Combined with the gleaming armour of his sculpted breastplate and greaves, it gave him a dangerous quality Rufus had not seen even on the hardest days in the arena.

Bersheba grunted beside them, and Rufus's face creased into a grin.

'I forget my manners. Mighty Bersheba, this is my friend Cupido, the greatest gladiator of his age, philosopher, wit and now in his most unlikely guise, unless I miss my guess, as First Spear of the Tungrian Cohort of the Emperor's Praetorian Guard.'

Cupido stepped forward and Bersheba's trunk swung out of the darkness to take his scent. She gave a 'harrumph' from deep in her chest.

'You are honoured, Cupido; you have been accepted into Bersheba's inner circle ... just as you have into the Emperor's.'

The last words were part statement, but with enough of a question in them for Cupido to remove his iron helmet and place it on the hay beside him as he sat with his back to the barn wall. He looked up at Rufus, his face a mask of shadows and hollows.

'You say you thought I was dead? I was certain of it. I don't have much time, but I will try to explain how all this' – he waved a hand that took in Bersheba, Rufus and himself – 'came about.'

In a steady voice he confirmed what Narcissus had suspected, but there was more. The guards had taken Cupido to a dungeon beneath the palace of Caligula, deep in the bowels of the Palatine, where they stripped him of everything he owned. It was a place known only to the Emperor's closest allies, his torturers, and, for a few mercifully fleeting hours, his enemies.

'It was a dreadful place,' Cupido confessed grimly, 'where the smell of burning flesh invaded the air I breathed, and the screams of the helpless tortured my ears. They took me past the chamber of the hot irons and sharp instruments and I had to turn my eyes away. I have seen suffering in many forms, Rufus, but what I glimpsed there still haunts my dreams.'

He was taken from his cell on the evening of the third day.

'They dragged me before the Emperor naked and coated in my own ordure, so my humiliation would compound my fear. But I called on my father's shade for courage and I stood before him, proud as on any day since coming to manhood, and bade him do as he willed. I expected to feel the kiss of a blade at any moment, but he did not give the order. Instead, he raised himself from his golden throne and stood before me, close as you are now, never flinching at my stink.

145

Then, I swear by the old gods, his mind entered mine and he knew me. Knew me past, present and future.

'At first, I felt more abused than if his torturers had returned me to the dungeons, but he has power, Rufus, great power, and he used it to overwhelm me.'

Cupido swallowed hard and shook his head in wonder.

'How long I was in his thrall I don't know. I felt dizzy with hunger, or perhaps the water they gave me was drugged. Eventually he returned to his throne and ordered his guards to bathe and clothe me. The clothes were these clothes, the uniform of the Praetorian Guard. When I stood before him in them, he returned to me my long sword and asked me for my oath. I gave him it.' His head dropped and he whispered the words again, as if he could barely believe their meaning. 'I gave him it.'

Rufus listened first with horror, then with disbelief. 'It cannot be. The Cupido I know could not pledge his loyalty to that man. He is a monster. I have witnessed it.'

Cupido snorted. 'Witnessed it? You have seen nothing. In this place and among these people you are a child, and you should pray it stays so. You don't know what he is capable of and if you did it would eat your mind and chill your guts. That is what I came here to tell you. You must find a way back to Fronto. It is not as unlikely as it seems. The Emperor's moods are fickle. He will soon tire of you and your elephant.'

Rufus shook his head. 'No. I will not leave you.

146

Teach me to fight as you do and together we can survive. You are right, you must have been drugged. You owe Caligula nothing. An oath administered without honour is an oath in name only.'

Cupido laughed gently. 'The way I fight cannot be taught, Rufus, though I will train you to a standard where you will at least be able to defend yourself when the time comes. But you are wrong: an oath is an oath as long as the oath-sayer believes it. In any case, I owe him more than my loyalty.'

'What?'

'My sister.'

Hours later Rufus sat in the darkness, still stunned by the gladiator's revelation.

Cupido had told of a day of fire and blood when the auxiliary cavalrymen of a Roman army cut down his fellow tribesmen like rows of summer corn and the booted feet of the legions smashed them into the mud of the fields where they made their futile last stand.

'My father was the last to fall. He fought them to his final breath and when the swords chopped him down, he died still shouting his war cry. I was young and had been left behind to defend our village and the women and children. My father said it was an honour, but I think he understood what would happen. When the Romans came I wanted to take my men out to fight, but the village elders knew the Roman way. If we resisted they would have killed everything. Man, woman and child. Horse, dog and pig. Nothing would have been left to mark the passing of my tribe save dry bones and old stories. Still,' his voice grew thick with pride, 'my sister Ilde, only twelve years old, stood on the walls and screamed her defiance until I carried her to our mother.'

He smiled his sad smile. 'The old men would have been better to let me fight. Those who were not fit for the mines and the quarries were put to the sword where they stood. The rest were taken as slaves. I can still feel the weight of the chains on my wrists and smell the woodsmoke from the burning huts. The last I saw of Ilde was in the slave market. I tried to talk to her – to explain – but she would not meet my eyes. I knew she despised me for not having the courage to die with my people.'

Then, three months after his last fight in the arena, and four long years since he had been taken into captivity, Caligula had called him to an audience.

'He told me: "I have a gift for my most faithful servant, Cupido of the Guard, who holds my life in his hands." A girl walked into the room, a tall girl with hair the colour of spun gold and the proud bearing of a princess. At first I thought his gift was a concubine to share my bed – he has re-warded others in this way – but then I looked into the girl's eyes and I knew it was Ilde. My lost sister.'

Rufus could not say when it happened, but there came a moment in Cupido's story when the realization struck him like a blow from Bersheba's trunk. He knew.

'Now she is an honoured member of the palace staff. She is maid to the lady Milonia, the Em-

peror's wife, and charged with the safekeeping of
his daughter. You would know her as Aemilia.'

Aemilia.

XVIII

He lay back in the great golden throne that
dominated the Receiving Room and wondered
why he didn't feel happy. Was it too much to ask?
After all, he was the leader of the most powerful
Empire the world had ever known. He looked
over the throng of appellants gathered at the far
end of the room. Did they realize how difficult it
was?

His surveyors were at work planning the canal
across the Ionian isthmus which would be his gift
to Greece. He had rebuilt the walls and the
temples of Syracuse. Soon there would be a new
city among the high peaks that would become the
economic driving force of Cisalpine Gaul.

But it was not enough. It was never enough.

They were all waiting for him, but this was
important. He was beginning to understand.

How could he have all he had and do what he
did and still feel empty?

Limits. It was all about limits.

Everything had a limit. You could have all the
pleasure in the world, but unless someone was
sharing your pleasure it was never enough. You
could eat the most exotic foods the Empire had
to offer and drink the finest wines, but eventually

they all began to taste the same. Men had their limits. There was a limit to how fast they could run in the games, or how high they could jump. There was a limit to how much pain a man could suffer before he died; he had tested that limit often.

Even love had its limits. Drusilla loved him, he knew, and Milonia had proved her love a thousand times, but was their love everlasting? He doubted it. He had thought of testing the limits of their love in his torture chamber, but he knew that if he did he'd lose them. And who else could he trust?

None of the men in this room. Look at them, every one wearing a mask, trying to hide their fear or their hatred or their greed. Any one of them could be part of the plots against him. Perhaps he should have them all killed? It would make life so much simpler. Clearer.

He looked towards the centurion in charge of the Guard. It was the Germans today. He liked the Germans because they hated the Italians.

The soldier came at his call.

'If I wished it, would you kill every man in this room?' he said quietly.

For an instant, the centurion's eyes went wide, but the discipline that had helped him survive a hundred combats quickly took over. His hand went to his sword.

'Of course, Caesar. At your order!'

Should he? He looked over the faces. Senators and knights. Praetors and tribunes. Men who called themselves his friends and others who did not try to hide their scorn. The Judaean who had

150

been boring him for a week about the problems of his benighted province. It would cause complications. He had another thought.

'If I ordered it, would you kill me?'

The soldier froze. What answer would he give to this unanswerable question?

He watched the man's face grow paler as the seconds passed. Tiny beads of sweat broke out upon his brow as he wrestled with the terrible implications of his next words. His mouth opened and closed like a dying fish, which was amusing.

Eventually, he became bored. 'You are dismissed. We will discuss this further another time.'

He picked at the platter of food by the side of the throne. Really, it was all so tedious. Had he tasted everything there was to taste? He let the long list slide through his mind. But there was a gap. Yes, there was one type of flesh he had never tasted. The forbidden flesh. He looked up. It would be interesting, exciting even. Who would it be? The fat one at the back? The athlete fidgeting by the wall? No shortage of choice.

He pondered the question for a full minute.

No, he thought, not today.

He smiled as he learned a new truth. Even he had a limit. He wasn't sure whether to be pleased or disappointed.

For a short time Rufus became an occasional guest at the Emperor's table. If he was not fouled or dirty enough when they came for him, the Praetorians would order him to rub himself down with dung gathered from the heap behind the barn.

The pattern of the evenings was always the same. The ritual humiliation of Claudius. The unbearable tension. The shocking moment of choice which reminded Rufus that slaves were not the only powerless of Rome.

He came to recognize the Emperor's favourites; the nobles who fawned over him as he raged against the mob and the 'baldheads' of the Senate he believed were working to deprive him of the money he needed to fulfil his ambitions. Chief among them were Appeles, the very young, overly powdered actor who had a laugh like a little girl, and was ever present at Caligula's side; Protogenes, his freedman and trusted adviser, unhealthily pale with a face that never smiled, who was never without the two scrolls the Emperor called his 'sword' and his 'dagger', which were said to contain enough secrets to execute a thousand men; and purple-cheeked Chaerea, the Praetorian tribune, a battle-hardened soldier with an unfortunate high-pitched voice, who had to bear being called a 'pretty wench' by his Emperor.

But, as he tired of everything else, the Emperor eventually tired of Rufus's presence. The 'invitations' stopped and he was left in peace.

When he was off duty, and they could find some quiet place where they would not be overlooked, Cupido would give Rufus the training in arms he had requested. It was a perilous business for them both. For a slave to be found with a sword in his hand on the Palatine the penalty was instant death. The man who gave him the sword would die screaming in the Emperor's torture cells. The hill was a small, compact and bustling community but the park in front of Bersheba's barn was close to the tree-lined walls and they discovered that among the trees there were suitable places to conceal their activities.

On the first day, Cupido handed Rufus a short wooden baton the approximate dimensions of a legionary *gladius*. 'Being so obviously harmless may not save us,' he explained. 'But at least it may make them stop and think.'

Cut, thrust, parry. Cupido began with the simplest moves, making Rufus repeat them again and again until his arms ached. 'Later we will study the more intricate manoeuvres, the feint to the groin, the back-cut and the gutting stroke, but for now this will do.'

Towards the end of the session, when Rufus began to tire, the gladiator laid down his wooden sword and ordered Rufus to do the same. 'A tired man is a dead man. I can teach you to defend yourself, but what use is that if your guard drops and you offer your life to your opponent like a sacrificial goat? You are strong, but you must be stronger.' He jogged across to the stone wall and in one smooth movement flipped himself upside down, so he was standing on his hands with his feet against the wall. 'Watch and learn,' he ordered. Rufus watched the muscles in Cupido's arms bunch and the tendons in them squirm like tree roots as, with quick easy movements, he bent at the elbows then straightened a dozen times.

'Now you.'

Rufus tentatively approached the wall and clumsily copied the gladiator's position, instantly feeling the strain on his arms. Cupido bent low, so his upside down face was close. 'Ten,' he said.

'Ten?' Rufus croaked in disbelief.

'Ten, and then we work on the abdominal muscles.'

When the session was finished Rufus's arms and upper body felt as if they were on fire, and his breath came in short gasps. He started to walk towards the barn, but Cupido's remorseless voice stopped him.

'So, you can fight. But what happens when the fighting is over?'

Rufus stared at him, puzzled. 'You celebrate?'

Cupido laughed. 'You're a slave. You run.' He trotted past, whacking Rufus across the buttocks with the pretend sword. 'You run. Twenty circuits of the park. Come on. No one is going to execute us for running.'

Rufus shook his head in disbelief, but his face creased into a grin and he forced his tired body into a trot. Staying alive was going to kill him.

The more time he spent with Bersheba, the more he appreciated his enormous charge's serene acceptance of life in captivity. She was happy to accommodate his wishes – if they coincided with her own – and her few complaints were made in what he chose to believe was a spirit of fellowship. They were both in this together, she seemed to be saying; they should make the best of it.

And she had a sense of humour. It was true. She played tricks on him, hiding things when he was not looking, placing small obstacles where he would trip over them. Afterwards, she would feign innocence. He could even look back now

154

and believe that she had been aware of exactly what she was doing when she had drenched Claudius on that fateful day.

Claudius.

Claudius the fool.

And now, Claudius the enigma.

It happened at a time when the Emperor retired to his villa in the hills above Rome to escape the savage heat that turned the city's streets into ovens.

Three days after Caligula left, Claudius appeared at Bersheba's barn.

At first Rufus wondered whether the limping patrician with the drooping eye sought revenge for his humiliation, but Claudius motioned him to continue his work and moved into the interior of the barn where he could study the elephant more closely.

This happened on three consecutive evenings. On the fourth night, as Rufus lay on his pallet, he heard the creak of the barn doors opening, and then closing again.

Claudius was back, standing in the darkness talking softly to the elephant, but what was more astonishing was the manner of his speech. The stutter that made him the butt of cruel jokes for everyone from the meanest palace slave to the Emperor himself was gone. This was a Claudius none would recognize. The tone was confident, the words flowed unhindered and the thoughts were articulately expressed.

And he was talking treason.

'Oh, Tiberius, what have you done to us? I know, I know, I had such high hopes for them too; the one so adventurous and full of ideas, the other a thinker, an organizer, and born to rule wisely. How naïve we were, how reckless. How long did we expect the stronger eaglet to share the nest with the weaker?

'Now your grandson Tiberius Gemellus is dead and Gaius Caligula holds Rome by the throat. Do you know what he said to me only a week ago? He said: "If the mob had but one neck I would sever it with a single stroke." He despises them, and they begin to hate him. Only the spectacle of the arena binds them to him, and they will only be blinded by blood for so long. Then we will all reap what he has sown.

'Yet I truly think he does not know the ruin he is causing. He is like a small child who has stumbled upon an ant heap. He is fascinated by the comings and goings, but how long before he decides to stir it with a stick and discovers he has the power to cause havoc among its populace? When he does, how much longer before, if he is that kind of child, he discovers he has the power of life and death over them? And how much longer before he uses that power? A certain kind of child might grow up to stick pins in the eyes of frogs and burn fledglings in their nests. Perhaps, as an adult, he would burn men.

'Caligula is curious to find out the limits of this power we have given him. But it has no limits; nor, I fear, does his curiosity. He will not listen to reason. Those close to him who spoke out are all long gone. The Senate lives in terror of his every pronouncement. I don't have the courage to stand in his way, and if I had I would be dead by now, "Uncle Claudius" or no. Only the army has the strength to rid us of him. But who gave him this childish nickname he bears so proudly, Caligula – Little Boots? No, the army loves him. But if not the army, then who?'

Having no answer, he left, shaking his head.

There were other such visits, and Rufus learned more than he wanted to know about the inner workings of the palace before the return of Caligula brought the encounters to an abrupt end. However, they did have one other consequence.

Narcissus appeared without warning on a fine morning when the dew still sparkled on the grass and clung to the gossamer webs the spiders had spun on the bushes.

'I am glad to hear you have settled in so well,' he called, as Rufus gave Bersheba her morning feed. 'You will no doubt have seen your friend? I understand he is high in the Emperor's favour. He has much to be thankful for ... as do you.'

Rufus stared at him. He had turned this matter over in his mind a thousand times and every time he had come to the same conclusion.

'This is your doing, Greek,' he said accusingly. 'It was you who had me brought here, to this place where the stink of death taints every hall. Do not expect my thanks for that. Cupido is my friend and I rejoice at his safety, but I would rather spend a thousand nights among Fronto's big cats than one more day on the Palatine Hill.'

'You think you would be safer with Fronto?' Narcissus laughed. 'Perhaps I should arrange to have you sent back to that fat oaf. We could have a wager. Will Rufus the slave live one week or two? Why do you think I suggested to the Emperor's chamberlain that an animal trainer of mighty talent could be bought to work with the Emperor's elephant? Sometimes, there is safety in proximity. You may not believe it, but you have the Emperor's favour, for what it is worth. None will harm you while you are here.'

'I still don't understand. Why should you do this for me? I am a slave. I am nothing to you, unless...' Rufus's face coloured and his eyes filled with horrified confusion. Visions of a day in the bathhouse with Albinius, the slave who ran Cerialis's household, flew through his mind. He could still feel the loathsome touch of the oily fingers on his upper thigh and the rubbery tongue pushing at his lips. He had eventually escaped, but it had cost him a night with the guard dogs.

Narcissus shook his head. 'No, not that. I can assure you I have interests in other directions. But have you forgotten already what you said? "I would always be in your debt." It so happens you might be able to repay your debt more quickly here.'

'How can I do that?'

'I understand you have had a night-time visitor. I hope he did not expose himself to any danger ... with your elephant?' Narcissus said, weighing each word carefully. 'It would not do if my master put himself into that situation. I don't suppose he said ... anything of interest while he was here?'

'I don't know,' Rufus lied. 'He comes at night. He spends time with Bersheba. He talks, but I don't listen.'

The Greek shrugged. 'No matter. There will be

158

other occasions, and perhaps you will find it profitable to listen. If you have something for me, hang a white cloth on the barn door. The next day, be at the little fountain behind the palace of Augustus at the seventh hour and I will meet you there. You can never have too many friends, Rufus. And I would make a very dangerous enemy.' The last words were said with a gentle smile, but Rufus understood the threat that lay behind them.

Narcissus then asked about Caligula's banquets. Of course, he knew Rufus attended. Who else was there? What was said? Who was chosen and what was her husband's reaction? Small things, but morsels that could be traded for other morsels. Here, Rufus was happy to supply the intelligence the Greek sought, and Claudius's freedman left satisfied. Rufus wondered if he would have been quite so sanguine if he had known what passed between Caligula and Claudius at the last banquet.

'Tell your Greek to keep his long nose out of other people's business, Uncle Claudius, or I will have the guards cut it off,' the Emperor had warned.

XIX

It had been more than three months since Rufus was last ordered to the palace and he allowed himself to believe he was safe from further summonses. So the shock was all the greater when he was shaken awake in the middle of the night to find a young legionary officer in a red tunic standing over his bed.

'You are to come with me,' the soldier ordered brusquely and hauled the blankets back.

While he followed his escort through the endless corridors and stairways, Rufus had time to wonder why the man wore the uniform of a regular unit rather than the black of the Praetorians, normally the only military presence in the Palatine complex.

His confusion increased when they reached their destination on one of the upper floors of the grand building originally built by Tiberius. He was certain he'd never been in this part of the palace before. A great gilt-inlaid door, intricately carved with scenes of hunting and the games, barred their way. The young soldier stepped forward and knocked gently, then turned and walked away without a word.

As Rufus stood with his heart thundering against his ribs, the door opened a few inches to reveal a pair of jet-black, almond eyes. Before he could say a word a slim arm slipped through the gap and a hand took his wrist and pulled him inside.

At first, the room was in complete darkness and his head spun as his senses were deluged by the musky scent of exotic perfumes so thick he could taste them on his tongue. A shiver ran through his body, but not one of fear. He heard a gentle rustling, which seemed to emanate simultaneously from both his right and his left, before the light of first one then a second tiny lamp pierced the gloom at opposite sides of the room. They were followed in quick succession by a dozen others until a paradise was revealed. The space before him was a vast treasure house. At its centre was a massive canopied bed hung with thick drapes of imperial purple. A hundred gold statues lined the walls, gods and goddesses vying for position with emperors and kings. But the object which drew his eyes was a human form, almost inhuman in its perfection. It stood naked on a plinth at the foot of the bed, the light of the lamps glinting yellow on the cold white of its marble flesh. From a handsome young face sightless eyes stared in concentration. The figure bent forward from the waist, his left hand close to his right knee and his right arm extended behind him, strong fingers curled round the discus he was about to hurl. With a genius it was impossible not to appreciate, the sculptor had created life from the lifeless. Each vein over his subject's tensed muscles stood out upon the flesh as if it pulsed with heart blood. Each rib was visible beneath the perfectly formed pectorals of his chest.

'Do you like my immortal?'

The voice close to his ear made him jump.

'He will always be as he is, frozen at his most beautiful. He will never grow old. His flesh will never wrinkle, nor his eyes grow dim.' Drusilla's voice was soft and Rufus could feel her breath on the back of his neck. 'If only human beauty could be so everlasting, instead of blossoming for a mere instant before fading into the ugliness of age. Do you think I am beautiful?'

Rufus hesitated, not sure he wanted to see what was behind him, but her hands descended gently on his shoulders and turned him to face her.

She wore a diaphanous robe that clung to her flesh like a second skin where it touched. Here too was perfection of the human form. Yes, he decided, she was beautiful, but it was a sharp-edged beauty that he understood could bleed him dry. He felt the heat radiating from her flesh and caught the slightest hint of the natural scent of her body in his nostrils. The robe highlighted shadows and clefts of unthinkable promise. For a moment, he forgot where he was and who he was with. Then his mind split in two. One part of him wanted what was about to happen with an urgency he had never experienced. Drusilla's blatant sexuality lit a fire in his lower belly that threatened to consume him. But there was another Rufus, Rufus the slave, who realized he was in more danger than he had ever been in his life. And this Rufus was screaming at him to escape while there was still time.

'My lady, p-please...' he stuttered.

Her lips parted and her face edged towards his. Then her perfect nose wrinkled and she gave an unimperial snort.

'Yeugh. You stink.' She clapped her hands twice and from behind a curtain at the far end of the bedchamber emerged the girl who had let him into the room, quickly followed by a second who was her exact twin. They were short and compact, with hair so black it was almost blue, and their slanted eyes twinkled with mischief.

'Bathe him and bring him to me,' the Emperor's sister commanded, turning her back on Rufus and disappearing behind the drapes of the giant bed.

The two girls looked him over and nodded to each other. Then, while the first, whom Rufus identified by the red cord she wore round the waist of her shift, disappeared back behind the curtain, the second approached and motioned for him to remove his tunic. He shook his head. She reached to do it herself, and, alarmed, he pushed her hand away. With a grunt, she stepped back and stared at him, perplexed.

Drusilla's annoyance was clear through the thick drapes. 'If you do not remove your clothing, I will tell my brother I found you hiding in my bedchamber. I'm sure you would not want that.'

Reluctantly, Rufus complied, pulling his tunic over his head as the first sister reappeared with a small basin, but he still hesitated before giving up his loincloth.

He closed his eyes as they bustled around him, turning him this way and that. More disconcerting than his nakedness, or the touch of the soft, warm cloths they used on every part of his body, was the way they cooed to each other like a pair of mating turtledoves. He tried to keep his mind empty. This was just another ordeal a slave must endure. But the more places they found that needed their attention, the more difficult it became to ignore their ministrations and he realized with anguish that his shame was literally growing with each passing second. He swallowed hard and thought desperately for some escape route from this pleasurable agony, then opened his eyes wide in shock as he felt a delicate hand take him in its grip and raise him up so another could have access to his scrotum. The touch of the cloth there had a gentle urgency and now there was no hiding his desire.

'Waste not a drop, or you will have the flesh off each other's backs.'

The voice was answered by a delighted twittering from Rufus's tormentors. The girls took a step back and surveyed their handiwork. They must have been satisfied by what they saw, for the sister with the red cord took him and led him towards the bed.

Rufus stood before the purple curtain knowing what was required of him, but without the nerve to take the next step. A small hand pushed him in the back and he pitched through the thick cloth and landed in an ungainly heap on a soft coverlet.

At first he was dazzled. The area within the curtains was a gilded sanctuary, lit by four scented lamps suspended from the poles which held the drapes aloft. It was dominated by a huge bed scattered with soft pillows, and the poles were carved with graphic sexual scenes featuring combinations of male and female figures involved in various erotic acts, many of which seemed unlikely, if not impossible. But it was the slim figure on the bed which held his attention. Drusilla was lying on her back, completely naked, with the tawny mane of her hair draped around her head and her arms thrown above it. Her pale flesh glowed like molten gold in the lamplight. Not a single hair blemished the smooth lines of her body and Rufus's eyes devoured every curve and hollow of that beautiful form. She had faultless, rose-tipped breasts that rose and fell as she breathed; a smooth, flat stomach and generous, wide hips. She smiled at him from under hooded lids, and for the first time he was aware of the scent of her arousal and noticed the liquid sheen on the fingers of her right hand.

'Am I not beautiful, puppy dog?' she asked, in a voice husky with desire. 'Am I not the treasure you have dreamed of, but could never have?'

He tried to reply, but his throat was so dry he couldn't speak. He was kneeling near the foot of the bed, just close enough for her to reach him. She put out her hand, but the enormity of what he was doing had eaten into Rufus's brain and it in turn sent a panic-stricken message to his body. That which had been so impressive only moments before faded away from her.

To his astonishment she laughed lightly and sat up, her breasts rippling with the movement.

'Better still, puppy dog. I relish a contest, none more. First we must both relax.' She reached to the side of the bed and picked up a vial filled with a red liquid. 'A massage, I think.'

She gave him the bottle, which was warm in his hand, before lying back with her hands behind her head, exposing the full length of that sensuous body to him.

'Now, shoulders first. Come, place yourself over me, with one knee to either side,' she instructed him. 'Now!' The sharpness in her voice as he hesitated startled Rufus and he almost spilled the precious liquid. He did as he was ordered, aware

165

of the closeness of her belly beneath him.

'Pour a little of the oil at the base of my throat, just there. That's right. Now place a drop on your hands and put them round my neck.'

Again, Rufus obeyed, as gently as he was able, conscious that his hands felt huge and rough against the slender vulnerability of her throat.

'Rub the oil in with your fingers. Mmmhhh. No need to be quite so delicate – I am not a toy. Yes, that is much better. Just think, you could choke the life out of me before anyone had time to stop you.' She laughed as he flinched. 'Now move out to my shoulders. Use your fingers. You have such strong fingers.'

Rufus felt her body shift beneath his hands as he smoothed the slippery liquid into her flesh and the sensation moved something in him, because he felt himself grow again, this time even more than before. She noticed it too.

'That's better, puppy dog. Now, some oil here.' She pointed to a spot between her breasts.

This time he responded immediately, and he did not need her instructions to smooth the viscous liquid right and left, his hands moving over the firm orbs and feeling her tiny nipples grow hard under his fingers. She shuddered below him.

'Yes, like that, puppy dog. You are a fast learner.'

He moved his hands over her, quickening the rhythm until she gave a little gasp: 'Lower.'

Lower, across the polished ivory of her abdomen and further, where he found he had been wrong: between her navel and that other place was a thin line of fine down. He tried to keep his eyes from her sex, but now he was drawn to it like

166

a moth to a nightlight. Instinctively, he reached to touch it.

'Not yet.' Her hand grasped his wrist. He looked up at her and saw that her eyes were no longer hooded, but wide open and aflame with a naked hunger. 'Start again at my feet, puppy dog, and move upwards.'

'Like this?'

He did as she ordered. He was becoming familiar with the game now, and he made his way over ankle, calf and the long silky curve of inner thigh with agonizing slowness, and when he eventually reached that place she shuddered again.

All the time his hands had been on Drusilla's compliant young body, Rufus's own desire had grown, and the molten feeling in his guts had moved inexorably into his groin. He was so hard now it was painful. He knew something had to happen and was just about to drop on top of her when she shook her body like a dog emerging from a river pool.

'Now you.'

She pushed him on to his back and took the oil from him. Now it was he who experienced the sensations which had so pleased her. The feel of the fingers first hard, then soft, forcing the oil into the very fabric of his body. And there was something else. With the oil came a slight burning sensation, intense and erotic, so that his whole body seemed to pulsate with energy.

When she reached the object of her desire, it throbbed and twitched in her hands.

'Now, puppy dog, now you are ready.'

She raised one knee and with an easy movement slipped on top of him.

Rufus immediately felt as if he had been enveloped in warm honey and he groaned with the pleasure of it. By now each was so aroused that the heat of her body on his could have only one outcome, and as she began to rock back and forth and her muscles contracted around him he exploded inside her with an agonized cry.

Undeterred, Drusilla maintained her grip on him and slowly increased the tempo of her movements until, grinding herself into his lower body, she too climaxed with a series of stifled gasps that ended in a long, drawn-out moan.

Rufus opened his eyes a few minutes later and realized he had been dozing. The warmth of the room, the softness of the bed and the power of their lovemaking had combined to rob him of his instinct for self-preservation. Now a thrill of fear shot through him as he absorbed the full extent of what he had done. He moved to raise himself, but a slim arm across his chest forced him back and he turned his head to find Drusilla staring at him with open curiosity.

'My brother would kill you if he knew you were here,' she said, as if she was discussing the next day's weather. 'He is terribly jealous.'

There seemed nothing to say, but to stay silent was to let her believe she frightened him, and he sensed a challenge in her words.

'And will he?'

'Only if he finds out, but he will only find out if I choose it. The only people who know you are here are my little doves and Lucius, the soldier who brought you here. My little doves will not tell, because they cannot – they have been dumb from birth. Lucius will not tell, because he has more to lose than you.'

Her hand stroked the length of his thigh. 'You really are terribly beautiful, puppy dog, almost as beautiful as my immortal. What a pity your beauty will not last as long as his. Life is so cruel, don't you think?'

She said the words wistfully, but they seemed to trigger a change in her because her eyes clouded and the pitch of her voice changed.

'My brother is cruel. He knows I love him, yet he sifts through my love seeking out imperfections which might displease him. Only yesterday he wondered aloud if he should have me tortured so he could measure exactly the extent of my devotion. When he places his hands round my throat, just as you did, he wonders at its slimness, and compares it to a swan's, then informs me it would take only a single word from him to have it severed by an axe.'

Rufus stayed silent. He understood that he had no need to speak. She was talking to him in the way Claudius talked to Bersheba. Using him as a reflector for her thoughts, so that she could consider them from a different perspective. To her, he was little more than a beast to be used for any purpose she thought fit.

'It can be a great burden to be an Emperor's favourite. Would it be an honour to die at the hands of a living god? Would it mean I, Drusilla, would be divine, a goddess in my own right? Or is death just death? An end.'

She looked puzzled for a moment, and he knew

this was a subject which perplexed her. But then it was as if a lamp lit behind her eyes.

'My brother's fame will be immortal, and Drusilla's name will be coupled with his. His greatness already outshines the combined light of Divine Julius, Augustus and Tiberius. His reign will last for fifty years and his deeds will be remembered for a thousand. Already people talk of him as a god, and soon he will take his place with the greatest of the gods. Should Gaius, saviour of Rome, bow before Jupiter? No!' Her eyes narrowed, and now an unsettling new persona revealed itself. 'But first he must destroy his enemies. Even now, when his people believe he leads his army to take Rome's bounty to the barbarians of Britannia, he marches to the Rhine to deal with the traitor Gaetulicus and his legions. This creature wishes to supplant him with my own husband, whose throat I will cut with this very hand. Gaius has so many enemies, even among those he would call his friends.

'They don't think I know,' she confided. 'But I see them sneering behind his back and plotting in their whispering nests. Cassius Chaerea, with his little girl's voice – a man, so-called, who will lie with woman, man or beast. Calpurnius, who still blames him for stealing away his wife, as if such a thing mattered. He cannot even trust his own blood. Uncle Claudius, who is a better actor than any on the stage, and that Greek who is never far from his shoulder spread their poison among the Senate and the guard. I have told him to kill them all, but he is too weak. Oh, Chaerea and Calpurnius will have their reckoning, but not

Claudius, who is the greatest danger of all. Gaius will spare him because he is *family*.

'My brother is weak, but I would be strong. I would wipe them from the face of the earth in a single day that Rome would remember for a lifetime. Their screams for mercy would be heard the length of the Empire and none would dare follow them in their betrayal.

'My sisters plot too, and my brother's wife, but against me, not him. They know I have his favour and as long as I do they will never rise. Livilla is harmless enough; she can be married off to a husband who will beat her regularly and painfully. And Milonia is but an annoyance. But Agrippina is different. We must watch Agrippina. Agrippina is a witch, and witches are dangerous. She can do more harm with her potions and poultices even than Uncle Claudius. Gaius has not been the same since she cured him of the head sickness. Cured? Poisoned, I say, or drugged to bend him to her will. We will deal with Agrippina in good time.'

As she talked, Drusilla's hand absently stroked Rufus's upper thigh. Now it stroked something else and she purred.

'Yes, puppy dog. We don't have much time and there is a service you can do your mistress before she sends you back to your kennel.'

She lay back and motioned him to her. Drusilla was hungry and practised, but Rufus was young and he was strong; more confident now, with wiles of his own. He had the arrogance of youth and he would not be bested. Their sweating contest of wills seemed to last an age, with each having periods of domination, but eventually it was she who cried out in defeat. A single scream that sent a spear of molten iron through his heart.

'Gaiiuuus!'

XX

It did not take long to discover that her confidence in their secret was misplaced.

Narcissus appeared at the doors of the barn a few days after the night-time excursion as Rufus trimmed Bersheba's feet, a process the huge animal seemed to find thoroughly satisfying.

Rufus had his back to Bersheba, with her left hind leg bent upwards between both of his so that he could work at the horny growth on the sole of her foot with a sharp knife. As he pared away, she shuffled slightly and gave quiet snorts of pleasure.

'I find it amazing that one can get quite that close to something so large, and so obviously dangerous,' Narcissus said after watching the operation for a few moments.

Rufus grunted and wrestled to slice off a particularly tough piece of hardened skin before replying. 'Bersheba may be big, but she is not dangerous – are you, girl?' he said, reaching behind him to pat a wrinkled hindquarter.

'Not at the moment, perhaps. But I have seen the beasts in battle and they can be very fearsome, even if they are facing the other way. You must remember, Rufus,' he added with exaggerated significance, 'you have a powerful weapon in your control.'

Rufus was surprised to hear Narcissus claim he had been in a fight. The Greek gave the impression of being ... not soft, but unworldly.

'No.' Narcissus laughed, reading his mind. 'I was not a military man. I was accompanying my former master – not Senator Claudius – on a diplomatic mission when the natives objected particularly violently to something. Taxes, probably. They didn't bargain for the squadron of war elephants the local potentate used against them.'

Rufus had cared for Bersheba for so long that he never thought of her as dangerous, not in a warlike sort of way. Clumsy, perhaps. An animal of her size could crush a man accidentally and barely notice it. And when she was in one of her moods...

'What were they like? Were they different from Bersheba? Bigger?'

'No, just the same sort of lumbering beast. Although I think they may have had smaller ears, and more of a humped back. They were armoured here,' he said, indicating the front of her head, 'and on their flanks. They were controlled by little brown men who sat on their shoulders, and they carried a ... a sort of basket, with a bowman in it.'

'I could see why they might be good against cavalry,' Rufus said, considering the matter. 'Any horse that comes anywhere near Bersheba gets nervous as soon as it smells her. I suppose it would take a lot to stop her?'

'Yes it does. I saw one elephant stuck so full of arrows it looked very like a large hedgehog.' Rufus grimaced at the description, but Narcissus affected not to notice. 'It was very angry and very effective for a time, and then it seemed to lose its mind.'

'What happened to it?'

'It turned on its own people and charged directly towards the potentate and my diplomat. The little man on its shoulders took a large spike and hammered it straight into the back of its neck with a mallet. It went down like a fallen tree. Stone dead.'

They looked at Bersheba in silence for a moment, considering the unlikelihood of such an animal being brought down with a single blow.

'I know, it doesn't seem possible. But I saw it with my own eyes. Now, have you anything for me? A little gossip perhaps? I understand you have been keeping interesting company.'

Rufus froze.

Narcissus smiled reassuringly. 'Oh, don't worry, your secret is safe with me. But the Palatine is a dangerous place, and nowhere is more dangerous than the quarter you entered three nights ago. The person who inhabits that room is beautiful in the way a sea snake is beautiful. It dances sinuously in the current and its colours enchant, but treat it with disrespect and you will be dead before you can blink an eye. Now, what do you have for me?'

Rufus hesitated. 'Gaetulicus.'

'Ah, our poetic governor of Upper Germany. What does she say of him?'

Rufus told how the British invasion was to be a deception, while the true target was the popular governor and the legions that followed him.

Narcissus greeted the news with a bray of laughter. 'How could she be so utterly wrong and so out of date? Gaetulicus is already dead at his master's hand, but Caligula lost his nerve when it came to taking his revenge on the legions. Instead, he added the First and the Twentieth to his army for this so-called invasion of Britain. Only a fool would believe he could lead a force across the sea at this season. He hadn't even arranged for ships to transport the army. It is all over the Senate. Just two days ago I heard one former consul declare that Caligula was more likely to collect seashells than ships. Of course, Rome being Rome, the story spread and now the mob believes their Emperor took four legions to the very ends of Gaul to gather clams. When he returns, he will find himself a laughing stock. Surely your meeting was more productive than this?'

'She said no one would know,' Rufus said miserably.

'Drusilla has her brother's power to protect her, but in the darker ways of the Palatine she is an untutored child.'

Narcissus raised his hands so Rufus could see them, and his fingers flickered through an intricate series of designs, tapping against the fingers or palm of his other hand.

Rufus stared. Was the Greek mad?

'It is a method of communication I discovered quite by accident,' Narcissus explained. 'How

175

does she think those poor mute sisters transmit information? By fluttering their eyelashes? But how I know is of little consequence. It is sufficient that I do know, and if I know you can be sure others will know.' Narcissus looked grave. 'You are in great peril, Rufus, if you do not find someone you can trust.'

'I would trust Cupido with my life.'

The Greek shook his head sadly. 'That might not be wise. I fear the honourable gladiator is not the man he was. The palace can destroy a person, but it also has the power to seduce one. Take the Emperor: vain, arrogant, unpredictable and cruel.' Rufus looked around instinctively to see if anyone was in earshot. Even to listen to this was treason. But Narcissus was not finished. 'But he can also be loyal, sympathetic, generous and brilliant. He is a little like the sun; those who stray into his orbit may burn like a moth in a flame or merely bask in the warmth of his presence. Your friend has seen an aspect of our Emperor few others are privileged to see. It may cloud his judgement.'

Rufus frowned. One part of him wanted to deny what Narcissus was saying, but another knew the Greek was right, or at least partially right. Cupido had changed, but Rufus sensed the change was not as deep-seated as Narcissus believed, and that there were other reasons for it.

'If I cannot trust Cupido, whom can I trust? Fronto might as well be in Africa for all the help he can be to me in this place. I have no other friends here, unless...'

Narcissus smiled like a teacher whose most

recalcitrant pupil has finally grasped a simple problem.

'Why should I trust you, who had me brought here against my will, and still refuse to tell me why? And how can you help me, when everyone but the palace mousecatcher appears to know that you and Claudius plot?'

The smile froze on Narcissus's face, and the corner of his right eye twitched. He opened his mouth to speak, but, for once, he didn't seem to have anything to say.

'Drusilla, who is but a child in the darker ways of the Palatine,' Rufus mimicked the Greek's cultured Latin, 'has been spying on you and just about everyone else in the palace. Even now she may be urging the Emperor to have you and your master arrested and taken before the inquisitors,' he added, enjoying the freedman's obvious discomfort.

'What else did she say?' Narcissus cleared his throat nervously.

Rufus shrugged. 'You are not the only ones she suspects. She mentioned the Praetorian commander Chaerea, and Calpurnius, husband of Cornelia. She despises the Emperor's wife and hates her sister Agrippina, whom she, accuses of witchcraft and dabbling in poisons. She believes Agrippina has drugged her brother.'

'It does not matter how many others are suspect. It only takes a single accusation for a man to be condemned.' Narcissus chewed his lip, thinking aloud. 'You say she believes Agrippina to be a sorceress. That is interesting. I was not aware of it. We will talk of this matter of trust again, Rufus, but for the moment I have urgent business to attend to.'

Narcissus scurried off, and as he watched the tall freedman's retreating back as he walked across the park, Rufus had a suspicion that he had said more than he should have.

XXI

The memory of his night with Drusilla ate at Rufus's mind like a swarm of fire ants. He would wake in his bed, sweating, with images of her lithe body dancing in front of him and the scent of her in his nostrils. When it happened, he'd spend the rest of the night in a fever, anticipating the knock on the door that would herald an invitation to return to the curtained bedchamber.

At other times, he would stop, paralysed, in the middle of some task, overwhelmed by what he'd done and the terrible retribution that might follow. On these occasions he would take Bersheba off to some far corner of the park, as if fleeing there would somehow save him from his fate.

And then there was Aemilia.

Milonia Caesonia had shown little interest in the elephant after that first encounter, but as the summer faded and the relentless heat abated it was not unusual for the royal family to spend time in the park, allowing the Emperor's daughter and Agrippina's son, Nero, to play together on the grass.

It was on one of these occasions, while he was mending part of Bersheba's harness in front of the barn, that Rufus noticed a shadow on the ground beside him. He looked up to see a tall figure watching him, her golden hair catching the sunlight.

'If you are busy, I will not disturb you,' she said in an accented Latin which reminded him of Cupido's. Her voice was not the only similarity. The way she stood, tall and straight, with the balance of an athlete and the awareness of a warrior, was evidence of her lineage. This was no pliant slave girl, bonded from birth and cowed by the powerlessness of her position.

'No, please.' He straightened to face her. 'Bersheba is not needed today.'

She was holding little Drusilla in her arms. The child must have been close to a year old, with a mop of dark curls and a face that permanently mirrored her mother's petulance.

Aemilia saw his look. 'She is growing heavier every day. Soon I won't be able to carry her any distance. She should be walking by now, but she is spoiled, I think, and if she prefers to crawl, then crawl she will.' She turned to look over her shoulder where Milonia and Agrippina sat on cushions on the grass, in the shade of a canopy held by two Nubian slaves.

Bersheba appeared at the door of the barn, sniffing the air with her trunk.

'She is a magnificent animal, but I would wish her back in the wild places of her childhood and not chained in the darkness to await one man's pleasure.' There was a hint of sadness in Aemilia's voice, and Rufus understood that she was linking Bersheba's position to her own. 'What would she do if you unchained her, do you think? Would she wander far and wide until she came to some stream she once knew, or some hill she looked out from? No, I am being foolish. Of course she would be hunted down and killed before she ever came close to the thing she once knew as freedom.'

'I think it more likely that she would stand where she was until the handler who had been so carelessly neglectful decided to feed her, for Bersheba's moods are ruled by her stomach, are they not, girl?' he said, trying to lighten the mood.

'Yes, you are right.' Aemilia smiled sadly. 'We must be thankful for the small gifts our captivity brings.'

Drusilla squirmed, almost dislodging herself, and Aemilia placed the little girl carefully on the grass. The child immediately began to explore her surroundings.

'Better here than near her cousin,' Aemilia said. 'Poor Nero, she scratches his face until he cries. I fear for the boy once all her teeth grow in.'

A cloud covered the sun for a moment, and Aemilia shivered, growing serious again. 'I thank you for being my brother's friend. I hope we too can be friends,' she said, and Rufus struggled to cover his disappointment. He wanted more than this girl's – this woman's – friendship. 'I came here to warn you that you may be in danger. Milonia Caesonia talks openly of a slave she calls Drusilla's puppy dog. She does so in the crudest terms and in the wrong company. I urge you to beware. Whatever your feelings for Drusilla, stay away from her. If the Emperor became aware of your relationship she could not save you.'

Rufus opened his mouth to deny he had any feelings for Drusilla. Who did this haughty German girl think she was, to come here and throw his shame in his face? Did she believe she was the only slave who still had pride? But before he could say anything, Aemilia gave a stifled scream.

Rufus looked round to see what had startled her.

Inside the barn Drusilla was playing in the hay directly between Bersheba's enormous legs. The elephant had only to shuffle her feet and Caligula's daughter would be crushed.

But Bersheba was Bersheba. She bowed her head to look at the interloper beneath her, and with the tip of her trunk gently pushed the laughing infant through the hay to safety.

Rufus picked up the wriggling bundle and plucked the straw from her tangled hair, while Drusilla hissed at him and demanded in childish gurgles to be allowed to return to her huge playmate. Aemilia, pale as a ghost, took the child from him.

'This is a dangerous place, Aemilia, and we must always be wary, but sometimes the fates contrive to undo even the most careful. I am a slave, and if the Emperor's sister demands it, I must attend her. But do not shame me by believing my attendance means anything more.' He turned to walk away.

'Rufus?' The note of apology in Aemilia's voice stopped him.

When he turned back she looked at him as if she was seeing him for the first time. What was he to her, this tall, fresh-faced young man with the untidy, russet-bronze mop of hair and the gentle, almost emerald eyes? She had noticed the way he looked at her; how could she not when he made it so obvious. He desired her, but then so did a lot of men. He was undoubtedly handsome, in a wholesome, rustic sort of way, and she liked him, but there were many people she liked. Sometimes, if they met by accident, she experienced an inner confusion and a fluttering in her breast she couldn't explain. Was that love? She knew of love; the palace ladies talked of little else. She was curious about the *act* but was in no rush to experience it. In any case, what could he offer her? He was a slave. Yes, she too was a slave, but Milonia had promised that when the time was right she would be freed, and that she would be found a suitable husband. So they could not be more than friends. But would that be enough for him?

'My words were ill-chosen and I beg your forgiveness. I meant what I said when I offered you my friendship, and I offer it again. Show me your hands.'

Puzzled, Rufus put out his hands, palms up. He was conscious of the roughness of his skin as she took his right hand in hers, still holding Drusilla in the crook of her left arm.

'When I was young, the women of my tribe believed I had the gift. I don't know if that's true, but I can read men's thoughts, sometimes, and see things I don't understand, and when I place my hand over another's, like this, I can some-times feel the future.'

She closed her eyes, and Rufus felt an energy pulsing in his right arm that had not been there before. Maybe it was the warmth of her hand on his that caused the effect, but it was there, and as the seconds passed he felt its power flow through his shoulder and into his chest.

She opened her eyes, and he was drawn into their fathomless depths. When she spoke it was in the measured tones of an oracle.

'You are strong, Rufus, stronger than you will ever know. You will survive this place while others will not, and you will travel far, over land and sea, to a place where you will witness the last stand of the tyrants.'

Rufus shuddered. He didn't understand why – or how – it would happen. But he felt in his heart it was true. 'Will Cupido be at my side? And you?'

She smiled distractedly. 'Perhaps. But our story is already written and our fate decided. If the gods will it, we will be there with you.'

XXII

From the highest to the lowest, the inhabitants of the Palatine went about their business in silence and in fear. The abortive invasion and the reaction in Rome had driven Caligula's always unpredict-able moods to even greater extremes. House slaves whispered of the Emperor's screaming rages and his favourites cowering for their lives at his feet. The two serving consuls took themselves on a tour of the provinces and sacrificed to the gods in the hope that he would not send for them.

Rufus was fortunately untouched by it all. He saw little of Aemilia, who still confused him, except from afar, and nothing of Drusilla, who, he now realized, had seen him as a compliant novelty. Once experienced, the novelty was gone for ever. He did not know whether to be grateful or insulted.

He was organizing Bersheba's feed on a cool morning that promised a perfect day a week after the festival of the Parilia, when he heard the clamour of voices and the sound of hammers. It came from the far side of the park, but hard as he tried he could not see what caused it. The massive marble-clad shoulder of Caligula's palace hid whatever was happening from his view.

As the day wore on his curiosity grew. He saw figures moving purposefully back and forth, but they were too far away to hail, or even for their actions to give him a clue as to what they were doing.

At the sixth hour, when he knew most of the Palatine would be at their midday meal, he harnessed Bersheba. 'Come on, girl,' he said. 'We'll go a little further than normal today.'

He directed her out into the park, but not towards the palace. Instead, he turned her right, so his route would take him across the face of the building, but would also allow him a clear view of what was going on beyond it by the time he reached the far end of the park where the trees were thin.

At first, it was difficult to make sense of what he was seeing, but gradually the chaotic scene in front of him took order in his mind. At the far end of the palace, where the Palatine Hill fell away towards the forum, was an ants' nest of activity. Hundreds of enormous baulks of timber were stacked in piles twice as high as Bersheba and some form of construction was already going on close to the palace walls. He could see teams of workers digging and others carrying the larger timbers, which needed a dozen men each to take their weight. He assumed the workers were slaves, but he was surprised to see men in the uniform of legionary officers scurrying among them, organizing and harrying.

He was about to turn away when a voice from behind almost made him fall from Bersheba's back.

'Impressive, isn't it?'

Narcissus.

'Don't you have anything to do but spy on people?' Rufus didn't bother to hide his annoyance.

'I might ask you the same. The Emperor's elephant seems to have remarkably few duties these days. Perhaps I could suggest something?'

Rufus flushed. Why did the Greek always get the better of him? He waited for Narcissus to bring up the question of trust, which had seemed to be so important to him during their last conversation, but apparently he was in no hurry to return to the subject.

'What you see is but a fraction of the Emperor's grand plan,' he said, shaking his head. 'Beyond the wall, the best part of a full legion is sweating and cursing to turn a dream into reality.'

'I don't understand.'

'Do you see the small fat man on the left? He is talking to a person who, unless I miss my guess, is a tribune of the Fourteenth Gemina. I imagine he sacrificed a large white bull at the temple of Jupiter this morning and prayed for an auspicious day. If he did not, he is a fool, or he has already mixed the hemlock in readiness for his failure.'

'He does seem troubled.' Even at this distance Rufus could sense the fat man's agitation.

'So he should be. One week ago the Emperor dreamed vividly he was the subject of an assassination attempt on the way from the Palatine to the Senate House. They say he felt the daggers entering his body and woke to find himself covered in blood. It was merely a nose bleed, but emperors tend to take such signs literally. He called a conference of his advisers, of whom, of course, my master, Senator Claudius, is one. He is a sensible man, and has a benign influence on the Emperor, and left to himself would have calmed the situation. But that dangerous fool Protogenes convinced Caligula the dream was a portent and that he must protect himself. This,' he waved a hand towards the builders, 'was the result. A million sesterces so one man can be carried four hundred paces from his table to the steps of the Senate without soiling his nostrils with the stink of the mob. It is a bridge,' Narcissus explained, 'probably the longest land bridge in the world. It will take the Fourteenth one month to build and that little fat man is responsible for ensuring it does not fall down with the Emperor upon it. Now do you understand why he is so agitated?'

Rufus grinned. 'I wouldn't be in his boots for all the gold in the Empire.'

Narcissus became serious. 'Now, to the question of trust we talked of, Rufus. I wish you would put aside your antagonism and place your faith in me. For better or worse, our lives are entwined, and if we slaves cannot work together we will all be like the little man building the Emperor's bridge: living in constant fear.'

Rufus thought for a moment, considering his response. 'Don't we live in fear in any case, Narcissus? I have lost friends who were blameless. If Drusilla convinces the Emperor you are plotting against him, your trust in your master will mean nothing. The only thing that will save you is to betray every person who ever put his faith in you.'

Surprisingly, mention of the Emperor's sister brought a smile to the Greek's face, a rather sly smile.

'Oh, I don't think Drusilla will harm anyone again. I thought you would be the first to know. She has taken to her bed. Some minor ailment, I understand.'

XXIII

Rufus returned the next day to see the bridge taking shape, and, as it grew, he became bolder and ventured closer. On the far side of the wall the largest timbers, massive baulks split from mature tree trunks and reaching six times the height of a tall man, were being buried deep in the ground to provide the foundations. Between each main timber, the legionaries jointed others, smaller, but still substantial, which Rufus could see would be the frame for the bridge deck. Finally, a double layer of thick planks was laid on the frame and nailed firm.

He marvelled at its progress as it snaked out from the Palatine towards the forum, forty feet above the ground. Across the intersection of Clivus Victoriae and the Via Nova; between the infant foundations of the temple of Augustus and the pillared frontage of the house of the Vestals; over the fountain of Juturna and past the temple of Castor and Pollux, until it turned to follow the path of the Sacred Way.

One thing struck him as strange. It had to be strong, because it was to carry the Emperor, but the little architect was certainly taking no chances. The scale of the wooden bridge was immense. The planking was so thick and the weight-bearing pillars so enormous, Rufus guessed the bridge could have taken the weight of two or three legions together. Perhaps, he thought, that was its true purpose: to provide swift passage for relieving troops if the populace rioted, as they had done so often during the bread shortages of Tiberius's reign.

Once the construction was completed, three days ahead of Narcissus's predicted date, carpenters appeared to turn their attention to the fine work. They smoothed the boards and the handrails with planes and erected carved pillars etched with gladiatorial scenes as gateways at each end. When their work was done, the painters replaced them, turning the entire length of the bridge a lustrous gold that hurt the eyes in the low autumn sunshine.

As the project proceeded, hundreds of onlookers gathered, curious to see the Emperor's latest wonder. On the evening the painters completed their work a rumour was born somewhere out in the suburbs beyond the Campus Martius that Caligula would make his first crossing the next day. Before he bedded Bersheba down, Rufus watched the first of the crowds stream in towards the forum, eager to secure the best viewpoints for the next day's spectacle. By the time he composed himself for sleep there were hundreds, but he anticipated that by the next day they would be in their thousands.

He intended to rise early, because he was as interested as any Roman to see the Emperor take his first steps on the marvel he had created, but he was still in his cot when a loud hammering on the barn door woke him, bleary-eyed and complaining, to find it was still full dark. He dressed as swiftly as he could, but the urgent hammering continued and Bersheba snorted with concern, shuffling in her chains.

'Don't knock the door down,' he shouted, rubbing the sleep from his eyes. 'I'm coming.'

He pushed up the beam barring the doors and pushed them open. Staring at him in the light of a dozen torches was a grizzled Praetorian centurion. For a second, Rufus wondered if he was finally being arrested and his eyes flicked among them, hoping the next face he set eyes upon would be Cupido's, but the gladiator was nowhere to be seen.

The centurion's barked order made him blink. 'Don't just stand there gaping, man. The Emperor requires his elephant to be at its most presentable by the second hour. Get to work, and if you need any help we've been ordered to provide it.'

With two of the soldiers holding lamps for him and another two lending a hand, Rufus prepared Bersheba's harness, polished her brass and buffed her tusks. He even managed to give her a manicure before the job was completed at first light. With a final flourish he threw the tasselled blanket of gold cloth she wore on ceremonial outings across her back. When he was done, he nervously asked the centurion where they would be needed.

'Just have the elephant outside and ready when the Emperor arrives. He will give you your instructions.'

As the hour approached, the centurion brusquely ordered his men into parade formation in front of the barn. Rufus unchained Bersheba and led her into the flat light of the early morning and wondered for the hundredth time what was going on.

The jingle of armour, and Bersheba's inquisitive 'sniff', gave warning of Caligula's approach. The centurion used his stick to straighten the line of Praetorians and Rufus fiddled uneasily with the elephant's harness, peering beneath her to get a good view of the imperial party.

The Emperor strode purposefully at their head, magnificent in a purple toga and with a wreath of laurel leaves fixed in his thinning hair. Behind him, almost cantering to keep up, was a short, barrel-like figure Rufus vaguely recognized, and a long-striding legionary officer wearing the badges of an engineer on his chest. To both sides of the mismatched couple marched a file of Praetorians, making the little group look suspiciously like an arrest party.

It wasn't until they were closer that the smaller man's nervous manner reminded Rufus who it was. Narcissus's architect. The man who had turned the Emperor's dream into a reality.

But why were they coming here?

Caligula stopped in front of Bersheba and ran an approving eye over her. The Emperor looked healthier than at any time since Rufus had known him. His skin had lost the sickly sheen that marked him as either a dissolute or an invalid, and the eyes, which Rufus remembered as being almost opaque, were a clear bright blue. He was hardly dressed for the part, but he had the ready look of an athlete on the morning of a games.

'Magnificent, isn't she?' Caligula said, to no one

in particular. He motioned the two men who accompanied him forward. 'Coriolanus, Sulpicius, I warned you this day would come. Do you believe me now?'

The smaller man hopped from one foot to the other, as if he was doing some sort of barbarian dance. 'W-we never doubted you, great Caesar,' he croaked.

The legionary officer said nothing, but Rufus noticed he was looking carefully at Bersheba with his forehead creased by a V of concentration.

'What do you think, Sulpicius? What does she weigh? Are you still confident?' There was a definite challenge in Caligula's voice that worried Rufus. He was beginning to understand that he and Bersheba might be at the centre of great things and he did not like it one little bit.

The officer shrugged, as if unconcerned. 'Say twenty talents, if I'm any judge. It will hold.'

'Oh, it had better. What about you, Marcus Petronius Coriolanus? Will it hold? And more important, are you willing to stake your life on it?'

The little man's face turned a similar shade of purple to the Emperor's toga, his eyes bulged and he began to choke as if he was having a seizure.

Caligula snorted. 'Someone help him. I don't want him to die on me yet. You,' he barked, pointing at Rufus, 'follow us and bring my elephant.'

The Emperor set off across the park, trailing Bersheba, Rufus and his escort of Praetorians. Rufus knew what was in his mind now, and his own was filled with fear for Bersheba. *She* was the test. She was to be the first to cross the Emperor's bridge. He tried to remember the dimensions of the pillars and the thickness of the planking. Had the engineers of the Fourteenth done their job well? Would it hold? That was the question. Would it hold? He had a terrible vision of Bersheba plunging through the planking on to the ground below; heard the sound of bones breaking and the shrieks of her agony clearly in his head.

No, he would not allow it! But here they were. The Emperor stood by the bridge, explaining his clever plan to the engineer and the architect. Rufus knew he had no choice. If he refused, Caligula would order someone else to force her across and he would be dead.

While they waited, he took the opportunity to look over the wall. The sight that met his eyes made him gasp. The great buildings below seemed to be floating on a sea of upturned heads. Every street was packed, every possible viewing platform filled to overflowing. The enterprising and the agile had even commandeered the roof of the Basilica Julia. It appeared that every Roman, from the highest senator to the lowest beggar, was determined to witness history.

'Now, Coriolanus, you will go first, but tread carefully, for you are almost as heavy as the beast.' The Emperor ushered the little fat man forward. 'Not too far. We don't want you to be at the other end before the elephant begins. You next, Sulpicius.'

The legionary officer needed no prompting. His nailed sandals rattled on the wooden boards as he marched briskly to where Coriolanus stood quaking. It was obvious from his manner that he thought the whole thing was a waste of his time. Rufus felt a tiny surge of hope. This man knew his work. He trusted his men.

'Come on, boy, what are you waiting for? Mount the elephant.'

Rufus stared at the Emperor.

'Quickly now,' Caligula snapped. 'You are keeping the mob waiting.'

Rufus gave Bersheba the signal to kneel, so he could use her knee as a mounting point. She bowed her head forward and he grabbed her huge ear for support.

'Wait!'

What now? He wanted this ordeal over quickly, whatever the outcome.

'I will mount the beast first.'

What? A murmur ran through the Praetorian ranks. Rufus was not the only person on the Palatine to be surprised this morning.

'Caesar, is this wise? What if...?' The Praetorian commander couldn't bring himself to finish the sentence. The reality was too terrible to contemplate. 'You are too important. To Rome. To your people.'

Caligula hitched up the folds of his toga, kicked off his embroidered slippers and prepared to mount Bersheba. He stared at Rufus, the ice-blue eyes boring into him like twin chisels.

'Get ready to help me, elephant boy, but bruise my dignity and I will have your head.' He turned to the Praetorian. 'I appreciate your concern, faithful Petronius,' he said theatrically, 'but am I to ask these men to risk their lives if I am not prepared to share that risk? It is a fine day for a ride and my public awaits. Can't you hear them? They grow impatient.'

Rufus watched the performance in bewilderment – for performance was exactly what it was. Here was the ruler of a vast empire preparing to risk his life in a ludicrous act of bravado before a multitude of his subjects, and for what?

Before he could think of an answer, he felt a hand on his shoulder as the Emperor used him as a support to climb on to the elephant's leg, and then slithered up between her shoulder blades. Once he was settled he looked down at Rufus, who still stood by Bersheba's giant knee.

'Come along, boy. I cannot drive this thing myself. It isn't a chariot.'

Rufus cleared his throat. 'You must move back, sir ... Caesar ... just a few inches. I must be able to sit in front of you so I can control her.'

The Emperor frowned, but didn't object. He shuffled backwards, creating just enough room for Rufus, who vaulted athletically on to Bersheba's shoulders and to his seat, with Caligula so close behind he could feel the man's breath in his ear.

'Forward! For Rome and for Empire.' The ruler of a million souls chuckled with anticipation.

Rufus used his knees to nudge Bersheba's ribs and tapped her on the left shoulder to turn her between the carved posts marking the entrance to the bridge. Coriolanus and Sulpicius walked ahead of them, the one tentative, the other confident. For the first few steps they were still out of sight of the crowd below, but then the Emperor's head must have become visible above the

Palatine wall. The distinctive murmur grew in volume, and Rufus could see them, and they, in their countless thousands, could see Bersheba, and the murmur mutated into gasps of disbelief before becoming a great shattering roar.

Bersheba shifted uneasily under him. He talked soothingly to her, knowing she was unlikely to hear him above the clamour of the crowd, but that the vibration of his voice would calm her. The first few steps took the elephant up a gentle slope, after which the bridge proper stretched out before them, a golden avenue ten paces wide with terribly fragile barriers on either side. At first, it was simple, for they were only a few feet above the surface of the Palatine, but soon the hill dropped away and what had seemed a solid, safe platform turned into a precarious, vertigo-inducing tightrope. Rufus glanced over the edge where the planks ended and his head began to spin. Forty feet below, ten thousand incredulous faces returned his stare. The bridge seemed to sway in front of him. They had to turn back. Instinctively, he reached out to Bersheba, knowing it was impossible for her to turn, but unable to help himself. Then he felt a pair of arms encircle his waist and an unlikely sound ringing in his ear.

Caligula was laughing, laughing with pure pleasure.

'Look at them – they love me. The consuls, senators and aristocrats all hate me and stand in the way of my great works, but it does not matter because these people are the real power in Rome. A single word from me and they would tear the

Senate House down stone by stone and bury its occupants in the rubble.' He squeezed Rufus's ribs. 'Did you hear me, boy? They love me.'

He laughed again, waving a gracious hand to the sea of upturned faces below, and Rufus realized with astonishment that the Emperor was speaking to him. Not at him, as Drusilla had, using him as a sounding board for her ideas and her fears, but *to* him.

A loose board protested loudly under Bersheba's massive foot and Rufus tensed, waiting for the entire edifice to come apart and pitch them to their deaths. He could see the fountain where Castor and Pollux had watered their horses far below and the temple dedicated to the two heroes close by. To his left was the foundation of the new temple Caligula was building to honour the God-Emperor Augustus. On the right, the suburbs of Rome stretched north above the frontage of the house of the Vestals.

Caligula loosened a hand from his waist and clapped him reassuringly on the shoulder.

'Do not worry, boy, you are safe with me. I cannot die this day; I have too much work to do. I will make Rome such a city that the world will wonder at its beauty and its magnificence for a thousand years. You see those buildings?' He pointed across Rufus's breast to the forum, which was just becoming visible before them. 'They are as nothing to the palaces and the temples I will build. And there will be more. Every citizen will have a home worth calling a home. Not slums and hovels that burn with the first spark. Real homes. Homes of stone, with running water from the new aqueducts I have commissioned. There will be a new arena, ten storeys high, and the games I hold there will make even the greybeards who remember Augustus's time gasp at the spectacle.

'But first I must clear the obstacles that stand in my way. Human obstacles. You don't know how fortunate you are, Rufus, the elephant boy, to have been born so low. You only have this splendid creature to look after. I am responsible for an entire Empire. I must feed a million people, pay my armies, build the temples and palaces that will ensure my immortality. Yet everywhere I turn I face obstruction and delay. They think I don't know who they are, but my eye is all-seeing. Drusilla' – the name made Rufus tense – 'wants me to kill everyone. Poor girl, she is ill, you know, but still she uses what strength she has to warn me against them. Sometimes I think she is quite mad. She gives me so many names I am confused. Can they all hate me? Why? Because of Gemellus? Tiberius, above all men, should have known that Rome can only be ruled by a single hand, and a strong hand at that. If I had not killed my cousin, my cousin would have killed me. Because I spend their money? What is an Emperor if he cannot make his mark? I will make my mark in stone and in deed, but even that is not enough, for I must make a mark substantial enough for two. My father, Germanicus, should have been Emperor before me. He was a great man, and good. I cannot match his goodness, but I will outdo his greatness.'

Bersheba's measured tread took them out towards the Via Sacra, over the edge of the forum, where the bridge took a diagonal turn to the left.

Despite himself, Rufus began to enjoy the experience. It was clear now that between them the engineer and the little architect had constructed the bridge so that it would take the weight of a dozen elephants. There was a sense of aloneness here, on this platform forty feet above the real world, even though the eyes of tens of thousands of living, breathing human beings never left them. He was even enjoying being in the Emperor's company. Oh, he was still wary, still prepared to be terrified by some leap of mood that would turn the quiet-spoken young man whose bare legs touched his into the cold-eyed monster he had seen enjoying watching men being eaten alive. But, for the moment, that persona was mercifully absent. The man behind him was the Emperor Caligula Romans had prayed for.

They could see the pillars of the Senate House now, and Rufus recognized the ranks of white-clad senators waiting on the steps. Caligula sighed heavily in his ear.

'This must be truly what it is to be a god. To stand above all. To look down upon all and know that a word of command will sweep all away. If only it could be so. It is a pity our journey must end so soon. I have enjoyed being with you and your elephant. But soon I will be once more in the company of vultures, whose sharp beaks you see yonder. If only it could be otherwise. How I long for the simple times on campaign with my father, when honest men treated me as an honest man, even though I was but a boy. I wore the scarlet tunic, and when I stood in line with them it was not in the silken slippers of a Roman knight, but in the very boots they wore themselves, so they gave me the name I bear to this day. And now Caligula must be an Emperor again,' he said, his voice taking on a new firmness as Bersheba descended the gently sloping wooden ramp at the end of the golden bridge.

'We could go back.' The words were out before Rufus knew he had said them.

Caligula laughed, a gentle, genuine laugh.

'If only it could be so. We could stand on our bridge and our people could worship us till the sun went down. But it is not for me. Take your elephant to be a god in my stead. She has done her Emperor a great service. She deserves her day in the sun.'

They reached the steps of the Senate House and Rufus ordered Bersheba to kneel. The Emperor slipped from behind him and down her flanks into the waiting protection of a Praetorian guard of honour. Among the stern faces, trying desperately not to look in his direction, Rufus recognized the handsome features of Cupido.

Later, he sought the gladiator out in his rooms.

'You have seen a side of him that few others see,' Cupido admitted. 'He could be a great Emperor and a fine man, but do not be fooled or seduced by what you witnessed. He can change in an instant from man to monster. I have seen it. Everyone in the palace, even those he calls his favourites, even the Praetorian Guard, go before him in fear, never knowing which Caligula will be waiting for them. You have seen them, those he keeps close. Appeles is not the only actor among

them. Each of them plays a part, even Protogenes, who is the only one he truly trusts.'

'Even Chaerea, your commander?'

'Especially he. Caligula knows the Praetorians
are his only true guarantee of power, but that
does not mean he is certain of their loyalty. That
is why there are two Praetorian Guards.'

'Two?' Rufus said, bewildered.

Cupido nodded. 'The Wolves and the Scorpions. There are the Italians under Chaerea; you
would know them by the scorpion symbol on
their breastplate, as you would know me as a German by the wolf that decorates mine. Caligula
plays the one faction against the other, so neither
knows who has his favour on any given day.
However, you should remember this: whenever
you see the sign of the wolf you will know you are
among friends.'

XXIV

A week after his outing on the bridge Rufus
experienced another of those heart-stopping
moments that accompanied a summons to the
palace. Unusually, the Praetorians who brought
it carried with them a new white tunic of fine
cloth and ordered him to clean up and put it on.

The two guards escorted him to a sumptuous
room deep in the palace where Caligula relaxed
on a couch overlooking a throng of richly dressed
noblemen and women. When he saw Rufus, the

Emperor rose, and greeted him with the savage, hard-mouthed grin of a cat that had just discovered a nest of sightless fledglings.

'Our guest is here at last. In recognition of your service to this household I have decided the time is right for you to wed and beget me a line of little elephant trainers. As you can see, I have gathered the finest families in Rome to witness the event and so do you the honour you deserve. Let me introduce you to your bride.' He clapped his hands.

Rufus turned to stare at the creature being led through the pillared entranceway. He was so astonished that he was able to ignore the brays of laughter which greeted her entrance.

She was beautiful.

The simple white dress contrasted with the delicate honey-brown of her skin and was designed to show off to best advantage the elegant curves of her perfectly proportioned body. Through it swelled surprisingly heavy breasts, elegant curves tapering to a trim waist, and the promise of a dancer's finely muscled legs. Her blond hair was swept back from a high forehead, with two tendrils trailing right and left to frame the face of a nymph, from which gazed the wide eyes of a frightened fawn. Directed by the Emperor, who fought to keep a solemn face amid the laughter echoing from the walls, she took her place by Rufus's side and placed her delicate hand in his.

She was three feet tall.

The wedding ceremony was unorthodox. Caligula, as high priest, clumsily contrived to combine tender love poems with crude references to the participants' differing heights and there were none of the formalities that would normally accompany such an occasion: no flame-red veil, nor knot of Hercules.

At first Rufus felt he was watching the proceedings from somewhere above, as if what was happening was actually being experienced by someone else. But there came a moment when the reality of it hit him like a hammer blow. He was being cheated. Aemilia should have been here by his side, not some ... some... For a moment he thought he might faint, but he forced himself to concentrate. He studied the Emperor as the latter performed for his audience, and wondered at the change seven days had wrought. Where was the composed and soft-spoken young man who rode Bersheba with him? Where was the concerned ruler now, who talked so passionately of *his* people? This Caligula's eyes were filled with an unnatural brightness and his face was the colour and complexion of well-kneaded dough. When he laughed it was the cruel laugh of a despot.

Slowly but relentlessly the resentment Rufus felt was replaced by anger. Yes, he was a slave and subject to his master's whims, but even a slave should not be asked to suffer this humiliation: paraded for the vicious entertainment of the crowd and as helpless as a chained bear baited by hounds. He raised his head and found himself staring into the Emperor's face. The mocking eyes locked on his and the lips twisted into a sneer, and suddenly, for the first time, Rufus knew true hatred. I could kill this man, he thought. I could put my hands round his neck and squeeze until the last breath was driven from his body. He saw the mocking eyes narrow, the glacial blue becoming shadowed, and he realized with a shock that Caligula was reading his mind – was challenging him. In that instant, the rage he was experiencing changed to a mindless, reckless exhilaration. The guards lining the walls seemed irrelevant and the crowd faded into a background haze. There were only two people in the room and one must die.

His mood was interrupted by a gasp from his side. He looked down to see the girl grimace in pain and realized he was gripping her hand so tightly he must be close to breaking her fingers. She stared back, her eyes filled with a desperate appeal. She had sensed the violence between the two men, and she knew it would be the death of her. He hesitated, but only for a second. How could he place this fragile creature in danger? He allowed himself a sad smile and saw the tension leave her. Caligula saw it too and roared with laughter. The moment was gone. He was a slave again.

It was a relief when they were led from the palace before the night's feasting began.

When their escort left they sat in silence in the shabby little room behind the elephant house. The girl was hunched on the cot as far from Rufus as was possible in that tiny space, and she looked more like a frightened child than ever. Rufus knew he should talk to her, reassure her in some way. Another man would surely vow to protect her and keep her safe. But somehow he could find no words that would not sound hollow, no promise that he could keep. It was as if he had been followed home by a stray street urchin who refused to be sent away. She was undoubtedly pretty, but it was impossible to forget she was a ... he struggled for a word that wouldn't make him as cruel as his Emperor, but gave up. He had no feelings for her beyond sympathy. She hadn't said a single word to him. He realized he didn't even know her name.

'Livia,' she said, as if she had read his thoughts. Her voice was soft and she had a lilting accent he found difficult to place.

'I am Rufus, keeper of the Emperor's elephant.'

'So that is the smell? I feared someone had spilled a pot of night soil.'

She turned to face the wall and curled up tighter, wrapping her arms protectively around herself. For a moment he was overwhelmed by a mixture of pity and concern and rose with the intention of joining her on the cot and giving her what comfort he could. But there was something terribly forbidding about that turned back and he stopped halfway. Instead he opened the door that linked the room to the barn, and spent his wedding night alone amongst the sweet-smelling soft hay and relentlessly crawling insects beside Bersheba.

In the morning he fed and watered the elephant and exercised her in the park. When he returned to the barn he saw the tiny figure of Livia watching from the doorway and led Bersheba towards her.

'No,' she said, backing away with a cry of fear.

'You are safe with Bersheba,' Rufus assured her. 'She may be big, but she's harmless. She won't hurt you.'

'What would you know of hurt?' she snapped and retreated inside the house, slamming the door behind her and leaving him wondering at the contrariness of women.

They spent that day, and the following one, in a sort of silent battle that could have no victor. He sensed there were things she wanted to say which pride or stubbornness stopped her from saying. This was his home, familiar and comforting in its humble way. For her it was an alien world filled with strangeness and potential dangers, not least the massive beast who shared their living space. But silence, like promises, only exists to be broken. It is impossible for two people forced to live together in a confined space not to communicate, at least by gesture, and gesture was eventually followed by words.

On the third day, they were taking their evening meal together when she began to talk about herself, and Rufus discovered in quick succession that she had been born in the province of Achaea, was probably about twenty years old, had lived the life of a nomad, and was now principal acrobat in a troop of dwarf entertainers.

He continued to sleep in the barn, where at first he dreamed dreams of Aemilia. But there came a point in his nocturnal reflections when Aemilia's heavy-bodied softness was replaced by a smaller, more delicate frame. He sensed a change in

206

Livia, too, and on the night when she reached out to touch him as he turned to go to his straw mattress he was almost expecting it.

It was Livia who took the initiative. She held his hand and led him to the bed, where she gently pushed him backwards. Then, never meeting his eyes, she shrugged off her dress and stood before him.

He was entranced. He had never seen anything so perfect. Her beauty took his breath away – and terrified him. The moment Caligula understood what he had given two mismatched outcasts, he would separate them.

Livia, meeting his gaze for the first time, read his thoughts in a glance. 'Come,' she said. 'We must make good use of what time we have.'

They lay together, cheek against cheek, her body tiny and vulnerable, but soft and tantalizing, against his. He reached for her, drawing her still closer, and bent his head to kiss her. She put her hand to his lips.

'First there are things you must know,' she whispered. 'I have sold my body. Men have sold me. Despite my size, perhaps because of it, men have always desired me. I have been used in ways that disgust me and would sicken you. If we are to be together, and stay together, you must first know this.'

He could feel the dampness where her cheek met his, and a tear rolled from the corner of his eye to mingle with hers. And as the grey of the early dawn began to show through the thin cracks in the wall, it was her head that came to his and there was no barrier to the kiss.

At first, he treated her like a fragile doll, afraid his size and strength would cause her pain. But she soon made him aware that, in her own way, she was as strong as he, and that she found his size, in every sense, a source of great pleasure. She taught him things, about her body and his, he would never have discovered for himself in a lifetime.

Rufus would remember the weeks that followed as the eternal summer of his life. Each day brought a new reason to be thankful, each night a new source of wonder. Livia was full of contradictions. He discovered that, although she wanted to be loved, she could not bear to be smothered. If he tried to help her with the household tasks she would snap at him with her teeth bared like an angry terrier. Yet minutes later another Livia would be revealed, the Livia who craved affection and could combine passion and compassion in a way that left him weak and bewildered.

She was determined to prove herself as a wife as well as a lover. She attacked the squalor he had been happy to live with, brushing like a tiny whirlwind, and did what she could with their meagre resources to turn the room behind the barn into a home. Only one thing came between them.

'Why must we live with that stinking animal?' she asked one evening as they lay together. 'You have the Emperor's favour. Surely you can ask for another position.'

'But Bersheba is my charge. She–'

Livia put a hand to his lips and rolled astride

208

him, laughing. 'Do you love the elephant more than you love me?'

Rufus hesitated only for an instant, but an instant was enough.

'You do love the elephant more than you love me!'

Nothing he said would change that opinion. His only option was to prove her wrong, and it was an exhausted Rufus who staggered from their pallet the next morning. At least Bersheba was less complicated.

But an elephant used to regular habits, who has found herself abandoned, is apt to be moody.

Bersheba ignored Rufus when he greeted her. Perhaps she was hungry; he should have fed her an hour ago. Turning his back on her, he began to pitch sheaves of hay into her feeding area. His thoughts returned to the hours before and the velvety softness of Livia's flesh and the way her small teeth had bitten into his lip as they both reached the height of their passion at just the right mo–

Why was he lying on his back on the packed earth floor with the crossbeams of the barn spinning sickeningly above him?

As the spinning slowed, he tried to stand, but only contrived to struggle as far as one knee before being overcome by nausea and sitting back with his head in his hands.

The next time his whirling head allowed him to look up, Bersheba stood over him, ominously close, her trunk swinging rhythmically. He thought she might be going to hit him again, for he realized now that what had felt like the roof falling in on him was a blow from that five-foot length of solid muscle. But the swinging stopped and instead she gently curled it round his arm and pulled him to his feet.

Rufus shook his head ruefully and went to where the fruit was stored. 'I apologise, mighty Bersheba.' He placed a bruised apple in the bowl formed by the end of her trunk. 'It is going to be more difficult than I had realized to look after my two ladies in the manner they deserve. But I have learned my lesson.'

Bersheba snorted her acceptance and went back to her hay. Rufus opened the big double doors to allow the sunlight of a glorious morning to stream inside, cutting through the thin clouds of dust rising from the elephant's straw floor. His heart filled with the simple joy of living as he stepped out into the clean air of the park. He took a deep breath, filling his lungs until they could take no more.

'Is the honeymoon over so soon?'

XXV

Lucius, the officer who had delivered Rufus to Drusilla's bedroom, sat on the damp grass a dozen paces up the slope towards the palace. He seemed in no hurry to rise, but lay back, staring at the sky with a contented look. Rufus walked over to him, stood for a while, until he realized how foolish he must appear and took his place on the ground beside the young soldier.

'Everything is so clean and pure on mornings like this, don't you think? Whatever happened yesterday is gone for ever and the day ahead holds nothing but promise. It reminds me of the hour before a battle when one sees everything much more vividly and each breath is precious because it might be among the last you take.' The words were directed at Rufus, but Lucius's eyes never left the solid blue dome above them.

'Have you fought in many battles then?' Rufus didn't try to hide his scepticism. Lucius had the kind of face that would always look boyish. It was impossible to imagine him in combat.

'You mean have I always been a princess's lap-dog? Then the answer is no. I have locked shields with my brothers and felt the power of the barbarian horde as they broke upon them. I have tasted barbarian blood on my lips, heard the screams of the dying and smelled the shit from bowels ripped by a blade.' He shrugged as if it was of no consequence, but Rufus heard the pride in his voice. 'But that was a long time ago in another place, in another life. I enjoyed campaigning. All you had to do was follow orders and look heroic even when your guts felt like ice.' He laughed and picked himself up, dusting the grass from his back. 'Perhaps it is not so different here after all. My orders now are to take you to a certain lady.'

Rufus followed him along the covered walkway connecting the Emperor's palace to that of his predecessor, Tiberius, but soon they turned north and into a small enclosed garden near the

211

Palatine library. Broad-canopied trees of a type Rufus didn't recognize threw wide circles of shade on the manicured grass, where a peacock, its brilliant rainbow-fan tail thrown proudly wide, shrieked its displeasure, and a herd of tiny deer grazed peacefully. Life-sized statues lined the paths, their stony gaze still focused on some epoch-making event a hundred years before. They were perfect, these toga-clad patricians; each face an individual, each marble cloak styled slightly differently from the others. Rufus quailed beneath their stern gaze, and wondered why he was here. What could she want from him she had not already taken?

She was waiting for him by a fountain in the centre of the garden. Lucius waved him forward and walked off to stand out of earshot beneath one of the trees.

Drusilla was cloaked and hooded, and stood with her back towards him. She seemed smaller than he remembered, somehow diminished. But perhaps that was a trick of the early-morning light.

'Walk with me.' The words were the merest whisper. She set off slowly towards the far end of the garden where he could see the red-tiled roof of the temple of Apollo rising above the trees. He kept pace just by her left shoulder.

'Do you fear me, puppy dog?' The words sent a shiver through him. Her voice was stronger, but he had to lean forward because it was muffled by the thick cloak which still hid her face from him. 'You should fear me. A single word from me would bring a dozen guards to cut you down and they would not stop to question why.'

She walked a little further before she spoke again. 'But the real question is, puppy dog, whether I should fear you. When I had you brought to me you were just another handsome morsel to be tasted. A tender piece of flesh to be enjoyed then discarded. How could it be otherwise? You are a slave and I am destined to be a goddess. You should be nothing to me.' She shook her head under the hood. 'Yet, since our meeting, my mind has been filled with your face and your body and your touch. I have pined for the sound of your voice and the feel of your hard flesh under my hands. At first, I believed it was weakness on my part, and I fought it, but in the fighting I have become weaker still. Then I understood. You had bewitched me. And now,' she swept the hood back from her face and turned towards him, making him step away in fear, 'I must decide whether to accept my bewitchment or to break the spell by having you killed.'

Rufus heard the words and understood their significance, but what she said was overwhelmed by the horror confronting him.

It was as if her beauty had been sucked from her like the moisture from an overwintered apple. The skin of her face was deeply wrinkled and the colour and texture of parchment, blotched with patches of darker, more lifeless flesh. Her yellowing eyes were sunk deep in their sockets. It was the face of death.

She laughed at his confusion, and he gasped at the ruin that was her mouth. The lips he had kissed were covered with weeping ulcerous boils and she had lost several teeth, while others dangled loose in her gums. And she was bald, or almost so. Only tufts of the silky auburn mane remained, standing out like sparse stalks missed by a careless harvester.

'Am I not beautiful?' she rasped, echoing the question that had greeted him in the room with the discus thrower. 'Am I not the treasure you always desired?' Then, more harshly still, 'Is this your gift to Drusilla, slave? Did you betray me?'

'No, mistress,' Rufus pleaded, hoping it was true, but remembering his words to Narcissus. Was this some sorcery of the Greek's? What was it he had said? 'I don't think Drusilla will harm anyone again.' Was there a terrible certainty there he had missed? His mind raced. He understood he was fighting for his life and he groped desperately for the words that would save him.

He found himself babbling, a near-incoherent jumble of inanity which, for some reason, appeared to please her.

'You gave me your love and I was grateful for it. For a few short hours you placed me among the gods and I was blinded by the glories I discovered there. When it was past, you left me in a shadow world where the darkness comes from within. I waited in vain for your call. I thought I had failed you in some way and that knowledge made my life worthless. I would give anything for this not to be. Kill me if you must, but know you have bewitched me as much as you say I have bewitched you.'

He dropped to his knees, not daring to look into her face. He knew he risked everything by offering her his life, but something in the memory of the time they spent together made him believe she wanted it to be so. He didn't see the single tear that ran down her ravaged cheek.

'You were the last of my lovers, Rufus of the elephant. Some would say you were the last of a vast legion, but believe me when I tell you it is not so. Drusilla was discerning in her choice of puppy dogs, at least give her that. And you did please her.' There was an infinite sadness in her words and the way she spoke them. She was talking of herself in the past tense, as if she were already dead, and even in his fear for his own life, Rufus could not help being moved. 'But Drusilla must ask herself if that is enough to save you? Would it not be fitting if you were to join her on her funeral pyre, in the manner of some terrible Babylonian queen in the texts of Herodotus, taking her most coveted possessions with her into the next world? I will think on that.'

Rufus felt the touch of her chilled fingers, and he rose awkwardly to find the sunken eyes piercing him.

'Would you burn for your Drusilla? A final fiery coupling before we join the gods in their endless dance?' She laughed, like dry twigs crackling underfoot on a forest floor, and drew his face to hers until their lips touched and he felt her tongue enter his mouth and tasted the vileness of her affliction. Despite himself he recoiled from her, giving her the answer she sought. 'No? I thought not. For you are but a slave and will always be a slave while Drusilla *will* be a goddess. Her brother does not understand the true nature of her sickness, but she has made him promise it.'

The strength seemed to drain away from her and she swayed drunkenly. Instinctively, he placed a hand on her arm to steady her and felt brittle bone beneath the thick cloth of the cloak, but she shrugged him off, staring at him as if surprised he was still there.

'Not the slave then, but who? The soldier? Surely his method would be more violent, less subtle. The spy? The very opposite. Milonia would not have the courage. Livilla does not have the hate. Agrippina has the skills, but she would not risk her brother's wrath. Uncle Claudius...'

Rufus listened to the rambling litany of names and backed away to where Lucius waited in the shade.

'You survived then?' the young soldier greeted him. 'I'm pleased.'

Rufus stared at him, puzzled.

'No, truly, I am pleased. All she had to do was raise her hand and I was to cut your throat, with this.' He pulled a curved dagger from his belt. 'I took it from a Parthian warrior, but I've never used it. When you were on your knees I thought she was about to give the signal.'

Rufus flinched at the sight of the knife. 'But why? I have done nothing. I am no danger to Drusilla or anyone else.'

Lucius shrugged. 'She believes she has been poisoned. Her physician told her she has a sickness, a cancer, but she would not listen to him. When the old fool insisted he was correct, she had him sent to her brother's executioners. She said she would know when she looked in your eyes if you had betrayed her. That was when I would strike. But you must have convinced her otherwise, because you are still here. As I say, I'm glad. It is too nice a morning to spoil by killing someone you hardly know. Here, take it.' He held out the short dagger and pressed it into Rufus's hand. 'I have no more need of it. You might find it useful some day.'

He turned to leave, but Rufus hesitated, his eyes drawn back to the slight figure in the shadows at the end of the garden.

'How long...?'

Lucius stopped and followed his gaze. 'She has been sick for more than a month. I have watched her wither as a flower does after a spring frost. First her beauty dulled; then it faded away. Her flesh fell from her bones and her hair from her head. I can scarce bear to look at her, yet she sends for me every night.' He shuddered at the memory and Rufus saw his eyes harden. 'I would rather endure the hot iron of her brother's torturers than the anticipation of another summons.'

'I loved her, I think.'

Lucius stared at him and Rufus feared the young tribune might strike him for his insolence. Then the look was gone. It seemed their similar ages and shared experience gave them a bond that bridged the void between slave and soldier.

'I didn't know it at the time, and it still confuses me, but Drusilla lit a fire in my heart even this cannot extinguish. At first I resented what she was taking from me; then I realized that in the taking she was also giving, if you can understand

217

that. I began as her slave, but by the end she said she was mine.'

'Then you are a greater fool than you appear. It is not a slave's place to love, but to obey.' Lucius snorted his disgust. 'Do you not understand she corrupts everything she touches? The ugliness you saw today was always there, but it was inside, and more disgusting still. The words that drip like honey from her lips are all lies, the kisses she bestows more poisonous than any viper. She is like her brother, a foul thing whose caresses are merely preparing your flesh for the blade or the pincers.'

The final words were forced through clenched teeth and Rufus realized with shock that Drusilla's was not the only bed the handsome tribune was forced to share.

'I am sorry. I did not realize–'

Lucius cut him off. 'Do not waste your pity on me,' he said. 'This sickness which afflicts Drusilla is a sign that the time of reckoning is close. I...' His voice tailed off as he realized what he had said. 'Forgive me, I talk too much. Forget Drusilla. She will be dead within the week.'

He was wrong. It was two more weeks before the announcement came and the Palatine held its collective breath and waited for the inevitable retribution.

XXVI

Rufus waited with the rest. Every hour of every day he anticipated the tread of Praetorian boots and the knock on the door, the grip on his shoulder and the bite of cold iron on his wrists. The fear ate at his spirit and chewed away his courage. Livia noticed the change in him, and tried without success to understand it. He did not give her any help. If he revealed what had occurred between himself and Drusilla he would drag her into the Emperor's net. At least if she knew nothing, her ignorance might save her, even if he fell. He knew it was unfair, but he had retreated so far inside himself he found it difficult to communicate with anyone. He spent more time with Bersheba than with his wife, but often could not bring himself to meet even the elephant's unruffled eye.

Narcissus kept him informed of events inside the palace. Claudius's freedman seemed unperturbed by the upheaval, even to be enjoying it. Clearly he believed himself above suspicion, and he revelled in the tribulations of his rivals.

'The Emperor uses Drusilla's death to rid himself of a dozen senators who oppose him. They have the choice of taking their own lives or enduring the glowing iron, with the knowledge that if they choose the second, their family will suffer with them. Of course,' he added complacently, 'their final decision is of little interest to Caligula. He knows they have nothing to do with his sister's demise. To solve that puzzle, he has tasked his chamberlain, who sees this as an opportunity to bring his own enemies low, but has neither the intellect nor the capacity to bring it about.' He shook his head in wonder at the man's bumbling. 'The old fool pinned his hopes on questioning the two eastern sisters who attended Drusilla's bedroom and kept her many secrets. As if he could force anything but screams from two mouths that had been silent from birth. Fortunately, someone else saved him the trouble. They were found in their quarters this morning with their throats cut. Convenient, is it not?'

Rufus had a curious dizzy-making instant when his brain was divided between relief that two potential witnesses to his midnight tryst with Drusilla were no longer a threat and guilt that his survival should be at the expense of the innocent dark-eyed twins who cooed over his body. 'My little doves.'

'I am sorry. They were harmless enough creatures. Their only crime was to serve their mistress.'

Narcissus skewered him with a look of disbelief. 'Harmless? Their crime was not to serve their mistress, but to know too much. Many people have died for lesser crimes. If they had been sensible they would have entrusted the fruits of their knowledge to someone who had the power to protect them. What a pity they did not.' His tone made it plain who should have been trusted, although Rufus doubted it would have saved them. He knew by now that Narcissus would never risk his position, never mind his life, for anyone. He looked carefully at the Greek: handsome despite his baldness, in a cultured, even decadent way. Educated and intelligent; cunning, certainly, or he would never have survived for so long. Claudius's spy, who also, to his certain knowledge, spied on Claudius. Ruthless? He recalled his momentary suspicion that Narcissus might have poisoned Drusilla, or at least manoeuvred it.

'If they knew so much about so many, then there must be any number of suspects?' he suggested hopefully.

Narcissus gave a knowing smile. 'That might appear likely, but apparently there is only one. He would have been swept up with the rest, so he very sensibly disappeared. But it does not matter where he hides, even if his aristocratic relatives are foolish enough to provide a refuge. Half of Rome seeks the Emperor's favour by providing his head, and the other half will betray him because they are too frightened not to.'

Rufus knew without asking who the suspect was. Only one link remained who could tie him to Drusilla; only one tongue could be persuaded to speak his name.

'It is only a matter of time,' Narcissus predicted. 'The life of the tribune Lucius Sulpicius Galba can be counted in days.'

But Lucius was not arrested that week, nor the next. Narcissus speculated that the young aristocrat might have vanished into the seething rabbit warren of lesser streets and dangerous, evil-smelling alleys of the Subura out towards the Esquiline Gate. 'He has done surprisingly well to survive for so long in a place where every man's hand is against him. Pray that he dies there and your secret dies with him.'

In the meantime, Narcissus watched, taking in every nuance, tasting every mood and studying every changing dynamic in the intricate web of hatreds and alliances that were the lifeblood of the palace.

'Drusilla was a friend and trusted adviser as much as a sister. Of all Caligula's passions, she was the greatest. He does not eat and seldom drinks. He keeps to his apartments during daylight and at night he barely sleeps. Callistus cannot get near him, and mistrusts anyone who can. He fears Protogenes, who fears no one, and in the background Chaerea smiles his scorpion's smile and waits.'

He reported that the Emperor was too distraught to attend his sister's funeral, but stayed in Rome until the Senate voted Drusilla the honours she was due, including a marble arch which he vowed would be the greatest the Empire had ever seen. This duty done, he left for Campania, with Milonia and his daughter and his closest advisers. Aemilia – who, despite his newly wedded state, sometimes invaded Rufus's dreams in the most disturbing of fashions – accompanied them.

When the imperial retinue returned to Rome in September, it was Cupido's sister who brought Rufus the news.

'He has declared Drusilla divine,' she said. 'She

is to be worshipped as a goddess.'

It was unheard of – sacrilege, even. The wives and mothers of emperors had been voted great honours in the past, but this was different. Drusilla was to stand beside Venus in the pantheon. Only an Emperor strong enough or feared enough could have achieved it. Caligula's opponents in the Senate were outraged. The priests warned of terrible retribution from the slighted deities. But the Emperor was unmoved. Drusilla would receive her divinity at the end of the lengthy formal period of mourning, in May, three days before the festival dedicated to Mercury.

Rufus's fears over his fleeting relationship with the new goddess subsided as the weeks passed. Lucius had not been sighted since the discovery of the murdered twins. There was still no body, which was vaguely worrying, but he breathed more easily and stopped looking over his shoulder every day.

'You are to appear before the Emperor's secretary at the seventh hour.'

Rufus almost dropped with fright. But the voice was wrong. Too polite. He turned and where he expected to find a squad of sword-bearing Praetorians stood a gilded youth in a fine-spun tunic held tight at the waist with a thin silver belt.

He must have been gaping, because the boy repeated his message, louder and more slowly, as if he was speaking to an old man or an idiot.

'You ... are ... to ... appear ... before ... the ... Emperor's ... secretary ... at ... the ... seventh ... hour.'

'I'm not deaf.' Rufus decided the young peacock before him presented no danger, and therefore insolence was not only required, but expected. 'Am I to … attend … the … secretary … like … this?'

The boy looked him over carefully, taking in the stained tunic and dung-spattered legs, and frowned. 'Perhaps you might like to change?'

'I don't have anything to change into.' It was a lie, he still had the tunic he wore for his wedding, but Rufus sensed there might be profit here, and sport. A slave was granted little opportunity for sport and he felt an intense desire to take advantage of this one.

The frown deepened. 'I … I could possibly find something for you.'

Rufus grinned. 'That might be wise.'

The boy sighed, and was about to turn away.

'I stink.'

'What?' The messenger blinked.

'I stink … of shit.'

'You could wash while I'm fetching you a new tunic,' the boy suggested.

'I would still stink. I always stink. It's from working with the elephant.' Rufus pointed to Bersheba, who was munching hay contentedly in the barn.

The boy bit his lip. This was a problem he hadn't considered. Secretary Callistus had famously sensitive nostrils.

'You could bring me some perfumed oil. A lot of it. I could smother myself in it, then the secretary wouldn't have to smell my stink. Or I could stand outside the door when he speaks to me,' Rufus suggested helpfully.

The messenger grabbed the solution as if he was a drowning man and it was the last plank from a burning galley. 'Yes, perfume,' he said, hurrying off before Rufus could come up with some new suggestion.

'Lots of it,' Rufus shouted to his retreating back. He would give the perfume to Livia, he thought; then, with a guilty shiver, *And if there is really a lot I might even keep some for Aemilia.* Callistus would just have to put up with his stink.

XXVII

Had anyone ever suffered as he did? Had anyone ever been more alone? Drusilla was gone. His only friend. His sister. The only one he had ever really trusted. How could she have left him?

He sniffed, blinking away a tear. He stank, but he did not care. His hair was slick with grease and undressed, but it was nothing. He hadn't shaved for three months and would not until her murderers were found, or he had given her the divinity she had craved when she was alive. She, above all, deserved immortality.

How he wished he could have accompanied her to that other life. There was nothing for him in this one but grief and pain, and he wanted neither. What were his accomplishments now, when there was no one with whom he could savour them? Every one a monument to vainglory. What was the point of the battles that were inevitably to come, when each victory would taste of ashes? It was she who had made all the effort worthwhile. In her, he could see the reflection of his greatness. But no more.

Who could he trust now?

As he recognized the answer, an unfamiliar sensation developed deep inside his body, and swarmed upwards into his brain. He felt the first breathlessness of panic.

It was a long time since he had felt fear.

When the seventh hour arrived Rufus was standing outside the door to the secretary's offices enjoying the feel of a silky cloth tunic finer than anything he had ever owned. His dark hair was damp and his nostrils were filled with the scent of some flowery perfume from the east that the boy had insisted on dousing him with. It didn't matter too much; there was plenty left for Livia ... and Aemilia.

'Enter.'

The voice was strong, the tone full of natural authority, and it had an edge that made Rufus stand a little straighter. He pushed the door, which swung back easily on its single wooden hinge.

Of all the great men who ruled Rome from the Palatine Hill and attempted to square the circle of the Emperor's chaotic brilliance, ever-changing moods and overwhelming ambition, Callistus, the imperial secretary, held the position of strength. No man crossed the threshold to Caligula's outer apartments without first being interviewed by the secretary. It was a privilege that had brought him immense wealth as well as power. But power did not come without a price, and the price was clear on the strained face of the man who sat across the scroll-filled desk from where Rufus stood.

Callistus had a wide, sloping forehead which swept down without obstacle to an identically angled, aristocratic nose, giving him the look of some long-beaked bird of the plains. The effect was emphasized by his hair, which had receded in a perfect half-moon leaving behind it a vast, open expanse. He was unhealthily pale, with an enormous bag of flesh beneath each eye and cheeks that sagged beneath the level of his lips, drawing them down in a permanent disapproving frown.

The secretary's eyes swept back and forth across an opened scroll on his desk, accompanied by repeated tuts of dismay, or disbelief, at the perceived failings of some far-off provincial official. Eventually, he rolled up the scroll with a sigh, deposited it in a leather case, and placed it carefully on the left-hand pile on the desk. Only then did he look up and acknowledge Rufus's presence, inspecting him with a jaundiced eye and not attempting to hide his disapproval.

'You are the keeper of the Emperor's elephant?'

Rufus nodded. 'That is correct, sir. I–'

Callistus waved him to silence. 'That is all I wish to know. And, for the moment, all you need to know is that the Emperor has decided you have an important role in the celebrations of his sister's divinity. You and your elephant.'

Rufus swallowed and tried to stay the panic

that filled his stomach with a ball of frantically mating toads.

'Since it is obviously beyond your capabilities to carry this out without supervision, the Emperor' – Callistus shook his head in resignation – 'has decided that among my numberless other responsibilities I must oversee your part in it. To that end you will have yourself and your elephant ready for inspection tomorrow at the second hour.'

'May I ask your honour what form this mission will take?' Rufus asked politely, adding hurriedly, lest his question be taken for insolence, 'in case any specialized preparations are required to ensure Bersheba is ready for the task.'

Callistus closed his eyes. Perhaps this was going to be more tiresome than he thought. 'Specialized preparations?'

'Yes, sir. Special harness, or perhaps a new basket. If Bersheba is to carry the Emperor he would need to be carried in something fitting. Something in the ceremonial line?'

The secretary pursed his lips. 'The beast will not be carrying the Emperor. However, it may be that you need to be aware of its burden. It is rather weighty, I'm told.'

Rufus spent a sleepless night preparing himself and Bersheba. At the appointed hour he and the elephant stood in front of the barn, she in her ceremonial finery and he in the tunic he had acquired from Callistus's gilded messenger. But it was another two hours before the secretary came puffing down the slope from the palace with an escort of soldiers.

The guards stood back as Callistus peered down his long nose at the elephant from a safe distance, holding a perfumed silk cloth to his face.

'No, no,' he huffed. 'This will not do. Not do at all.'

Rufus shuffled his feet and tried not to look round. What was wrong with her? He had spent the entire night scrubbing her down, polishing her teeth and tusks and brushing the great gold-cloth mantle that now covered her back. What more could he have done?

'Bring it closer,' Callistus signalled. 'But not too close.'

Rufus did as he was asked.

'Turn it round.'

Again Rufus complied.

'No. No.' Callistus pulled a small writing block and a stylus from the sleeve of his toga and spent a few moments scratching on the block. 'Soldier! Yes, you. Take this to the Emperor's armourer. Tell him the job must be completed in ten days, that I already know it is impossible, and that he must consult me before he makes a single rivet.'

It was clear the inspection was over, so Rufus returned Bersheba to her stall. He knew he could have done nothing more, but the secretary's reaction had angered him and he was rougher with the elephant than he intended. Bersheba in her turn made her feelings plain with a gentle slap of her trunk that almost knocked him off his feet and changed his mood. Grinning, he began to undo the harness which kept the cloth mantle in place.

'You have no time for that.' Callistus's voice was sharp with impatience. 'Attend me now, slave.'

Rufus had never been inside a closed carriage before. Few Romans, even senators, had been inside one which clattered through Rome's streets during daylight hours, unless they happened to be on imperial business. He would have enjoyed the feel of the soft cushions as they bounced over the road surface more if it was not for the presence of his travelling companion and the fact that he could not see, thanks to the blindfold that had been carefully tied in place over his eyes.

A barked order and the sound of a gate squealing open signalled that they had reached their destination. A firm hand guided him down from the carriage and he felt the air change as they swapped the open for indoors. The cloth still covered his eyes, but his nose was giving him a message. There was a distinct quality to the smell that made his nostrils twitch. It was a long time ago, but it was there, somewhere in his memory. Then his mind filled with red sparks as a hammer pounded on the super-heated blade of a short sword. That was the smell. He could taste it on his tongue. The smell of an armoury. The faded smell of enormous heat.

'Reveal this secret, to your wife, your lover or your elephant, and the Emperor's vengeance will seek you out to the ends of the earth.' The words came from behind him as hands fumbled at the ties of the blindfold.

He blinked as the cloth was removed. He was in a high-ceilinged windowless room of similar proportions to Bersheba's barn. At first his vision was blurred and all he could make out was the flicker of torches around him and an enormously powerful source of light at the far end of the building. Then the blurring cleared and he was staring at one of the wonders of the world.

In death, she was even more beautiful than in life. She was taller, more perfectly proportioned, and any physical imperfection had been carefully removed or ignored. Her head was held high, and her hair fell in ringlets to her bare shoulders. She was regal, but not aloof, staring sightlessly into the middle distance. Those who looked upon her might at first have found her cold, but the golden eyes glowed with a warmth their owner had never emanated in life. The surfaces of her body drew in the light of the torches and reflected it a thousand-fold, so that from some angles it was like staring into the centre of a furnace.

When he had recovered from the first shock, Rufus realized that Drusilla had achieved her ambition. She was immortal.

Where had they found so much gold? The statue Caligula had commissioned to cement his sister's divinity was eight feet high and set on a plinth of pink marble. The artist had dressed his subject in the vestments of Diana, but had posed her in the manner of an earlier Greek rendering of Venus. For a few moments Rufus looked upon the statue in wonder. Then he was back in the room with the curtained bed and her glistening, sweat-sheened body was beneath him, breasts rising and falling, every shadow a temptation. And the statue was just that: a lifeless piece of metal that could never compare with the living, breathing being that had once inhabited that body.

Callistus brought him back to reality. 'Can the

elephant pull her?'

Rufus looked at him for a second in confusion before his mind accepted the challenge and he attempted to calculate the enormous weight of the gold and the carriage needed to transport it.

'She cannot take the statue over the bridge to the Senate,' he said decisively. 'It would never hold. You would risk destroying everything.'

Callistus's face paled at the thought. 'That will not be required. The route is necessarily secret, but think of a circuit of the forum and perhaps a procession as far as the Circus Maximus.'

'Then, yes, Bersheba can pull her.'

The ceremony was timed for the final day of the restrictions imposed by Caligula for her period of mourning, which ensured an outpouring of joy such as Rome had not seen since the day of the Emperor's coronation.

But Callistus had one last surprise for Rufus.

A dozen slaves carried the heavy bundles, all carefully wrapped in soft leather, to the elephant house and laid the curiously shaped objects on the grass. The secretary supervised as Rufus unwrapped them, counting each item as it was revealed in front of the barn.

'But Bersheba can't wear this.' Rufus could hardly believe what he was seeing.

Callistus winced. 'It must. The Emperor insists.'

The bundle with the strangest shape contained what Rufus eventually worked out was an elaborate gold-plated chain-mail headdress. It combined eye and trunk protection for the elephant and was fitted with leather straps so it would not slip out of position. From the forehead, just between the shield-boss-sized openings for her eyes, he was horrified to see jutting a dangerous two-foot golden spike.

Next there emerged a set of four equally extravagant knee protectors, again each with its alarming spike.

Finally, from the burden which it had taken four of the slaves to carry, was unrolled an enormous mantle of interlocking leaf-shaped segments of gold-plated metal that would have covered the entire floor of Rufus's modest home. It was designed to protect Bersheba's back and flanks.

'Oh, and there are also these,' the secretary remembered, and reaching beneath the folds of his cloak he pulled out two pointed, hollow golden horns that fitted snugly over the ends of Bersheba's tusks.

'She will look foolish,' Rufus pleaded.

'Not foolish, magnificent,' Callistus insisted, 'You will accustom the beast to wearing this ceremonial armour, so that when it pulls the golden statue of the Emperor's sister it will provide a spectacle such as Romans have never witnessed. There is one more thing.'

Rufus bit his tongue. He knew Callistus would not forget his outburst. The only reason he was not on his way to a whipping post was that no one else could control Bersheba.

Callistus gestured to one of the slaves, who unrolled a small parcel which had lain forgotten, but now revealed what was plainly the gilt armour and dark tunic of a soldier of the Praetorian Guard.

'You should be honoured, slave. The Emperor

has seen fit to appoint you an honorary soldier of his elite guard. Temporary and unpaid, of course.'

Of course.

Bersheba detested her new finery, and she let him know it.

When he attempted to fit the intricate head-dress, she would allow him to reach a point where he was ready to tighten the final strap before giving a shrug of her head that left it hanging untidily from one ear.

If anything, the plate-armour mantle looked as though it would be even more difficult. Not only was it huge, it was awkward, and he realized immediately he would need more help. Callistus tutted and waved him away, but six slaves arrived at the elephant house within the hour and he put them to work.

In the event, Bersheba was suddenly a model of cooperation. She did exactly what she was asked and they worked the enormously heavy metal blanket over her back. Even when he ordered her to stand, she did so with such care that the covering stayed exactly where it was, and he was able to get underneath her and, using all his strength, tighten the leather straps to keep it in position.

He had never felt so satisfied as when he stepped back to survey his achievement, a smile splitting his face. The secretary was right: she did look magnificent.

He looked into the soulful brown eyes. 'I thank you, Bersheba. You have made me proud.'

Bersheba looked back. Was there a twinkle there?

'No!'

Yes. It began as a twitch of her shoulders and rippled down her massive flanks as an almost imperceptible wriggle, ending in a profound shake of her huge backside and a twitch of her tail. Slowly, infinitely slowly, the golden mantle slipped sideways, until it finished up hanging between her legs.

The roar of frustration that echoed across the Palatine scared the pigeons from the trees and rooftops.

But the one thing Rufus had learned in his years with Fronto's animals was perseverance. He knew he would win in the end, and a day before they were due to lead the parade Bersheba stood before him, a sight to chill the blood, her ceremonial armour firmly in place; a living mountain of glittering golden fragments which sparkled individually in the sunlight.

He sent for Callistus. The palace official narrowed his eyes and studied Bersheba from every angle then nodded with satisfaction.

'Wait,' he ordered.

A few minutes later he returned with the Emperor at his side, followed by Protogenes and a small weasel-like individual Rufus realized must be the Emperor's chamberlain. Rufus was shocked by Caligula's appearance. He had not seen the Emperor since his sister's death and the interval had wrought a dreadful change in the young man. His hair was long and lank, his beard matted, as if he had been neither shaved nor barbered in many months. His eyes were sunk deep in his head and his cheeks had the sallow complexion of candlewax.

Caligula stopped so suddenly when he saw Bersheba that Protogenes almost ran into his back and had to throw himself clumsily sideways to avoid the collision. The Emperor stared wide-eyed at the elephant as if he had never seen her before.

'Truly this animal is worthy of my sister,' he cried. 'If only I had a dozen, no, a hundred, like this, I could do her the honour she deserves.' Rufus could see his eyes were moist. Caligula gave a huge sniff and addressed him directly. 'Do your duties well, slave, and be sure your Emperor will reward you.'

Later, while Rufus sat in the little room behind the elephant house with his stomach twisted by doubts, Livia questioned him.

'If the Emperor offers you a reward, what will you ask?' she said seriously.

He shrugged. 'It is too early to think of such things. If anything goes wrong tomorrow I could be dead by nightfall.'

'But there must be something you wish for more than anything else?' she insisted.

She was right. Rufus knew exactly what he would ask. But to say it out loud seemed to be to risk losing it. The gods liked to have their little jokes with the ambitious and the proud. They enjoyed giving hope and then replacing it with despair; he had had experience of that. But Livia would not give up and eventually he capitulated.

'I suppose I will ask to buy our freedom,' he said casually, as if it was not the most momentous thing in the world. 'Fronto still has the money he was saving for me. It might not be enough on its own, but I think he will advance me what I need. We could make a good living together.'

Livia struggled to hide her disappointment. How could he not understand?

For the first time in her life she had escaped. For the first time in her life she possessed something. It was not a lot. Only a draughty little room that stank continually of elephant dung, with a husband who was more boy than man and was sometimes naïve to the point of foolishness. But it was hers.

She had had her fill of loneliness. Reviled as some kind of monster as soon as it became clear she would grow no taller, she had been sold into slavery by her father. Treated at first as a toy, then as a sexual plaything, by her master, she had been discarded as soon as he tired of her and slipped to his next level of depravity. Other masters and similar experiences followed, but when she was sold into the troop of dwarves she thought she had finally found, at the very least, companionship. She was wrong. For she, young, pretty and with a recognizably human form, was as different from them, with their overdeveloped arms and legs and stunted bodies, as they were from normal adults. They hated her.

Only her aptitude as a performer, one who enhanced their reputation, brought her acceptance. And if she was desired by the men who eyed her greedily as she danced and tumbled, at least they ate the better for it.

Rufus, and the Emperor, had saved her from

that life. And now her husband was threatening her security – their security – to follow some impossible dream.

Could he not see that Caligula would never set him free? There was only one Emperor's elephant, and only one man who could control it. He had as much chance of freedom as Bersheba did. She opened her mouth to tell him so, but was interrupted by a knock at the door.

Rufus stared at her. The knock came again, harder this time, full of authority. He got up and cautiously opened the door just a crack.

'A man could get a warmer welcome in Dacia.'

'Cupido!'

Livia glanced up as the German came into the room. He looked very young and impossibly handsome in his gleaming wolf breastplate, his golden hair contrasting with the sinister black of his tunic.

'I came to wish you good fortune, Rufus. Aemilia and I sacrificed a white cockerel to the old gods and the signs were good. My sister threw the sticks for us. They foretell that both you and I will face trials but united we will overcome them and be victorious. The gods will it.'

Rufus felt an involuntary shiver. Something in the way Cupido spoke the word contained a shadow of warning. 'Trials? What kind of trials?'

'It is but a word.' Cupido shrugged, but Rufus could see he was not entirely convinced. Was his friend keeping something back? He knew Aemilia claimed to have the sight, but messages from the gods came in many forms and were not always straightforward.

'What kind of trials?' he repeated.

Cupido glanced towards Livia, but Rufus read the meaning in his eyes. *Do not press me on this. Trust me.*

'Know only that I will be at your side when the need is greatest,' the gladiator said, attempting to lighten the mood. 'The Tungrian cohort will provide close escort to the Emperor tomorrow. Make sure Bersheba does not drop anything on my line of march – I have just bought new sandals.'

Rufus stared at him for a few seconds, then smiled. What did it matter? What the gods willed, the gods willed, and nothing mere men could do would change it. The only certainty was that his friend would be only a few feet behind him when Bersheba led the procession to the new temple of Drusilla which Caligula had dedicated on the Capitoline Hill. And that was enough.

Cupido stayed only a little longer. When he had left, Rufus turned to Livia with a smile, but she was concentrating on her sewing and did not look up.

He would make her and the Emperor proud. Trials and a victory.

XXVIII

Rufus opened the barn doors the next morning to be greeted by a sun that seemed to have been created specifically for Drusilla. It shone with an extra lustre, as if the gods had polished it in honour of the newest member of their pantheon. When he led Bersheba out, the plates of her ceremonial armour shimmered like a golden skin, and he knew Drusilla's statue would blind and awe everyone who looked upon it this day.

Bersheba was on her best behaviour and had accepted her awkward accoutrements without any sign of rebellion. When Callistus came to the barn at the fifth hour to pass judgement he tutted disapprovingly and instructed Rufus to polish a joint here, a plate there, but Rufus could see the secretary was almost as proud of the elephant as he was. Rufus too, feeling uncomfortably martial in his guard's uniform, passed Callistus's inspection, and they were ready.

A small escort of Praetorians led them to the foundry where the statue of Drusilla waited, already firmly roped and wedged into a formidably strengthened four-wheeled wagon decorated with the gold-leaf motifs of the imperial family. Rufus harnessed Bersheba to the cart, took his seat between her shoulders, and the double doors swung back.

The crowds had been gathering since before

240

dawn and there was not one of them who had not anticipated the day of Drusilla's divinity with the greed of a starving man. It was not that everyone welcomed her accession to the godhead; far from it. Many felt it a violation of every known code, and others feared divine retribution for the insult to the established order. But for what seemed an eternity they had been bound by the draconian codes imposed by the Emperor for his sister's mourning. Since her death, to be found laughing, bathing or even dining in the company of friends had been to face instant execution. Today the bondage would be over and the Empire would celebrate.

The foundry was close to the start of the official procession route, near the junction of the Nova Via and the Via Sacra. Most people were already in their chosen places, but a slow stream of tardier revellers still made their way along the Via Sacra hoping to find vantage points from where they could get a decent view of the Emperor.

Rufus gave Bersheba the signal to walk. She was accustomed to pulling the cart with her hay, and now she leaned forward to take the weight of the wagon with Drusilla's statue at its centre. She was tremendously strong, but still Rufus had expected her to strain when presented with the unexpected weight of the enormous golden figure. Yet it was obvious when she took her first step that the effort was much less than he had anticipated and the wagon rolled smoothly forward, its iron-rimmed wheels rattling over the cobbles.

Puzzled, Rufus looked over his shoulder. The wagon was sturdily constructed, but even so it

241

should be bowed under the weight of precious metal it carried. It did not seem possible that something which looked so heavy could be pulled so easily – unless... He almost laughed out loud. It was hollow. The Emperor's tribute to his sister was nothing but an empty shell.

As they made their way through the big double gates on to the Nova Via, Rufus tapped Bersheba on her left shoulder and she turned sharply into the wide street. At first it was the Emperor's elephant in all her armoured magnificence that drew every eye. Then he heard shouts of amazement ringing along both sides of the street as the crowd realized what was in the wagon.

'Divine Drusilla! Look, look, it is the goddess! A goddess of pure gold!'

The crowd surged towards them, those at the rear pushing those in front, but Callistus had taken no chances with his Emperor's divine sister. Two full centuries of Praetorians lined either side of the road, and now they drew their short swords and the mob jostled in confusion just out of reach of the points.

The cries of astonishment grew as Bersheba made her stately way past the ornate columns of the temple of Jupiter Stator, the Praetorians keeping pace on either side, slashing at anyone who threatened to come too close to the priceless cargo. At the intersection of the Nova Via with the Via Sacra, the Emperor waited, invisible behind the curtains of a golden carriage. Behind him, positioned by rank and lineage; the aristocracy of an Empire stretched up the Clivus Palatinus. Consuls and governors, senators and generals,

242

kings and princes. They had travelled from all over the world to be here this day to see Drusilla enter the realm of the immortals.

Cupido was in his place beside the Emperor's carriage along with a dozen others who formed the Emperor's close guard, the wolf emblem on their breastplates gleaming in the sunlight. Beyond the carriage Rufus could see Callistus rushing about like a panic-stricken mouse, jostling, hustling and straightening. Bersheba snorted, and the imperial secretary gaped as if he was surprised to see her, making Rufus wonder if they had arrived early. Arms flapping, the little man manoeuvred Bersheba and the statue into position in the place of honour at the front of the procession. The original Praetorian escort marched off to take their places among their comrades who waited along the route at six-foot intervals.

With one last darting look along the line, Callistus took a deep breath and gave the order to march. With fluttering heart, Rufus set Bersheba in motion.

All Rome seemed to be crammed into the overflowing streets around the forum. The crowds on the Via Sacra could be numbered in their tens of thousands and they perched on every possible vantage point on the temple steps and among the statues. Ahead of Rufus, columns of fluted marble marked the road at intervals, each with its solemn carved figure at its peak. From his elevated position on Bersheba's back, the great thoroughfare stretched out before him all the way to the massive bulk of the records office at the foot of the Capitoline. Close on either side were the great temples and public buildings which made this the most important of all Rome's streets. Already he was approaching the long frontage of the house of the Vestals. Beyond it was the *regia* and the temple of Divine Julius, with its rostrum where the great orators sometimes drew crowds of hundreds, even thousands.

As Bersheba advanced step by patient step, the crowds threw flower petals beneath her massive feet and the scent of them filled Rufus's nostrils. Cheers from a thousand throats rang in his ears. He did not dare look behind him, but he felt the comforting presence of Cupido close by, keeping pace with the imperial carriage where Caligula sat alone and unseen behind the silken curtains. This was Drusilla's day and the Emperor wanted nothing, not even himself, to distract attention from the great golden figure of his sister.

Now they were approaching the Rostrum Julium. Rufus could see the distinctive prow beaks from ships captured at the battle of Actium jutting from the wall on either side of the niche that held the shrine.

Bersheba was directly opposite the rostrum when they struck.

Rufus had been concentrating on the splendours surrounding him and, at first, didn't realize what was happening. Then, above the roars of the crowd, he heard Cupido's shout. 'Guards, to me.'

The sight that met his eyes when he twisted in alarm didn't seem possible. Twenty sinister figures had emerged from the still-cheering crowd and somehow breached the line of alert Praetorians. Each man wore a hooded cloak of brown wool that covered his face and each carried a drawn sword. The professional way they held the weapons marked them as soldiers, or ex-soldiers, and they moved silently towards the gilt carriage with an intensity of purpose that made their intention unmistakable. Assassins! They were trying to kill the Emperor. Rufus watched incredulously as a dozen more followed them, still unmolested.

'Guards, to me.' Cupido's shout was shriller, more desperate. Why were the Praetorians who lined the route not reacting? They stayed frozen in place, as immobile as the statues on their marble plinths.

Three or four of the faceless killers already surrounded each of Cupido's dozen men and still more were working their way between the individual conflicts towards the carriage. The fighting ebbed and flowed but Cupido somehow managed to stay between the assassins and the Emperor. Rufus saw the long sword flash and one man was down, blood fountaining from a gaping wound in his throat. But he was instantly replaced by another of the hooded figures and Rufus realized the attackers were trying to manoeuvre Cupido away from the carriage.

Without thinking, Rufus leapt from Bersheba's flank and sprinted towards his friend. 'Here, Cupido,' he shouted as he ran. Cupido stole a quick glance towards him and Rufus recognized the battle light in his eyes. Overwhelming odds or not, this was the young German's natural element, with a sword in his hand and an enemy at his front. The fallen assassin's weapon lay at his feet and with a flick of his wrist Cupido used his blade to send it, grip first, sailing into Rufus's hand.

'Remember what I taught you,' he shouted, his sword slicing up to parry a slashing blow with a clash that made Rufus's ears ring: 'the eyes, the throat and the balls.' The grim order must have sent fear through the hearts of his opponents, because their attack wavered. It was only for the merest instant but enough to give him his opening. He screamed his war cry and rammed his sword point into the mouth of the stocky figure in the centre, spraying gore as he back-cut it free, leaving the man to drop like a stone.

Rufus managed to work himself into position at Cupido's right side, blocking access to the carriage just as another group of the hooded killers broke through the Praetorian line. His friend's easy confidence helped still the icy panic churning in his stomach, but the truth was he was terrified. He swallowed hard and tried to concentrate as the assassin lying in a pool of blood at his feet twisted and uttered a choking scream before giving a convulsive shudder and going still.

Repeating Cupido's instructions over and over inside his head, Rufus kept his sword low and point up, darting with little jabs towards groin and stomach as the gladiator had shown him. It didn't seem very warlike, but it was enough to keep his nearest opponent at a safe distance. Rufus could see his assailant's eyes beneath the hooded cloak. He seemed very young and very frightened and he gave the jabbing blade more respect than it deserved. At first, Rufus wondered why, then he remembered the uniform he was wearing. The Praetorians were the Emperor's elite and among the best-trained soldiers in the Empire. His opponent must have believed he faced a battle-tested campaigner.

Cupido was fighting hard, but Rufus realized his friend was using his speed and agility to ensure that most of the assassins were forced to face him rather than the clumsy amateur at his side. Another of the killers fell before his sword, and the survivors stepped back, the courage that had brought them through the line quailing before the arena-honed skills of the man who confronted them.

'The carriage! Remember why we are here.' The shouted order had the ring of desperation. The voice came from beneath the hood of the tallest man, and stirred a memory in Rufus, but before his mind could search for it the assassins rushed the two defenders with swords flailing. Cupido speared one of the attackers in the chest, and somehow parried a sweeping sword cut with a dagger that appeared in his hand like a prop in a deadly conjuring trick. Rufus could hear the clash of iron behind them, and realized a similar battle was being fought on the other side of the Emperor's carriage, but it meant nothing to him. He had to concentrate on staying alive. Then there came a strange moment in the desperate battle when his immediate opponent moved away and he found himself in an oasis of calm at the centre of the maelstrom. Fighting for breath, he was able to look about him for the first time in many minutes.

Despite being outnumbered Cupido's wolves

were holding their own. Bodies lay thick around the carriage, some still, some writhing in their death agonies, bleeding and groaning. The Emperor's coachman had been dragged from his seat and cut to pieces and one of the milk-white mares harnessed to the carriage was down in her traces, her hooves thrashing as she fought to regain her feet despite the spear that pierced her belly.

Puzzlingly, the Praetorian line was still holding back the crowd, though several were looking round in alarm and were obviously wondering why they didn't receive the order to join the fight. Surely they could see their comrades were hard pressed and the Emperor was in mortal danger? It was unfair, Rufus felt, that he and Cupido appeared to be doing most of the work.

The glint of a blade broke the spell and he ducked low to allow the scything cut that would have taken his head from his shoulders to pass harmlessly above him. Then the battle closed in again and he was fighting for his life.

Now his hooded opponent was bigger and stronger and had none of the caution of the fearful young man he had faced earlier. He was forced back inch by inch until he stumbled over the legs of an injured man who had crawled between the wheels of the carriage for safety. The world turned upside down as he fell backwards and he had a momentary glimpse of a wide-eyed face behind the carriage window. He grunted as the attacker planted a hobnailed sandal on his chest and used him as a platform to get into position to hack at the gold-leaf pattern on the door of the coach.

Rufus felt himself being crushed and instinctively lunged upwards with his sword. He experienced an instant of resistance, then an obscene bucking as the man above him squealed and twisted as he felt the needle point angle upwards into his body. Horrified, Rufus pulled the blade free and was rewarded with a howl of agony. At the same time a flood of warm liquid spattered across his face and chest, and the assassin toppled sideways.

He suddenly felt very tired, but Cupido was still locked in combat a few feet away and he forced himself to his feet, using the carriage wheel as a prop. He could see it was almost over. The Praetorians who had tamely allowed the assassins through their line had finally stirred themselves from their lethargy and six or seven of the killers were struggling to escape their grasp.

Cupido chopped at one of his surviving opponents and the man spun away with blood pouring from his neck. That left only the tall man; the leader who had shouted the order. He fought well, with the skill of an experienced swordsman, but he was no match for a former gladiator. With a twist of his blade, Cupido ripped the man's sword from his hand and sent it spinning into the air. He put his point to the assassin's throat and forced the man to his knees, before flicking back the hood.

Rufus gasped.

Lucius.

'Kill me.'

It was not a plea – he was too proud for that. The words were addressed to Cupido, but

Lucius's eyes were fixed on Rufus's. He knew his fate if he fell into the hands of the Emperor's torturers.

'Kill me,' he repeated, and Rufus knew one of the names screamed out when the hot irons were applied again and again would be his own.

Cupido heard the words also, but he knew his duty, and it was not to grant a merciful death to a man who had just tried to kill the Emperor. He took the sword away from Lucius's throat.

'Your fate was written the moment you crossed the line of guards. How did you do that? It will be the first question they ask and I will be interested to hear your answer. Because you will answer, friend. Brave man or coward, they always answer.'

Lucius dropped his eyes, but not before Rufus recognized the despair in them.

'Look out, he has a dagger.' The words were out before he realized he had said them. Cupido stepped back and his sword came up, but it was Rufus who moved first, plunging his blade deep into Lucius's chest. The young tribune opened his mouth as if he had something important to say, but a flood of crimson filled it and he fell forward, dragging Rufus's sword from his hand.

Rufus turned away, to find himself looking into Cupido's accusing eyes.

'There was no dagger.'

Rufus drew out the ornate knife Lucius had given him beneath the tree in Drusilla's garden. Using Cupido to shield his movements from the occupant of the carriage, he bent down and placed the weapon in Lucius's lifeless fingers.

'There is now.'

Cupido stared hard, but did nothing to stop him. 'We will discuss this later.'

A shattering roar reminded Rufus that he had abandoned Bersheba. As he walked painfully back towards the elephant, he was forced to pass beneath the shocked gaze of the consuls and senators who had watched the combat in impotent horror. His eyes caught those of the Emperor's uncle. Claudius was blinking nervously, like an elderly owl caught in bright sunlight.

'Send for Nestor and tell him to bring his most fearsome instruments.' The shouted order was accompanied by a clatter as Caligula kicked back the door of his carriage, his face almost scarlet with fury and suppressed fear. 'We will set up the triangle and the forge here, in open show, and Rome will see how an Emperor rewards those who would do him ill!'

Rufus shuddered, but kept walking. Nestor was Caligula's most experienced and refined torturer. Was it his imagination, or did Claudius's face go a little paler at the mention of the name?

XXIX

He had killed a man. No, he had killed two men.

This air he breathed seemed more of a privilege now he had robbed Lucius of its gift. Yet the very fact of the deaths seemed to diminish him. Was this how Cupido felt each time he left the arena? Did he experience this emptiness, as if some part of another man's going had taken with it an essential element of his killer?

Rufus sat at the rough wooden table. He had spent an hour at a public fountain trying to wash the blood from his skin and his clothing, but it seemed to leave an indelible stain. From time to time he would rub his fingers absently over patches on his arm only he could see. Livia watched her husband anxiously. She had heard of the assassination attempt, but not the details. She could see he was affected by what had happened and she wanted to comfort him, but Rufus had created a barrier around himself that she could not penetrate.

She had another reason for wanting to speak to him. She had news of her own. But there would be another time.

Eventually, he broke the silence. 'Why did they do it?'

'Who?'

'Lucius must have known he would fail. It was as if he expected the guards to stand aside. Some of them did, but not Cupido. Not me.'

'Who is Lucius?'

'I killed him. I think he might have been my friend, but I pierced his heart with my sword and he died thanking me for it.' He shook his head and looked at her with empty eyes. 'I killed them both. To save the Emperor.'

Livia's eyes lit up. 'You saved the Emperor?'

Rufus stared at her in confusion. He found it difficult to remember the details. Everything had happened so quickly. The dazzling patterns as Cupido's long sword carved the air, the terrible certainty as he drove the point home into another victim. The accusing eyes. Had that been Cupido or Lucius?

'It was Cupido. Cupido saved the Emperor.'

'And you?'

'Yes. And me.'

'Then there will be a reward.'

Rufus suddenly felt sick. 'I want no reward.'

He walked out of the room to sit with Bersheba ... and wait for Cupido.

The Cupido who came to the barn at dusk the following day was almost unrecognizable as the young man he had watched dazzle his opponents in the arena, or even the hard-eyed killer he had fought beside in the shadow of the Rostrum Julium.

The gladiator stumbled against the barn door and would have fallen beneath Bersheba's feet if Rufus hadn't stepped forward to catch him. His eyes were glazed and his breath was heavy with the fumes of the rough red wine they served in the worst type of tavern. Rufus attempted to support him, and lead him through the barn to the living space, but the gladiator shrugged him off, mumbling wearily to himself.

'We were betrayed.'

Rufus opened his mouth to reply, then thought better of it.

Cupido blinked at him, and brought his face close, as if his eyes were having difficulty focusing.

'The Praetorians were tricked,' he slurred bitterly. 'Tricked! A legionary officer of the palace went to the barracks and warned the centurion in charge of the guard that the Emperor had ordered a test to entertain the mob. He must tell his men to stand and let certain men pass – certain men who could be identified by their hoods.'

Rufus winced as the gladiator continued.

'The centurion was surprised, but such things have happened in the past. He was a good officer, and he checked the order diligently. He recognized the hand, which was that of Callistus, the Emperor's secretary, countersigned by Cassius Chaerea, of the Guard. So he gave the order.' Cupido shook his head to clear it. 'Naturally, the order was a forgery. How he must now wish he had been more suspicious, if he is not already dead.'

'The legionary officer?' Rufus spoke for the first time, already knowing the answer to his question. 'Lu – arrgh.' He fought for breath as a hand like an iron claw gripped his throat.

'Yes, Lucius. Lucius who betrayed his Emperor. Lucius who could have condemned another hundred, or another thousand, if he had lived. Lucius ... who ... you ... killed.' With the final four words the fingers tightened on Rufus's windpipe and the hand raised him until his feet dangled inches from the floor. He tried to speak, to explain, to plead for his life, but not a single word came out. His vision first blurred, then faded...

He felt himself flying through the air, and for a second he truly believed he had been summoned by the gods, before the flight ended with a bone-rattling crash.

He opened his eyes to see Cupido in a crumpled heap among the straw by the barn door and Bersheba standing over him with her trunk swinging menacingly. There was something in her posture that told him she was preparing to step forward and crush the gladiator beneath her massive pads.

'Easy, girl,' he croaked, massaging his throat. 'Easy.'

He crawled over to the prone body and raised Cupido's head, his hands finding a pronounced lump behind the left ear beneath the golden hair. He looked up to find Livia standing over them, her hands held protectively over her stomach and her eyes wide with fear. Between them, they settled Cupido on the bed and waited.

He opened his eyes two hours later, but it was clear he wasn't aware where he was or how he arrived there. Rufus brought water from the cistern and the gladiator drank it, sitting on the bed. He lifted his head, and the look he gave Rufus was haunted by demons that could not be explained by the events they had witnessed together.

Then, in a voice devoid of emotion, he told them of Caligula's vengeance.

'First they broke the legs of the surviving assassins, so they should be brought low before their Emperor. Not just one break, mind, but smashed up and down with iron bars, so there was no possibility they would ever walk again.

'When this was done and they writhed on the ground below him – for they had brought his throne so he should see the spectacle more clearly – they took the first and hung him from the triangle. He was a young man, well set and handsome...' Rufus remembered the scared eyes beneath the hood and wondered if it was the opponent he had faced. 'The Emperor joked he would be favoured by the ladies. Then he ordered Nestor to remove his manhood, since he would have no further need of it. This Nestor did with a single cut of his razor, and the youth's squeals chilled the blood. There were no questions, you understand, for this was mere instruction for those who watched and waited their turn.'

Caligula had discussed the next entertainment with Nestor as the young man bled to death within feet of him.

'When they trussed up the next he was already babbling with terror, and when Nestor placed the instruments before him – the hooks, the shears and the impaling irons – he wailed that he would tell all and they need not put the fire to him. So the clerks took down the names and the dates and all the minutiae of treason. Once he had given all he knew, he thanked the Emperor for his mercy, but the Emperor asked him reasonably how he could be certain this was all, since he had not been tested. Could he not, for instance, have omitted the name of his mother or his sister, out of love and compassion? And the assassin had no answer, for none would do. So they put the hot irons to him anyway, and he expired still listing the names of his loved ones.

'And so it went. Each one gave a dozen names, and a dozen more, and when they ran out of names, the Emperor helpfully suggested other names: the names of aristocrats and knights with land and riches who would give them up to their

Emperor to prove their loyalty or to save their lives. When there were no more assassins they brought the first of the men and women they had betrayed, and it went on, and on, and on. All afternoon and into the night they screamed, sometimes one at a time, at the end in twos and threes.

'Only once did the Emperor show compassion, of a kind. When they brought the actress Quintillia to the triangle she was beautiful, perhaps the most beautiful woman in Rome. She was brave – you would be surprised how many of them were brave at first – but Nestor knows his business and in her beauty he saw opportunity. He removed it one piece at a time, and still she did not answer. So he did things which I will not speak of here, and her courage was such that the Emperor wept, and had her taken down. She could not stand, but he knelt by her side and placed eight hundred thousand sesterces in her hand, as if it was enough to buy her beauty back.'

Cupido closed his eyes then and slept. When he rose before dawn to return to his barracks, Rufus accompanied him to the doorway.

'Should we have let him die, Cupido? Think how many lives it would have saved, how much suffering it would have avoided.'

The gladiator's face was hidden in the shadows when he replied, and Rufus could not read his expression.

'If we had let him die it might have saved a thousand lives, Rufus, but not ours, and not Livia's, and not that of the child she carries.'

Rufus thought he had misheard. 'Child?'

'Are you really so blind?'

Rufus shook his head. It could not be. He was too young. He was not ready. He remembered his own childhood, before Fronto and before Cerialis. The beatings and the hunger. What right had he to bring a child into a life of bondage?

Cupido turned into the light and laid a hand on his shoulder. 'Life was much simpler in the arena.'

XXX

When Cupido left, Rufus turned back into the barn and walked past Bersheba to where Livia waited.

'Is it true?' he asked.

'Yes,' she admitted, surprised he knew without being told. 'I have consulted old Galla, who understands these things. My time will be in the spring. We have much to do.'

Her eyes shone and she took his hand and led him to their bed, where they made love for the first time in many nights. When it was over and Livia chattered her plans and hopes for the child, Rufus nuzzled her neck ... and tried to clear his mind of Aemilia's face.

He attempted to come to terms with his new status, but his mind spun in a demented chariot race of doubts and fears. There was so much to consider, so much he didn't know. Whom could he turn to? Not Cupido, who in his own way was as naïve as Rufus himself in this area. Certainly not Narcissus. There was only one answer.

Fronto.

Cupido arranged the meeting for three evenings later at the warehouse where Rufus usually collected Bersheba's hay. Rufus was loading her cart when the flicker of torchlight on damp cobbles warned him that someone was approaching. It was the animal trader, accompanied by two men who had all the wary reserve and muscle-bound confidence of bodyguards.

Rufus ran forward to take his old friend in his arms, but his pleasure quickly faded. Fronto had changed, and not for the better. It was not only the white of his thinning hair and matted beard, or the deep lines etched in his cheeks, that made him seem older. The bulk that had reminded Rufus so much of a bear had melted away, leaving only the emaciated husk of the man he knew. The hands that held him shook like reeds in a strong wind.

But Fronto still had some of his old spark.

'So this is the reason the Emperor took you away from me,' he said, waving towards Bersheba, who stood placidly in front of the cart. 'If I had a few like her I would not have half the worries I do now. Perhaps he would sell her to me? You could come too, of course. No? No, I don't suppose he would. Never mind, never mind. We'll manage somehow.'

'Is your business going so badly?' Rufus's voice betrayed his concern. 'I was certain you would be a rich man by now.'

'Oh, I am rich enough,' Fronto replied airily.

'But success has brought burdens as well as rewards. Burdens I could never have imagined.'

'Is that why you must be followed everywhere by a pair of beaten-up old gladiators? Look at that one. Cupido would squash him as Bersheba would a butterfly.'

'Yes, I suppose he would at that. But even Cupido, with his great talent, was eventually undone by that man.'

'That man?'

'The Emperor. I fear he has turned against me, or more precisely been turned against me. Protogenes has spies everywhere. Everything I touch, every bargain I conclude, is recorded in those two ledgers he always carries around with him.'

Rufus shook his head. 'But that should not concern you. You have always been honest in your dealings.'

'Perhaps, who knows? Did I occasionally take more than a lion was worth, or sell an antelope I knew was injured? Yes, I probably did. But so did everyone else and we all laughed about it together over some wine. But now...'

'Now?'

Fronto's voice dropped and Rufus could see he was struggling to avoid looking behind him like a bad actor in one of the interminable dramas at Pompey's theatre.

'Now I am dealing with Caligula's creatures, Protogenes and his like. They stink of corruption as a bull buffalo stinks in the heat and the smell lingers, Rufus. Whenever I am near them I return home and scrub myself until my body bleeds, but I can still smell that stink in my nostrils. I can smell it now and it sickens me.

'The Emperor has an insatiable appetite for the games. He can watch a hundred – no, five hundred – animals die, and he is still not satisfied. And who must replace those animals, and more like them? Fronto.' He slapped his hand to his chest.

'You understand how difficult it is to find good stock these days? But I, Fronto, always manage to find a source, and, because I have the Emperor's sanction, the suppliers have no choice but to sell them to me. It is a power I have never known before. If I had had it ten years ago I would be the richest man in Rome.'

'But now?' Rufus repeated.

'Now every bargain I make must be guaranteed by Protogenes, or one of his slaves. The money goes direct from the Emperor's coffers to the seller and I get my cut later.'

'So Protogenes is cheating you?'

'Surprisingly, no,' Fronto admitted. 'I receive what I am owed and sometimes a little more, a bonus perhaps, or more likely to buy my silence, although nothing is ever said. But suddenly people avoid me. Old friends will not look me in the eye. I hear whispers. Fronto is a thief. Fronto is a cheat. I have even been threatened, Rufus, threatened for my life, which is why I always have my companions with me these days. I think Protogenes and his gang are cheating the suppliers at one end, and the Emperor at the other. With all the stock that comes across from Africa they must be making a fortune at the expense of my honour.'

Rufus pondered this for a moment. 'But you are the key to their supply; it is in their interests to protect you. They would not threaten you?'

'No, the threats come from the suppliers they have cheated out of hundreds of thousands of sesterces, and who believe I am to blame. But protect me? I don't know. Maybe I have said too much in the wrong company. Complaints. Accusations.'

Oh, what have you done, my old friend, Rufus thought, and how can we get you out of this cesspit?

'The Emperor must know,' he said.

Fronto's eyes opened wide in terror. 'No. No. It cannot be. If Protogenes had the merest hint of suspicion that I was going to denounce him I would be dead before I could catch another breath. Have you not heard how he destroyed Proculus? And Proculus was a senator, not a mere businessman. Protogenes condemned him as a traitor within the very walls of the Curia and the poor man was torn apart by his fellows.'

'Then the denunciation must not come from you,' Rufus said. The statement hung in the air for a moment between them before Fronto realized its true significance.

'I will not allow you to do it,' he said. This was the old Fronto speaking and the command was back in his voice. 'Do you think I would ask you to endanger yourself for me? You were like a son to me, Rufus. I only wish that I had been more like a father to you. But this father's duty I will accept. My son will not die before me, if it is within my power to prevent it.'

Rufus struggled with his emotions, and they stood in silence for a while. At last Fronto said: 'But I forget. It was you who summoned me here. What did you want of me? I would deny you nothing. Your inheritance is still safe.'

Rufus smiled at him. How could he add another burden to the load already carried by this man? 'Oh, it wasn't important. I only wanted to see you again.'

XXXI

Rufus waited for the summons that would bring him the reward he dreaded for his part in the Emperor's deliverance. But if Caligula had noted his presence during the defence of the golden carriage he gave no sign of it or, more likely, regarded it as nothing more than his due. In the meantime, the Emperor filled the cells below the palace to overflowing and the taint of death hanging over the Palatine grew stronger with every passing day.

Rufus and Livia settled into a domestic rhythm which had the child growing in her belly at its centre and irritated her to distraction. He followed her around the house as she cleaned and cooked, offering to do this task or help with that chore, until she screamed at him in frustration. The tension between them in their narrow bed meant Rufus increasingly spent his nights beside Bersheba.

One night he was lying awake, buried in the

straw at the rear of the barn, when he heard the rattle of chains. Bersheba gave a sniff that Rufus recognized as a welcome for someone she knew. At first, he feared it was Cupido, whose experience of Caligula's justice at the temple of Julius had created conflicts between duty and honour which made him more and more unpredictable. But the steady voice that reached him from the darkness was not in the German-accented Latin of the gladiator.

Claudius was back.

Rufus lay still as death as the Emperor's uncle addressed his uncritical audience. He was being dangerously indiscreet.

'What has Rome done, that it must destroy itself in this way? Our brightest and our best sent to the axeman and the impaler while the Emperor's jackals compete among themselves to discover who can be the cruellest or the most foul.' He gave a long sigh. 'Everything I have put in place, every stratagem and scheme, threatened by the impetuosity of youth. How many times did I tell them that one opportunity and one only would be granted to bring about that which is so imperative? Yet they throw everything into a hopeless gamble the Emperor has hysterically drowned in blood. Why? Lucius was no fool; he would not have acted without guarantees. But who could have given them? Bassus might have had the means, but would he have been so foolish? Guilty or innocent, it made no difference to his fate, since he died in front of his father's eyes. Asiaticus? No. Our aspirations run parallel: the return of the Republic by peaceful means; rule by democracy, not dictat.

Pomponius had the means, but not the motive. Narcissus? Surely not. Yet can even I truly trust Narcissus, who is privy to my most inner thoughts, when he takes those thoughts and uses them to his own advantage at every opportunity? If not Narcissus, who?'

He paused for a moment and Rufus could almost feel the power of his mind picking the conundrum apart a piece at a time.

'Chaerea,' he announced, pleased with his own cleverness. 'Yes, Cassius Chaerea, or more likely someone acting on his behalf. Perhaps his signature on the order to hold back the Praetorians when the assassins attacked was not forged after all. He has become so warped by the Emperor's jibes he has been driven beyond rage to blind hatred. It was he who persuaded Lucius he could attack without fear of retribution. And when the deed was done, who would rise beyond his intelligence and his powers, beyond blood and ability? Who would take the mantle of Caesar and sully it beyond redemption, if it is not sullied beyond it already? Why, Cassius Chaerea, loyal commander of the Guard. And where is he now? Up to his elbows in blood in the place where he is most visible and of most use to his Emperor. Yet even as he performs his duty, he is quaking inside lest the next name screamed from the rack be his own. For he too was betrayed, or why did the German guards fight when they were meant to flee? Only one man was in a position to ensure that outcome, and only one man will profit from it.'

He paused again, and when he resumed it was clear from the change in his voice that he was talking directly now to Bersheba.

'All the unruly strength of your kind lies within you. Yet for all that strength, what are you but an ornament to reflect your master's power? But in times past you were a proven weapon of war, a champion of the battlefield. Be thankful your master has not used you so, or used you worse. He has not bent his mind in that direction thus far, but it may come to it. Unless? What if, by some accident, your might was employed not for but against him? Could even Caesar survive the strength of your caress, or the weight of your body upon his? Think upon this, mighty one: an Empire may depend on it.'

By the time the door closed behind Claudius, Rufus was in a cold sweat. The names he had heard were among the most influential and powerful in Rome. And here was proof of their treason. Proof of Claudius's treason. He wanted to unhear what he had just heard, but no matter how hard he tried it gnawed at his brain. So he did the only thing possible. He put it away in a compartment inside his head where it would stay until it could be used as a bargaining chip – or he felt the bite of the executioner's blade.

With few official duties and a wife who wanted little to do with him, Rufus spent each waking moment of the coming weeks pondering how he could help Fronto. He knew there was only one person he could go to, but could he trust him when even his master did not? There was only one way to find out. He put a white rag on Bersheba's door and the next day set off for the

266

little fountain.

Narcissus was still in the benign mood he had affected since Drusilla's death and it was clear he felt Claudius's patronage placed him above harm from the purges.

'We really must find somewhere else to meet. It stinks here.' He sniffed at Rufus. 'It's not you, so it must be the drains. Have you something for me?'

Rufus mentioned a few things he had heard among the servants, but nothing seemed to interest the Greek. Then he said hesitantly, 'I would like to ask your advice. A friend is in trouble. Fronto. I thought you might be able to help.'

'Mmmmm.' Narcissus let the syllable linger, and stared at Rufus as if seeing him for the first time. 'Fronto is an acquaintance,' he conceded. 'But I have so many acquaintances. Advice? Yes, I can probably provide advice. But help you? Why should I help a slave?'

Rufus thought the answer was self-evident: 'Because I tell you things.'

Narcissus actually laughed. Did Rufus really think the palace gossip he provided was of the least importance? Did he not understand he was merely a minute part of a larger whole? A tiny worker ant who could be crushed underfoot in an instant and not even be remembered, never mind missed.

'I don't believe you have told me anything that would warrant ... help.' The final word emerged slowly, as if it was something distasteful, and he turned to walk away.

Rufus let him get halfway along the path.

'I can tell you what Claudius says to Bersheba,' he said.

Narcissus stopped, hesitated for a second, and turned back with a broad smile. 'Yes?'

Rufus gave him the information one titbit at a time and watched the Greek's eyes light up. Only one thing did he hold back; the knowledge that Claudius did not trust his faithful servant Narcissus would be useful in future. When he finished, he explained Fronto's dilemma.

The Greek shook his head in mock sorrow. 'You really are terribly innocent. And Fronto. Of course Protogenes is corrupt. Everyone in Rome from Caligula down is corrupt. The Emperor squeezes the aristocracy to fund his lunatic schemes, so the aristocracy squeezes the middle class, and the middle class squeezes the plebeians. The only people who don't get squeezed are the slaves, because they have nothing to give.'

'But surely you can help?'

'I may drop a word here, or a hint there, if I am certain it will do me no harm,' Narcissus said dismissively, indicating the interview was at an end.

XXXII

Now they feared him. All of them. He could see it in their eyes when he attended the Senate. The baldheads would not meet his gaze and their bodies cringed as they wondered what Nestor might have in store for them. He could see it in the streets when the mob bowed so low their noses touched the earth. Even his generals did not dare oppose him.

He was above them all. Drusilla had confirmed it.

The voices began when the headaches stopped, in the weeks after they tried to kill him. After she joined the gods in their heavenly paradise, she had come to him in the night when he was in dire need of her reassurance. The attack had shaken him more than he would ever admit. It was all very well to see violence from afar, or to see it inflicted on others at your command, but when you could smell the blood and the torn vitals, and at the same time were aware that the heart the blades sought was beating inside your chest, it was different.

But it did not matter now.

Drusilla had spoken. He was the match of any member of the pantheon, even Jupiter himself. It was time to have done with earthly things. To claim his place among them.

He would become a living god.

They came for Rufus in the deepest hour of the night, and without warning. A hand across his mouth and a sword at his throat ensured his silence and he was dragged from the room naked and shaking with fear. Livia lay with her face to the wall, apparently sleeping, but he knew she was awake, and terrified.

Outside in the moonlight, one of the men put his tunic in his hands, but they didn't stop to let him dress and he had to do his best as he was hustled along. The questions raced through his head. Who were they? Where were they taking him? He expected to be escorted to the palace and the unspeakable place in its depths from which no one returned, so he was surprised when his captors took pains to stay among the trees and guided him to a little-used path which led them down the hill and into the city. They weren't gentle: the sword never left his back and, if he slowed or stumbled, they hastened his progress with kicks and punches. Each man was heavily cloaked and they took care to stay just behind him so he didn't have the chance to dwell on their faces, but a glimpse of armour beneath a flapping cloak gave them away.

Scorpions.

Now he understood where he was going, but not why.

The Castra Praetorium was more fortress than barracks; the massive main doors would have stopped an army. But there was another, lesser known entrance on the northern face, and it was to this that Rufus was taken. Once inside, they pushed him along endless empty corridors and finally down a set of steep steps to a single door which led to a tiny windowless room. His captors threw him inside and the door clanged shut behind him, leaving him in impenetrable darkness, blacker and more frightening than any night.

He sat for a few moments allowing the panic to recede and listening to the sound of his own breathing. Only the beating of his heart gave him an indication of the passing of time, but he knew that the strength of his fear made his incarceration seem a dozen times longer than the reality. It was difficult to say what scared him more, the thought of being locked in this airless dungeon for ever, or what awaited him when the door finally opened again.

He tried to think of anything but where he was. Fronto and the rhinoceros. The day of his triumph with Africanus in the arena. Livia and the child that was to come. But he found that when he tried to conjure up Livia's face it was always confused with Aemilia's. Could it be true that he did not want what he had and could not have what he wanted? It was all too confusing, so he gave up and allowed the misery to wrap itself around him like a shroud.

Eventually he must have fallen asleep, because he missed the sound of footsteps and the rattle of the deadbolts shocked him awake. He looked up to find Cassius Chaerea standing over him with a gently flickering torch in his hand.

'Not too uncomfortable, I hope?' The Praetorian commander smiled and the words were solicitous, but Rufus took no comfort from them. He knew this man would have his throat cut and his body thrown in the Tiber if he uttered a single wrong word.

At close quarters Chaerea was a curious amalgam of strength and softness. He wore his grey hair cut short and he had the blunt face and stocky build that characterized so many hardened military campaigners. He was well into his fifties now, having been a young man when he fought in the German frontier battles where he had made his fearsome reputation. Yet he had a curiously high voice and a light, dancing walk that made him a figure of fun among Caligula and his favourites.

'I am sorry to have brought you here like this, but it is safer this way. Better to be able to tell your little wife of a wrongful arrest and a night in a cold cell than to be forced to lie. And if another should ask, why, you would only be telling the truth.' The voice was the essence of reason, but it was belied by Chaerea's granite-chip eyes.

'You were very heroic that day on the Via Sacra. At first I could not fix you when you ran to the German's side and placed yourself between your Emperor and his killers. I am an old soldier and I pride myself on knowing every man who wears the uniform of my unit. Then I saw you fight and knew you were no soldier. Brave, yes, but no swordsman. No tactical understanding, or you would never have stayed to face such odds. You see, a soldier must know not only when to stand, but also when to retreat. What made you do it, by the way? As I say, you were heroic, but I think you are not naturally of heroic mould.' He smiled as he saw Rufus bridle. 'No, do not be insulted, I meant no slight. To place oneself in danger when one has no training in arms is brave indeed. But tell me, why did you do it? I am genuinely interested.'

Rufus gave himself time to think. 'The Emperor was in danger and I did what any loyal servant would do.' A lie, but only a little lie. 'I didn't know the odds when I ran to the carriage. All I saw were a few cloaked figures breaking the line. Once the fight was on, all I did was save myself.' Which was the plain truth. Rufus closed his eyes and his head was filled with slashing swords and falling bodies, gaping wounds which exposed things that should never be exposed.

'A good answer. A soldier's answer,' Chaerea said appreciatively. 'Not I think the whole answer, but let us consider the day from another angle. Do you agree?'

He waited until Rufus nodded.

'You and your friends saved the Emperor, we are in no doubt about that. Without your intervention, the assassins who attacked him would have cut him to pieces. Yes?' Rufus was not so sure. The mob may not have loved Caligula, but once they realized what was happening they would not have stood back and let him be butchered. But that was not the answer Chaerea wanted, so he nodded again and the Praetorian continued: 'What would that have meant to Rome?'

'Havoc. Ruin. A republic.' They were all words Claudius had used. 'What would Rome be without an Emperor?'

'No. What would Rome be without *this* Emperor?' Chaerea's voice was as hard as his eyes now, each word hammered out as if it was a nail into a cross. 'What if the assassins had succeeded and another Emperor was raised in his place by those with the best interests of the Empire at heart? An Emperor who would rule with strength, but also compassion. An Emperor who would use his power for the good of all. An Emperor who would build, but not bankrupt.' Rufus listened carefully for any hint of irony. Surely even

Chaerea could not create this image of himself as Caesar. 'An Emperor like Senator Claudius.' Chaerea stared at him, and Rufus realized his mouth had dropped open.

'Do not underestimate him. He may look a kindly old man, but there is iron in him. Where others saw a drooling imbecile, I discerned genius. Tiberius saw it too. Under Claudius there would be no more killings, no more madness.' All of this sounded familiar, and Rufus remembered hearing similar words from the mouth of Narcissus. Was it coincidence, or was the Greek being spied upon more closely than he knew? Whatever the truth, it made him all the more wary of Chaerea. He remembered Claudius's words to Bersheba. The old senator was certain Chaerea planned to take the throne for himself. And, despite the Praetorian's carefully chosen words, Rufus's instinct told him Claudius was right. But Chaerea had not finished his wooing.

'With the Praetorians at his back Claudius would not have to concern himself with his enemies in the Senate. He could govern with strength and Rome and Romans would benefit. But you made it impossible, you and your German friend. He is your friend, is he not, the gladiator Cupido, whom the Emperor holds in such high esteem?'

Rufus nodded. 'He is...' *But he holds the Emperor in no higher esteem than you do.* He almost said it, the words touched his lips, but a warning bell in his head stopped him.

Chaerea's patience was plainly wearing thin. 'Then you must be my messenger to him. As a friend it is your duty. You will tell him that the next time – and there will be a next time – he should stay his hand, like the rest. Make no move to stop what is happening. For Rome.'

'Why should Cupido listen to me? He is his own man and the Emperor's. If his honour dictates he stand and fight, that is what he will do. You would do well not to underestimate him.'

Chaerea reached out and touched Rufus's cheek. The fingers were cold and clammy and Rufus shivered with disgust.

'But I don't underestimate him,' the Praetorian said softly. 'That is why you are here and he is not. What price the gladiator's honour? What would it cost to make him allow what must happen to happen – or better yet, what would it take to make him strike the fatal blow? Threats?' He shook his head. 'I don't think a man like Cupido would respond well to threats. I could have him killed for a thousand sesterces, but what would be the point? The Emperor would only appoint another like him in his place, and the place matters as much as the man. Money? Caligula pays him more than he can spend. Freedom? Once he completes his service he is free already.

'No. Nothing I can do to him or offer to him would convince him to do my bidding. But there is one thing he loves more than any other, is there not? His mother is dead. His father is dead. His sister ... is not. Surely he would do anything for her. Anything at all.'

Rufus felt a sudden urge to take Chaerea by the throat. Aemilia's face filled his mind. The solemn eyes and the perfect mouth. The smile that melted

275

his heart. He thought of her at the Praetorian's mercy, and knew he would kill Chaerea first.

'His sister means nothing to him. They were apart for years after their capture. She despises him for allowing her to be taken,' he said.

'How very loyal. But there is really no point in lying to me. My friends and I know everything, you see. But perhaps it is not your friend you are protecting; perhaps the German bitch means more to Rufus, the elephant man, than she does to her brother? What would your pretty wife think if she knew the way you mooned over her?

'But come, I did not bring you here so we could disagree. Narcissus trusts you with his intimacies, so we are not altogether on different sides. I ask only that you repeat what has been said here to your German friend. He is in a position to do the Empire a great service. A single blow from him could have the impact of an entire army. He has only to strike it and he will be the most honoured man in Rome. Will you do this for me?'

'And if I don't?'

Chaerea shook his head sadly. 'Your wife carries the continuation of your line inside her. It would be unfortunate if that line were to be … cut.'

It was after dawn when the escorts returned Rufus to the barn on the Palatine, by the same narrow stairway which was so fortuitously unguarded.

Wearily, he opened the double doors, to find Bersheba looking miserable and shuffling in her chains.

276

'An hour late with your breakfast, girl. No wonder you're pining.'

He spent fifteen minutes filling her hay bags and managed to find some of the bruised apples she liked so much. Satisfied she had everything she needed, he slapped her on one enormous buttock and quietly opened the door of his home. To find another man in his bed.

XXXIII

He was old, and very thin, and he rocked back and forth mumbling almost inaudibly to himself. Livia sat by his side, bathing his forehead with a damp cloth. She looked up as Rufus entered, the relief written clearly on her face.

'I ... I feared you might be gone for longer.'

He almost smiled at the understatement. The truth was she had feared he might be gone for ever.

'Did they harm you?'

He shook his head. 'No. I was never in any danger – at least I don't think so. It was a mistake, but a mistake which took all night to correct. Once I convinced them who I was, they freed me. Who's our new friend?'

Livia chewed at her lip. 'I don't know. I found him.'

Rufus laughed. It sounded so unlikely. If you were lucky you found a sesterce someone had dropped. An addled old man was different.

Livia explained: 'I went out this morning hoping to see you, or at least hear news of you. He was lying on the grass near the wall babbling to himself. I think he must have tried to climb it and fallen.'

'Then he's doubly fortunate. If he had managed to get over it, the fall on the other side would have killed him. And if you hadn't found him when you did he might have died of cold. He looks very frail.'

'I'm frightened of him. He keeps talking about some terrible river. He was wearing this round his neck. Is it some kind of strange charm?'

The object she handed him was a piece of metal, about six inches in length and in the shape of an elongated T, except it also had two prongs protruding horizontally from the bottom end, slightly shorter than the upper arms of the T.

He shook his head. 'I don't know. I've never seen anything like it. I don't recognize him, but he must belong somewhere in the palace. Someone in the guard will know him. I need to talk to Cupido. I'll ask him if anyone has lost an old man.'

The object of their discussion gave a start, as if he had been listening, and his eyes opened in alarm as if he could see something they could not.

'So many. So many I cannot count them all,' he groaned, rocking his head from side to side. 'But I must help them on their way. Where is the ferryman? There must be a ferryman. Have they not paid him? Have they not paid him to make the journey over the river?'

The words emerged in one long, rambling sentence and Rufus could barely make them out. He knew he should have felt pity, but his long night with Chaerea had robbed him of any capacity for sympathy.

'What river? Tell us what river?' He shook the old man by the shoulder, and for a moment the eyes focused.

'The Styx.'

Rufus pulled his hand away as if he'd been burned, and when he looked at Livia her eyes were as wide as he knew his must be. She was making the sign, and, belatedly, he followed her example.

'What can we do with him?' she whispered. He was tempted to say 'Take him back where you found him and leave him there,' but he had seen enough death recently not to want to add to it, even by natural causes.

'What else can we do? Give him a bowl of broth and hope he gets better and goes back where he belongs.'

A few hours later, Rufus called at the guard-room and asked for Cupido. One of the Praetorians he knew by sight answered. 'He's on watch, but if you come back later he should be here around the eighth hour.'

He spent the rest of the morning exercising Bersheba, and he was surprised when, close to midday, he turned the elephant to find Callistus watching them. For once, the palace secretary wasn't accompanied by his normal entourage. Instead, a small boy who looked about five years old stood at his side, pointing excitedly at the elephant.

Rufus brought Bersheba to a halt a few paces from them and slid from her back. He approached Callistus and bowed.

'My son has been asking to see the elephant ever since I told him about her,' the imperial secretary explained, smiling indulgently at the child. 'I promised to bring him today, though he should be at his lessons.

This was a different Callistus from the one who organized the parade for Drusilla's divinity. The cloak of official menace he habitually wore was missing and his voice held a deep affection for the boy that surprised Rufus.

The child stared wide-eyed at Bersheba, as if he could not quite believe what he was seeing. He had short-cropped dark hair, and his father's long nose was already making its presence known, but there was a glint of mischief in his eyes that Rufus liked. He had an idea.

'Would he like to ride her?'

The boy grinned shyly but Callistus's face took on an expression heavy with paternal protectiveness. 'Will he be safe?'

Rufus laughed. 'Bersheba has carried the Emperor himself. He did not complain.'

Callistus nodded. 'Of course. In that case, yes, but only for a short time.' He ushered the boy forward. 'Do not be frightened, Gnaius. This is the Emperor's elephant and she is very tame.'

Rufus ordered Bersheba to kneel and lifted the wriggling child on to her back, then settled into place behind him. He slapped the elephant on her shoulder. 'On, Bersheba.' As they lurched forward he felt the boy laughing, and when he turned to Callistus the imperial secretary's normally solemn face was split in a wide smile.

By the time they were finished Rufus and the boy were firm friends. He had difficulty persuading Gnaius to dismount, and it took an order from his father before the child would get down from Bersheba's back.

Rufus returned Bersheba to the barn and tried to prepare himself for the meeting with Cupido. The encounter with the strange old man and the morning with Callistus's son had allowed him to put the dilemma to the back of his mind, but now he could not hide from it.

How could he tell his friend that they had become involved in a plot against the Emperor and, perhaps more important, how would Cupido react towards the man who had involved them?

The Cupido who ruled the arena dealt only in certainties. On the bloodstained sand the simple choice was between life and death and he killed without hesitation in order to stay alive. But in Caligula's Palatine, there were no certainties. Here Narcissus, and his rival, Protogenes, were the masters. Their weapons were information and intrigue and they used them with the same deadly subtlety with which Cupido wielded his long sword. Chaerea might believe he was their equal, but Rufus sensed the Praetorian commander was out of his depth. He was too blunt an instrument to challenge the rapier intellects arrayed against him. Rufus now realized that his arrest was a measure of the veteran soldier's desperation in the wake of the failed assassination attempt.

But he was still dangerous.

'I should kill him,' Cupido said reasonably.

They were sitting in a small annex to the guard quarters Cupido shared with his comrades. The young German had produced a flagon of rough wine and Rufus was enjoying the unfamiliar warmth of it in his belly.

'Yes, you probably should ... if you don't care whether you live or die. And Aemila, of course. Chaerea's friends would never leave her alive.'

'You think Chaerea's Scorpions could best me? I'd squash them flat and take pleasure in doing it.'

'Not the Scorpions, the Emperor. Caligula believes Chaerea has served him well. It wouldn't look good if he allowed some rogue gladiator to slaughter the commander of his Praetorians. When you are dead, Aemilia will have no one to protect her.'

'But he is a traitor and I have the Emperor's favour.'

'True, but the only evidence you have against him is my testimony of what was said at the Castra Praetorium, and if you kill Chaerea I will be dead before I can give it. Do not concern yourself too much, though. The Emperor will no doubt show his favour by allowing you to flavour your wine with a little hemlock.'

Cupido's handsome face creased in a frown. 'So Chaerea lives, for the moment. Do you have any other clever suggestions?'

Rufus thought for a second. 'You can't confront Chaerea for the same reasons you can't kill him. I am the only leverage you have and my life wouldn't be worth a bent sesterce if Chaerea discovered that. I don't know what else we can do.'

'Kill Caligula.'

Rufus choked on his wine at the words, which came from the corner of the room.

'Well, do I have no say in this because I am a mere woman, even though I am the only one this ... this piece of vermin has actually threatened?' Aemilia demanded. 'Am I to sit here awaiting my fate while you dither over a decision which is already made for you?'

Cupido took the outburst with remarkably good grace. He had sent for Aemilia as soon as he heard of Chaerea's threat, and she had been sitting quietly and listening. Now her eyes were lit with righteous outrage, and Rufus realized for the first time that any man who shared his life with this woman would not have everything his own way. Perhaps it might help if Cupido could be persuaded to take a stick to her.

'If the decision is so simple, what should it be?' Cupido asked his sister.

'Do nothing. What can you do but wait? If Chaerea is going to act it cannot be soon. Callistus is now responsible for the Emperor's security and you are agreed it is tighter than ever. Only the Wolves who fought for him when Drusilla was deified are assigned to him for any period of time. All the other Praetorian units can be rotated at short notice. Chaerea cannot afford to strike until he is certain of success.'

The gladiator looked thoughtfully at Rufus. 'What she says is true.' He winked. 'Even if she is a mere woman.' He ducked as a leather cushion narrowly missed his head. 'But we cannot wait for ever.'

'No. But time is on your side. Wait, and who knows what might happen? The Emperor's investigators have an endless supply of victims. It is not unlikely that one of the names they hear will be Chaerea's, in which case he would be wise to fall on his own sword. Also, we know Chaerea and his fellow plotters are not the only people seeking change. Others have more subtle methods. Remember Drusilla.'

Rufus grimaced. 'Drusilla died from some sort of sickness. The only person who thinks she was poisoned is her brother.'

Aemilia snorted. 'Believe what you like, Rufus, but Agrippina thought her sister was murdered, and who should know better than she, who understands more about the properties of mushrooms than she needs for the kitchen.'

'You think she had something to do with Drusilla's death?'

'No, but perhaps you should look to your own friends.'

'What do you mean?'

'Only that you keep strange company. It is well known in the palace that Narcissus is Claudius's spy. Why would a slave spend so much time with him, unless it was because he was a spy in his turn? Tell me,' she said sweetly, 'will you report our conversation to your Greek master?'

Rufus leapt to his feet. 'You–'

Cupido put a hand on his chest. 'Enough. We did not come here to quarrel. Aemilia, Rufus is my friend and yours. He risked his life to warn us. We are in his debt. You should apologize.' He waited for a reaction, but Aemilia only stared all the harder at Rufus. 'In any case, there may come a time when it is to our profit to keep Narcissus informed. We will see,' he said thoughtfully.

'And now?' Aemilia demanded.

'Now we do as you suggest. We wait. But first we let Cassius Chaerea believe I am considering his offer. He will accept the lie at face value because it suits him to do so. At the very least it will keep you safe, Rufus. And you, Aemilia.'

'I don't need any protection from Chaerea or anyone else,' she said contemptuously. 'The royal household is more secure than any other in Rome. Look to yourself, brother, and you, elephant boy.'

Rufus ignored the insult. 'Don't underestimate Chaerea. He may be a brute, but he is not stupid and he has a soldier's eye for an opportunity. If he strikes, it will be when you least expect it.'

Her eyes caught fire. 'I am a princess of the Tungri, and I can protect myself.' Suddenly her mood changed, her face and her posture softened and she laughed and moved close to Rufus, so he could smell the scent of her body. 'Forgive my harsh words, Rufus,' she whispered. 'But know this: if Chaerea strikes he should look to himself, for I too am not to be underestimated.' He felt a slight prick at his throat and looked down to see a jewelled dagger she had produced from the folds of her dress.

Cupido laughed. 'You look a little pale, Rufus. It appears my sister's company does not agree with you?'

Rufus swallowed. 'It is just that I am not used to dealing with naughty children. Do you know of a crazy old man who wanders the palace grounds talking of the River Styx?'

The change of subject caught Cupido by surprise. 'Only one old man walks the palace grounds talking to himself and that is Senator Claudius.'

'No, not Claudius.' Rufus explained how Livia had discovered the old man by the Palatine wall. He tried to describe him. 'Very thin, with long white hair. He wore this on a piece of leather round his neck. Do you know what it could be?' He produced the strange piece of metal. Cupido looked at it for a few moments.

'Yes, I have him. I don't know his name and from your description he has changed since I saw him last, but I believe he has a room in the Domus Augustus. He's certainly a little strange. He walks the grounds with his head down as if he is forever looking for something. The guards call him the Scavenger, but I think he has something to do with the water supply.' He took the metal T from Rufus and studied it. 'I have never seen anything like it, but he has had it specially made. Look, you can see the smith's mark just below the crosspiece.'

'Could you visit his quarters and find out if there is anyone who can come for him? His ravings are beginning to frighten Livia.'

'Do I look as if I have nothing better to do? I will provide you with a pass to get you to his rooms. Why don't you go with him, Aemilia? But leave your little sword behind – you might hurt someone with it.' He left the room and returned a few minutes later. 'Take this,' he said to Rufus. 'It gives you authority to enter and asks the guard to show you where you wish to go. Do not lose it.'

XXXIV

The Domus Augustus lay on the far side of the Palatine, and their route took them through covered walkways and little parks, past shrines and fountains. Aemilia was wearing a long red dress, in a style fashionable among the ladies of the court, and Rufus wondered if she had been given it because Milonia had tired of it. The Emperor's wife was notorious for the enormous amounts she spent on clothing, and, he reasoned, must have plenty to spare. The dress left Aemilia's milky shoulders bare and he could see a light scattering of dainty freckles across them. The sun caught the tiny golden hairs at the base of her neck and he found himself wondering what it would be like to touch them. She was beautiful, sometimes extraordinarily so. Just being with her made him feel more alive. He grinned to himself.

'What are you smiling at?' she demanded. 'Is there something wrong with my dress?'

'No. I was just thinking how easy it is to forget.'

'Forget what?'

'Nothing. Everything. The things that seem to matter most don't seem so bad on days like these.'

'What is so different about this day?' she asked suspiciously.

'Nothing,' he replied, infuriating her further.

'Sometimes you are such a fool, Rufus,' she snapped, but he kept smiling anyway.

The guard at the main entrance of the palace gave their pass a cursory glance and allowed them inside. It had once been the largest and most prestigious building on the Palatine Hill, but now the main apartments housed Caligula's lesser relatives, and the smaller rooms were home to a variety of minor palace officials.

Rufus described the old man and the guard laughed.

'That's Varrus. He has a place close to the back near the kitchens.' He reeled off a bewildering list of lefts and rights, corridors and stairs. 'If you get lost just follow your nose.'

The directions were less confusing than Rufus feared, but they were still forced to ask one of the kitchen girls for the exact door to knock.

'Don't worry, darling. Varrus doesn't have a door. It's the third curtain you passed on the way here. Wife? Don't think so. Anyone know if Varrus has a wife?' she called across the ovens.

Rufus thanked her, and she laughed coarsely. 'Not planning to stay and taste a little of what you fancy, then? We can always do with an extra pair of hands around here, especially hands like yours, pretty boy.'

He backed away, face flushed, and bumped into something soft and warm that seemed to yield for a second before pushing him off with surprising strength.

'We can always do with an extra pair of hands,' Aemilia mimicked. 'Well, you can keep your

288

hands to yourself. Which door is it, pretty boy?'

For the fifth time that day he revised his opinion of her. She really was insufferable, spoiled, annoying...

'Third on the right.'

'Come on then,' she ordered, leading the way.

It was immediately obvious Varrus didn't share the room with a wife or any other kind of companion. It was tiny, smaller even than the space Rufus shared with Livia behind the elephant house. Against one wall, under a shuttered window, was a narrow bed covered by a piece of sackcloth. A few unwashed bowls were stacked beside a larger basin, obviously used for fetching water. Apart from the bed, the only piece of what might be called furniture was a large wooden box standing in a corner near the bed, which must have served as a table.

Rufus shrugged. 'There's nothing here to tell us who he is, or who might take him off our hands.' He turned to leave, but Aemilia stood her ground.

'How do you know without looking?'

He waved at the room. 'Because there's nothing to see.'

She gave him the look women reserve for men they think have the mental capacity of a dull mouse.

'What?' He followed her stare. 'It's only a box.'

'There might be something in it that tells you who he is. Do you still have the key?'

'What key?'

She gave him the look again. 'His key. The one he had round his neck when Livia found him.'

'How do you know it's a key? It doesn't look like any key I've ever seen.'

'Try it.'

He knew it wouldn't work, but something told him it wasn't worth arguing. 'Look, it's too big.' He held the T-shaped metal against the small lock on the chest. 'We can't open it, and anyway, it wouldn't be right. Come.'

She reached past him and grasped the lid, which lifted easily in her hands.

'Look, I was right,' she said triumphantly, peering into the depths of the box. 'There are documents and another key and ... what do you think this is?'

He didn't want to give her the satisfaction, but his curiosity got the better of him.

It was a piece of parchment, but like nothing he had seen before. Thin lines in different colours criss-crossed and joined each other, superimposed on other fainter lines which he could barely discern in the poor light. Only one feature was more prominent than the rest, a line marked in red, which snaked its way from one side of the parchment to the other with a distinctive zigzag halfway along its length. As he looked more closely, he could see that at the point where the red line zigged left, it was joined by a green line thicker than most of the others, which cut off at an angle to the right.

'I think it must be some kind of map, but it is difficult to make anything out of it. Maybe if we could look at it in a better light?'

'Let me see it again.' He handed it to her and she moved under the window. She pursed her lips and traced the thick red line across the map with her finger, squinting to try to interpret the faintest contours, which were almost lost against the old parchment. The expression on her face made her look very young, and he could not stop himself smiling again. She looked up and caught him. 'You're laughing at me. You think I'm stupid,' she said.

'No, I–'

'Why don't you take it to your friend Cupido? I'm sure he's cleverer than his stupid sister.' She threw him the parchment. 'What else is in there?'

He looked into the chest again. It contained three more documents. Two of them seemed to be covered in complicated calculations he did not understand, but the third caught his eye. It was another map, less complex than the first, and the main feature was marked in the same green as the secondary feature on the original.

'It seems to be a detail from this one, focusing on the green line. Look, there at the edge, that's where it must join the big red line. I wonder what it is?'

'And what are those?' she wondered, looking over his shoulder. He could feel her softness against his back and suddenly he had difficulty thinking straight. 'Those.' She prodded him in the ribs and he noticed that what he'd thought was a line of smudges were actually tiny symbols which marked the length of the green line at regular intervals.

'I don't know. There is too much information here to take in at once. We'll have to leave them and return another time.'

'There may not be another time,' she insisted. 'Take them with us. We can let Cupido see them, and if he doesn't know, you can always ask the old man when he recovers.'

'The guards won't allow us out of the palace carrying documents. They'll think we've stolen them, and they'll be right. It's probably just the scribblings of a crazy old man. Random drawings on an old map.'

She gave him the look again.

He sighed. 'All right. Where will we hide them?'

She grinned and pulled up her dress. He had a glimpse of two unsettlingly long legs before he was able to turn his eyes away, and was astonished at the feelings of desire she awoke in him.

'You can look now.'

He glanced up and saw a demure Roman maiden in a red dress that fitted a little more snugly than before. She returned his look, and the maiden dissolved into a naughty, laughing schoolgirl.

'You have no idea how these things scratch.'

They were on the way back across the Palatine when Rufus noticed Narcissus walking in their direction.

'Take the documents to Cupido and tell him I'll contact him later today, or when he is off duty tomorrow. Go quickly now, or Narcissus will suspect something,' he whispered.

The tall Greek increased his speed and marched purposefully towards them. He opened his mouth to greet them, but Aemilia gave him a disdainful stare and sailed regally past, leaving him gasping like a beached fish in her wake.

Rufus suppressed a smile, but, when he recovered, Narcissus's face was serious.

'She is a pretty thing, but she has airs far above her status,' he said sadly. 'I fear she does not realize just how dangerous it is to be a thing of beauty in a place where the acquisition of beautiful things is a competitive sport.'

Rufus had never seen Narcissus show interest in a woman. 'What do you mean? Is Aemilia in danger?'

'Your naivety never ceases to astound me, young man,' the Greek replied. 'In Caligula's shadow we are all in danger. Perhaps she is in less danger than many, but that would depend on your definition of danger.'

'I don't understand. You talk in riddles.'

'You don't need to understand,' Narcissus said dismissively. 'You are a slave – all you need to do is obey. Have you anything for me?'

Rufus thought back to the hours in the little cell below the Praetorian barracks. Yes, he had much he could tell, but now was not the time. He still did not fully understand his meeting with Chaerea. Any missed nuance could have serious consequences. If some of the information reached the wrong ears, those consequences would be fatal. First let Narcissus show his faith.

'No, but have you been able to help Fronto?'

The Greek's eyes went hard. 'He is beyond help. Forget him,' he said coldly, and turned away.

But Rufus was not to be allowed to forget Fronto.

XXXV

The summons arrived one evening two weeks later during preparations for the chariot races that would mark the festival of Consus.

The guards who came for him ordered that he wash and dress in his best clothing, and, with Livia watching apprehensively and holding her swollen belly, escorted him through the park to the palace.

Their destination was the room with the great silver table, but this time there was a difference. Rufus was the first guest to arrive.

Caligula lounged on his padded couch on a raised dais and studied him closely. 'Here, elephant boy.' He waved a hand in the direction of the couch closest to him. 'But first I have some questions for you.'

Rufus felt his bowels turn to ice as the two Praetorians pushed him in front of the Emperor.

'You wouldn't plot against me, would you, elephant boy?' the Emperor enquired in a voice as honeyed as the confections that sweetened the end of his feasts.

'N-n-n-no, majesty,' Rufus quaked, ashamed of his fear.

Caligula laughed lightly. 'N-n-n-no,' he mimicked. 'You sound just like Uncle Claudius. Not that it would save you. Claudius plots, you know, Claudius and that scheming Greek of his. I'll get rid of them both soon. So you don't plot?'

Rufus shook his head, not trusting himself to speak.

'You see, a little bird – well, a little spy, actually – tells me you have been consorting with that old master of yours, the hairy one. What is his name? The animal trader? I forget. You too? Never mind. Not thinking of returning to him, are you?'

Rufus shook his head again.

'Good. That would be a mistake. Protogenes tells me the hairy animal trader is a plotter. Isn't that right, Protogenes?'

'Yes, majesty,' a harsh affirmation rasped from somewhere to Rufus's right and he realized Protogenes must have silently entered the room while Caligula was questioning him.

'So if you were to plot with him, that would make you my enemy and I'd have to have you executed. Do you agree?' Caligula continued.

Rufus didn't know whether to nod in agreement that it would be perfectly reasonable for the Emperor to execute him or shake his head and risk calling Caligula a liar. He did neither.

'But you aren't a plotter?'

Now he shook his head until he thought it was going to fall off.

'Excellent. If I had to kill you, who would look after my elephant? Protogenes says he once saw an elephant walk along a rope suspended above the ground,' he added conversationally. 'I don't believe him, though. You're a liar, Protogenes,' the last in a great shout that almost made Rufus faint with fright. 'How big a rope would you need to support an elephant? Come, sit here, at my side.'

From his vantage point to the left of the Emperor's dais, Rufus was able to see the other guests enter the room by a doorway behind the couch where Protogenes lay with a sneer of anticipation on his ravaged face: Chaerea, who greeted him with a cold smile of recognition, and a beautiful girl much too young to be his wife; Appeles, the third of the ever-presents, sporting a purple bruise on his cheekbone, new scars just visible through his blond hair, and darting scared glances at the Emperor; and Cornelius Aurius Fronto.

There were further arrivals, but Rufus barely noticed them.

Fronto was visibly terrified, his whole body racked by spasms. The only colour in his sweat-sheened face was in the purple rings beneath his eyes, and his toga hung on a skeletal frame. Rufus swore he could hear the old man's heart thundering against his ribcage, until he realized the galloping rhythm was that of his own.

The banquet began as normal, each course removed almost before it was touched. Caligula chatted languidly to Chaerea, the pale blue eyes running lazily over the Praetorian commander's partner in a sensual way that suggested he had already chosen his companion for the evening's entertainment. The other guests draped themselves across their couches and tried to look relaxed, picking at a morsel here, a sweetmeat there. Rufus touched nothing.

Protogenes's dull, merciless eyes never left Fronto.

Finally, the Emperor eased himself into a sitting

position and turned to face the animal trader. But it was to Protogenes that he spoke.

'Tell me, Protogenes, how does our business prosper?'

Protogenes picked up the thicker of his scrolls and unrolled it with exaggerated care, studying it closely before he replied. 'It prospers, majesty, but perhaps not as it might.'

Caligula reacted with mock surprise. 'And why, Protogenes, why do we not prosper?'

'I fear we are being cheated, majesty,' the imperial aide said solemnly.

Fronto, becoming more agitated with each sentence, let out an agonized croak: 'No, it is—'

Caligula raised a palm to silence the old man. 'Cheated? Who dares cheat your Emperor?'

'I do not know, majesty,' Protogenes admitted, obviously pained by his ignorance.

'But surely your little books know everything? What do they inform us?'

With feigned reluctance, Protogenes again consulted his scrolls. 'It appears the animal trader, Fronto, has been using his position to divert your majesty's profits into his own hands,' he said.

'And how much do you calculate he has defrauded us of, Protogenes? You must know, you are so clever with figures,' Caligula added with overstated irony.

'This Fronto has been particularly devious, majesty. Much is hidden, but I would say he has stolen several thousand sesterces which should have gone to your treasury.'

'Such a sum?'

'Yes, majesty.'

'And what is the penalty for this crime?'

Protogenes thought for a moment, providing a theatrical pause. 'Death, majesty,' he pronounced with finality.

Rufus saw Fronto flinch as if he had been struck. On the underside of his couch beads of yellow liquid gathered and then dripped to form a small pool on the marble floor. A familiar yeasty smell made itself known over the aroma of the perfumed candles. From the corner of his eye, Rufus noticed Chaerea slip from his couch and vanish into the shadow of the room's outer edge.

'Yes, death,' confirmed Caligula. 'But did you not inform me that this man was a diligent servant before he strayed from the path of honesty?'

'That is true, majesty,' Protogenes admitted.

'Then we are inclined to be merciful.' Caligula smiled at Fronto, who stared at him with the wide eyes of a rabbit trapped by a hunting weasel. 'You are fined ten million sesterces.'

A gasp came from the Emperor's dining companions, astonished at the enormous sum, quickly followed by dutiful laughter.

'Of course, you must pay immediately,' Protogenes informed the bewildered Fronto, who had, for a split second, been overwhelmed by hope. 'You can't? Such a pity.'

Rufus watched the unfolding drama with growing dread. Now it was time to stand up for the man who had befriended him. He would accuse Protogenes. But his body would not respond. He was paralysed by fear. No matter how he struggled, nothing would break the iron bonds of self-preservation that held him to the couch. Suddenly he found it difficult to breathe and his head began to spin.

Through his panic, he barely heard Caligula's chilling whisper in his ear. 'Watch, elephant boy, watch every moment and understand how the Emperor rewards those who betray him. Look away but once and I will have your eyes sewn shut.' Then he heard the rattle of the chains.

Fronto heard them also, and began to plead his innocence in an incoherent babble of words. At first Caligula found his ravings amusing, but he quickly became irritated.

'If that man says one more word you will slice out his tongue, and if he raises his hands to his Emperor you will cut them off,' he told Chaerea, who had appeared behind Fronto with two of his Praetorians.

Chaerea ordered his guards to bind the condemned man with the heavy chains they had brought, but Caligula's fertile mind had concocted something more entertaining.

'No, it would be much too fitting to chain a man who has spent his life chaining animals. Let him be beaten instead.'

Chaerea, puzzled, looked round for his thick wooden staff of office.

'Let him be beaten with his chains.'

The Praetorians looked at each other, then doubled the long chains into manageable lengths. Chaerea nodded.

And the beating began.

The two burly Germans concentrated their aim on Fronto's shoulders and body, drawing grunts of pain from the old man, though the thick folds of his toga absorbed much of the force.

'No, no,' Caligula shouted impatiently. 'His head.'

Now Fronto learned the true meaning of horror. The heavy metal links smashed into his unprotected face and head, gouging into his flesh and pulverizing bone and sinew. His agony must have been terrible, for a high-pitched mewing began in the back of his throat, rising to a full-blooded scream. The scream changed instantly to a choked gurgling when a roundhouse swing by one of the Germans hammered into his open mouth, smashing teeth into fragments and shattering the bones of his lower jaw. In minutes, the Praetorians had trouble gripping chains that were slick with bright crimson, spattered with slivers of bloody scalp and clogged with matted strands of Fronto's long hair.

All this Rufus watched from some place of refuge deep inside his mind. A place where he was safe from Caligula and all his kind. A place only a membrane from screaming madness.

He noted that when Fronto, or the thing that had been Fronto, slumped forward, making it difficult for the chains to strike where Caligula, bright-eyed with excitement, directed them, the Emperor ordered the two senators closest to the animal trader to hold his head up. He noted how, as the beating continued, the top of Fronto's head, now mostly white skull decorated with just an occasional tuft of hair, was transformed from a solid dome into a soft, amorphous mass. And he noted that in the background, among the

Praetorians surrounding the walls to ensure that none should interfere with the process of Caligula's justice, one stood more rigid than the rest. Cupido watched helpless, his eyes mirroring Rufus's agony and blood running down his chin from the gash where he had bitten through his lip.

Finally, the Emperor waved a hand and the Germans paused, breathing heavily.

Caligula approached the piece of human wreckage that had been Fronto slowly, peering for some sign of life. The animal trader's eyes were swollen shut and the once-proud hawkish nose was beaten flat across his face. A triangular piece of skull had been knocked from the right side of his head just above the ear, leaving a hole through which could be seen a yellowy-pink mass that, on closer inspection, appeared to quiver.

Drawn to this window into the human head, Caligula delicately placed his forefinger in the opening, and was rewarded by a raw, rasping noise from the approximate position of Fronto's nostrils, accompanied by delicate bubbles of blood which expanded then burst with a gentle click, a phenomenon which clearly delighted the young Emperor.

'Quite amazing. He still lives. He must have been very strong; Protogenes. I wonder how long you would have lasted?'

Protogenes's ravaged face paled, but the question was clearly a rhetorical one, because the Emperor continued wistfully: 'A pity, really. Who will seek out our animals now?'

Chaerea motioned to his guardsmen to remove

the dying man, but Caligula intervened with a smile. 'No, leave him where he is. He has been fine company. He deserves to enjoy the rest of the evening.'

Fronto was still in his place on the couch when a dream-walking Rufus was escorted from the palace that night. There were no tears when he returned to the elephant house. The animal trainer's living death was beyond mourning. Some instinct made him create a nest of hay in the barn itself. It was not until later that he remembered Caligula's words. 'A little bird tells me ... a little spy.'

In the in-between world Rufus now inhabited it seemed appropriate to be summonsed a second evening.

Fronto remained in the seat of honour opposite the Emperor and Caligula introduced him animatedly to a reluctant group of aristocrats who tried, with difficulty, to hide their disgust.

The hideous form still fought for every tortured breath, but only the gods knew how. His battered head was terribly swollen, and the tight-stretched skin varied in colour from bright blue to black. From the wound above his ear a thin stream of yellow pus ran down the side of what had once been a face.

The Emperor was clearly as captivated by his living exhibit as he was by the gold statues lining the walls, or the rich paintings adorning them. When the old man at last let out a final snoring breath, he wept as if someone else had caused his death.

Rufus did not have the luxury of tears. For him

the moment of parting had come when the first blow was struck. The rest was nightmare.

But he was still able to register surprise when Caligula, eyes damp with tears, turned to him and said: 'Here is your former master. He was our friend and companion. Take him from here and give him an honoured funeral as a good servant should.'

Then the Emperor and his guests stood in dignified silence as the same Praetorians who murdered Cornelius Aurius Fronto, the animal trader, wrapped him gently in a white shroud and carried him from the room.

The little group was bathed in moonlight as Rufus directed them across the grass and through the trees to Bersheba's barn. There the soldiers deposited their burden on the ground and stood for a moment in silence.

'I have no wood to cremate him,' Rufus said.

The Germans looked at each other. 'You'll have to bury him. Can't just leave him lying about,' the taller of the two said. 'Over by the wall would do. Not too many tree roots.'

'Can you help me?' Rufus pleaded.

'Not us, lad – we're soldiers, not gravediggers. He was your friend, you give him a nice send-off.'

'I will help you.' The voice came out of the darkness. The Praetorians turned, each right hand on its owner's sword, but they relaxed when they recognized one of their own.

Rufus stood over Fronto's body while Cupido fetched a pair of shovels from the barn. They dug in silence because there was nothing to say. The ground was hard and the tall Praetorian was wrong about the tree roots. They spread tentacle-like through the earth, and Bersheba was roaring grumpily for her morning feed by the time they filled the grave over the shattered remains of Cornelius Aurius Fronto.

Rufus knew there were words that should have been said, and dedications he ought to have made, but he did neither. Instead, he stood, with Cupido at his side, over the raw earth mound that was Fronto's only memorial, fleeting images of their time together flashing through his mind. Fronto and the rhinoceros. Fronto laughing as yet another circus trick ended in disaster. Fronto with the great heart and the endless generosity. That was when the tears came, dripping steadily from his chin to form small patches in the disturbed soil. As he wept, Cupido laid a hand on his shoulder.

'Perhaps Chaerea is right. Perhaps it is time.'

Rufus turned to him, his face set hard. 'Do you think Chaerea would be any different?'

Bersheba picked up his mood when he returned to the barn to replenish her hay racks, and she took to throwing trunkfuls of her food over him in an unsubtle attempt to dispel his gloom, but she eventually realized it was a hopeless task and gave up. After the elephant had been fed and watered, he returned to his wife for the first time in two days.

XXXVI

Livia came to him and took him in her arms. She held him for a moment, her face resting on his stomach and her swollen belly against his knees. When she looked up into his face he saw she knew.

Little bird. The thought came unbidden into his head.

'I am sorry,' she said simply.

He looked at her, unsure how to reply; caught somewhere between the extremes of physical collapse and terrible violence. 'You did not know him.'

'He was your friend.'

'No. He was more than my friend.'

'Then I am sorry.'

Did you betray him? The words touched his lips, but went no further. 'He once promised me my freedom. But when I was with him I was always free, so it did not really matter. Do you understand?'

Her face became a blank wall. 'No, and neither do you. He bought you and sold you. He was not some kindly old man who put a roof over your head and fed you because he loved you. He used you.'

'He would have freed me and I would have been his partner in business.' Rufus shook his head in frustration. 'He saved money for me.'

305

'Then where is this great fortune?' she demanded. 'Where is the legacy of Cornelius Aurius Fronto to Rufus, the slave? Perhaps I have missed something, but we do not appear to be rich.'

'He would have given it to me, but—'

'But? But? But he cheated the Emperor and now he has died for it. I am sorry, truly sorry, that Fronto is dead, Rufus, but he died because of his greed. Would you rather have been the victim? He was not your father. He was a rich merchant who wanted to be richer, and he used everything he could, including you.'

'No. He would have freed me,' Rufus insisted, but his voice had lost its certainty.

Livia continued her attack. 'What is freedom to you and me, Rufus? Perhaps it is different for you, but for me freedom is just a word. Do I need freedom to starve? Freedom to sell my body until some dog-breathed pervert decides it would be more fun to squeeze the life out of me than fuck me? We are slaves and we must live with that. We must make the best of what we have. For our child's sake we must bend like trees in the wind, not invite those who have power over us to break us. Do not risk your life again, Rufus.'

'Fronto was my friend.'

'Yes, he was your friend, but he is gone. We remain. We must survive.'

She made as if to take him in her arms, but he eluded her grasp and stumbled from the room, past the huge bulk of Bersheba and out into the sunshine where the air was cleaner and the world less confusing.

Why had he done nothing? He would have

given his life for Fronto, yet he had watched him die without lifting a finger in his defence. The answer seemed simple: he was a coward.

He walked on, head down and unseeing, his shame weighing on his shoulders like an iron yoke, until he bumped into a slight figure and the force of the collision knocked the other man flat. With a thrill of fear he recognized the Emperor's uncle.

Claudius lay on his back in the grass, arms and legs moving in uncoordinated jerks that reminded Rufus of an upended tortoise. He reached down to help the crippled senator to his feet. The old man shrugged him away, managing to turn awkwardly on to his hands and knees and push himself upright. His clothing was streaked with grass stains and stuck with leaves and twigs, but when Rufus tried to brush them off he flailed at him.

'G-gct away f-f-from m-me,' he stuttered furiously, spittle dripping from the drooping side of his lip. 'I-I-I-I...'

'Forgive me, sir. I did not see you ... I was clumsy ... I...'

Claudius focused on his assailant for the first time. 'You again? You have a t-talent f-f-for abusing an old m-m-man.'

'No, sir,' Rufus said anxiously, before he remembered the drenching Bersheba had given the old senator. 'I mean ... yes, sir.'

For the first time, Rufus thought he saw a flicker of humour in the old man's eyes; then it was gone as quickly as it had come.

'You have b-b-been dining at the E-E-Emperor's table?'

For a moment the change of subject confused Rufus. 'Yes, sir.'

Claudius looked thoughtful, as if weighing up a decision. 'Narcissus will c-call on y-you. L-listen t-to him. You m-may hear something t-to y-your advantage.' He waved a hand in dismissal and limped off, muttering to himself

Rufus frowned as he watched him go.

It was two full days before Narcissus fulfilled his master's prediction. Rufus realized it was no coincidence the tall Greek arrived only a few minutes after Livia had left the house.

Pleading an unlikely indisposition because of the heat, Narcissus asked if they might talk in the shelter of the barn.

'It was unfortunate about your friend,' he said once they were safely hidden in the cool darkness. 'I did what I could for him, of course, but his fate was already sealed. Protogenes presented his evidence to the Emperor some weeks ago. Caligula trusts him as no other.'

Rufus did not hide his disbelief, but Narcissus pretended not to notice the cold stare.

'Truly, nothing could have changed what happened. Such a death,' he added, watching Rufus's face carefully for any kind of reaction. 'How could anyone not hate the man who did this to a friend?'

Rufus saw the trap and could smell the bait. What had old Claudius said? 'Listen to him' – this was a time to listen, not to bark like an angry dog.

Narcissus took his silence as assent to continue.

'Of course, forgive me. You are asking yourself

which "man" I mean? Could it be Protogenes, who designed it? Or Chaerea, who ordered it? Or even the two Tungrian oafs who wielded the chains? I understand your confusion and I acknowledge that each is culpable in his own way. *And* that it would give me great satisfaction if Protogenes, in particular, were to pay for Fronto's death and certain other crimes I could list. But what is the sword without the hand that wields it? Protogenes will be taken care of in good time. Our discussion – our debate – must concern his master.'

He waited for a response, but continued when none came.

'Protogenes's master, then. You have suffered in small ways at his hands. Many have suffered more, and I don't just mean your friend Fronto. The number of those who have suffered, and watched their loved ones suffer, at his hands is countless, Rufus. You are not alone in your hate, never believe that.'

Rufus noticed that it was permissible in the game Narcissus played to reveal any name but that of the subject of the conversation. He was so deep in his own thoughts he didn't realize that Narcissus had stopped talking and was standing patiently, watching him.

'You and I should have no secrets, Rufus,' the Greek said reasonably. Rufus shook his head. He did not want to hear any secrets. 'We are everywhere. Senators and soldiers, freedmen and philosophers, in the streets and in the palaces. If you need names, I will give you names.'

'No names,' Rufus said firmly. 'If you have the

support of so many, why do you need one more? Senators and soldiers, you say, but no slaves. Why do you now need a lowly slave?'

Narcissus considered the question. He knew the answer: a lowly slave could reach places and do things, unnoticed, that a senator or a soldier could not. A lowly slave was expendable, where a senator was not.

But there was another reason.

'Perhaps I was too subtle. It is one of my faults. Did we not once talk of a weapon, an unstoppable weapon that can crush a man with a single blow? There is only one person here who has the knowledge and the power to wield that weapon. Only one who can say when the time is right to use it. Do we understand each other?'

Rufus's throat was suddenly desert-dry. A voice in his head screamed at him to walk away. Even to speak of this was death.

'What if...?'

Narcissus waved away his question. 'We will ensure an opportunity arises. It will be your decision whether to take it. He will visit you, as he did with my master that first day. No guards, just you, the elephant and him. Think on it, Rufus. The man who killed Fronto. Not many are granted the opportunity to change history. To save Rome. You should be proud.'

Rufus stared at him, this arrogant courtier who so blithely dispensed life and death. Did Narcissus really think he was such a fool? The fate of Caligula's assassin was as certain as the next day's sunrise. The man who laid a hand on the Emperor was already as good as dead. And he knew something the Greek did not. Bersheba was as incapable of delivering the fatal blow as he was of manoeuvring it.

He stood deep in thought for several minutes after Narcissus left, but he could find no way of escape. The Greek had caged him as securely as any big cat held in the bowels of the arena. When the cage door opened it could lead only one way. To death.

XXXVII

Cupido laughed incredulously when Rufus told him about Narcissus's fantastic scheme.

'Is there no one in this place who is not involved in a plot? He wants Bersheba to kill Caligula? I have never heard anything so insane. If the Emperor knew how many hands were raised against him the streets of Rome would run with blood.

'I have thought of what you said. About Chaerea. You are right. He is a foul creature with flint for a heart and the morals of a jackal. He would set himself up as the new Caligula and deem it a challenge to outdo his cruelty. But Claudius? He is an old man with an old man's weaknesses. Chaerea would swat him like a fly and his spy Narcissus would be screaming on a cross before the purple touched his shoulders.'

Rufus remembered the Claudius who talked with Bersheba, and shook his head. 'I think you may be wrong about him. It seems to me he is like an actor who changes character between scenes. He has one guise for his friends and another for his enemies. The crippled drooling fool is a cloak that covers the true Claudius, and I believe that that Claudius may well be capable of ruling.'

He told Cupido of the old senator's nocturnal visits to the barn. The gladiator looked thoughtful.

'That is useful to know. If you are correct, he covers his true self well. Yet there are contradictions in what you report. He appears to oppose Chaerea, but he was well informed of his intentions. Well enough informed to know that Lucius was the intended assassin. Does that mean he is part of Chaerea's plot, but does not trust him? Or is there someone in Chaerea's inner circle who informs him of his rival's intentions? And where does Narcissus stand, if Claudius doubts him, but Chaerea speaks of him as an ally? Is this one plot with many strands, or many plots intertwined?'

'What do we do?'

'Do? What can we do, but what Aemilia suggested? We wait, we sacrifice to the old gods and we pray that time is on our side.'

He picked up his long sword and began to sharpen it, the whetstone singing its way up and down the blade.

'Chaerea believes he owns me, Narcissus believes he owns you. It appears to be a trap from which there is no escape, but it contains certain elements that might yet be in our favour. They each see half a picture, while between us we have the whole image. There may come a time when we can turn the one against the other.'

312

'Maybe we should just run?'

Cupido gave his sad smile. 'And where would you run to, Rufus? For myself, I have nowhere to go. Grass grows tall above the ashes of my home and I have no wish to see the bones of my father in the field where they lie scattered. If I am to die, I would rather die here with a sword in my hand and a friend at my side than cornered in some stinking alley. No. We stay and, if need be, we fight.'

Rufus envied him his certainty. How was it that one man could contain so many contradictions and endure what he had endured, yet emerge not only sane but even noble? He turned to leave, then remembered the documents.

'Did Aemilia bring you the parchments?'

'She did, and I told her you were fools for taking them. What did you think you were doing? They are imperial property and the penalty for having them without permission is death. We must get them back where they belong.'

'But did you look at them? She thought you might be able to decipher their meaning.'

Cupido nodded, and went to a small cabinet, where he retrieved the two scrolls. 'Remember I told you Varrus had something to do with the water supply? The smaller of the documents is based on an old map of the Palatine. See. Here is the palace of Augustus. And here? These are the old houses where Caligula built his palace that outdoes all the others. The thin straight lines are all pipes or conduits that feed every house on the hill with water. Varrus is the overseer of the work gang which maintains them.'

Rufus studied the map carefully. He could see it now. The faint outlines of the buildings. The pipes that were all connected to the great aqueduct system which had served Rome for centuries. Even the little fountain where he met Narcissus. But one thing still puzzled him.

'What is the green line? It is much larger than the rest. It appears important. Look, it joins this red line on the main map.'

'I don't know. But you can ask Decimus when you give them to him.'

'Who?'

'Decimus is one of the men who work with Varrus. Arminus, who fought with us at the Rostrum Julium, is friendly with him. He is coming to collect the old man from you later. Tell him Varrus was carrying the parchments when Livia found him.'

Decimus turned out to be a slightly built youth with a face that might have been handsome had it not been pitted with the evidence of some kind of childhood pox. At first he was more interested in Bersheba than in recovering his overseer, but once he had stood beside her in awed silence and been given leave to touch the wrinkled skin of her trunk, Rufus reminded him of the purpose of his visit.

Varrus appeared to have recovered physically, but his mind was still in a place only he could go. Decimus shook his head sadly.

'He's been like this for weeks,' he said. 'Ever since the last inspection.'

'He was carrying these when we found him.'

314

Rufus handed over the two parchments, and received a sharp look from Livia. 'We wondered what they are.'

'This one's the map we use to check the pipes around the hill. If the water pressure goes down in one of the houses or fountains, we can trace it back until we find the leak. Then we replace it with a new section of lead pipe. You'd be surprised how often it happens. Some of the plumbing up here hasn't been replaced since Romulus.'

'And the red and green lines? They must be the main water supply?'

Decimus shook his head. 'Nah, not water. Shit. That red line there is the big one, the Cloaca Maxima,' he said proudly. 'Every sewer between the Capitoline and the Palatine, and the Argiletum and the Forum Boarium, empties into her.' He noticed Rufus's look of bewilderment. 'The Cloaca is the main sewer. A man could walk from one end of Rome to the other and never come above ground – if he could stand the smell. You've seen the shrine to Venus Cloacina up on the forum? Well, Cloacina is our protector when we're down there. Only she didn't protect old Varrus.'

'What happened to him?'

'He was inspecting the Palatine spur, that's the green line, what we call the Cloaca Palatina. You can tell where it goes from above by the drain covers – they're marked by these little symbols. Well, Varrus went down one day sane and came back up like this. Keeps talking about a river of dead. Nobody will go near the place now. It's frightening enough down there on your own in the dark, but the lads reckon he encountered

315

some monster and the sight drove him mad. Me, I think it's more likely to be the fumes. Sometimes the combination of stinks can make you dizzy. Whatever it was, you won't get me down there again.'

Rufus thanked him and told him he was welcome to visit Bersheba whenever he wished. They could still hear Varrus raving as Decimus led him off towards his quarters.

Fronto's death created a barrier between Rufus and Livia which at first appeared insurmountable. They occupied the same space in the way animals of different species inhabit the same territory, eyeing each other warily and seldom communicating. But the child growing in Livia's womb could not be ignored. Slowly, the wounds that scarred their relationship healed, at least partially. They became friends who slept together, and, when the mood took them, they made love with a passion and inventiveness that surprised them both.

He did not know when he became aware Livia was watching him. It was not something he saw or heard, nothing solid or tangible; somehow he just knew. He could feel her eyes on him. When he was with Bersheba in the bright sunshine of the exercise yard. When he talked with the noble visitors the Emperor graciously allowed to watch the great beast put through its paces. Whenever she thought he might have the opportunity to contact someone?

When he was certain it was true, he took Bersheba away from her normal exercise area to a position among the trees across the park where, although he had an angled view of the barn, they were outside the line of Livia's vision. He waited patiently and was rewarded by movement in the shadow just inside the barn doors. As he watched he saw Livia looking around distractedly, wondering where he had vanished.

The game became a regular feature of his day. Was it cruel? Perhaps. But it was how he discovered the identity of her true master.

It did not happen until two weeks later. That morning, he spotted a palace servant approaching from the opposite side of the park. Rufus did not recognize the man, but it was obvious from his manner that he too did not want to be seen. He entered the barn by the side door and disappeared from view. After a few minutes he reappeared, accompanied by Livia. Rufus could sense her fear. Moments later, another furtive character took the stage.

Chaerea.

As Rufus watched, the Praetorian commander began an animated discussion with Livia, who shook her head emphatically in reply. Chaerea's frustration visibly grew until, with the speed of a striking snake, he twisted a hand in Livia's hair and pulled her into the shadow of the barn. As Livia struggled in his grasp, the Roman commander twitched aside his tunic and pushed the struggling woman's head into his groin.

A red veil descended over Rufus's eyes. He began to move into the open, his only thought to kill the man defiling his wife. But he stumbled to a halt just before he broke from the cover of the trees. This was not one of the pampered princes who rose to command a legion because of his aristocratic connections. This was Cassius Chaerea, survivor of a dozen combats; a man who had killed with his bare hands. To act now would be to sign both their death warrants.

By the time Chaerea had completed his assault, wiped himself clean on Livia's hair and thrown her limp body to the ground, the murderous rage which had surged through Rufus had turned to a ball of cold stone. He would kill this man. If it was the last thing he did on this earth, he would kill him.

He watched Livia struggle to her feet, her bulging belly making it difficult for her to balance. He wanted to run to her, to hold her and comfort her. But there was still a chance Chaerea might be watching.

Instead, he continued to exercise Bersheba, marching her mechanically back and forth across the bone-hard ground. He was becoming the accomplished conspirator, and he despised himself for it.

When he returned much later to the cramped room behind the barn, she greeted him with a smile that would have deceived him entirely had he not seen what he had seen. Only the damp of her recently washed hair and a slight reddening in the corners of her eyes betrayed her.

He returned her smile with one of his own. And, just for a moment, he did truly love her; Livia, his wife and companion, bearer of his child, his lover and betrayer. And he knew she loved him. The façade of normality she had somehow created was not to protect her from him. It was to protect him from them.

As she turned her back he stole a glance at her, marvelling at the perfect proportions of her body even in pregnancy, and the sharp intelligence of her mind. How often must she have cursed the fates that halted her growth? How often did she lie awake in the night and wonder again and again, what if? What if? Who would she have been and what would she have done?

For the first time he truly understood her frustration at being trapped in that tiny body and he vowed he would do everything in his power to help her escape, if not from it, at least from the life to which it had condemned her. Fronto had promised him the money to buy his freedom. He did not know how much, but he knew his friend would never cheat him. He would have left it with someone he could trust or somewhere only Rufus could find it. Somehow he would track it down and would make it free them both.

But first he must prise her from the clutches of Chaerea.

Narcissus owed him.

The Greek's eyes narrowed when he heard of Chaerea's bungling attempts to gather intelligence.

'So the simple soldier has decided to dirty his hands,' Narcissus said. 'But why would he choose your wife? No doubt he too has heard of my master's visits. He wonders what was said, and to whom, and how he can profit from it. If he knew Senator Claudius had been having conversation with an elephant he would die laughing instead of on an impaler's spike as he deserves. You have done well, Rufus. This could have been fatal to us. Now we know where the danger lies we can protect ourselves against it. Perhaps we can even use the knowledge to our benefit.'

'We must find a way to stop him using Livia. Use this information to free her from his hold,' Rufus pleaded.

Narcissus looked at him with disappointment. 'That would not be very subtle, and it would probably be the death of both of you. Livia's safety lies in her usefulness to Chaerea. We must be patient. She must know nothing.'

'But what can I do? If Livia has nothing to give him he'll no longer regard her as useful and then...'

'Exactly,' Narcissus said. 'And that is why we must ensure she gives Chaerea what he wants.'

Rufus was confused. 'But how will we do that?'

'Not we, Rufus. You. Let me think on it and I will provide you with some tasty pillow talk that will make your pretty young wife Chaerea's most treasured possession.'

'There is something else.'

Narcissus raised a cultured eyebrow, and Rufus explained to him about Fronto's legacy.

'I think you may be putting too much faith in Fronto's friends.' Narcissus frowned and thought for a moment. 'It would take someone remarkably honest to hold so much money for a dead man and then hand it over to a slave. Fronto was too clever to trust the people he dealt with. If he left the money with anyone, it was with a lawyer, and if that was the case Protogenes will track him down and the money will disappear. I will have Fronto's acquaintances approached in such a way that they will not know why or by whom, but I hold out little hope, Rufus. Can you think of anywhere else it could be?'

Rufus considered for a moment. It seemed so unlikely that he had not dared think of it.

'There is one possibility.'

Later, Rufus lay side by side with Livia on their straw-filled mattress, he stroking the curve of her stomach, she with her head on his shoulder. They talked into the night.

The next morning, she left the barn early with the excuse that they needed bread, even though Rufus could see there was ample for both of them.

He was filling the water barrel when he was distracted by a buzzing sound that grew noticeably louder as the minutes passed. Eventually, his curiosity became too much to withstand and he decided to investigate.

Giving Bersheba the command to kneel, he mounted her shoulders and directed her towards the palace wall. There, her great height afforded him an unobstructed view down on to the city streets below the Palatine. He had never seen so many people. They came in their thousands, a river of life that flooded the narrow streets and packed them so tightly that he was surprised they could move at all. But move they did, in a constant stream towards the forum.

Far below him, as the masses moved in one

direction, Narcissus moved in the other. The timing was perfect. All Rome was converging on the Senate to hear the Emperor's announcement. Caligula was about to declare himself divine.

In a way, it was not surprising. The more malleable sections of the mob already treated him as a god and dedicated shrines to his spirit. In this, they were only following a tradition set by his ancestor Augustus. But the declaration he would make today was a step further, further even than his elevation of Drusilla to the pantheon. Already he spoke daily to Jupiter in his temple on the Capitol. He had begun to remove the heads from statues of the gods and replace them with busts of his own. Now Roman citizens would be required to worship him alongside Mars, Hermes and Apollo. The nobility would bankrupt themselves to build temples in his honour and make expensive sacrifices to him. They would hate him even more. Narcissus smiled his cold smile, and quickened his pace against the flow of the crowd.

The villa Rufus had described was to the east of the Circus Maximus, on the edge of the city. The animal trader's property and goods had been confiscated and divided among the Emperor's favourites, but Narcissus was aware that the villa had not yet been formally occupied by its new owner, Protogenes's effeminate nephew.

The house was locked, but Narcissus had come prepared. From beneath his tunic he drew a selection of keys tied together by a piece of cord. They would not be missed before the hired thief who stole them for him returned them. It took three attempts before he found the correct key to unlock the gate, then a further two to locate the smaller key to the entrance door of the villa.

Fronto's home was a Spartan place, exactly what Narcissus would have expected of an uncultured oaf who lived alone and spent his life purchasing animals destined for death. No opulent or ostentatious decoration here, no great paintings or statues, but what was this? An extensive library. Perhaps Fronto was not the buffoon he seemed.

He looked around. What was it Rufus had said? The red urn with twisted vine decoration at the neck. A souvenir of one of the trader's trips to the east. There it was, in the corner. It was heavier than it looked but, using all his strength, Narcissus was able to move it out of position. Yes, the cracked tile. Despite himself he began to tremble with excitement. He prised up first one jagged portion of the patterned stonework, then the other, and bent forward to look into the dark cavity below.

Rufus knew from the moment he saw Narcissus's face that the news was bad.

The Greek spread his hands in a gesture of helplessness. 'None of Fronto's acquaintances admits to any knowledge of your money, Rufus. Of course, one may be lying, but I don't think so. Fronto was too clever to trust them.'

'And the villa?'

Narcissus shook his head, defeat in his eyes. 'Nothing. I checked it myself and there was nothing beneath the floor but spiders and mice.'

Rufus bowed his head. 'Perhaps it was too

much to ask. It was only a dream.'

Narcissus clapped a hand on the younger man's back. 'Don't give up, Rufus. You can win your freedom. I am the living example of that.'

Rufus looked up at him, the pain of failure reflected in his eyes. 'But you are cultured and intelligent. You won your freedom with the talents the gods gave you. What gifts do I have? I was born to be a slave.'

Narcissus shook his head sadly and turned to walk back to the palace. As he did, he struggled to control a smug grin.

You could never be too rich. He had done Rufus a favour, really, by saving him from a difficult decision. The gold in the two leather pouches would not have been enough to buy freedom for the young man and his pretty wife. In any case, Caligula would never have freed him. Who else would look after his elephant?

XXXVIII

Now the door into Narcissus's clandestine world opened more fully for Rufus. The volume of information he passed to Livia increased and the messages themselves became more complex. Claudius's secretary could no longer impart what he needed during short visits to the elephant keeper's house. Instead, Rufus would wait until Livia made her excuses and waddled off to see the woman who was monitoring her pregnancy (and, no doubt, to pass on the fruits of their previous evening's discussions to Chaerea) before departing for a previously arranged meeting with Narcissus.

Here he would be instructed, not only in the wording of the message, but also in the way it should be imparted. Do not give it all at once; let her tease it out of you. A did not meet B in the alley behind the kitchens of the palace of Tiberius. No, A was seen by C loitering. C said A gave the impression of *being up to something*. Then change the subject. Livia will go back to it, and then, only then, do you reveal that when C was leaving, he saw B approach A and they disappeared together talking animatedly.

Rufus did not question what he was told, but he sensed each message was a building block in some intricate structure Narcissus's devious mind had designed – part of a giant puzzle in which each piece would only interlock in a certain way. But the messages were so innocuous he couldn't see what use they would be to Chaerea.

What he could not know, and what Narcissus would never tell him, was that the information Livia passed to Chaerea was being relayed to different sources in the palace hierarchy. They in turn would feed their titbits to the other members of the select circle of Caligula's hated favourites: Protogenes, Helicon and Callistus (harmless Appeles was long departed, flayed alive for failing to laugh sufficiently loudly at one of the Emperor's jokes), each of whom would seek to outdo the others in the speed and the drama with which they would present the information to the ultimate recipient.

At first, Caligula would accept the whispers for what they were, nails in coffins; specifically, and here was the dangerous part, nails in the coffins of Senator Claudius and his faithful freedman, Narcissus.

Yet the Greek gambled that Caligula's paranoia was so acute, it would allow him to perceive the seeds of treachery sown in the messages. On their own they were simply a series of denunciations by his faithful servants of plots by those he had long suspected. Yet each was subtly different in emphasis, and, taking all together, the young Emperor could only come to one conclusion: he was being betrayed by one or more of the men he trusted most.

Somehow, Rufus discovered, it was possible to live two lives. The seething undercurrents and ever-changing alliances of palace politics occurred in a dimension somewhere close by, occasionally intruding on what he called normality. But it never felt as real as his dull little everyday routine.

His reputation as an animal trainer had followed him from the arena to the Palatine, and occasionally he would be asked to use his skills to help the handlers at the little zoo the Emperor had established in one of the palace courtyards. It was one of the great mysteries of Caligula that he took as much pleasure from studying the exotic animals captured in Africa and Asia as he did from watching them being slaughtered in their hundreds in the arena.

'We're having trouble with one of the tigers, the big female,' the head keeper explained one day.

'She's usually quiet as long as you keep her fed, but she almost took Rodan's arm off yesterday and nobody's been keen to go anywhere near her since. Can you have a look at her?'

At night, the big cats slept in cages surrounding a deep, stone-lined pit, but during the day the cages were opened and they roamed free where the Emperor's privileged visitors could view them.

Rufus was surprised to see Callistus and his son among the watchers by the low wall overlooking the pens. He smiled in recognition. Callistus ignored him, but the boy – what was his name? Gnaius – grinned back, before turning again to watch the big cats that so obviously enthralled him. Rufus made his way to the narrow stairway leading down to the cages. The sharp, pungent scent of the cats thrilled him, as it always had, reminding him of his days with Fronto, but that memory brought with it an overwhelming sadness he struggled to throw off. Fronto was gone. There was nothing he could have done. Nothing he could do. Unless... No, he must not even think of it.

'This way.' The voice of the Gracus, the head keeper, brought him back to the present and he buried the image of treason where it belonged. 'She's over here. We didn't let her out with the others.'

Rufus approached the cage slowly, careful not to surprise or antagonize the tigress. She was lying on her side in the straw, and managed only a lethargic snarl when she noticed him. He stood for a few minutes, studying her carefully in the poor light from the torches which lit the chamber. Her eyes had none of the demon fire that characterized her kind, and he could see she breathed in short bursts, the way an animal does when it is in pain. As if to confirm his diagnosis, she turned to lick the pale fur of her belly. He waited a little longer, but he was already confident that he knew.

'Either she is pregnant, in which case you must let nature take its course, or more likely she has colic.' He explained how the condition could be treated, and Gracus thanked him.

The forlorn little cry came as he turned away towards the stairs. On its own, it was an innocuous sound, but his disbelieving mind knew it for what it was and it froze him to the spot. It was followed a second later by an anguished scream that seemed to fill the chamber.

'Gnaius!'

The blood drained from the handler's face. 'The boy! I told him to stay away from the edge.'

Rufus was first to recover. 'How can I get into the pit?'

'But the cats, they–'

'We don't have time.' Rufus gripped him by the front of the tunic. 'How do I get in?'

Gracus pointed. 'Through here.'

The handler fumbled with the padlock holding shut an empty cage, and was about to lead him through when a thundering roar shattered the silence.

Rufus recognized the sound, knew he had only seconds to act.

'Get out of the way.' He shouldered past the

handler and ran through the cage until the length of the pit was spread out before him.

It was almost fifty feet across, with smooth stone walls two and a half times the height of a man. Still that might not have been proof against a springing leopard, so they had placed two-foot iron claws all the way round the rim to stop any potential escape. The claws were situated just under the low parapet that topped the wall.

The boy must have been leaning over the parapet when he lost his balance. The fall should have been enough to kill him, but Rufus could see he had landed on a thick bush growing against the base of the wall. It saved him from serious injury, but he was badly stunned, and, worse, bleeding.

It was the scent of blood that had triggered the hunting instinct of the lioness.

There were three of the big cats in the pit, and Rufus took time he couldn't afford to study them.

Two of the tawny cats, a black-maned male and a lioness little more than a cub, showed more curiosity than aggression towards the small intruder on their territory. His first instinct was to ignore them. The mature female was different. She was crouched, head and shoulders low over her front paws, muscles bunched, ready to attack. Only the fact that the boy was not moving had saved him so far. Rufus watched him closely, saw the little chest rise and fall. Then a tentative hand reached up towards the wound on the boy's head and he let out a loud groan as he felt the graze on his scalp. The lioness's ears twitched.

Experience had taught Rufus to recognize the

signal of an impending attack. Very slowly he walked into the centre of the pit.

He kept his eyes on the big female, willing her to stay where she was. At the edge of his vision he could see Callistus's ashen face among the ring of watchers round the parapet.

Each pace took him further from safety.

A snarl ripped from deep in a massive chest close behind him, then again a second later from his right. The dark-maned male was stalking him. His back tensed at the thought of the raking claws and gaping mouth. He was level with the crouching female now, and perhaps fifteen paces from Gnaius. It might as well have been a mile.

She had been concentrating on the prey before her, and only now realized there was another presence in the pit. She turned her great head towards him, spitting her fury, nostrils flaring, and he could see the smoky hatred in her eyes. But captivity had made her familiar with humans and Rufus knew that gave him a slim chance. If she would only hold off her attack until he reached the boy he might somehow get him to one of the hands now reaching down from above.

He maintained his steady pace, ensuring his eyes never met hers and willing himself not to show the terror that seized his muscles and chilled his blood. Ten paces, five; he was going to reach the boy. He was close enough to see the blood matting the dark hair where he had struck his head on the stone floor. At the very least he might be able to protect him until the handler brought help. Then Gnaius gave a little whimper and tried to stand.

The lioness roared and he knew the next time she gave song she would charge. He increased his pace but didn't dare run, even though he knew his time was measured in moments. He was a few steps from the boy when she roared again and he heard the skitter of her long claws on the stone as she came.

She moved so fast she was little more than a blur and he barely had time to pick Gnaius up. No chance of throwing the boy towards the reaching hands now. His mind only had time to register gaping jaws filled with yellowing fangs before he raised his free hand in a hopeless gesture of defence.

The lioness was quick, but the black-maned male was quicker. He hit her in the ribs just as she was taking off in the leap that would have brought her teeth to Rufus's throat, and his weight and momentum knocked the breath from her body and bowled her head over heels to the far side of the pit. The blow stunned her, but she got shakily to her feet, snarling at her attacker, and Rufus heard his black-maned saviour roar his defiance as he ran with the boy for the open cage where he had entered.

Once he reached the safety of the bars, he slammed the cage door shut behind him and sat with his back to the lion pit with the slight figure of Gnaius warm in his arms. He felt sick, but he also wanted to laugh. Now the danger was past it seemed so funny, so utterly atrocious, to have walked unarmed and unprepared into the den of three grown lions.

'I...'

He looked up to see Gracus. The handler would not meet his eyes and Rufus realized he had not moved since Gnaius fell. There would have been no rescue. That made him want to laugh even more.

Gracus reached for the boy, but for some reason Rufus found he could not let him go. He raised himself to his feet and pushed past the handler towards the exit. He was almost at the stairs when he remembered.

'Make sure you give Africanus something special for his meal tonight. He earned it.' He shook his head slowly, amazed at his own stupidity. How could he have failed to recognize the animal he had trained from a cub?

As he made his way towards the upper level, the euphoria drained from him and suddenly he felt very tired. He staggered as he reached the light and only retained his footing when a hand caught his shoulder.

'How is he? Is he…?' Callistus's voice quivered with emotion.

'He hit his head, but he is a strong boy. I think he will be all right, but you should take him to a physician right away.'

The imperial secretary's eyes filled with tears as he lifted his son gently from Rufus's arms. 'I owe you a life,' he said, in a low voice, so none of the watching slaves could hear. 'Visit me in my quarters tonight and perhaps I can go part way to repaying it.'

He walked away with his head bowed protectively over his son's, leaving Rufus as mystified as he was dazed.

XXXIX

Information was power, Narcissus had taught him that. But now he possessed this information what was he to do with it?

In the right hands it could unquestionably destroy his enemy. Yet the right hands belonged to a man who was a greater enemy still. Then there was the question of survival. If the information came from a source close to the heart of power, it would be endowed with the power of that source and its effect would be multiplied. But coming from a slave would it not raise doubts? Yes. First doubts, then suspicions. Rufus shuddered as he considered the consequences of arousing the suspicions of the man with whom he was considering sharing the secret. No. Not that route then.

Time was on his side. He could hold it until he needed a bargaining chip. Then again there was the danger that its power might be devalued, or his need so dire he would be forced to sell it for less than it was worth.

Narcissus, or his master, would pay well for it – he had no doubts on that score. It would give the Greek power over his greatest rival. Who knows, it might even open the door to an Empire, but what kind of Empire? He had witnessed Narcissus at work, seen the cold calculation in the Greek's eyes. Would he trust Narcissus with the gift he had just received? Again, the answer was no. In truth, there had always been only one choice. But the thing he had in his possession was of such momentous significance it was imperative to consider every option.

'It is very pretty, but why should I want it?' Cupido studied the object in his hand. It was a small, intricately worked metal box of the sort ladies of consequence kept their most valued rings in. The box itself was crafted of silver, but the lid had been worked with gold wire inset in the shape of a dragon being attacked by a leopard. It was very beautiful, and obviously very valuable. 'Did you steal it?' he demanded suspiciously.

'It is a poor creature who has so little faith in his friends,' Rufus commented.

Cupido raised one eyebrow. 'I remember a tale of a boy who was told he could pat a rhinoceros as if it was a dog. This' – he held the box between two fingers – 'looks suspiciously like a rhinoceros.'

'Then your eyesight is patently not what it was. I have been close enough to a rhinoceros to know what one looks like. But, please, let me tell you a story. It begins, as most stories do, quite a long time ago. Almost thirty years, in fact.'

'Then you had better get on with it, because I have important duties, even if you do not.'

'Of course.' Rufus picked up the box with a flourish. 'The tale concerns a certain Germanicus.'

Cupido's head came up sharply as he recognized the name of Caligula's father, and Rufus knew he had his friend's full attention now.

'This Germanicus was generally considered to possess the highest qualities to be desired in a man. Handsome, brave, clever. Orator and warrior. Friend to many and inspiration to all. When the German legions would have disowned Tiberius, he held them to their oaths. When they stared defeat in the face, he turned it into victory by the strength of his own character. Surely, you may ask, such a man would be loved by all?

'But when lesser men look to the heavens and see a star so much brighter than their own, or men less well favoured look into a mirror and see a face less handsome, their minds become twisted. Thus it was with those who regarded Germanicus as a rival.

'It was not enough that he restored order to the Orient, that he vanquished the king of Armenia, and bestowed upon Cappadocia the honour of a province of Rome. No, he must no longer be allowed to cast a greater shadow than his Emperor, or hold greater power than his Emperor's closest adviser.

'So a soldier was dispatched to Antioch, where his deeds and his honours ensured him a welcome and a place in his general's counsel. It was unfortunate that, soon after, Germanicus, who had stood so tall and was so loved, was brought low by a most loathsome disease. His golden skin withered and became covered in dark pustules. The mouth from which so many honeyed words had poured instead spewed froth. And he died, mourned by all, but none more than his Emperor, his Emperor's closest adviser, Gnaius Piso, and the good soldier who had come so

335

untimely to his service.'

'Who told you this?' Cupido demanded.

'But there is more. Do you not want to hear it? Does it not enthral you?'

Cupido's nostrils flared, so that he reminded Rufus of the lion he had confronted. He wondered if he had gone too far, but the gladiator nodded for him to continue.

'Such illnesses are not uncommon in the Orient, or so I am told. Those who grieved for their general would have been content to believe his death was mere fate – but for two things. When his body was reduced to ashes in the fierce heat of the funeral fire, his heart was found entire among his bones, which, as your witch of a sister will no doubt have told you, is a certain sign of poison. And among his effects was found something which was pretty,' he raised the little box so it glinted in the lamplight, 'but seemed an unlikely trinket for a commander who lived a simple life.'

He handed the box to Cupido and the young German stared at it, as if he was trying to unlock its secrets by sheer force of will.

'One among the general's staff was not content. He took the pretty trinket to a certain medical man with knowledge of things he did not care to advertise among his friends. This medical man carried out tests, I know not how, which proved that the contents of the little box you hold had included some distillation of the red-spot mushroom. Even the slightest dose would have proved fatal to anyone who consumed it.'

'Narcissus!' Cupido exclaimed. 'It was Nar-

336

cissus who revealed all this to you. Only he with his contacts in the east could have unearthed such a detailed report. You did this for me? You placed yourself even deeper in his debt for a friend?'

Rufus smiled modestly and recalled Callistus's final words when they had parted the previous evening. 'Let him believe anything, as long as it is not the truth.'

'And who was this simple soldier,' Cupido asked, though he knew the answer already, 'who was so trusted by his general, but whose appearance proved a harbinger of such tragedy?'

Rufus smiled coldly. 'Why, our good friend Cassius Chaerea.'

They spent the rest of the night discussing the best use of what Rufus had discovered. From time to time Rufus noticed Cupido giving him a strange look, as if he could not quite believe him capable of providing this deadly combination of intelligence and evidence.

'You are certain of its provenance?' he demanded at one point. 'You trust the source of this information with your life?'

'More than that. I trust him with your life,' Rufus said evenly.

In the end it was decided. Cupido would seek a meeting with Chaerea in some neutral place, repeat the story as Rufus had just told it and show him only the slightest glimpse of the silver box. If Chaerea reacted as they hoped, Cupido would tell him he wanted nothing to do with his plots, and leave him in no doubt that if there was any further interference in either his or Rufus's affairs, the information would reach Caligula.

'You must convince him it will come from someone in power,' Rufus repeated for the third time. 'If he thinks a senator like Claudius, or Helicon, the chamberlain, is ready to denounce him at your signal, he will not dare act against us, for to do so would be death.'

'It is your death I will think on if I am left with Chaerea thanking me for the gift of a pretty jewel box for one of his whores,' Cupido said wryly.

'You won't be. But don't rush into the meeting. Set it up for four days from now and let Chaerea fret about your intentions. He is still looking over his shoulder after the last attempt on Caligula's life. This will unsettle him even more.'

Cupido nodded, his expression grim. 'I have something to give Narcissus in return for this gift.'

Rufus stared at him. Cupido seldom revealed information about his dealings with the Emperor. This was a sign of the true extent of their peril.

'The guard is split. Cassius Chaerea has suborned many with his promises of wealth and position, but not all. There are some who see him for what he is, a jackal who feeds on the carrion others provide. They know it will be Chaerea who dons the purple if his plan succeeds, and not the mysterious other he claims to support. And when he does, they understand what will happen to his enemies. Some of these are officers held in high esteem by their men. They are not innocents, but Caligula has disgraced them by using them as executioners instead of soldiers. He has lost their loyalty. They will not act against him directly.

They wish him gone, but not to be replaced by Chaerea. They need someone to follow, someone worthy of their support. Claudius.'

Rufus's head spun with the enormity of what he was being told and the opportunity it represented. Then reality intervened.

'But Claudius would never agree to be Emperor. Remember what I told you of his conversation with Bersheba. He wants a return to sanity. A republic.'

'I understand that, but the Guard, those who are against Chaerea, will not support a republic. They believe it will weaken the Empire and lead to anarchy. They seek a return to the prosperity and security Augustus brought. Only one of Augustus's blood can provide it.' He shrugged. 'Claudius is not perfect, but he is available.'

'But I told you. He will not do it.'

'What if someone engineered it so he had no choice?' Cupido suggested. 'Someone who had much to gain if his master rose to the very pinnacle of power?'

Someone like Narcissus.

But before Rufus could arrange a meeting with the Greek, their lives would hang by a thread...

He and Livia were sitting in their little home three nights later. It was the eve of the sacrifice of the October Horse and there was a festival air to Rome which had even penetrated the room behind the barn. The couple had mellowed lately, and Rufus was trying to come to terms with the enormous upheaval about to occur in his life. An upheaval that drew closer each day as Livia's belly grew rounder and fatter. His stomach was just dealing with the disturbing detail of childbirth when the door burst open.

His hand darted for the knife he kept beneath the bed and he rose ready to use it. But he froze when he saw the figure in the doorway.

This was an Aemilia Rufus barely recognized. Her eyes were wide and her blond hair was matted, with small twigs and leaves tangled among it, as if she had just spent a night on a forest floor. Her breath came in short, desperate bursts and her chest heaved against the thin cloth of the expensive dress she wore.

'I didn't know where else to go,' she gasped. 'You must help me.'

The words were directed at Rufus and it was apparent that she had not even noticed Livia was in the room.

Rufus opened his mouth to reassure her, but it was Livia who spoke. The Palatine was a small community and she knew Aemilia by sight, knew too that she was Cupido's sister. But they had never met and she slightly resented the girl's position in Milonia's household.

'What has happened that you must enter our house without invitation in the dead of night?' she demanded in a voice that was, if not frosty, certainly not welcoming.

Aemilia looked from the tiny figure to Rufus as if she was a deer seeking escape from a pack of hounds.

'Enough of this,' Rufus said. 'She has come to us for aid and we will give it. Bring water. Aemilia will explain herself in her own time.'

'But she is right, Rufus: you must know. My presence here is a danger to us all.' Aemilia's voice shook and her head drooped so she did not have to meet their eyes. 'The Emperor. I was dining with Milonia – a favour to her, she said. He came to her quarters as we ate and placed himself on the couch beside me. I was a fool, because I was honoured by his attentions. Then he began to touch me. First my hair.' She took a handful of the golden mass in her fist as if she wanted to tear it from her head. 'Then my skin. He touched my skin and it crawled as if a serpent had been placed upon it. Then he spoke to me of things I did not understand, or want to understand. Of the nature of love. What do I know of love, or care, in this place where each of us is a commodity to be bartered? He said I must share their bed. I looked to Milonia for aid, but she only smiled, and there was something in her smile that chilled me. She knew. She knew and she approved. The Emperor took me by the hand, and said, "Come." But I could not. I shook myself free, and I ran.' She sobbed, a great heart-wrenching breath from deep in her body. 'I have nowhere else to go.'

Rufus listened in silence. He was appalled. Not because of his sympathy for Aemilia's ordeal, but because she had placed them in mortal danger. And for no reason. How could she be such a fool? This was no sanctuary. It was a trap.

As if the gods were able to read his mind there came a thundering knock at the door.

'Open up, quickly.'

He breathed a sigh of relief. Cupido. Cupido

341

would know what to do.

Rufus opened the door cautiously and the young German, wearing a long cloak over his armour, bustled past him.

'I heard she had come this way, and I decided to check before the patro–' He stopped, open-mouthed, staring at Aemilia. 'You? I was only told it was a girl.' He shook his head in disbelief. 'I didn't... No one said...'

Aemilia ran to him, crying his name, and he took her protectively in his arms. But the eyes that met Rufus's across her shoulder were filled with confusion.

'You must get her out of here, now.' Livia's voice was cracked with tension. 'The child... If they find her here, you know what they will do.'

'It is too late,' Cupido said, and Rufus heard something in his tone that was as out of place in Cupido the warrior as snow in a Tuscan summer. Defeat.

He was right. Already they could hear the clash of weaponry as the soldiers of the Emperor's guard made their way down the slope from the palace.

'Wait. I will talk to them.' Cupido tried to thrust Aemilia away from him, but she held tight and forced him to look at her.

'No,' she said. Her face was set in a savage expression that reminded Rufus of tales of fierce women fighters who were as deadly in battle as any man. 'Kill me.'

Cupido recoiled as if he had been punched. 'No. Never.'

'Kill me,' she repeated. 'If you cannot save me,

at least save my honour.' But he shook his head helplessly, and she pushed him away. 'You were a coward when we were taken and you are a coward now,' she said, her voice dripping with scorn.

Cupido's face turned ashen, and she looked at Rufus.

'Then you must kill me. If my brother does not have the courage I ask a friend.'

'If she dies we all die. But if we are going to die, let us die fighting.' Cupido drew his long sword from under his cloak and threw a short dagger to Rufus, who caught it awkwardly. Aemilia made a grab for the blade, but he pushed her away, knowing what she intended. She collapsed sobbing beside Livia, who lifted her head and looked deep in her eyes.

'You are so young,' she whispered. 'So terribly young. He is only a man, Aemilia, and there will be many other men. There is no need to be frightened of him. You will find he has a man's pride, but requires a woman to appreciate it or it has no value to him. He also has a man's doubts, and he must prove himself with many women or those doubts will turn into certainty and he will no longer be the man he thinks he once was. He is an Emperor, therefore his pride and his doubts are multiplied a thousand-fold. But still, he is only a man.'

Aemilia stared at her. 'Have you..?'

Livia smiled sadly. 'I have been with so many men, it is difficult to remember.'

The younger girl shook her head. 'I cannot. My honour...'

'Remember,' Livia said fiercely. 'It does not matter what he does to your body, as long as you resist in your mind. Stay true to yourself, and you will survive.'

'But Milonia...'

'In this, Milonia is your ally. If she is with him, then he is not with you. With Milonia you will at least find affection, if not pleasure. Do not look so shocked. It is not unknown. Some women even prefer other women to men.' She looked at Rufus and Cupido standing awkwardly by the door, from behind which came the unmistakable sound of soldiers preparing for action. 'It is not difficult to understand why.'

'Inside.' The shout from outside filled the room. 'You inside, open up or we'll smash our way in.'

Cupido tensed, and Rufus went to his side. 'I am ready to die,' he said quietly, 'but I wish it was for a better reason.'

Cupido shrugged. 'There are worse reasons.'

'On the count of three.' They heard the Praetorian prepare his men for the attack.

'Wait!' Aemilia's cry caused shuffled confusion beyond the barrier of the door. 'I am ready to attend the Emperor.' She turned to Cupido and wiped the tears from her eyes. 'I will go then,' she said, all emotion suddenly vanished. 'But know this: I no longer have a brother and I no longer have a name.'

She made to brush past him, but he stopped her and she did not struggle as he unwrapped his cloak and folded it around her. As she fumbled with the latch, he touched her hair and removed a small twig from it in a gesture of brotherly affection that was so alien to the circumstances Rufus almost believed he had imagined it.

At the door, Aemilia turned to Rufus and it was as if they were alone in the room together. He knew then she understood his passion for her. She had never been able to return it, but she could use it. When she spoke her voice was flat, cold. 'If you will not give me the mercy of a quick death, at least promise me this – when the opportunity arises you will kill him.'

She stood there for a moment, tall and proud once more, her eyes demanding an answer he couldn't give. Then she was gone.

XL

Aemilia changed. She would never speak of what happened that night, or in the ones that inevitably followed. The carefree girl was gone, replaced by a hard-edged young woman with a painfully sharp tongue. She was still beautiful, but it was a different beauty; colder. Occasionally Rufus would see her in the park with the Emperor's daughter and try to catch her eye. Where once she would have smiled and called out, she ignored him as if he didn't exist. He cared too much for it not to hurt, but knew better than to force his company on her.

A few weeks later – at the end of the three-day festival of the Compitalia – when he thought the wound might have begun to heal, he asked

Cupido if he had spoken to her. The gladiator's face turned bleak. 'I have no sister,' he said.

Whether it was the weather, which was making its heartless jump from autumn's end to full winter, or something in the air, Rufus came down with an indefinable sickness. It never quite laid him low, but it was always there, a cold, clammy ball deep in his stomach, which made him lethargic and miserable. He struggled to cope with tasks that, a week earlier, were quite routine, and found himself sighing for no reason. Livia noted the change in him, and, being a woman, soon worked out the cause. At first she was angry, but then anger turned to a sort of disconnected, pragmatic acceptance. Aemilia was not her rival. Rufus was still her man. Until either of those situations changed she had more important things to concern her.

Rufus was talking quietly to her as they lay on the straw pallet late one evening, ready to give her the latest piece in one of Narcissus's puzzles, when she told him her time was near.

She had tried to prepare him, and he had believed himself prepared, but he found the change hurtling towards him as terrifying as a mountain avalanche. He hid away in his work with Bersheba as Livia gathered the necessities required for the birth. When she spoke of the baby as a living being, it was as if she talked a language he could not understand. He did not think he could ever be a father,

He tried to change the subject, to pass on Narcissus's instructions, but she placed a child's finger tenderly over his mouth.

'Enough of that. We have other things to concern us. Now, you will know when the baby is coming when my waters break – from here.' She took his hand and placed it deep between her legs beneath the overhang of her belly. 'Don't grimace like that.' She laughed. 'It is what happens to every woman.'

She was still giving him instructions – how to contact Galla, the palace slave who had advised her through her pregnancy – when he drifted off to sleep. Smiling, she shook her head and kissed him on the lips. He was still such a boy, really.

The screams took time to penetrate his sleeping mind. He never discovered whether the meeting had been prearranged or whether Chaerea had somehow managed to circumvent Bersheba's vigilance. But when he stumbled, blinking, past the grey bulk of the elephant and into the night, the Praetorian commander was visible fifty yards away in the moonlight, kicking purposefully at a screaming white bundle that squirmed at his feet. Livia.

Rufus launched himself in a hate-blinded charge as Chaerea completed his assault with one final, carefully aimed boot into Livia's exposed belly, and turned from his victim. He had covered less than ten paces when Rufus caught him in a flying tackle around the shoulders. But Chaerea, the legionary veteran, was not going to be taken so easily. It was laughable. Had he become so old that this beardless slave believed he could surprise him?

He pivoted his body so the younger man's

347

momentum sent him flying over his shoulder to land with a sickening thud six feet away. Rufus was stunned and winded, but even if he hadn't been, Chaerea would have been on him before he could move. He felt the razor edge of a curved dagger across his throat.

'I should kill you now, elephant boy, you and your midget whore, but somehow you have acquired friends I can't afford to annoy at the moment,' he grunted, filling Rufus's nostrils with the stink of his breath. 'You think you can sink old Cassius with a few whispers and a piece of junk, eh? You think you're clever? Well, at least I can give you something to remember me by.'

Rufus's mind filled with a white light and a lance of pain scored his forehead before his vision vanished behind a sea of red. For a second he thought Chaerea had blinded him.

The Praetorian laughed and his weight shifted, allowing Rufus to breathe. Rufus explored his face to discover how much damage had been done. His tentative fingers found a thin, four-inch slash.

'You'll live. Not that I care. Tell the gladiator he's not in my class. Tell him he has until the ninth day before the Kalends of February to strike the blow or his sister will die. She's safe for the moment, but she won't be for long. If he doesn't do what I ask I'll kill her, slowly, and enjoy it. If he tries to get to her, I'll roast him alive over an open fire and make her watch while my men have her. And I want a meeting with the old cripple.'

Rufus felt a calloused hand grip his chin and

raise his face, while another wiped away the blood that had masked his eyes.

'Did you hear me? A meeting.'

Rufus nodded.

'Ruuuufuuuuss.' The shriek was filled with a naked terror that chilled his heart.

Chaerea laughed again. 'Looks like you're going to need a midwife.'

Rufus pushed himself to his feet and stumbled to where Livia lay on the grass, writhing in agony.

'Galla,' he said.

But Livia gasped: 'No. No time. Help me. Such pain.'

Another scream froze him where he stood, helpless, lost, searching for aid he knew would not come.

Think.

Livia's dress, now stained with grass and blood, rode up above her thighs, exposing her splayed legs. The tiny crevice that had given him such joy was now distended and opening further before his eyes, a blue-veined dome forcing its way from deep within her body. This was impossible. It could not happen. She was too small.

Livia moaned and her breath came in short desperate explosions. Her eyes bulged as she shook her head from side to side.

He must do something.

He knelt between her legs and frantically tore a piece of cloth from his tunic and wiped hopelessly between her thighs. She screamed again. And again. He stopped the wiping as a mucus-covered head slipped from the opening.

'Please,' she begged.

He manoeuvred in front of her tortured body and tried to take the head between his hands, but it was too slippery.

With all his being he wanted to run. Anywhere. But he could not leave her. He tried again, with just as little success. If he could only get a purchase on the head, he might be able to pull it with enough force to help her move it.

But that might kill the child. His child.

It took an hour.

In the end, nature and his Livia provided the force. First the baby's shoulders, then the waist and finally its legs squirmed through the narrow gap of her pelvis and on to the grass between her legs. And with it came the blood. More blood than Rufus had ever seen. Even in the arena.

Of course, he tried. He pushed the torn cloth from his tunic deep inside her, ripped another, and another, until he stood naked. But the blood kept coming.

Throughout it all, he spoke to her; an unending litany of love and hope and lies. She could no longer reply. But the reproach in her eyes told him she knew she was dying, and that it was his fault, but that she forgave him.

Her golden skin turned first grey, then marble white. Her breathing grew gradually shallower, until, with one last exhalation, she was gone.

He wanted to scream his hatred to the world. He wanted it to know how worthless it was. He wanted revenge. But he could only stand over her, brain refusing to acknowledge his loss, even though she lay lifeless before him.

The baby cried; a long annoyed wail that cut the morning silence like a knife.

It was a boy. A tiny, ugly, wizened thing with a shock of dark hair and a penis the size of his little finger from which there arched a curve of golden liquid. Rufus picked up his son and carried him to the elephant house.

Bersheba moved uneasily as he entered the barn, shying away and pulling at her shackle. It was only then that he realized he was covered in blood from head to foot. He laid the baby carefully by the cistern and washed himself down with the icy water, shaking spastically from the cold and delayed shock.

But there was one more thing. He knew what he must do.

He had no choice.

He fetched a piece of cloth from the dusty room he and Livia had called home and soaked it in the cistern. Bending down over the baby, he carefully wiped away the dry mucus and blood from its face. It grizzled in irritation and glared at him with piercing blue eyes, then it twitched its tiny flat nose and the glare transformed into something akin to a toothless smile. Yes, a smile. Today, my son, *my son*, smiled at me for the first time.

His head spun, a palpitation hammered his chest and he collapsed on the mud floor. He curled up in a foetal ball by the tiny wriggling body of his son, lost in a maze of contradiction.

But he had no choice. He had no way to care for the boy.

Steeling himself, he forced himself up, made certain the cloth was well soaked, then very

351

gently placed it over the baby's face.

It wriggled and struggled for breath, tiny limbs jerking as it fought for life.

He almost gave in. His hand moved to within an inch of the cloth before he willed it back.

It had to be done.

'No.'

The voice came from behind him and he turned to find the Emperor standing in the doorway flanked by two of his guards.

'Let the child live.'

Rufus looked at him, dazed.

'Let the child live.' The words were a command.

One of the guards moved towards the baby, but before he could reach it Rufus removed the cloth to reveal a tiny face mottled blue and red and gasping for air.

'Find a nursemaid,' Caligula ordered the guard. 'There must be plenty of them in the palace. If not, seize one from elsewhere.' He turned back to Rufus. 'I have heard of your loss and I am sorry for it.'

Rufus stared at the Emperor. He was confused. Was this a joke? Some kind of trick? He looked around. If it was, where was the audience?

'You are surprised?' Caligula asked, but he was no longer the Caligula who inspired terror. 'You should not be. Today, I am a god, but once I was a man, with all the frailties that make a man weak. I too had a wife. Her name was Junia Claudilla. She was beautiful and kind and she died giving birth to my son. Perhaps, if she had lived ... if my son had lived ... things would be different. I would be different.' The voice became sharper again. 'You will receive help to look after the child. If you are not given enough, send word to me. Here, a gift to celebrate his birth. You will call the boy Gaius, of course.'

The remaining Praetorian handed Rufus two large gold coins. Rufus stammered his thanks, but the Emperor waved a hand in dismissal and turned to leave.

'Chaerea.' The word hung in the air between them like wood smoke on a still autumn after-noon. The Emperor turned and looked directly into Rufus's eyes. Caligula the predator was back. Was this insolence? Was it worthy of punishment? It seemed not.

'Cassius Chaerea has overstepped himself,' he said. 'I gave him my friendship, but he has not repaid it with faith.'

'Let me face him in the arena.'

Caligula looked at him quizzically. Should he allow it? It might be interesting. But in the end he shook his head. 'I think not. Who would look after my elephant when he killed you?'

With Cupido's help, Rufus dug a child's grave for Livia beside the mound beneath which Fronto rested, while the boy, Gaius, gurgled in the arms of his new nursemaid, a plump, mousy girl, who said little and expected less from life. She had lost her own baby to red throat disease and was satisfied to have another to hold in its stead.

When they had placed the last sod on Livia's grave he told the gladiator what Chaerea had said about Aemilia, and watched his face set hard as granite.

'We are agreed. Chaerea will die. At my hands or yours, it does not matter which, but he will die and his death will not be quick. I swear it by the old gods. First we must find Aemilia before they kill her.' And there the gladiator halted, because they had no idea where Chaerea held Aemilia. She could be in the Castra Praetorium, but Cupido doubted it. The presence of a female captive would not be a secret for long in a barracks holding five thousand men. But if she was not there, where was she? Chaerea was a rich man, with a dozen houses in the city. She could be in any one. He also had plenty of wealthy friends who would give him the use of an out of the way place where a meeting of like-minded individuals would not attract the wrong kind of attention.

Rufus's mind was still numb, and he struggled to focus on the living rather than the dead. Livia was gone, he understood that, but he knew the full impact had still to come, along with the loneliness it would bring. He would mourn her in his own time. First he had to help Cupido save Aemilia's life. His chest filled to bursting with a cold rage and he vowed he would find her, and avenge Livia at the same time.

But how to find her?

'I think I know someone who might be able to help us.'

Cupido stared at his friend. Could it be that simple?

'You were unwise to involve Claudius in your plans. I would have counselled against it.' Callistus sat behind his desk looking down his long nose at the two men standing side by side in front of it. 'Chaerea may act like a fool, but he does not lack intelligence, or support. He has spies among the opposition faction in the Guard. He was bound to discover any conspiracy against him involving someone so senior, and once he did he was bound to act. His fear of the information I passed to you was overcome by his fear of this greater threat. He blamed your wife,' he nodded to Rufus, then looked at Cupido, 'and he took your sister as a hostage to ensure your cooperation in the other matter he believes is so secret.'

'You know so much about Chaerea's affairs it is difficult to believe you are not part of them,' Cupido said harshly. 'If so, you know where Aemilia is being held.'

Callistus gave a tight smile. 'That is possible, but why should I tell a broken-down gladiator and a rancid animal handler? What have I to gain?'

'Your life.' Cupido's sword appeared a hair's breadth from Callistus's throat. The imperial secretary frowned, but didn't flinch from the blade.

'You owe me a life,' Rufus said, gently pushing the sword to one side. 'I am here to collect it.'

Callistus swallowed and rubbed his throat. 'It is always a pleasure to deal with a reasonable man.'

He described a large white villa, close to the temple of Minerva.

Cupido's brow creased as his mind dissected the information. 'I know that house,' he cried. 'It is on the Argiletum out by Augustus's forum. It belongs to Chaerea's lieutenant, Sabinus. It will be difficult to approach by stealth, but not impossible.'

'No, not impossible,' Callistus agreed. 'But dangerous, for you and your sister. Chaerea has placed six of his men there to guard her – or to kill her, if that should become necessary.'

'Then we have no time to waste here.' Cupido turned to Rufus. 'Meet me in my quarters. Wear your Praetorian uniform – it will disguise you and give us greater authority. We can be there within the hour.'

'Wait!' Callistus said. 'If you go uncloaked you will not get off the Palatine. Chaerea has issued a warrant for your arrest. He has guards on every corner. The only way you will reach the villa is to fly like a bird or burrow underground like a mole.'

Underground? The thought came to both of them simultaneously. Rufus could see it forming in Cupido's eyes, even as the image of the map filled his head. The green line and the red. The one leading from the Palatine to the Velabrum below the Vicus Tuscus, and the other slicing north *under* the forum and out past the Senate House towards the Argiletum and the white villa.

He felt a thrill of fear. 'The Cloaca.'

Cupido's voice was brittle with excitement. 'Even if it does not take us all the way, it will get us close enough to ensure we reach the villa un-molested. We will need torches and...'

Rufus heard his voice, but the words faded away. He couldn't rid himself of a vision of crazy old Varrus and the horror etched on his face.

They would save Aemilia – but only if they survived the river of the dead.

356

XLI

Was he losing his mind?

Only yesterday he had demanded that Julius Canus, the Stoic philosopher, be brought before him so they could continue their discussion of the previous week, only to be reminded that Canus was already dead, executed at *his* order. He had liked Canus. The man had a sense of humour. Too many people laughed only because he, Caesar, laughed. Canus laughed because he thought something was funny.

Had he become such a monster he could kill a man and not even remember it?

He felt like crying. He despised self-pity, but he had often felt like crying since Drusilla died. More so since she had abandoned him – for she had abandoned him. They had all abandoned him. The reassuring voices had stopped on the very day he declared himself a god. Had he been wrong? Had he gone too far? And if he had, what would be the gods' revenge?

He winced as a fiery streak of pain scored its way across his brain. Agrippina's medicines no longer helped him. Was this their doing?

What could he do to appease them? Surely there must be something? But he had tried, tried so hard, and they had rejected him. When he had sacrificed a white bull to Mars, the fool of a priest had botched the stroke and blood had spattered his cloak of imperial purple. The augurs had stared at each other and whispered that it was an omen of ill fortune. He had laughed at their fears, but inside he knew they were right.

Then the answer came to him and it was so simple he wondered why he hadn't recognized it earlier.

He had lost his way. Been blinded by the plots and the tragedies, and goaded into the terrible retribution that inevitably followed. He must find it again, find that magical thing that had made Rome love him in those few short months after he and Gemellus had been crowned. He sighed. If only he could bring Gemellus back.

But there was a way. The old way. He would hold a games, such a games as the world had never seen. The crowd would not witness a few duels, or even a battle. They would see a war. And not gladiators. Soldiers. The Emperor's own Praetorian Guard. The Wolves against the Scorpions. To the death. He would fill the Circus Maximus to overflowing, not once, nor twice, but a dozen times. Every Roman, rich or poor, would attend, and when it was done they would love their Emperor as never before.

He would announce it tomorrow. After the theatre.

It was raining steadily by the time Rufus was ready. At Cupido's suggestion he wore the dark Praetorian tunic Callistus had supplied him with on the day of Drusilla's divinity. He would have felt much braver in the sculpted iron breastplate normally worn with it, but when they met outside his quarters the gladiator counselled against armour.

'We will certainly have to fight when we reach the villa, and they will outnumber us, but first we have to get there,' he explained. 'We don't know what we face in the Cloaca. We only have the word of Decimus that it is passable at all. We should travel light. Weapons, torches, a cloak, for it will be cold below ground, but no armour.'

Rufus carried the torches and flints in a cloth bag. Cupido gave him a short sword of standard legionary pattern, and he strapped the belt round his waist with the scabbard on his hip.

They waited until it was fully dark before they set out, using the time to piece together their memories of Varrus's two maps. They knew the general line of the Cloaca Palatina, but not its exact location. Cupido was certain they would recognize it when they reached the main shaft of the Maxima.

'There must be an entrance somewhere on the hill, but how do we find it?' Cupido wondered. Rufus didn't give him an answer until they were outside, with the rain in their faces. He pointed to the little runnels between the cobbles of the path, which trickled to gather in a shallow gutter.

'The Cloaca is a sewer, but it is also a drain. We follow the water. Decimus said it is visible on the surface. We will know it when we see it.'

They searched for less than five minutes before Cupido gave a cry of triumph. 'Here,' he said, pointing to the ground at his feet. Rufus ran to see what he had discovered.

Staring up at him, slick with rain, was a heavily

bearded half-human face, with empty eyes and a slit for a mouth. It was a face meant to frighten; a water god guarding a hidden kingdom. The face was cut into a circular stone drain cover, about two and a half feet across, and the run-off from the paths disappeared into a narrow gap round its edge. They could hear the water falling into some sort of empty space below.

'Here, let me open it.' Cupido pushed Rufus aside. He bent low over the drain cover, but recoiled gagging. 'Jupiter! Even for a sewer this stinks.' He tried to work his fingers below the gap at the rim, but there was not enough room for a proper hold. Undeterred, the gladiator shifted position and reached for the mouth slit.

'There's only room for one hand,' he grunted. 'I can't get enough purchase to move it, never mind lift it. Maybe we can use your sword to lever it up?'

'I think I might have a better answer,' Rufus said, reaching into the cloth bag. 'Move aside.'

Cupido was reluctant to concede defeat. 'If I can't lift it, you won't be able to,' he said sourly.

Rufus grinned at him. 'This is a time for brains, not muscle.' He held up the object he had retrieved from the bag so Cupido could see it. It was the strange T-shaped metal tool Varrus had worn round his neck.

'I thought it might come in useful,' he said, taking over Cupido's position. 'See, the bar at the bottom fits perfectly in the mouth slit, and if I turn it like this...' Using the upper bar of the T as a handle, he rotated the key 90 degrees, so the bottom bar hooked below the stone at both sides.

'Now I should be able to lift it.' He heaved two-handed, using all his strength, and the cover rose until he could move it to one side.

'Ugh.' He choked and took a step back. With the cover out of place the stench from the Cloaca Palatina hit him in the face with almost physical force. He looked at Cupido, and then both stared into the menacing black void at their feet. It was as if they had uncovered the door to the under-world.

For a moment it seemed simpler to walk away.

Cupido sensed his dread. 'Remember, Rufus, when you waited in the room below the Taurus? I saw you struggle with your demons and over-come them. To step into the unknown took true courage and you found that courage within your-self. Whatever is down this hole is less frightening than walking out in front of five thousand of the mob. You can do it. For Aemilia. I am just as fearful, but I would face Hades himself rather than leave her in Chaerea's hands.'

At the mention of Aemilia's name, Rufus felt the empty space within him fill up. Was this cour-age or simply conviction? It didn't matter. It was enough. He gave Cupido a half-hearted smile.

'All right, but you can go first. You are better prepared to meet Hades than I will ever be.'

Cupido nodded grimly. 'So be it,' he said, and lowered himself into the darkness. Rufus slung the bag across his shoulder and sat on the lip of the hole.

'There are hand and footholds cut into the wall,' Cupido's disembodied voice echoed up from the shaft. 'It's a little awkward to reach the first one, but once you are on it you will be able to lower yourself. Take care, though – the steps are slippery. I don't want you to land on my head.'

Rufus felt with his foot for the first notch. When he found it, he turned and lowered himself over the edge until he felt the second foothold.

His head was at ground level when he remembered the drain cover. He couldn't just leave it where it was. Anyone who discovered it would realize where they were. It was possible their enemies might send a patrol after them. He twisted awkwardly until he could get both hands around the cover. Maybe if he could just perch it on one edge?

He succeeded in moving it almost to where he wanted it, then worked his way down a step. Just another inch would do it. But gravity was working against him and the full weight of the cover was on his arms and he had his back to one wall of the shaft with his feet in one of the notches. It was too heavy! He couldn't hold it. He had moved it too far and if he tried to push it back any longer he would lose his footing and plummet down the shaft on to Cupido. He strained and grunted, but the ache in his shoulders and his arms turned into spears of agony and the drain cover settled into place with a sharp crunch.

'What's happening?' Cupido demanded. 'What was that?'

Rufus put one shoulder to the cover, but it felt as if it was cemented into place. They were trapped.

He made his way down the vertical shaft a foot

at a time. In his imagination it was bottomless and it came as a surprise when there were no more notches, but solid ground beneath his feet. He calculated he must have descended twenty-five to thirty feet.

He turned slowly, arms in front of him like a blind man. He knew instinctively he was in a wider space than the claustrophobic drainage shaft, not because he could see anything, but because the darkness was a deeper shade of black. A sort of darker darkness that was almost solid.

Down here it was a different kind of cold; rawer and hungrier, and he was glad Cupido had thought to bring the heavy cloaks. He heard the trickle of water down the shaft, and, close by, a heavier rushing sound.

'Are you going to get the torches out or are we going to stand here all day?'

The words came from six inches in front of his face and he almost fell over in surprise. He fumbled in the cloth bag for the first torch.

'Take this,' he said, holding the torch out in the general direction of the invisible Cupido.

'How can I take it if I can't see it?'

Ah! With his free hand, he located the flint. Ideally, he needed a third hand to strike metal against stone while holding the torch close enough to light, but somehow he managed it. The flame flickered for a second then blossomed until it illuminated a dozen paces around him.

They were standing on a paved walkway beside a dark brown stream composed of things he didn't like to think about, which flowed along a stone culvert perhaps three paces wide. The culvert ran down a tunnel which stretched away into the darkness under a barrel-vaulted roof of dressed stone blocks about a foot wide and three times as long. The roof curved six or seven inches above their heads, slick with hundreds of years of accumulated slime which hung in obscene feet-long tendrils, like wisps of a witch's hair. For a few seconds Rufus's astonishment overcame his fright. How could this marvel, another world, exist beneath his feet and he not realize it?

A shuffling noise from beyond the circle of light reminded him of his earlier fears and his hand flew to his sword.

'Rats,' Cupido said. 'Rats and sewers go together.'

Rufus laughed nervously. He looked around him. 'Which direction do we take?'

'Follow the flow. It's only going one way, to the Cloaca Maxima, and that's where we want to be. Let's go – we have wasted enough time. I want to reach the villa before dawn. Keep the second torch dry, and don't lose the flint. I wouldn't want to be stuck down here in the dark.'

Rufus mouthed a short prayer. He wished Cupido hadn't said that.

They started off down the tunnel, Rufus leading with the torch. At first, he set a good pace, but it quickly became apparent that the section into which they had descended gave a false impression of the Cloaca. The passage was not uniform. It had evidently been built and reconstructed, repaired and repaired again, over different periods, with different standards of workmanship and by men working to different ends.

The air in the tunnel was damp and fetid, rank with the stink of corruption and other people's shit. It became fixed in his throat like a solid thing, and he had to keep swallowing in order not to gag. Soon, the shaft narrowed, becoming ever more claustrophobic, until the walkway. was little more than a shelf and they had to inch forward one foot in front of the other to save from falling into the loathsome stream on their right. Rufus noticed it seemed a little swifter now and the height had risen marginally. At least the rain would wash away the filth more quickly.

The tiny walkway was an irritant at first, but quickly became a danger. The flickering torch gave off an uneven and barely helpful light, which, in places, seemed to be absorbed by the algae-slick walls. Pieces of stone crumbled beneath their feet, threatening to pitch them into the sewer. At one point the roof suddenly dropped to half its height and they had to crouch low with the torch held straight ahead in order to make progress. This happened at regular intervals and Cupido suggested it might have some architectural purpose.

It was also clear they were descending, almost imperceptibly, deeper into the earth.

They had been walking for perhaps ten minutes when they heard the voices.

'Douse the torch,' Cupido whispered.

'What?'

'Put the torch out or they'll see it.'

'But we'll be in the dark. We can't fight them if we can't see them.'

'Better in the dark. We can hear them, but they

won't hear us.'

Reluctantly, Rufus placed the torch on the walk-way and gently stamped out the flames, doing as little damage as he could. He had a feeling they would need every flickering spark of both torches before the night was out.

He felt Cupido's reassuring hand on his shoulder. 'Now we wait.'

They sat in the darkness, listening; waiting for the voices to come closer. But the only things that approached them were the rats, which had been wary of the light, but now scampered by in ones and twos. Rufus jumped as he felt something touch his hand.

'Aaah!'

'Shhh.'

'I hate rats.'

'You told me you loved animals.'

'Not rats.'

'They can't hurt you.'

'Not even when they're the size of cats?'

Silence.

There was a strange, unearthly quality to the voices. Sometimes they were clear, as if they were close by, but then they would fade as if the wind had changed direction. Only there was no wind.

And then there was the stench. At first it had been sickening; a putrid, stomach-churning miasma so thick you could almost chew on it. But soon after they started walking their sense of smell had either become accustomed to it, or been overwhelmed by it. Now the smell was back, more powerful than ever.

Rufus felt Cupido stir behind him. 'We can't

stay here for ever. We have to move,' he hissed into the darkness.

'Go, then, but carefully. No light.'

Rufus thought this was foolish and said so, but began to feel his way along the wall. He had gone no more than half a dozen steps when the wall disappeared as the tunnel took a sharp left turn, and he ended with one foot in the ooze, cursing his ill fortune and his friend. It was only when he recovered that he noticed the light.

Only it wasn't a light, more a disturbance in the darkness; a place where the black was a little paler. He crawled slowly towards it.

It was at a section of wall where the tunnel made another turn, this time to the right. The pale patch was a dim reflection of some stronger light source a little further ahead.

He had almost reached the bend when the scream froze him to the tunnel wall. It was high-pitched and terrible, and it seemed to last an eternity before ending in a choking rattle, only to revive a second later in a new shrieking crescendo. Rufus felt for his lion's tooth charm and muttered another prayer. He hoped no human could scream that way, but he knew it was a vain hope. The cry had shattered his nerves and his legs shook as he rounded the corner, unwilling to confront whatever horrors awaited him there.

They had passed several of the slim drainage shafts at irregular intervals along the tunnel. This was different.

Before him was a large, bell-shaped chamber carved out of the rock. At the top of the bell, perhaps fifty feet above them, a shaft of flickering red light pierced the darkness and partly illuminated the space below. The base of the bell was a pool measuring twenty paces across, where the sable waters of the stream gathered before being channelled down a wider and deeper culvert. The reason for the pool became clear when he looked to left and right. This was the gathering place of the Cloaca Palatina, where the stinking waters met. Entering on either side were further tunnels, which helped keep the pool filled and the stream flowing.

The voices were quite distinct now, emanating along with the light from above. Cupido came up beside Rufus and whispered in his ear.

'Caligula's torture cells. I was chained there for two nights and witnessed his executioners at work. I thought the shaft was a well – now I know otherwise. Quickly, we are vulnerable here. We must move on.'

Cupido led as they worked their way silently towards the outlet channel.

Rufus turned to take a last look behind him. The surface of the pool was almost pretty, dancing in the soft glow from above. It happened so suddenly his mind didn't have time to register the details: a thundering explosion a few feet from his side that blinded him and showered him in a column of stinking, brown water. He froze, terrified that he was about to face the monster Decimus had spoken of, the one which had driven Varrus beyond the edge of sanity.

Trembling, he waited for it to rise from the waters to claim him, but, instead of some scaly dragon, a flash of white like the belly of a dead fish became visible just below the surface. As he watched, the white grew clearer and formed human shape. At first it floated face down, with its arms hanging beneath it; then, very gently, it turned over, as if to take a last look at the life it had left behind. Only it couldn't see, because it had no eyes.

Rufus swallowed hard, his throat filled with bile.

The toothless mouth was open wide in a rictus of sheer horror. As well as the eyes, the man's nose and ears had been removed. For it was a man, or had been before they had torn his sexual organs from his body with the red-hot pincers.

As he watched, the broken body continued its gentle roll and, with hardly a ripple, disappeared below the surface.

'Come.' Cupido shook him by the shoulder. 'Now I am certain we have no time to lose.'

Rufus shook his head to clear it.

'Hurry,' Cupido repeated. 'Did you not recognize him? Before the Emperor's executioners improved his looks he was Marcus Agrippa, a decurion of the Guard and one of Chaerea's closest allies. The net is closing. If Chaerea does not act soon he too will feel the hot kiss of the torturer's blade.'

Rufus relit the torch when they were clear of the chamber and to their relief they found the going easier as the tunnel and walkway widened to cope with the greater flow of water. And, Rufus noted, it was a much greater flow. Where before the waters had been slow-moving and their surface placid, they now rushed past and the surface was whipped to a filthy brown froth. A little further on, he noticed with alarm that the waters were lapping at the very edge of the culvert, and soon his feet were splashing in inches of sewage.

He stopped and turned to Cupido. 'Something is wrong here.'

The gladiator's eyes flashed in the torchlight. 'We have no choice. We have to go on. This is the only way we can reach Aemilia.'

Reluctantly, Rufus forced his way forward even though the flood rose first to his knees, then his thighs and finally to his waist.

He stopped again, and Cupido pushed him in the back. But this time Rufus did not move. He held the torch out in front of him.

'It's impossible. We have to go back. Look!'

Cupido followed his gaze and his heart quailed.

A dozen paces in front of them the torchlight was reflected by the surface of a new pool. This was one of the places where the roof shelved sharply away. At the far end of the pool only inches separated the glittering surface from the roof. The tunnel was impassable.

Rufus shook his head in despair. They had failed.

'Come, we will find another way,' he said, although he knew there was none. He put a hand on Cupido's shoulder, but the gladiator shrugged it off.

'No. This is the only way. Something has blocked the flow. If I can find what it is, I may be able to unblock it. Take this.' He shrugged off his cloak and unbuckled the long sword, then untied his tunic and removed it. 'Keep them dry. I will need them when we continue.'

Naked, he walked forward until the waters reached his shoulders, then began to swim through the noxious brown flood.

As he approached the far wall, he felt his hair touch the roof. For the first time he noticed more rats, swimming back and forth between a heap of white rubble jutting above the surface and the nearest dry land. Whatever the white thing was, it must be part of the blockage.

He was at the very edge of the torch's range and the sight that met him was so outrageous that at first his mind would not believe what he was seeing. But it was real. The white globe that first drew his attention was revealed as a grinning skull. Around it were other remains he recognized as vaguely human, and working steadily to strip them bare of flesh were the rats who had shared his swim.

This was Varrus's river of the dead. Caligula's army of victims. They had dammed the Cloaca Palatina solid.

Treading water, he turned to where Rufus stood up to his waist with the bundle of clothes and weapons over his shoulder.

'It is the way of these things that there is a keystone,' he shouted. 'If I can find it, the whole thing should collapse.'

Rufus heard his friend's words, but only had a vague understanding of their meaning. He looked on aghast as Cupido took a deep breath and dived.

Cupido knew it would be impossible to see and he feared the effect of the filth on his eyes, so he

371

kept them closed and felt his way cautiously towards the dam until he touched cold flesh. He was thankful the bodies beneath the water were at least whole, and fortunately had not been there for long or they would have come apart in his hands. There also did not seem to be as many as he had feared. The layer at the top was wider than that at the bottom, probably due to the buoyancy of the bodies and the action of the water.

He tugged at a cold arm, struggling to contain his disgust at the feel of the wrinkled, water-worn dead flesh, but whatever it was attached to was stuck fast. He felt his chest tighten as his air began to run out and he kicked himself to the surface, where he gasped in two or three breaths before diving straight under again.

This time he had some idea where he was going and soon he had a good grip on a clammy leg. At first it seemed as firmly wedged as the first body, but as he worked at it he felt it move, and as it did so he felt the others move around it. He hauled at it for another twenty seconds, levering the leg back and forward and feeling the movement become easier. His air was almost up. Noting his position as well as he could with his eyes shut, he resurfaced, gasped in the air he needed, and immediately dived back.

Now, where was the leg? His fingers touched a face. It was a woman's face and he recoiled in disgust. He thought of Quintillia and her ravaged beauty. Why was it so much worse when it was a woman? Not there. To the left. Yes. The leg. He took it and, bracing his feet against the other submerged bodies, hauled as hard as he could. At

372

first, nothing happened, so he heaved again. With a bubbling sound of trapped air being loosed the leg and the body attached to it came free, and the dam of death collapsed in upon itself.

For the merest heartbeat Cupido experienced a surge of elation. Then he felt the power of the flood and realized that in freeing the dam he had doomed himself.

Fool! Why had he not foreseen this – prepared for it? The incredible force as tens of thousands of gallons of backed-up waters found release gripped him tight and sucked him in among the bodies. It was as if the dead were clinging to him, were determined to keep him with them until he was as dead as they. His chest tightened and the pressure to breathe became overwhelming. He was drowning. With the strength of despair, he pushed himself free and attempted to swim to the surface, but he was too weak. The current would not release him. He raised an arm and felt it break clear, but by then it was too late. He was propelled into a whirling vortex of flailing limbs and empty-eyed faces, just another powerless piece of flesh among the human flotsam.

XLII

Rufus was too far away to see what had caused the blockage, but he knew his friend would never give up. Not in this life. While Cupido was submerged, he held his breath as if it would somehow help the gladiator. When he had to gasp for the next breath before Cupido resurfaced, he feared he would never see the young German again, but then there was a splash and the golden hair broke into view for a few precious seconds.

After what seemed an incredibly long interval, Cupido surfaced again, only to disappear as quickly as he had appeared. When the water suddenly swirled in the centre of the pool he knew Cupido had defeated the odds. It was only when he realized what was happening below the surface that the elation turned to fascinated horror. He screamed out his friend's name and a moment later a despairing arm broke the surface as if reaching for an invisible handhold. Then the entire pool vanished through the tunnel in a single almighty rush.

Rufus saw what happened, but his mind wouldn't accept it. What had been six or eight feet of water was now a small stream bubbling between the two walls of the culvert. And he was alone.

He dropped the torch and slumped against the wall, staring at the empty space where the pool had been. The road ahead was open, but he couldn't move. He could think, but not act. He told himself to get up, but his legs would not accept the order from his brain.

The reality of what had happened was too awful to take in. Cupido gone? It did not seem possible. Cupido couldn't die – he was bigger than death. But his own eyes had seen a man he loved – yes, he understood now that what he felt for Cupido had gone beyond friendship and respect to something that could only be called love – swept away in that unstoppable wall of water.

The torch spluttered and went out, leaving him in darkness, but he made no attempt to locate the second.

So this was despair, a physical force that crushed him into the earth and robbed him of will. The courage that had sustained him in the long walk through this underground nightmare had drained away. He could barely find the strength to breathe. He resigned himself to death.

But deep within him the unquenchable thing that was his spirit wouldn't allow it. It chewed at his brain with a message. Time. There was something he had to do and time was important. His head was filled with coloured images, but none of them meant anything to him. Then the colours merged and from their centre a face appeared. Aemilia. He had to find Aemilia.

But what was the point? Without Cupido he was nothing.

With that thought he felt failure wrap itself around him once more like a shroud. He giggled hysterically. If he didn't move the rats would feast on his flesh. The thought galvanized him, but still he could not find the strength to move.

Then the voice whispered in his ear. It whispered of honour and of duty, of loyalty and of courage. And when he still did not move it flayed him with scorn and mocked him for his weakness. He willed it to go away, but it was relentless. He was disappointed it was not Aemilia's, but he knew in his heart she could never have shamed him into movement. Only Livia could do that.

Gradually, his mind repaired itself and he raised himself on shaking legs. He located the second torch and lit it, and as it flared in his hand it reminded him of the time he had wasted. He set off downstream towards the Maxima.

The tunnel seemed to go on for ever now he was alone. Cupido's presence had sustained him; now each leaden step felt pointless. It didn't matter how Cupido had intended to attack the villa, Rufus knew he could never do it. He did not have the skill or the courage to fight six trained soldiers, and, if he tried, Aemilia would be dead before he reached her. Cupido would have used his strength. He would have to use stealth. There would be a way. There had to be a way.

When he finally reached the outlet where the Cloaca Palatina met the Cloaca Maxima, he was faced with a featureless wall. He knew he had to turn upstream, to the left. The walkway was now on the far side of the channel. He threw the cloth bag and the two cloaks across first, then followed them.

He felt his confidence returning. At least the going was better in the main sewer, the walkway wider and kept in good repair. He would find a way out, and when he did he would meet each challenge as it came. Even if it meant his death.

He had gone less than a dozen paces when he heard the noise behind him. Another rat? No. It sounded like...

He turned, pushing the flaming torch in the direction of the sound, drawing his sword with his right hand. It had been a human voice. A whisper. They had followed him down here. They must still be in the Palatina spur. Idiot! Put the light out, remember what Cupido said about fighting in the dark. He extinguished the torch against the wall and laid it carefully on the ground.

Silently and in complete darkness, he made his way back to the junction of the two sewers. That was it! He would ambush them as they came out of the Palatina into the Maxima. Even better, downstream of the junction he had noticed a buttress where he could stay hidden while they passed. He would follow them in the darkness and take them by surprise, one by one. Who knew how many he would be able to kill before they discovered him?

He felt his way along the wall past the gushing inlet of the Palatina until he came to the buttress. He edged round it carefully – he'd look a fool if he fell in the sewer in the dark – and froze.

He was standing on something alive!

Slowly, he raised the sword and took a deep breath as he prepared to chop down on the thing below him.

'Is this how you treat a friend?' a voice croaked weakly. 'As if he was a doorstep?'

Rufus almost fainted away. 'Cupido!'

'Please fetch a torch. When I saw the light I thought you were coming for me, then when the torch went out... I have had enough darkness to last a lifetime.'

When Rufus returned, he saw that the gladiator was lying naked against the buttress, his face lined with pain and his left hand cradling his right shoulder. He shook uncontrollably as his body fought the raw cold eating at it. Rufus picked up the cloaks and tried to wrap them around him.

'Careful,' Cupido cried. 'My shoulder.'

'Is it broken?'

Cupido shook his head. 'I think it became dislocated when I was thrown against the wall by the force of the flood, but it saved my life. If I had followed my new friends I would be food for the Tiber catfish by now.'

'I can reset it. I have done it with antelope.'

Cupido gave him a weary smile. 'We can test your medical skills later. Heat first. I am as cold as a week-old corpse. Unless you can warm me I will be going nowhere this night, perhaps ever.'

At the gladiator's instruction, Rufus wrapped one cloak gently around him. The other he used to rub Cupido's flesh, which was puckered and wrinkled and in places almost purple. His back was scratched to the bone by contact with the rough sewer walls and Rufus at once marvelled at his survival and feared for the long-term effects of his immersion in Rome's filth.

He quickly realized the rubbing was doing little good. If anything Cupido's face grew paler. Taking the big cloak, he wrapped it around them both and gently took his friend in his arms to allow the heat from his own body to warm him.

Cupido opened his eyes and Rufus saw a glint of humour in their grey depths.

'Am I so weak it has come to this? I pray my father is not looking down on me now to see how low I have fallen.'

He closed his eyes again, but now Rufus noticed that at least there was a hint of colour in his cheeks.

After about ten minutes Cupido stirred again. 'This romance has gone on long enough. Bring me my tunic,' he croaked. He shrugged the cloak from his injured shoulder. 'Now you can do your worst. Don't stop if I cry out.'

Rufus felt his friend flinch as his fingers searched the taut muscles for the pressure point he needed.

'I... I don't know if I can do it. It's different. The bones...'

'You must. Here, I will show you. One hand here,' he indicated a point on his arm, 'and the other here.' He placed Rufus's hand on the bone sticking out of his shoulder. 'Now push, hard, with the one and pull with the other.'

Rufus heaved with all his strength and his friend grunted in agony, but the bone returned to its proper position with an obscene popping sound.

'If that is the extent of your medical knowledge I pity your animals. The arm will be useless tonight, but if I live it will be as good as it ever was.' He put a hand on Rufus's shoulder and raised himself to his feet. 'Truly this is the river of the dead Varrus spoke of. Working each day with the sights I have seen, in the stink and the darkness, would drive any man out of his wits.'

Rufus helped him with his tunic and belted the long sword round his waist. Cupido drew the weapon from its scabbard with his left hand and attempted a couple of practice cuts.

'That is better. The iron gives me strength. Perhaps one arm will be enough after all, but if it is not,' he looked at Rufus steadily, 'you must be my right hand if the need arises. Now let us go, and with speed. I fear we are behind schedule already.'

'How will we know when we have reached where we need to be, and how will we get out?' Rufus asked the two questions which had been worrying him since the drain cover closed over his head.

'We will know,' Cupido said and there was a comforting certainty in his voice. He took his dagger and scratched on the stone at his feet. 'We are here, under the Velabrum near the Vicus Tuscus, just below the Emperor's palace on the Palatine Hill. If I remember it correctly, the Cloaca turns left beneath the forum, and then right past the Senate House. Any time after that right turn we will be within striking distance of the villa. While I waited for you tonight, I prayed to Venus Cloacina and made a sacrifice to her. It was a worthy sacrifice and I asked her help in this thing of Aemilia. Cloacina will provide.'

After about twenty minutes, they came to the stairs.

Rufus might have missed them. They were just another dark shadow on the wall to their left. But Cupido's senses were so acute he halted directly in front of them. It was clear the ground level was now just above their heads, because there were only half a dozen steps leading up to a drainage cover similar to the one by which they had entered.

'This must be one of the main accesses,' Cupido noted, pointing to the well-worn stairs.

Rufus put his shoulder to the drain cover. He expected it to be difficult to move, but because of the steps he had the leverage he needed and it shifted easily at his first push. He extinguished the torch and climbed out into the steady drizzle of a grey winter dawn.

When Cupido saw where they had emerged, he laughed with pleasure. They were standing in a small stone circle about five paces across, with walls of waist height. On one side of the circle was a little altar with a marble statue of a woman holding a myrtle branch. 'Look, it is the goddess. She has favoured us as I asked.'

He was right. They were in the little shrine dedicated to Venus Cloacina, goddess of the sewers. In front of him, beyond the corner of the nearby basilica, Rufus could make out the walls of the forum of Augustus and the distinctive roof of the temple of Mars Ultor, where the sword of Julius Caesar was kept. To the right of it, two hundred and fifty yards away, would be the temple of Minerva, and beyond that the villa of Sabinus. And Aemilia.

'I had hoped to arrive here in full dark,' Cupido said. 'But we must make use of what little we have.'

They pulled the cloaks over their heads and moved cautiously up the deserted street. Rufus knew they were close when Cupido pulled him into the shadow of an apartment doorway.

'You would think, with the bribes at his disposal, Sabinus could afford something better,' the gladiator chuckled. Rufus knew Cupido was attempting to put him at ease, but he could hear the hard-edged excitement of the coming fight in his friend's voice. In truth, the villa was not massive, but it was substantial enough, a two-storey white-stucco house set back from the roadway in its own grounds. A wall surrounded it, but one built for privacy, not for defence. From their hiding place they could see the orange glow of a substantial fire.

Cupido ignored the main gate, a stout wooden structure that was firmly closed, and no doubt barred on the inside. 'We will go in at the corner of the wall, see, where the top of that big tree is just visible. The guards have lit the fire to give them better visibility, but also to stem their fears. Yet it might count against them,' he said thoughtfully.

They moved stealthily across the street and slid along the length of the wall until they reached the point Cupido had indicated.

'Stay low when you reach the top, and wait for me,' the gladiator whispered, boosting Rufus up with his good hand, so he could lever himself on to the top of the wall. Despite his injured arm, Cupido joined him with the practised ease of an acrobat. Silently, they dropped into the villa's courtyard.

XLIII

Cupido's instincts hadn't let him down. Four men in Praetorian uniform huddled close round a pile of blazing logs in attitudes that indicated they'd spent more time than they wanted with the damp winter chill eating into their bones.

They seemed mesmerized by the dancing golden flames at their front, and the columns of sparks that danced upwards whenever a log cracked. Even if the shadows from the trees and shrubs hadn't hidden them, Rufus thought it unlikely their entry would have been noticed.

'Too long in barracks,' Cupido whispered in his ear. 'But they are still dangerous. Stay by my right side and use your sword as you did to defend the Emperor and we will win through.'

For the first time, Rufus felt the flutter of fear in his chest. Cupido sensed it and placed a hand on his shoulder. 'Have faith, Rufus. You hold their attention and I will take them. But remember they have Aemilia inside. If we are delayed they will execute her. Speed is all, not clean kills.'

With that he set off, crouched low among the bushes – like a hunting panther, but infinitely more deadly. The guards were only twenty paces away, but they had no clue to his coming until he was upon them. By then it was too late.

Rufus had seen Cupido fight many times before, but this was different. Here was cold, merciless fury matched by clinical execution. The big sword took the first Praetorian's head off at the neck with a single sweeping blow and sent it spinning into the fire. Two of the survivors were raw recruits and froze, paralysed by the sight of their comrade's face melting among the flames, but the third spun towards his attacker. He was a veteran, and when he saw Cupido he knew he was already dead. But he was brave. He snarled his defiance and his blade chopped upwards at Cupido's defenceless belly. The gladiator parried the blow almost effortlessly and with a twist of his wrist left the soldier staring in disbelief at the stump of his severed sword arm.

The remaining guards were still well armed, but their shock and terror rendered them defenceless. Together they dropped their swords by the fire and fell to their knees in surrender. But Cupido had neither the time nor the inclination for mercy. He swung right and left and the men fell screaming among the glowing embers at the fire's edge.

'Finish them,' he said, and ran towards the doors of the villa.

For a moment, Rufus stood open-mouthed at the order but logic told him the three men were already as good as dead. The first fighter sat in a growing pool of his own blood with a dazed expression, and the others were expiring noisily and roasting at the same time. It was a mercy, really.

When he entered the villa, time might have been standing still. The only movement came from the young Praetorian mewing pitifully beside the door as he attempted to push his intestines back into the great tear Cupido had just carved in his stomach.

Beyond him, Cupido's back was to Rufus, and eight paces beyond him was a scar-faced soldier, evidently the leader of the guard detachment. And Aemilia.

She stared at her brother with a look that might have been irritation. It certainly wasn't fear, although fear would have been perfectly justified given the short sword that pricked beneath her chin and only needed one good push to skewer her. The sword was held by scar-face, who stood

384

with his back to the russet-painted plaster wall and was scared enough for both of them.

'One more step and I kill her,' he rasped.

'I thought you were supposed to rape her while she watched me roast alive?' Cupido said conversationally.

The challenge in Aemilia's captor's face changed to a frown of confusion.

'That was what Chaerea planned for me, wasn't it? That I would cook over an open fire while you had your way with Aemilia.'

The soldier spat. 'If you drop that sword maybe we can come to a different arrangement. Something that suits both of us?' The words were an offer of negotiation, but there was a glitter of anticipation in his eyes that betrayed his true plans.

'I don't think so.' Cupido smiled, and the glitter in scar-face's left eye was extinguished as it magically sprouted a four-foot sword that transfixed his skull and pinned him to the wall.

Rufus hadn't even seen Cupido move. The stroke was so impressive he felt like applauding. He was never certain whether it was an arena trick honed by a hundred hours of practice, or a sleight of hand Cupido learned at his father's knee. However he came by the skill, it was horrifically effective. The gladiator had whipped the long sword up underhand with a flick of his wrist and speared a target an inch across only a hand-span from Aemilia's right ear.

'You took your time, brother,' Aemilia said, unwrapping the stricken man's arm from her throat. She looked at him with detached interest. He wasn't dead, but it couldn't be long. His body jerked and shook as he hung there, held fast by the iron blade through his head. His remaining eye went through a range of emotions: dread of what was inevitably to come, puzzlement at how he had been so careless, and perhaps a mute plea to have this dreadful alien thing removed.

Aemilia spat in his face and wrenched the sword free, allowing him to drop like a stone.

'I thought you said you didn't have a brother?' Cupido said.

She stuck out her tongue and handed him his sword. 'Phawwww! You stink.'

'That's a nice way to talk to your saviour. But you're right, where is the bathhouse? And do they have any other clothes?'

She gave him instructions and he went off muttering to himself about ungrateful women, leaving Rufus and Aemilia alone apart from the unfortunate, sword-gutted youth who was now attempting to crawl out of the door.

'Ah, yes,' Aemilia said, as if she had just re-membered something important. She bent over the young soldier and pulled at a pouch at his belt.

'I thought you had it,' she said triumphantly, recovering her jewelled dagger. 'Where are your lusty promises now, Marcus?' And she drew the blade across the boy's throat with appalling sud-denness, so that his blood painted the mosaic floor bright red. She looked up and saw the horror on Rufus's face.

'What do you think he would have done to me if you hadn't come, he and that pig over there?' She pointed at the one-eyed veteran. 'Do you want me to tell you what they planned for me? I'm sure you'd find it instructive.'

Rufus shook his head. He suddenly felt very tired. He swayed on his feet and might have fallen if Aemilia hadn't taken him in her arms.

'I am sorry, Rufus. I wasn't thinking. They told me what that brute Chaerea did to Livia. He will follow these swine over the Styx in his own good time.' She lifted his mouth to hers and before he realized what was happening she kissed him, long and hard, so the breath was driven from his lungs and his hammering heart tried to escape from his chest. 'You saved me, you and my brother. Accept this as the first part of my reward, but not the last.'

He stepped away from her, confused by the contradictions going through his mind. A second ago this woman had cut a dying boy's throat, and now...

'I...' He stopped at the sound of approaching footsteps. Aemilia raised her still bloody dagger, but he waved her away and stepped to the side of the door, sword in hand. He allowed the intruder to walk past him into the room before putting the sword point to his spine with enough force to pierce the cloth of his tunic.

'Is this the way you greet a friend?' Narcissus demanded irritably. 'Callistus informed me you might need help. He has at last decided which way the wind blows. However, I see you don't require my aid. I am most impressed.' He indicated the prone bodies of scar-face and his comrade and the bloody floor around them.

'What help would you have provided, eunuch?'

Cupido appeared in the doorway dressed in fresh clothing, his hair plastered like strands of gold against his skull. 'I see no sword.'

Narcissus greeted the jibe with a tight smile, but his eyes gleamed dangerously. 'You are right, of course: not all of us are so adept at dealing death as you. Yet even a simple scribe might be of use in times of danger. I bring a message as well as offering aid, and it is this: the Praetorian tribune Cassius Chaerea and his assassins plan to murder the Emperor today. They must be stopped. You must stop them.'

Cupido shook his head. 'Why me? I have as much reason to hate Caligula as any man.'

'It is simple. He trusts you as no other because you have already saved his life. If you need a reason: you have given him your Oath. If you need another: you would be stopping a civil war in which thousands of innocents will undoubtedly die. Would you care to have the death of innocents on your conscience along with so many others?'

The long sword was at his throat before the last word was out. 'Have a care, Greek. One more death would not weigh too heavily.'

'I have brought a horse,' Claudius's freedman choked, as if the metal had already pierced his flesh. 'The Emperor attends the theatre. You must persuade him to leave before the sixth hour. The sixth hour, you understand, no later. Yet do not act too hastily. The assassins intend to strike at the end of the performance, but if they become aware of your purpose they may take fright and attack early. Caligula normally leaves the theatre to take a noonday meal. That may provide an excuse to manoeuvre his departure by a route which will surprise the plotters.'

'What about the guards on the road?' Cupido stared at him hard.

'Chaerea has called off his dogs. He will have other work for them if he succeeds today.'

Cupido sheathed his sword and picked up his cloak.

'No,' Rufus shouted. 'Don't trust him. It is a trap!'

The gladiator smiled sadly. 'He is right, Rufus. I have given my oath. Perhaps by this act I can atone for everything that has gone before. Join me if you can. I will bring him by the shortest route. There is an underground passageway between the theatre and his palace; Aemilia will direct you to it.' Then he was gone.

'You might remove that thing from my backbone now?' Narcissus suggested testily.

'Better to fillet you with it. There is something wrong here. Why do you and your master, who would have had me use Bersheba to kill Caligula, suddenly want to keep him alive?'

'It is a matter of timing,' Claudius's freedman said. 'I will explain in the carriage.'

He had come in one of the imperial carriages, splendid with gold leaf and fine metalwork. It had right of passage through Rome at any time of day or night and no one would stand in its way. As they passed through the courtyard Rufus realized that the hour was later than he thought. The sentry fire had burned down to ashes, with the blackened remains of two vaguely familiar shapes smouldering gently at its edge and giving

389

off a strong smell of roasted pig. The aroma made his mouth water, a fact he found profoundly disturbing.

As they clattered across the cobbles towards the vast bulk of the Palatine hill, Narcissus explained why it was so imperative the Emperor stayed alive.

'Chaerea believes nothing stands in his way if he kills Caligula today, but he is wrong. If the Emperor dies without a successor a dozen generals will descend on Rome with their legions, each with a better reason than the one before for taking power. The German guard, who oppose Chaerea, hold the key, and it is all about power and timing. If they can be persuaded to proclaim a member of the imperial family as Caligula's heir and march with him to the Senate, he will have the power of both the army and the people behind him. The generals will stay in their provinces and we will have peace.'

'And a new Emperor. Claudius.'

The Greek shrugged. 'My master took much persuading, but he realizes the times are too' – he searched for the right word – 'too turbulent to convince the Senate of the wisdom of a republic. Now all that remains is to agree a price with the Germans – you would be surprised how tedious avarice becomes – but for that I need time, which is why Cupido must save the Emperor today.'

'But Caligula must die in the end?'

Narcissus smiled. 'We all must die in the end, Rufus, but yes, Caligula will die – at a time of our choosing. Does our bargain still hold?'

'No.'

The smile didn't falter. 'I thought not. You always were an unlikely assassin. You see too much good in people.' He glanced across the carriage at Aemilia, who appeared to be sleeping. 'It is a trait that will get you into trouble one day.'

XLIV

By the time they reached the Palatine it was already close to midday. Rufus jumped from the carriage. Narcissus took his arm. 'Remember. You must win me some time. If you can escort the Emperor to his palace he will be safe there. The guard are all Germans and loyal.'

Rufus turned to Aemilia. 'Go there and wait for me,' he ordered.

The look she gave him would have felled a bullock and her voice fairly dripped with contempt. 'Do you think you can keep me from my Emperor?' The change in her left him utterly confused. Where was the girl with the sweet lips who had kissed him an hour earlier? He tried to make his voice as hard as hers.

'Very well, but if you slow me down I will leave you.'

'I am my brother's sister. It is not I who will slow you down.' She set off at a soldier's jog, and even though her skirts hampered her he had difficulty keeping up.

By the time they reached the pillared entrance to the passageway she had slowed to a more sensible pace. Rufus tried to discuss with her what had happened in the villa and the contrast in the way she had treated him minutes earlier, but she refused even to acknowledge him. Her mood had shifted again. Now she was quiet and withdrawn, but her face bore a look of resolute determination. They walked side by side through the corridor in silence. It was wide enough to take half a dozen soldiers marching abreast, but it was a gloomy cavern of a place lit only where sunlight filtered through tiny square windows that pierced its roof every twenty paces or so. In some ways it reminded Rufus of the Cloaca Palatina, but the air was fresher. The walls were lined with white marble and the mosaic floor – at least where it could be seen in the poor light – was astonishing. It had been decorated in sections by the finest craftsmen in the Empire. They had created wonderful scenes featuring angry gods and wild-eyed monsters so finely wrought it seemed sacrilege to walk upon them. At one point Rufus glanced down to see a sinuous sea-dragon with emerald scales and rows of fearsome teeth entwined round a great whale which was struggling for its very survival. A few steps onwards Jupiter fired bolts of jagged, golden lightning across a perfect Tyrrhenian sky towards a bearded giant holding a trident who must have been Neptune. Set into the corridor walls were large curtained alcoves containing statues of the famous emperors and generals who had made Rome great. The interiors of the alcoves were shadowed and hidden and Rufus grew more nervous with every step. Narcissus had been certain Chaerea had called off his men, but if they met a stray patrol of Scorpions their lives would be measured in seconds.

They were almost halfway when Aemilia stopped abruptly. Rufus halted beside her and tore at his sword with his mind screaming panic. What had she seen that he'd missed? He stood at her side, blade in his right hand, and waited, his ears filled with the sound of his own thundering heart.

Slim, warm fingers clutched at his free hand and held it tight. He turned in surprise to find her staring at him with a look of infinite sadness that scared him as much as anything he'd experienced this terrible day. It was the look of someone who had lost everything but her soul; the look she must have worn on the day when she was taken into bondage as her whole world burned around her.

She reached up to touch his face with the palm of her left hand. When she spoke, her voice was the voice of a child. He realized he'd forgotten how young she was. Somehow the sadness made her even more beautiful.

'Whatever happens, please don't think badly of me, Rufus. Whatever pain you suffer, I will suffer more, and I could not bear it if you hated me. There are times in a person's life when they do not control it; it controls them. Once I thought I could have loved you, as you loved me. But first there was Livia and now there is the Emperor. Even to share a smile would be death.'

He attempted to reply, but his mind was a whirlpool of confusion, thoughts forming and shattering, hopes dashed against the diamond-hard certainty of her words.

She put a finger to his lips and said softly: 'You must live your life and I will live mine, whatever that life brings. Promise me.'

He shook his head, still struck mute by confusion and conflicting emotions. He wouldn't allow hope to die, even if it might mean his own death.

She would have spoken again, but the sound of raised voices echoed down the passageway and Rufus stepped protectively in front of her, his sword raised.

'Why can we not wait for my litter bearers? It is unseemly for an Emperor to walk when he can be carried.' Caligula's strident, complaining voice was instantly recognizable, and when Cupido replied his words came back to them clear and strong.

'I am more concerned for your life than I am for your dignity, Caesar. You must keep moving.'

Rufus almost sobbed with relief. Cupido was here. Now they were safe. The gladiator would take charge and his indomitable presence and nerveless courage would see them through. A few seconds before he had been scared of his own shadow, but with Cupido by their side he knew they could overcome any odds. He held the sword tighter. Already it felt more comfortable in his hand.

Two figures appeared at the far end of the shallow curve of the corridor. At first it looked as if they were wrestling, but Rufus quickly realized that one held the other and was hustling him along the passage as fast as he was able.

'Unhand your Emperor, you fool,' Caligula

shouted, struggling against Cupido's grip on his toga. 'Mnester was just reaching the climax of Cinyras and I have seen him dance but once. The public expect to see their Emperor at the games and the public will see him.'

'I have told you, great Caesar, and I will tell you again: if we do not reach the palace you will never have the chance to see Mnester dance again because you will be dead. Don't you understand the Scorpions are at our heels? You have been betrayed. My Wolves are too few to hold them for more than a few minutes, and if we do not hurry Rome will not have an Emperor.'

The last words seemed to penetrate the wall of outraged dignity and Caligula allowed himself to be carried along for a few more steps.

'Who?' he asked in a tone of mixed bewilderment and disbelief. 'Who has betrayed Rome?'

'Narcissus will name the conspirators when we reach the palace,' Cupido said. Caligula went rigid and the gladiator knew instantly he had made a mistake.

'Narcissus?' The Emperor's voice was shrill. 'My uncle's pet Greek spy? Why, I have the order for his arrest in my litter. What trickery is this that you drag me to meet my enemy?'

'Cupido!' Rufus cried.

The young German froze, the long sword instantly at the ready. Caligula looked puzzled. 'Why is my slave here when he should be with my elephant?'

Cupido smiled and sheathed his blade. 'They are friends, great Caesar. You need have no fear.'

Rufus sensed Aemilia stiffen at his side. He

could feel the tension in her as if they were connected by some physical bond. Finally he realized why her moods had fluctuated so disconcertingly. He cursed himself for an insensitive fool. How could he not have seen it? She was on the cusp of some momentous decision. With every fibre of his spirit he willed her to remain where she was. Where she belonged. At his side. Please, he thought, let her rule her own life. The Fates would have their day, but let it not be this day.

'Caesar!' she cried. And his heart turned to ice.

He watched her run towards the Emperor in her long skirt, the golden tresses of her hair flying free behind her. It was as if the gods had slowed time. Each beat of his heart seemed to take an eternity. Breath became unnecessary. With each step she took he felt her spirit floating away from him. He had to bite his lip to keep from calling her name.

Caligula stood to Cupido's right, hands tugging at the folds of his toga in an attempt to return it to its proper shape. The expression on his face betrayed his bewilderment. It seemed Aemilia's public show of affection was as much a surprise to him as it was to Rufus, and to a clearly mystified Cupido.

The running figure finally reached the Emperor and Rufus felt the first prick of tears as Aemilia took Caligula in a lover's embrace, reaching up to kiss him with her left hand behind his head bringing his lips down to hers.

They were spotlighted in the rays of one of the little square windows and it happened so fast that Rufus at first didn't recognize it for what it was.

When Aemilia's right hand came up almost gently towards her lover's cheek there was a vivid flash of purple and green, as if a starling's wing had been caught in the sunlight. In the same instant the Emperor screamed and reared back with one hand to his throat.

Caligula's mind had been busy trying to solve the conundrum presented by the slave he had used so badly who was now declaring her love so publicly, while at the same time being diverted by the sensuous working of her tongue within his mouth. The bee sting at his neck came as a complete surprise.

An instant later he realized it was more than a bee sting and his bowels turned to liquid. It was a razor-edged, death-bringing, invasive thing powered by a strong hand that worked it deep into his flesh. His panic grew and the sting grew with it, turning into a red-hot spike that was being forced through his neck, filling his throat so that he found it difficult to breathe. Aemilia's lips left his and he found himself looking into the crazed light that filled her eyes. She stepped away from him with a smile of satisfaction on her lips.

He reached up with a shaking hand to inspect his neck and flinched as his fingers found the bejewelled hilt of Aemilia's little dagger. His head swam with the enormity of what was happening to him and he swayed and almost collapsed. He tried to speak but all that emerged was a strange gurgling sound. He willed his fingers to grip the knife and with a tug pulled the short blade from his neck, leaving a small-mouthed wound that leaked blood in jerky bursts that stained the shoulder of his toga. Dark, ruby red on pristine white.

'What have you done?' Cupido cried, dragging his sister away from the Emperor's side.

Caligula coughed and spat blood. It seemed to clear the obstruction in his throat. He found his voice.

'Done? The bitch has killed me. Do your duty and execute her.'

Cupido ignored him and turned to Aemilia. 'Go, now. Find Narcissus and tell him I will do his bidding if he saves you. Remember that.' He shook her by the shoulders. 'Cupido will do his bidding if he helps you escape.'

But his words had as little effect on Aemilia as a bird's singing. She seemed to be frozen to the spot.

'Help her,' Cupido pleaded with Rufus. 'Get her away from here. I will buy you time.'

Rufus's mind reeled in confusion. He looked incredulously from Aemilia to Caligula and back again. She had tried to kill the Emperor they had come to save. To save him was now to condemn her, but not to save him was to condemn the thousands of innocents Narcissus believed would die in the civil war which would inevitably follow.

'Hurry.' Cupido's strong hand gripped his shoulder. 'You must get her away from here. Find Narcissus.'

Rufus nodded, but as he did so he heard the sound of a sword singing clear of its scabbard. They had forgotten the Emperor. He had reached forward and taken Cupido's weapon by the hilt.

'If you won't kill the bitch, I will,' he raged,

398

bringing the long sword up so its point was feet from Aemilia's chest, poised for the thrust that would send the blade through her.

She stared back at him contemptuously and Rufus was reminded of a statue he had once seen of a doomed Galatian princess protecting her children from the vengeance of the legions, her stance and her expression a mix of defiance, courage and despair that shamed her attackers.

'Strike like the serpent you are,' she spat.

Caligula's bulging eyes filled with fire at the insult. His face twisted into a snarl and he screamed his hate as he rammed the blade towards her unprotected body.

Rufus did not see Cupido move. For an instant the gladiator was back in the arena making one of the effortless transitions through space and time that had kept him alive for four years in the most dangerous place on earth. In less than a heart-beat he was a human barrier between Caligula's sword and his sister, one hand stretched out directly in front of him towards the Emperor.

It appeared so harmless. Cupido's chest was protected by the wolf breastplate he wore, but the sword found the gap beneath his armpit with all of Caligula's strength behind it and vanished into the gladiator's body with as little resistance as if his flesh had been satin.

Cupido felt his head explode as the needle point ripped through his body. Strangely there was no pain, only the heart-stopping shock that froze a man when he dived into an ice-bound river. So this was it, he thought. This was what it had been like for all those other men he had faced, and

399

fought, and killed. How many times had he woken sweating in the night, wondering? And now it was here. In the moments before his consciousness faded he realized with surprise that it was almost welcome. Strange that he should meet it so objectively. Without fear. He listed the organs the long sword had pierced: lung, then heart, then lung again. Death.

Rufus saw his friend shudder as that terrible iron blade entered his body. Heard Aemilia's scream. For a second there was no Emperor before him, no ruler of Rome – only the enemy. He howled, a mindless wolf's howl that filled the corridor with hate and fury and a lust for revenge. The sword in his hand sliced upward as if it had a life of its own, chopping Caligula's lower jaw almost in two and cutting through his cheek. The Emperor staggered back, a hand to his ruined face, but the other still held the long sword and in one movement he drew its bloody length from Cupido's body and the gladiator slumped to the floor as if it had taken his life force with it.

Rufus lunged forward, but a sideswiping slash of the long sword made him leap aside and the cut that should have disembowelled Caligula merely found the thick cloth of his toga. A horrible grunting noise, like a pig rooting for acorns, emerged from the Emperor's mouth, but the dreadful wound, even coupled with the one Aemilia had inflicted, didn't appear to have slowed him.

Caligula's sword flailed in a lethal half-circle but Rufus always managed to evade the edge, even if it was only by the width of a piece of parchment. Time and again he found himself in position for a killing stroke only for that vicious razor-streak of bright silver-blue to arc from the limit of his vision and force him to leap back as the blade that would have gutted him hissed inches from his belly.

He knew that the longer he fought, the more likely Caligula was to defeat him, but it was as if an army of ghosts stood at his back willing him onwards. Varro, Fronto, Quintillia and the countless other victims of this monstrous man whispered in his ear for justice and demanded vengeance. Vengeance. Cupido's face appeared before him and he heard a calm voice inside his head. In the next seconds his movements became more controlled, more subtle, the tip of his sword dancing in lightning strokes that dismayed and deceived his opponent. Suddenly it was the Emperor who was forced backwards and when he stumbled Rufus was on him, sword slashing for his exposed neck. Somehow, Caligula parried the blow and a muscular arm shot out like a cobra's strike and a hand with fingers of double-forged iron closed upon Rufus's throat. Now it was he who croaked and gurgled.

Frantically, he stabbed with his sword at any part of the Emperor he could reach, sometimes feeling the point pierce flesh, but never quite enough to inflict a serious wound. The iron grip tightened and his vision first blurred, then faded.

He was dying.

Caligula's arm, muscles bunched with the effort of killing him, was directly in front of Rufus's face. He had all but given up the fight. His mind was blank, but it seemed his body still contained some deep-buried instinct for survival. The short sword stopped its hopeless stabbing and, seemingly of its own volition, very slowly and deliberately began to saw at the taut tendons of the Emperor's forearm. Caligula grunted at this new and unexpected assault and the insane light in his eyes was replaced by doubt.

Suddenly his grip slackened and the arm flopped and Rufus could breathe again. He felt his opponent's weight shift as Caligula reared back. The Emperor still had Cupido's long sword in his right hand and now he lifted it for one final killing blow. Rufus knew he would never be able to react quickly enough to parry the heavy blade, understood it must cleave his skull in two. Then a slight hand appeared from nowhere to grasp Caligula's wrist, making the Emperor half turn in surprise. Rufus saw his opportunity and with every ounce of his remaining strength he plunged the *gladius* under the Emperor's ribs and forced the point upwards and into his heart.

The ruler of a million Romans screamed in mortal agony and his face was etched with a look of horror. Rufus felt the moment his spirit fled from his body like water escaping a breached dam. The Emperor flopped down alongside him, twisting as he fell so that his lifeless eyes stared at the roof. Caligula was dead. He had lived twenty-eight years and ruled Rome for three years, ten months and eight days.

Rufus lay back, chest heaving, for what seemed an age, his eyes drawn to the clouds passing above the little window in the roof of the passageway that proved the unlikely truth: he was still alive.

He tried to work out what he should do now, but it was as if his mind had been overwhelmed by the enormity of what had gone before. Each thought simply melted away before it formed any substance, like water draining through the fingers of a cupped hand.

'Rufus!' Aemilia's disembodied voice was urgent in his ear and somehow his sanity returned. He stared vacantly at her. 'Rufus, they're coming. If they find us here they will kill us.'

He heard the shouting voices and the clatter of armour. He was too tired think, but Aemilia was thinking for both of them.

'Help me,' she hissed. Cupido. Now he remembered. Cupido had been hurt. She was trying to drag her brother towards one of the curtained alcoves. He stood to help her, but his foot slipped and he looked down. The corridor was like a slaughterhouse. He realized his clothing was soaked in blood, and his arms and face, even his hair, were coated in it.

The voices were closer, but this wasn't right.

'Your sandals,' he said, removing his own. 'You're leaving a trail a child could follow.'

She looked down at her bloody footprints, and did the same. Together they wrestled Cupido up and laid his body gently against one wall of the alcove. There was barely room for the three of them crammed in beside the statue, but fortunately the velvet curtain was long enough to reach the mosaic floor.

They sat in silence, each holding one of Cupido's hands.

Footsteps approached cautiously and there was

a shout as one of the approaching men recognized the torn body. It was followed a second later by a voice Rufus recognized, high and lisping and crackling with urgency.

'Someone's done our work for us, and by Marius's arse they've done it well,' Cassius Chaerea cried. 'Those bastard Wolves, I knew they were up to something. They've got their own plan, and their own Emperor.'

'Who?'

'It doesn't matter who, Sabinus. All that matters is that we have to kill them, kill them all. It just means we'll have to do it more quickly. Take the west side of the hill as we agreed. Hunt down Milonia and the brat. I want none left of his line. His sisters too, if you can find them. You have the lists, you know what to do.'

'And Claudius? I did not see his name on any list.'

'Leave Claudius to me. I have plans for him and that Greek snake of his. Hurry. We must act quickly.'

Rufus held his breath as a dozen men clattered past only feet from the curtain. He knew they had to find a safer refuge, but waited a few moments pondering whether to make a move. Narcissus was their only option, but would the Greek risk giving them aid? There was only one way to find out. He was reaching slowly for the curtain when a solitary voice stopped his hand and almost his heart.

Chaerea must have delayed, gloating over his tormentor's body, while his men went on their murderous mission.

'Not so brave now, my young lion?' The Praetorian's sneering tone was sharp and clear in the empty passageway. 'A pity the Wolves got to you first. A quick death was much more than you deserved and I've long dreamed of killing you myself. Have so many insults ever gone un-avenged? Still, a man must do what he can.' There was a short pause before the unmistakable sound of splashing liquid echoed in the silence.

Once Chaerea was done with defiling the Em-peror's body, a single set of nailed sandals marched steadily towards the hiding place. Rufus untangled his hand from Cupido's to grip the short sword and his eyes locked on Aemilia's, willing her to stay still.

The measured tramp halted immediately out-side the alcove. Rufus realized Chaerea was study-ing the blood pattern on the gore-thick floor. He tried to remember if there had been a trail of blood from Cupido's wound. He didn't think so, but if there were it would be as good as a signpost.

The silence seemed to last for an eternity before the ringing footsteps continued on their rhythmic way. When they were out of earshot, he let out a long breath and slumped beside Cupido. The gladiator's face was a waxy grey, but he was barely bleeding at all. Rufus checked him and found a little ragged wound under his left armpit. It seemed almost insignificant.

'Why?' he asked.

'You would not understand,' Aemilia said. 'You are a man.'

'I need to understand.'

'He was a foul thing. Fouler than you will ever

know. He deserved to die a dozen deaths. I would kill him again if I could.'

What might have been a soft chuckle came from between them.

'You have been cheated, sister. What is death to a god? I am but a man and I have seen death in a thousand guises. I do not fear it.'

Rufus gripped Cupido's hand tight. It was as cold as when he held him in the sewer. Corpse-cold.

The gladiator's mind drifted between past and present, between reality and illusion, until he wasn't certain which was which. He knew he was dying. Accepted it almost gratefully, and with acceptance came a strange euphoria that suffused his body with an imagined warmth. He felt his father's strong grip on his waist as he was lifted on to his first pony. Tasted the strawberry sweetness of the first lips he kissed. Finally understood the desolation in his mother's eyes on the day he picked up his first sword. He reached out to her, to ask her forgiveness, but before their hands touched a lance of pain seared his chest and he was back in the alcove with Aemilia and Rufus looking down at him, their faces filled with concern.

He coughed and tasted blood. 'Don't grieve for me, Rufus. A legion of the dead awaits me in the halls of the Otherworld. We will feast there and boast about our great battles. I...' he faltered and gave a child's laugh, 'I will be great among them.'

'Why, Cupido, why will you be great among the champions of the Otherworld?'

The gladiator's fingers tightened on his. 'What

greater honour than to die by an Emperor's own hand?'

Rufus blinked away tears as he watched the life light fading in his friend's eyes. He felt the grip relax and for a moment he thought it was over. But Cupido used the last of his strength to choke out one final request. 'Remember,' he gasped. 'A sword in my hand and a friend by my side.'

Rufus bent to kiss the cold flesh of the gladiator's forehead and at the same time placed the hilt of the *gladius* in his open palm, closing the lifeless fingers around it. Cupido's expression relaxed, making him seem quite boyish, and he gave a prolonged, almost wistful sigh. The greatest gladiator of his age was gone.

Aemilia stroked her brother's golden hair and whispered to him. Curiously, she shed no tears. Rufus wondered why. Had her time in Caligula's palace so inured her to death that even Cupido's passing did not move her?

She read his face. 'He was marked for death. This was his fate. I saw it when I threw the sticks for him on the eve of Drusilla's procession and I did my grieving then. He saw it too. He said that if it came he would welcome it. There was a stain on his soul that could never be removed in this life. Only by being reborn would he truly be free. Be glad for him.'

Rufus remembered Cupido's face the night he had come to the little room behind the elephant house. Trials, he had said; trials and a victory.

'There is more.' He stared at her. What more could there be? 'I am with child.' Rufus closed his eyes. He felt as if Caligula's sword had pierced his

407

heart. He didn't ask the question, but she answered it in any case. 'Yes, it is his child. Caligula's child. If he had lived he would have murdered both me and the baby. He has done such a thing before. Now do you understand why he had to die?'

He choked back tears and nodded, but the truth was he didn't understand anything any more. She was carrying Caligula's child. How much stored-up sorrow was there in that simple five-word sentence? What awful horrors did the future hold? It was the child of a monster. Maybe it would have been better to have killed it.

But he didn't say that. 'No one must ever know. The child must have a father, but it must never learn its true lineage. It will be the offspring of a simple palace servant.'

She stared at him. She understood that his statement contained an offer, but why did the offer feel like a trap?

He waited for her answer, but none came. Eventually he knew they could wait no longer. 'We have to move. If we stay here they'll find us.' He shrugged. They both knew what would happen then. 'We have to leave Cupido.'

She protested, as he knew she would, but he persuaded her that the only way to stay alive was to remain together. He stepped out of the alcove, meaning to start in the direction of the palace, but he was drawn to the still figure on the bloody mosaic floor.

Caligula lay with his head in a ring of sunlight, in that boneless pose adopted only by the dead. Rufus stood over him wondering at his lack of feeling. There were so many questions he could have asked that would never be answered. Or perhaps only one question. The question he had asked Aemilia. Why?

They both heard the running footsteps, but a night and a day of fear and tension had sapped any will he had to react.

'There! The assassin.'

There were four of them, burly Praetorians with the battle madness in their blood. They had spent the last hours chasing shadows and not knowing who was friend and who enemy. Three wanted to cut him down where he stood, but their leader ordered them to put up their swords. They disarmed him and two of them bound him, while the others took Aemilia by the arms.

'Caesar will have his justice and it will not be as merciful as a blade.'

Rufus's bonds were so tight he wondered his hands did not come off. The soldiers pushed him roughly towards the palace, taking turns to prick him with their swords if he lagged. He tried to meet Aemilia's eyes. At least he could say farewell. But she had her head bowed and her expression was hidden behind the curtain of her corn-gold hair.

They had gone barely a hundred paces when they stopped abruptly.

'Kneel, slave.' The commander kicked him in the back of the knees and forced him down with Aemilia at his side. 'Kneel before your Emperor.'

Rufus heard the footsteps approaching, but didn't raise his head. What did it matter if Chaerea killed them? He had lost so many friends: Fronto, his father and mentor; Livia, whom he had not loved enough; and Cupido, best and bravest of them all. Would it be such a hardship to join them? Then he remembered Gaius, the son he had barely known, and felt a stab of pain as he realized the boy would grow up alone and a slave. For a fleeting moment he considered giving up Aemilia's secret, but what was the point? It wouldn't save him, and it would undoubtedly condemn her. Chaerea wouldn't leave a single one of Caligula's line alive. At least this way there was a chance she would survive.

'He is one of the assassins, Caesar,' the Praetorian leader said. 'We found him standing over the Emp– the former Emperor, with blood on his clothes and a sword in his hands. Should we execute him now, or do you want him with the rest?'

Rufus's tired mind tried to send him a message. Something wasn't quite right, but he was too exhausted to work it out. Assassin? Yes, he was an assassin, but how did they know?

'Execute him?' Rufus recognized that voice, but it was different, changed somehow. The muscles in his neck bunched as he waited for the sword to fall. 'Should we execute him?'

Seconds passed and he found he was still alive, so he looked up. Not Chaerea. Claudius. A taller, straighter Claudius who stood between Callistus, wearing a charitable smile his face was never intended for, and Narcissus, who contrived to look bored and conceited at one and the same time. They were surrounded by Praetorians, whom Rufus now recognized as Cupido's Wolves.

'Execute him?' the new Emperor of Rome repeated. 'No, I don't think so. Who would look after my elephant?'

Acknowledgements

Special thanks to my editor, Simon Thorogood, and the team at Transworld. Stan, my agent at Jenny Brown, guided me through the minefield of a first novel. I would also like to thank Edward and all at Youwriteon.com who helped turn a writer into a novelist, and Sara O'Keeffe for her encouragement and advice. And John Wyllie, who read it first and liked it, which was encouragement enough.

The publishers hope that this book has given you enjoyable reading. Large Print Books are especially designed to be as easy to see and hold as possible. If you wish a complete list of our books please ask at your local library or write directly to:

Magna Large Print Books
Magna House, Long Preston,
Skipton, North Yorkshire.
BD23 4ND

This Large Print Book for the partially sighted, who cannot read normal print, is published under the auspices of

THE ULVERSCROFT FOUNDATION